It Lives Again!

Horror Movies in the New Millennium

It Lives Again!

Horror Movies in the New Millennium

Axelle Carolyn

First published in England in 2008 by
Telos Publishing Ltd
61 Elgar Avenue, Tolworth, Surbiton, Surrey KT5 9JP, UK
www.telos.co.uk

Telos Publishing Ltd values feedback. Please e-mail us with any comments you may have about this book to:
feedback@telos.co.uk

ISBN: 978-1-84583-020-5 (hardback)

Internal design, typesetting and layout by Arnold T Blumberg
www.atbpublishing.com

All images used in this book are for promotional and publicity purposes and grateful thanks are given to those individuals and collections who supplied them.

Printed in India

1 2 3 4 5 6 7 8 9 10 11 12 13 14 15

British Library Cataloguing in Publication Data.
A catalogue record for this book is available from the British Library.

Contents:

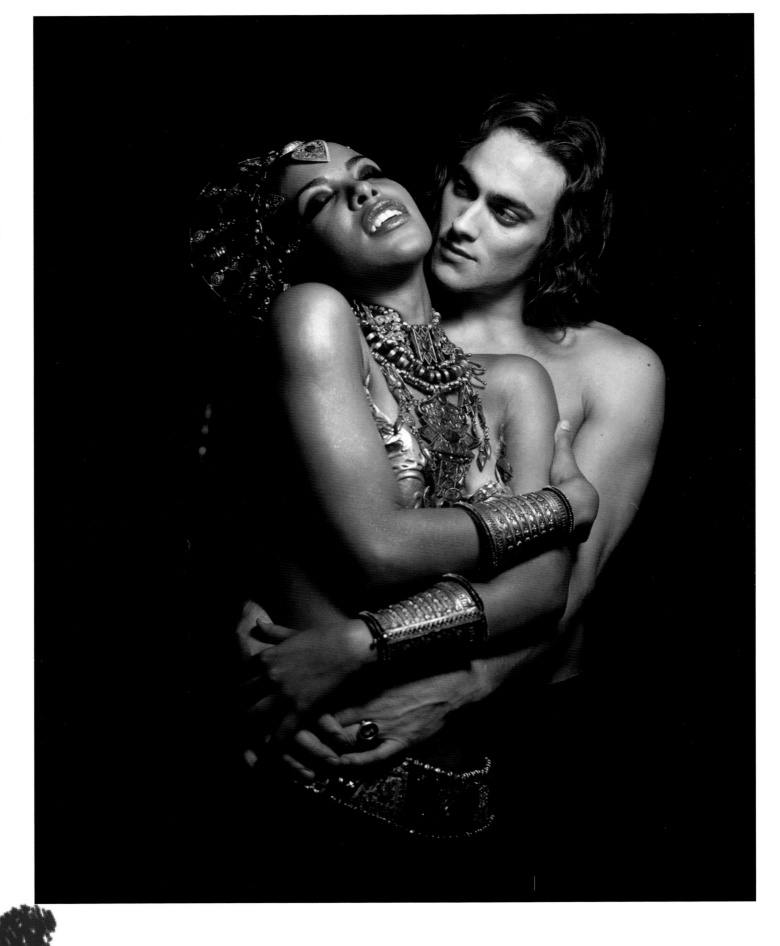

Foreword:

of Fear and Death

(Neil Marshall)

WHY CHOOSE TO LIVE IN FEAR?

It's a question I'm often asked. Why do horror movies continue to be so popular? Why have audiences loved being scared at the movies, ever since that first flickering footage of a train pulling into a station sent them running out into the street in blind terror? The only answer I can ever come up with is … because we secretly crave it. It's human nature. It's carved into our hearts and our minds, part of the DNA of our blood and bones. It's who we are, and it's because of who we once were.

Thousands of years ago, long before we settled into our mundane routine of day-to-day life, when we still lived in caves and rubbed two sticks together to make fire, we lived on the ragged edge of existence. Every day was a horror movie. We had to fight to survive, to eat, and to protect our territory and our tribe. We lived in fear of death at any moment. The stakes were high and very real, and yet for all its downsides, it must have been a hell of a thrill ride. Every chase, every fight, every hunt brought its own reward. Not just a meal and another day of life, but an adrenalin surge that empowered us with a lust for life.

Today we get up, go to work, come home, watch TV and go to sleep. To combat the monotony we chase the death rush by other means, as perilous as base or bungee jumping, or as sanitised as roller coasters and theme parks, while for most the simple thrills of the horror movie are more than enough to satisfy and provide a little taste of fear.

That's just one theory. Another is that we watch horror movies because they offer us a challenge – to look fear and death in the face and survive the ordeal.

Axelle loves a good scare as much as the next person, but her passion for horror goes far beyond these base instincts and primal urges. I'm sure she's probably forgotten more about this genre than I'll ever know. This is her field of expertise. She lives and breathes horror, and as

such I can't think of a better person to write this book. Her rise as a film journalist and writer has almost run in parallel to the ascendance and growing popularity of horror cinema since the start of the new millennium. It's certainly a fascinating trend in contemporary society and it's long overdue an in-depth and objective analysis. With this book Axelle does just that, and over the last year I've watched her sitting at the keyboard, hour after hour, day after day, piecing together this meticulous volume. Utilising tireless research, she looks at the social and political climate into which these movies fell over the last 8 years, and discusses the merits of the movies themselves or, in some cases, lack of them.

I feel incredibly proud to be a part of my wife's work, a part of this book, and a part of the recent history of horror cinema.

So, switch off the television, dim the lights, and read on … but only if you dare!

Neil Marshall
London, June 2008

Introduction:
Horror's Endless Cycle
(Mick Garris)

THE HORROR FILM, THROUGHOUT ITS SHADY, REBELLIOUS HISTORY, HAS earned more money than respect. Though these days there are film festivals, websites, books, magazines, Masters theses, and even film distributors devoted entirely to the consumption of the dark side of entertainment, the mainstream media and self-appointed intelligentsia of pontificators cluck their tongues and blame the fall of society on these nasty little gutter-dwellers we call our own. In truth, the horror film may be the best mirror of the world's *zeitgeist* we have, reflecting, rather than creating, the ills and crises of the planet's collective psychology.

It's been said before, and it bears repeating, that horror is to cinema what rock'n'roll is to music: rude, abrasive, pushy, and anti-establishment. No wonder, then, that it is so embraced by the young. What better way to break away from the parental chains than to blast distorted guitars on the stereo, and revel in disembowelled damsels in distress on the widescreen plasma? The young are immortal, right? And who can blame them for gathering tribally in front of the Cineplex screens to cheer on the latest adventures of the newest teen-gutting horror franchise star? They know it's not real, that they are thumbing their noses at mortality. Yes, deep-seated fears are faced on the screen, from a safe distance, allowing the audience to safely play tag with what scares them.

But horror is not just the playground of the adolescent and young adult. There is a long and defensively proud history of dark storytelling, from the cave-paintings through Shakespeare's bubbling, troubling witches (yeah, I know that's a big jump in the time machine), the *Grand Guignol*'s 75-year run in Paris, Lon Chaney's silent classics, the Universal monsters in their heyday, the big bug movies of the 1950s, winding through the anti-establishment, independent offerings of Hooper and Carpenter in the 1970s, all the way up through the constellation of franchise sequels and remakes that brighten the silver screens of neighbourhood multiplexes around the globe.

Even today, the only respect you'll find behind studio walls for the horror film is in the accounting department. Few studio executives actually like the films, if they see them at all, and you can probably count on your fingers the number that understand them. Despite being responsible for actually foisting the films on an audience, all too many of the mucky-muck powers-that-be behind the walls of Black Towers and studio gates believe that 'it's the kills that pay the bills'.

A good horror movie has all the elements of a good drama: creative storytelling, compelling characters placed in relatable plots, an artist's point of view. But a *really* good horror movie, the *best* horror movie, can take you far beyond: it can take you to a place you've never been, a shadowy chamber of the mind outside of your worldly experience, with story twists and turns that will make you squirm until the lights come on and you emerge victoriously from your two hours in the dark. A great horror movie can be a revelatory experience.

A great way to take a society's pulse is through the arts and entertainment of the time. And the horror film makes a great thermometer. As Axelle Carolyn makes so abundantly clear in the chapters to follow, a national or global health is particularly well represented by its fright films. At times of political upheaval, war, depression and recession, the horror cycle runs to a particular high. Adam Simon's remarkable documentary, *The American Nightmare*, about the horror boom of the 1970s arising out of the international upheaval that surrounded the war in Vietnam, is a terrific examination of how one relates to the other.

But as we close in on the end of the new millennium's first decade, we find ourselves in another long-lasting terror boom in a post 9/11 world. Obviously, most of these films are not artistic reflections of social strife, or the primal screams of the mad artist who paints in blood. As they have with everything else that makes money, the corporate kings have co-opted the popular cycle on their own terms. Where brilliant artists contribute excellent and exciting new ventures, the screens are also littered with the latest iterations of franchises nobody asks for, but are easy to market. In recent years, it's been far easier for an industry that isn't interested in or has any understanding of the horror genre to take familiar titles, and remake and sequelise them until the law of diminishing returns proves itself, and they move on to the next title.

There are great horror films being made today amidst the dross. But it's not really quality that's being discussed here, though it obviously plays a part. It's that there is a new and ravening audience for the spilling of blood. Again, there's nothing new about this: filmgoers filled the cinemas during the Depression to see the Frankenstein monster toss an innocent little girl into the pond, to see Count Dracula sup on the blood of lovely blondes; during World War II, Frankenstein's monster met everyone from the Wolf Man to Abbot and Costello, and Universal cranked out one monster fest after another, while a quiet, well-read producer named Val Lewton churned out intelligent, atmospheric shockers for RKO; in the 1950s, when the Cold War and Air Raid duck-and-cover drills were the order of the day, nuclear tests gave birth to the giant ants of *Them*, the humungous grasshoppers of *The Beginning of the End*, and the radioactivity-breathing Japanese dragon beast of *Godzilla*; the early sixties turned internal, with human monsters like Norman Bates infesting our souls and killing on behalf of the sexual battle within on the newly blossoming psychological terror train; the Vietnam apocalypses were brutal, fed

as they were by nightly news imagery of burning bodies and human torture, in a toe-in-the-water test of loosening censorship that led to a free-for-all; the eighties were all about cheap: no stars, gore effects and creative kills being the entire *raison d'être* for a horror film's existence; the complacent, Wall Street frivolous 1990s were mostly in a horror lull, but ended with a bang of excellence with films like *A Stir of Echoes*, *The Sixth Sense*, and *The Blair Witch Project*.

In the new millennium, a new generation of filmmakers is finding its voice, raised on ubiquitous film courses in high school and beyond, computers that can provide in-home editing and sound mixing, mobile, high definition cameras that lead everyone to believe they can be the next John Carpenter. But it is ingenuity that best raises the profile among hordes of wannabes, as well as a point of view.

The world, under the shroud of George W Bush, Tony Blair and their brethren, is dangerous, complicated and nervous. And the boom in horrific storytelling, even when controlled by the mass-media collective out to squeeze every last buck out of it, will reflect a world on edge in its unforgiving mirror … at least until the next cycle.

Mick Garris
Los Angeles, May 2008

1990s:

'Someone has taken their love of scary movies one step too far!'

(Tagline for *Scream*, 1996)

Horror wasn't dead, but it certainly was in bad shape.

In the last few years of the 20th century, scary movies were few and far between, and their success marginal. With the exceptions of *The Blair Witch Project* and *The Sixth Sense* in 1999, none had been box office hits since Wes Craven's *Scream*, which had grossed over $100 million in 1996, and followed a similar period of drought for genre films. Blood and guts were out of fashion and studios no longer invested in real, hardcore horror movies, preferring to mix the scares with comedy or action. As they had done countless times before, critics and online reviewers, these movie coroners of the modern age, pronounced horror dead, no longer able to draw audiences to theatres or give birth to original ideas.

But the phoenix-like genre always had a way of coming back to life during post-mortem examinations, and it returned from the grave in a big way after 11 September 2001. By showing the Western hemisphere that it was not invulnerable, the terrorist attacks also revived old fears in its inhabitants; fears that would somehow have to be channelled and exorcised. As Craven once put it, 'all that bad karma has got to go somewhere …'[1]

Bad Karma

From campfire tales to gothic literature to cinematic frights, scary stories have always been a way for listeners, readers and viewers to purge themselves of emotional tensions by approaching their fears in a controllable way: anxieties become concrete, visible, and can be examined and kept in check without any harm. The process of catharsis is unconscious and has to remain so: get too close, and you'll get burnt – that is why horror movies are rarely produced in times of war at home, or fail to attract audiences if they remind them too directly of their troubles.[2] On

Night of the Living Dead.

an immediate level, these stories play on personal, instinctive fears: fear of dying, of getting old, of getting hurt. On a global level, they can also reflect more complex concerns, particular to a community – be it local, national or international – and linked to that community's state of affairs: fear of communism, of terrorism, of religious fanaticism. It is when horror films tap into the latter, or when primal fears are exacerbated by a particular societal crisis, that they are most likely to reach a wide audience – even though viewers may not be able to pinpoint the exact reason why they relate to what they've seen.[3]

So beyond gross-out special effects and easy jump-scares, scary movies – just like novels, comic books and any horror medium – exploit and reflect the fears of the moment they are created. Recessions bring about doubt and anxiety, feelings that fuel horror cinema, which thrives on troubled times. International peace and economic stability, on the other hand, can be fatal to the genre. Horror feeds on the tensions of society; it starves to death then fattens up along with the world's never-ending cycle of upswings and depressions.

The horror film in its present incarnation arguably emerged in 1968 – a difficult year if there ever was one, with the successive assassinations of Martin Luther King and Robert Kennedy, ghetto insurrections and campus revolts, and the growing involvement of the United States in Vietnam. Between '68 and the end of Ronald Reagan's eighties, America saw its defeat against the communists in South East Asia, the OPEC oil embargo, the Watergate scandal, the general slowdown of the economy in Western countries, the Iran hostage crisis, and the assassination attempt against Reagan, to name but a few key events. The very confidence of the United States as a great, leading nation was shattered at the beginning of the period; its perceived invincibility and supremacy, once core beliefs of the American spirit, were now brought into question for the first time since the World Wars. Interestingly, never before that time had horror movies been so bold.

George Romero's *Night of the Living Dead*, released in October 1968, marked the beginning

1 Quoted in *The American Nightmare*, directed by Adam Simon, 2000.

2 As illustrated by the UK box-office underperformance of Neil Marshall's underground drama *The Descent*, released the day after the London underground bombings of 7 July 2005, which killed 52 commuters and injured over 700.

3 Since the late seventies, countless books and articles have analysed the link between real-life horror and scary movies; this understanding of their function as mirrors of contemporary social and political events has slowly led to a new acceptance of the genre as a legitimate object of study. See for example *The Monster Show: A Cultural History of Horror*, David J Skal, Plexus, 1994; and Stephen King's excellent history of the genre, *Danse Macabre*, 1981, Everest House.

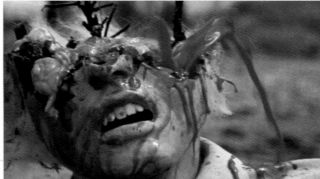

of horror movies as we know them today; set in Anytown, USA, in the present day, it contrasted with traditional period pieces and brought horror close to home and into everyday life, breaking many taboos along the way – cannibalism, daughters attacking their mothers, and, the supreme novelty, a black man as the only survivor. Shot on a shoestring budget, Romero's classic changed the genre – and the zombie subgenre, as we will see later – forever, and launched a series of increasingly violent and gory movies throughout the seventies, from Italian living dead and cannibal movies to Wes Craven's *Last House on the Left* (1972) and Tobe Hooper's masterpiece *The Texas Chain Saw Massacre* (1974).

Horror's popularity peaked in the early eighties with the advent of the slasher film, following John Carpenter's *Halloween* (1978), which, on an estimated budget of $325,000 and after a modest opening, went on to gross over $47 million in the US alone. Sean Cunningham's *Friday the 13th* (1980) and Wes Craven's *A Nightmare on Elm Street* (1984), movies in which few believed originally but which turned out to be huge box-office hits, also left a lasting mark on horror.

As America slowly rebuilt its confidence and pride throughout the Reagan years, the genre spiralled downwards with a series of sequels that turned Jason Vorhees, Michael

Last House on the Left. Evil Dead II. A Nightmare on Elm Street. Bad Taste. Friday the 13th Part VIII Jason Takes Manhattan. The Shining.

Myers and Freddy Krueger into familiar and amusing figures, and was soon reduced to parodying itself, most movies – *Return of the Living Dead* (1985), *Evil Dead II* (1987), *Bad Taste* (1987) – having to include some degree of humour to be successful. Originality was no longer required. Relentless killers and gory murders had been done to death. The decade that began with Stanley Kubrick's *The Shining* (1980) ended with *Friday the 13th Part VIII: Jason Takes Manhattan* and *Toxic Avenger Part III* (both 1989).[4]

Violence of the Lambs

The fall of the Berlin Wall in 1989, the swift victory of the US-led coalition against Saddam Hussein in the Gulf in 1991 and the break-up of the USSR the same year all reinforced the nation's confidence and started a new era of economic growth, thereby putting the final nail in the coffin of the genre. Known to the Western world as its 'most prosperous decade'[5], the nineties were a time of compromise for scary movie fans, who had to make do with teenager-

friendly flicks and horror comedies. Granted, under the Clinton administration, US troops were slaughtered in Somalia, the United Nations let millions die in Rwanda and the American air force bombed civilians in Kosovo, but these fiascos occurred far from home, while the country prospered, none of these conflicts posing a real threat to the United States. In the absence of global anxieties to tap into, filmmakers couldn't as easily strike a chord in the collective mind of the masses as they would in times of tension; its audience limited to a small congregation, horror didn't disappear, but learned how to please the new generation by avoiding shocking and upsetting.

The decade began with high profile 're-imaginings' of classic horror tales. Francis Ford Coppola's *Bram Stoker's Dracula* (1992) vowed to be the most faithful adaptation of Stoker's classic novel, but depicted the Count as a man who lost his soul for love, rather than the frightful creature he is in the book. This retelling of one of the world's most famous scary stories was introduced with the tagline 'Love never dies,' and sold as a horrific romance or a drama. Similarly, Kenneth Branagh's *Mary Shelley's Frankenstein* (1994), and Stephen Frears' *Mary Reilly* (1996), a 'new twist' on Robert Louis Stevenson's *Strange Case of Dr Jekyll and Mr Hyde*, were sold as period dramas, and showed the legendary characters as doomed human beings rather than monsters. Horror was out of fashion, its very name considered a dirty word by marketers and studio executives, and only presentable if bastardised with other genres. Jonathan Demme's 1991 American *giallo*, *Silence of the Lambs*, the story of an imprisoned cannibal and a loose serial killer who skins his victims, was seen as a thriller and went on to win five Academy Awards, the ultimate sign of its mainstream acceptability. The studios continued to hide the true faces of their monsters and to couple them with comedy, adventure or crime throughout

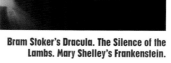

Bram Stoker's Dracula. The Silence of the Lambs. Mary Shelley's Frankenstein.

4 On eighties horror movies, see J Stell, *Psychos! Sickos! Sequels!*, 1998, Midnight Marquee.

5 See *Roaring Nineties: A New History of the World's Most Prosperous Decade*, by Nobel Prize winner J E Stiglitz, 2004, W W Norton and Company.

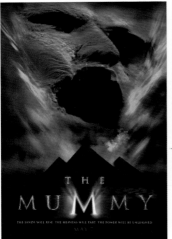

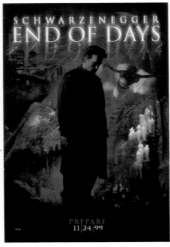

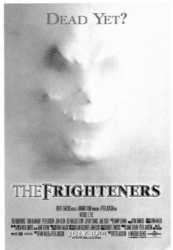

Interview with the Vampire. The Mummy.
End of Days. Braindead. The Frighteners.
OPPOSITE: In the Mouth of Madness.

6 Thomas Schatz, *Hollywood Genres: Formulas, Filmmaking and the Studio System*, Random House, 1981, pp 37-38.

7 Leo Braudy, *The World in a Frame: What We See in Films*, Anchor Books, 1977.

the decade; *Interview with the Vampire* and *The Crow* (both 1994) were labelled 'supernatural thrillers'; *The Mummy* (1999) and *The Devil's Advocate* (1997), as well as *End of Days* and *Stigmata* (both 1999) offer a few more examples of watered-down chillers. Even Peter Jackson, who had broken all blood and guts records with his 1992 gorefest *Braindead* (also known as *Dead Alive*), released in 1996 *The Frighteners*, which frightened viewers much less than it made them laugh.

It's a *Scream!*

The introduction of VHS in the early eighties, and of DVD in the mid-nineties, meant that horror fans were finally able to watch their favourite movies over and over again – enough times to know them by heart, quote them regularly, and most of all, detect and study the tricks used by filmmakers to make them jump. Mirroring the advent of this new film-savvy generation, a series of self-reflective movies came out in the first half of the decade. John Carpenter's *In the Mouth of Madness* (1995) and George Romero's *The Dark Half* (1993) looked at the link between horror literature and real life; Wes Craven's *New Nightmare* (1994), the seventh outing of the *Nightmare on Elm Street* series, analysed the influence of scary movies on their makers. Their plots mixed fiction with elements of fiction-within-fiction; clearly, the goal of these post-modern *mises-en-abyme* was to acknowledge the audience's understanding of moviemaking techniques, and try and play with the viewers' expectations.

The trend culminated with Craven's *Scream* series, in which the killers used the now well-known rules of slasher films to decide who was to die next. Filled with references to the classics, *Scream* (1996) biopsied the genre and twisted and bent its clichés with humour and intelligence. The second instalment dealt with the very fact that the murders had resumed, like in a sequel (when Randy's school teacher asks him if he believes someone is making a 'real-life sequel,' he replies, 'Why would anyone want to do that? Sequels suck!') and with the impact of fictionalised violence on society. It also featured a movie within a movie – *Stab*, an account of the events of the first *Scream* film: in effect, a fake *Scream* taking place within its sequel.

This tendency to expose stereotypes corresponds to perfection to what film historian Thomas Schatz calls the baroque phase of genre evolution[6]. After an experimental stage, where its themes and conventions are isolated and established, a classic stage, during which they are understood by the filmmakers and their audience, and a refinement stage, a genre goes through a baroque or self-conscious phase, where its formulas and iconography are examined and inverted, to the point where they 'themselves become the substance or content of the work'. This phenomenon happens when viewers have assimilated the genre's inner workings well enough that they no longer react the way they are meant to – in our case, the tricks have become so obvious that they no longer scare. As Leo Braudy put it, 'change in genre occurs when the audience says, "that's too infantile … Show us something more complicated."'[7] Self-reflection is thus a logical and necessary – if often unpleasant – step in the evolution of a genre, opening the door to new possibilities.

The Dark Half. I Know What You Did Last Summer. Scream. Urban Legend.

Craven's groundbreaking chiller broke the sacrosanct $100 million barrier in the United States, turned screenwriter Kevin Williamson into an instant sensation, spawned two hit sequels, and was followed by a series of largely inferior copycats. From *I Know What You Did Last Summer I* (1997), *II* (1998) and *III* (2006), to *Urban Legend I* (1998), *II* (2000) and *III* (2005), *Final Scream* (2001), or *Wishcraft* (2002), these pointless follow-ups plagued the genre with low-quality, self-aware, tongue-in-cheek teen slashers for the rest of the decade. The trend was subsequently parodied in *Scary Movie* (2000) and the adequately named *Shriek if You Know What I Did Last Friday the 13th* (also 2000). As for Williamson, once considered the saviour of horror, he crashed and burned after the failures of his directorial debut *Teaching Mrs Tingle* (1999) and of his last collaboration with Craven, the fatally flawed *Cursed*, in 2005. Given the unfortunate immediate consequences of *Scream*'s success, genre fans may have had the feeling Craven had indeed taken their love of scary movies 'one step too far' …

The only exception to the general mediocrity of the sub-genre, Joss Whedon's brilliant hit TV show *Buffy the Vampire Slayer* rocked both the horror and high school worlds from 1997 to 2003. Referential and aimed at young adults, *Buffy the Vampire Slayer* was undeniably a product of the decade, but its clever mix of supernatural adventures and teenage situations and of humour and serious battles, as well as its complex and endearing characters and its fearlessness (which other series can claim to have had both musical and silent episodes? How many haven't been afraid to kill several of their most beloved protagonists?), won over the hearts of millions of viewers. The series ended after seven successful seasons, when lead actress Sarah Michelle Gellar refused to renew her contract to pursue a career on the big screen. Buffy continues to fight the forces of evil in a series of comic books.

Last Twitches

The second half of the decade saw the emergence of another new and somewhat disturbing trend: the remaking of classics. *The Haunting*, Jan de Bont's 1999 update of the Robert Wise masterpiece, traded the subtle, atmospheric thrills and growing sense of dread of the original for computer-generated shocks. Rated PG-13, it raked in $91 million in the States – not that much of a success considering it had cost $80 million to make, opened on over 2,800 screens nationwide, and featured two of the hottest stars of the time, Catherine Zeta-Jones and Liam Neeson. Released five months later, Gus Van Sant's verbatim remake of Hitchcock's 1960 masterpiece *Psycho*, with Vince Vaughn as Norman Bates, barely paid back its $20 million investment. A very weak start for a concept which would become all the rage a few years later …

The same year however, the agonising genre twitched a couple of times, with surprisingly favourable results.

First, *The Blair Witch Project* (1999), shot in 8 days on a shoestring budget, in black and white, with a hand-held 16mm camera, grossed over $140 million in the States, becoming the world's most profitable independent movie of all time. If the quality of the film itself divided critics and moviegoers alike – some claiming it was the scariest cinematic experience they'd ever had, others seeing it as 'the biggest con trick that the world has ever fallen for'[8], it's the clever Internet marketing campaign surrounding its release that turned it into a phenomenon. According to its official website[9], the events depicted in the movie were true and the film footage had indeed been found in a forest where three film students went missing while shooting a documentary on a local legend, the Blair witch. The site gave details on the myth, the filmmakers, and various pieces of evidence of their disappearance; the Internet Movie Database[10] listed the actors as 'missing, presumed dead' before the release. The stunt paid off; intrigued by its verisimilitude and curious to see what the buzz was all about, audiences crowded the theatres, and the film and its makers became a topic of discussion on- and offline all around the world. Writers-directors Daniel Myrick and Eduardo Sanchez were not involved in the 2000 sequel, *Book of Shadows*, a bitter artistic and commercial disappointment for its production company Artisan Entertainment, previously responsible for another successful 1999 scary movie, *Stir of Echoes*.

The Haunting. The Blair Witch Project. The Sixth Sense. Candyman.

Secondly, in 1998, a 28-year-old director with the unusual and hardly pronounceable name of M Night Shyamalan was granted $50 million, final cut, and a major star – Bruce Willis – by Disney Pictures for a ghost story (of course described as a 'psychological drama') called *The Sixth Sense*. Released in the US in the middle of the summer, a time usually monopolised by blockbusters, the movie was expected to be a mid-level hit, but went through the roof – $293 million nationally at the end of its run – and made Shyamalan one of the most sought-after filmmakers of the moment. Its twist ending, in the *Carnival of Souls* tradition, set a new standard for the resolution of genre stories; followers include *The Others* (2001), *Saw* (2004) and its sequels, and *High Tension* (2003). Shyamalan himself unfortunately felt compelled to repeat the trick *ad nauseam*, using it as a signature in *Unbreakable* (2000), *Signs* (2002), and the abysmal *The Village* (2004).

Strangely, the consecutive successes of *The Blair Witch Project* and *The Sixth Sense* did not seem to push producers and studios to invest in the genre. The world wasn't quite ready yet …

A Cut Above the Rest

In all fairness, the nineties also gave birth to a few rare treats. Largely overlooked, rarely granted wide theatrical releases, sometimes made for TV only, they have nevertheless contributed to shaping the genre in one way or another.

A first example would be Peter Jackson's 1992 *Braindead*, already mentioned, which drove

8 *The Rough Guide To Horror Movies*, Alan Jones, 2005, Rough Guides, p 51 (Jones doesn't say which category of viewers he falls into.)
9 http://www.blairwitch.com
10 http://www.imdb.com

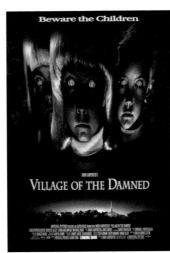

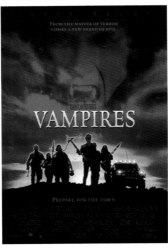

Village of the Damned. Vampires.

a stake through the heart of the gore sub-genre. With over 300 litres of blood used for its final scene, and more gross-out jokes than any previous horror comedy, this splatstick classic was simply impossible to top. Jackson himself moved away from the genre with his following film, and to this day, has never looked back.

The same year, *Candyman*, directed by Bernard Rose and adapted from a short story by Clive Barker, scared audiences while examining the link between an urban legend and the ghetto environment which had created it. A minor box office success, it was followed by two sequels.

Premiering on ABC in May 1994, the Stephen King miniseries *The Stand*, directed by King specialist Mick Garris, was seen by an unprecedented average of 50 million viewers on each of its four episodes. The format allowed many of the book's developments and subplots to be included in a particularly complex end-of-the-world epic, and its impeccable cast – Gary Sinise, Molly Ringwald, Ossie Davis, Rob Lowe – created multi-dimensional and endearing characters. Although made for TV, *The Stand* is one of the decade's biggest genre achievements. Another would be *Storm of the Century* (1999), also a miniseries, but this time from an original screenplay by King. Few may have seen or heard of it, but this story of a supernatural killer blackmailing the inhabitants of an island during a snowstorm is one of the best movies ever made from King's material.

Also on the small screen, Twentieth Century Fox's *The X-Files* premiered in September 1993, and soon turned into an international phenomenon. The names Mulder and Scully and the slogans 'The Truth is Out There' and 'I Want to Believe' quickly became well-known pop culture references; the series aired for nine seasons and a hit feature film, *X-Files: The Movie*, was released in 1998 (a sequel is expected for the summer of 2008). The show's realistic approach to supernatural themes also inspired countless TV documentaries on UFOs and other mysteries. Creator Chris Carter launched another series, *Millennium*, in 1996; though dealing with similar topics in a comparable way, the popularity of this dark and underrated gem was largely inferior, and it ended after only three seasons.

Featuring impeccable performances by Corbin Bernsen in the titular role, Brian Yuzna's *The Dentist* (1996) and its sequel (1998) were as much black comedies and social satires as they were horror films. Most famous for producing Stuart Gordon's *Re-Animator* in 1985, Yuzna was one of the most prolific directors of the 1990s. Other titles with his name attached included *Bride of Re-Animator* (1990), *Return of the Living Dead III* (1993), *Necronomicon* (1993) and *Progeny* (1998), all of decent quality.

With a cast of unknowns, a single location and a very clever script, Vincenzo Natali's 1997 *Cube* might well be the decade's most original genre production. It won well-deserved awards in festivals all around the planet, but only received a limited theatrical release in the States (16 screens!). Still, two sequels followed, and the movie is today considered a cult classic.

It's also in the nineties that horror's luminaries – John Carpenter (*Halloween*, 1978), Wes Craven (*A Nightmare on Elm Street*, 1984), Dario Argento (*Suspiria*, 1977), George Romero (*Night of the Living Dead*, 1969), Sam Raimi (*Evil Dead*, 1981) – released their last genre hits to date.

In addition to the aforementioned *In the Mouth of Madness*, one of the most frightening and powerful movies of its time, Carpenter directed (and starred in) *Body Bags* (1993), a brilliant made-for-TV anthology, filled with good old fashioned scares and dark humour, and whose last segment was directed by Tobe Hooper (*The Texas Chain Saw Massacre*, 1974). Carpenter's 1995 remake of Wolf Rilla's 1960 film *Village of the Damned* and his 1998 *Vampires* are also worth a mention.

Romero and Argento collaborated in 1991 for *Two Evil Eyes* (*Due Occhi Diaboli*), another anthology film based on short stories by Edgar Allan Poe. The former also released *The Dark Half* in 1993. A box-office failure, it is nevertheless a good adaptation of the eponymous Stephen King novel.

Besides the major successes of *New Nightmare* and the *Scream* series, Craven also directed *The People Under the Stairs* (1991), another hit ($24 million in the US) and a return of sorts to his 1970s work, though slightly lighter in tone. The filmmaker intended the movie as a political allegory, and was quoted saying 'the two antagonists … are conservatives … people who would elect Nancy and Ronald.'[11]

Finally, Raimi's *Darkman* (1990) was among the first in a new trend of dark superheroes, continued with *The Crow* (1994), *Spawn* (1997), *Batman Begins* (2005), and the same director's *Spider-Man* series, starting in 2002. Grossing $48 million worldwide, this Universal production was another success for Raimi, who went on three years later to release *Army of Darkness* (1992), a sequel which took the *Evil Dead* series further down the comedy and mainstream roads, auguring the direction the filmmaker's career would soon take. 'We tried to make a cool summer movie primarily for boys fourteen to sixteen years old,' star and co-producer Bruce Campbell told *Cinefantastique*[12] at the time. 'It's not docu-horror like the first one. It's more like an adventure story.' Raimi returned to horror once more, in 2000, with *The Gift*, and since then has only contributed to the genre in a producing capacity, though his return to horror direction is announced for 2009 with *Drag Me to Hell*, starring Justin Long.

R is for Restraint

It is a common misconception that during the nineties, distributors were reluctant to release R-rated films, and that in the nineties scary movies had to obtain PG-13 certificates to stand a chance in the market. Actually, most big successes of the time – *The Blair Witch Project*, *Scream*, *Scream II*, *Bram Stoker's Dracula*, *Wes Craven's New Nightmare*, *Stir of Echoes*, *The Crow*, *In the Mouth of Madness* to name but a few – as well as many independents – *Cube*, *The Dentist* – were rated R (Restricted – no-one under 17 without parent or adult guardian). This erroneous conclusion probably comes from the fact that the films were generally less bloody than their more recent counterparts; the R-rating granted both to the gothic chills of Tim Burton's 1999 *Sleepy Hollow* and to the tortures of Eli Roth's 2007 *Hostel: Part II* is a clear example of this evolution.

Created in 1968 after the abolition of the Hays Production Code, which imposed censorship on movies that didn't conform to its rules, the ratings system of the Motion Pictures Association of America (MPAA) is one of self-regulation. The certificate is intended as an indication for parents of whether a film is suitable for their children. The evaluation is flexible, and is 'meant to consider parental attitudes at the time the picture is rated'[13]; in other words, to reflect the opinion of most parents at a given moment. In a time of relative peace and quiet such as the nineties, with televised real-life atrocities as well as fictional horrors few and far between, the public's reactions to on-screen violence were bound to be harsher and less permissive; therefore the R certificate was harder to obtain if your picture contained any elements of graphic violence.

The People Under the Stairs. Sleepy Hollow.

Contrary to what happens in many other countries (including the UK), the MPAA does not have the power to prohibit the distribution of a movie, and filmmakers don't even have the legal obligation to submit their work to the board; but the implications of an NC-17 (No Children – no-one under 17 admitted at all) certificate – or of the absence of any – on the commercial potential of a movie are such that the rating, or lack of, inevitably has an impact. Advertising for NC-17 movies is extremely difficult, and giving them wide releases nearly impossible. Even if such a film were to receive good publicity and a decent amount of screens, teenagers under seventeen constitute such a big percentage of the movie-going population, that returning profits would be much harder. Producers are therefore less inclined to invest large sums in such films, and in a time where mild violence such as *Sleepy Hollow*'s was likely to get an R certificate, they were not inclined to increase the amount of fake blood, since they had to stay within the limits of the R to have a shot at success. The situation hasn't changed much since; studios and investors still have to obey the laws of the market and aim for the same middle-ground rating. Only what is considered acceptable within this category fluctuates constantly, according to the public's perception.

Horror movies of the nineties were thus generally non-threatening: true products of their time.

11 Quoted in *Screams and Nightmares, The Films of Wes Craven*, B J Robb, Titan Books, 1998, p 152.

12 *Cinefantastique*, vol 23, number 1, August 1992, p 52.

13 See http://www.mpaa.org/Ratings_FAQ.asp

Ring.

Asian Nightmares

While America and Western Europe prospered, Japan, on the other hand, entered its first economic recession since the end of World War II. After decades of continuous growth and the boom years of the late 1980s, when the yen soared and companies expanded and invested massively, the bubble finally burst around 1991 when the property and share markets, until then used as securities for loans, suddenly crashed, leaving investors with insurmountable debts. Companies and financial institutions went bankrupt, jobs were lost; and despite many government initiatives, demand remained low.

Depression turned to nightmare when on 20 March 1995, Japan faced its first major terrorist attack. On that day, over 5,000 commuters were exposed to the nerve gas sarin in the subway system; the attack, perpetrated by members of the Aum Shinrikyo sect, claimed twelve lives, injured fifty and gave another 900 temporary vision problems. The incident marked the end of a golden age for a nation until then considered virtually crime-free.

Inevitably, these changes in Japanese society would find an echo in local horror productions, which suddenly expanded in the second half of the decade. According to Norio Tsuruta[14], creator of the influential *Scary True Stories* (*Honto ni atta kowai hanashi*, 1991) video series and director of *Ring 0: Birthday* (*Ring 0: Bâsudei*, 2000) and *Scarecrow* (*Kakashi*, 2001), 'After the sarin episode, the Japanese people knew that sudden unreasonable death could be a part of everyday life … Without this change of consciousness, I think Japanese horror would not have caught on.'

Of course, Japan wasn't new to the genre. Ghosts and apparitions played an important part in Japanese folklore, and for the main part of the 20th century, horror movies brought local legends to the screen. These atmospheric tales were replaced by a wave of gorier flicks in the eighties, such as the *Evil Dead Trap* (*Shiryo no wana*, 1988) and *Guinea Pigs* (*Za ginipiggu*, 1985-1992) series, but planted the seeds for a new type of scary movies which would develop in the nineties.

In 1991 indeed, Tsoruta released the aforementioned straight-to-video (known as 'v-cinema' in Japan) adaptation of a manga based on real-life encounters with ghosts, *Scary True Stories*. Shot on an extremely low budget ($60,000), it returned a handsome profit and was followed by two sequels. The series' restraint, after the excesses of the 1980s, and its slow-building suspense would influence other filmmakers, among whom Hideo Nakata who, after the v-flick *Curse, Death and Spirit* (*Jushiryou*) in 1992 and *Don't Look Up/The Ghost Actress* (*Joyû-rei*) in 1996, released his surprise hit *Ring* (*Ringu*) in 1998, which would turn the trend pioneered by Tsoruta into the worldwide phenomenon known as J-Horror.

Based on a 1991 novel by Koji Suzuki[15], *Ring* tells the story of a reporter investigating the mysterious deaths of a group of girls who died at the hands of a vengeful spirit, Sadako, exactly a week after watching a cursed video. She ends up seeing the tape herself and having to break the curse in less than a week to avoid meeting the same fate. Combining urban legend and traditional ghost story in a contemporary setting, *Ring* doesn't feel the need to explain every detail of its deceptively linear plot, but leaves room to interpretation; its gradual building of tension culminates in a now legendary final scene in which Sadako crawls out of a television screen to catch her victim, leaving viewers to wonder if the sofa in front of their TV set is still a

14 Quoted in *J-Horror: The Definitive Guide to The Ring, The Grudge and Beyond*, D Kalat, Vertical, 2007, p 67.
15 Suzuki's book had already been adapted for television in 1995 (*Ring: The Complete Edition*, Chisui Takigawa) and in a 1996 manga by Koujirou Nagai.

safe place to be.

'I went to five or six theatres and saw kids calling each other on their cell phones right after the screening, telling their friends how scary it was and to go see it,' Nakata told *Fangoria* in 2000[16]. Made for a mere $1.2 million, *Ring* grossed over $15 million in Japan. It was not only followed by the American remake we will review shortly, but also by a Korean retelling (*The Ring Virus*, 1999), two Japanese TV series (*Ring: The Final Chapter* (*Ringu: Saishûshô*, 1999) and *Spiral* (*Rasen*, 1999)), three Japanese sequels (Joji Iida's *Spiral*, 1998, Nakata's *Ring 2*, 1999, and Tsoruta's *Ring 0: Birthday*, 2000), and several manga adaptations.

Ring's success set Asian horror production into overdrive. In the following years, dozens of J-Horror movies would see the day, mainly in Japan and Korea; in 1998 and 1999 only, Ataru Oikawa's *Tomie* and Toshiro Inomata's direct-to-video *Tomie: Another Face* (*Tomie: anaza feisu*), Kiyoshi Kurosawa's *Seance* (*Kôrei*), Shunichi Nagasaki's *Four Countries* or *Land of the Dead* (*Shikoku*), and Tae-Yong Kim and Kyu-Dong Min's *Memento Mori* (*Yeogo goedam II*) would

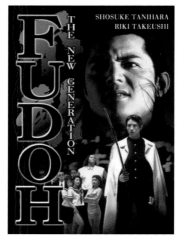

be released with varying success. All share the same characteristics: long-haired female ghosts looking to avenge their violent death, female heroines, curses that cannot be ended or contained, slow pace, low degree (if not absence) of gore and graphic violence. Thematically, J-horror reflects the main issues of modern Japanese society: the questioning of traditional gender roles and its impact on women, fractured or dysfunctional families, child abuse. If Western anxieties are derived from international tensions, Japan's problems are essentially internal, and it's no wonder horror movies explore the very issues their audiences have to deal with every day.

Nakata's movie (and to a certain extent, its sequel) toured festivals around the world to unanimously positive responses. Bootleg copies spread in the States very much the way Sadako's videotape circulates in the story, which gave the film an underground flavour horror fans appreciated. *Ring* was eventually released on DVD in 2003, along with its remake, Gore Verbinski's 2002 *The Ring*.

Fudoh: The New Generation. Audition.

In parallel with the development of J-Horror, prolific filmmaker Takashi Miike, who'd already directed the 1996 Yakuza epic *Fudoh: The New Generation* (*Gokudô sengokushi: Fudô*) and two dozen straight-to-video outings since the beginning of the decade, got his first big break in 1999 with *Audition* (*Ôdishon*), the shocking story of a widower who sends a casting call to find a new wife, and ends up getting horribly tortured by the woman he chooses. If the first half of the movie is a slow-paced love story, the second part is by contrast strikingly violent, not so much through an excess of graphic horror than thanks to Miike's masterful use of sound effects and Eihi Shiina's chilling performance as sadistic *femme fatale* Asami. Although light years away from J-Horror's understated scares, *Audition* nevertheless shares some of its themes: loneliness ('The whole of Japan is lonely,' says one of the protagonists), the frustrating role of women in society, and once again, child abuse. 'I don't feel it's the specific responsibility of a director to tackle social issues,' Miike told the BBC in 2001[17]; 'with *Audition* however, I was pleased that I was able to touch upon something that is prevalent in Japanese culture.' Unsurprisingly, this may well be the movie he will be remembered for. *Audition* was officially released years later in Europe and America, but it would soon have a profound influence on Western horror filmmaking. As for Miike, he would keep pushing the boundaries of gore and kinkiness outside of horror throughout the 2000s.

16 'Ring in the New Fear', Donato Totaro, *Fangoria* 193, June 2000, p 20.
17 Takashi Miike interviewed by David Wood, BBC website, http://www.bbc.co.uk/films/2001/03/13/miike_takashi_interview.shtml

2000:

'The Millennium Starts Screaming'

(Tagline for *Scream 3*, 2000)

THE START OF THE 2000S PROVED RELATIVELY QUIET ON BOTH THE SOCIO-political and horror fronts, but planted the seeds of change for the years to come. Having avoided the predicted crash of the Year 2000 Computer Bug, the world continued for a while to invest confidently in new technologies. In January 2001, America half-heartedly welcomed a new president, Republican George W Bush, after one of the closest and most controversial elections in US history. And in theatres, the first post-*Scream* scare of the 2000s came from a New Line production called *Final Destination* …

'You can't cheat death' (*Final Destination*)

James Wong's *Final Destination* follows a high school student, Alex (Devon Sawa), who has a vision of his plane crashing as he's about to fly to Paris on a school trip. He and a few classmates get off the plane, only to see it explode after take-off with the rest of their companions on board. In the days that follow, the survivors start to die under strange circumstances. Alex soon understands that his premonition has allowed them to elude their intended deaths, and that fate is now reclaiming their lives one by one.

Final Destination marked the feature film debut of director James Wong, who, along with writing and producing partner Glen Morgan, was until then known as Chris Carter's collaborator on *The X-Files* and *Millennium*. Wong's TV work allowed him to develop a feel for moody atmospheres, and the inventive death scenes, increasing sense of foreboding, dark tone and sinister soundtrack he brought to the film all greatly contributed to its success.

The movie's true originality, however, lies in the twist it puts on the teenage slasher genre that was all the rage after the success of *Scream*. Rather than a visible killer, the threat the heroes face is

Death itself, an unstoppable force that kills its victims through chain reactions of everyday events that lead to their demises. But what is now regarded as the story's best idea did not please the studio. Newcomer Jeffrey Reddick[18], who scripted the original drafts, explains[19] that New Line 'was extremely nervous about having a horror movie without a tangible killer. I read in *Entertainment Weekly* that the other writers scoffed that my original version had a hooded psycho with a sickle, hacking up teenagers, which isn't true. After New Line bought the treatment and had me write the script, they insisted that I visualize the threat at the climax of the movie. I went with the idea of an Angel of Death, a force that claimed people who cheated Death. Throughout the story you got hints of this force, either by an eerie gust of wind … or a ripple of shadows. And in the final showdown, Alex and Clear briefly saw the Angel.' Morgan and Wong fought to avoid showing this apparition and eventually won the battle. In the final movie, there is no identifiable threat the protagonists can hide from; death can strike anytime, anywhere, in an unlimited series of ways. The idea hit a nerve amongst the youth of the time, particularly aware of their own mortality after the Columbine High School massacre on 20 April 1999, where two schoolboys went on a shooting rampage that claimed the lives of twelve students and a teacher. Both this tragedy and *Final Destination* reminded young people that even they can die at any time, for no logical reason, during the most trivial moments of their everyday lives.

The opening scene at the airport is certainly the most memorable of the movie. Introducing the characters and situation in a very realistic way, it builds a sense of impending doom by filling the screen with hints and premonition signs: the use of the words 'terminal' and 'departed' on the announcement board, the departure time matching Alex's birthday, a John Denver song playing in the men's room, the number of the gate echoing the number of students embarking the flight … Through this sequence, *Final Destination* taps into another great anxiety of its time: flying. Released a year and a half before the terrorist attack on the World Trade Centre changed civil aviation forever, the movie was originally called *Flight 180*, 'because a flight number these days

18 Ironically, Reddick originally intended the script as a spec episode of *The X-Files*; it was later optioned by New Line, where Reddick worked at the time.

19 Email interview with the author, December 2007.

HARRISON FORD   MICHELLE PFEIFFER

He was

the perfect husband

until his one mistake

followed them home.

WHAT
LIES
BENEATH

What Lies Beneath.

has a sort of death connotation,' Wong said in a March 2000 interview[20]. Indeed in 1999 and the first two months of 2000 alone, close to 600 people lost their lives in plane crashes and hijackings around the world. And on 25 July 2000, only thirteen days after the French release of the movie, Air France Flight 4590 from Charles de Gaulle to JFK (the opposite direction to the flight in the film) crashed shortly after take-off – as in the story – killing all one hundred passengers and nine crew members as well as four people on the ground. The cause of the real-life explosion was eerily similar to that of the film's: a piece of disintegrating tyre struck a fuel tank, whose leaking fuel was ignited by a part of the engine (its exact nature is disputed)[21], against a leak of combustible fluids ignited by a spark beneath the coach cabin. There were no students on a school trip on Flight 4590, but a group of Germans on their way to a luxury cruise. Speaking of premonitions …

Not only does *Final Destination* rely heavily on its sense of dread, it further throws the audience off balance by making the deaths happen slightly before or after we expect them. The scene where Clear and Alex meet the other survivors at the terrace of a coffee shop exemplifies this well: no one dies when the car almost crashes into Billy's bike, and Terry gets run over by the bus a split second before we realise she's in danger. This emphasis on timing and anticipation rather than on the red stuff also separates the film from other *Scream* followers. If Kevin Williamson's influences in writing *Scream* were the slasher movies of the late seventies and eighties, Wong and Morgan's roots go back further in time, as evidenced by the names they gave their characters: Murnau, Lewton, Browning, Weine: all are genre filmmakers from the first half of the twentieth century, while Hitchcock (Billy's last name) is one of the writers' main sources of inspiration.

Also unlike the *Scream* saga and its imitators, there is no humour in *Final Destination*, and no real resolution: it's obviously easier to stop a killer of flesh and blood than to put an end to Death's actions … But this dark tone didn't please everyone. After the ending tested poorly with audiences, New Line ordered a reshoot, replacing a scene where Alex sacrificed himself to save Clear, with another that gave a different interpretation of Death's design and left the ending open in a more traditional way.

Surfing the teenage slasher wave, but bringing new ideas and a fresh outlook on the sub-genre, Wong's story of death and doom grossed over $53 million in the US alone: less than pure nineties production *Scream 3,* released a month earlier, but still impressive for a feature without stars or franchise name, at a time when horror didn't seem to welcome originality. It was followed by two sequels (in 2003 and 2006) and a series of novels; and although it may not have started a new trend in horror, it did show studios that supernatural stories were still popular. As Reddick observes[22], 'If you look at the films that came out in 2001 and beyond, you do see an increase in this sub-genre after *Final Destination*: *Thir13en Ghosts* (2001), *Soul Survivors* (2001), *The Others* (2001), *The Mothman Prophecies* (2002), *Darkness Falls* (2003), *Ghost Ship* (2002) and so on. I think after the surprising success of *Final Destination*, studios realised you could do a horror film that didn't revolve around an axe-wielding maniac slicing and dicing pretty teenagers right after they had sex.'

Supernatural Thrills

The same year, two well-known filmmakers directed genre features, light enough on gore and scares to be released at unusual times for horror: the summer for Robert Zemeckis' *What Lies Beneath*, and the run-up to Christmas for Sam Raimi's *The Gift*.

Released 21 July 2000, *What Lies Beneath* is an uncomfortable mix of Hitchcockian suspense and mild supernatural scares. Convinced that her next-door neighbour has murdered his spouse, a scientist's wife, Claire Spencer (Michelle Pfeiffer), believes she's haunted by the ghost of the presumed victim. But when the woman turns up alive, Claire understands that the spirit in her house may be linked to a dark secret her own husband Norman (Harrison Ford) has kept from her.

What Lies Beneath opened at number one at the US box-office and went on to gross over $155 million, on a budget of $90 million. Walking in the footsteps of *The Sixth Sense* (1999), it is however considerably less scary than its successful predecessor. In the first part of the story,

20 In Sarah Kendzior, 'Wong Time Coming', *The 11th Hour* Web Magazine, 10 March 2000, http://www.the11thhour.com/archives/032000/features/wong2.html
21 Wikipedia, http://en.wikipedia.org/wiki/Air_France_Flight_4590
22 Email interview with the author, December 2007.

where the spirit is most present, the focus is on Claire and Norman's reactions to her visions rather than the visions themselves, and their consequences for their relationship. Is Claire going crazy? Will her husband understand her? Who can she trust? The ghost is little more than a way to lead Claire to uncover Norman's past; Harrison Ford declared to the BBC[23] that 'the ghost … can be seen as an effort by the subconscious mind of the character Michelle plays to remind her of the events that she has repressed.' The supernatural elements of the story aren't used to build up tension; the ghost merely appears in jump-scares, more or less out of the blue, and vanishes just as soon. Zemeckis takes his time to develop the characters' personalities, but doesn't bother creating a scary atmosphere.

In the second part of the film, we discover that Norman is the actual threat to Claire's life, the real villain. The ghost practically disappears from the story until the final scene where she takes Norman down to the bottom of the lake with her, and the movie turns into a much more classic thriller, with Claire being chased and almost killed by her husband and escaping at the eleventh hour. Hampered by the ghostly elements of its plot, *What Lies Beneath* is a rare case of a movie that actually deserves to be considered a supernatural thriller, a suspense story that simply borrows techniques and themes of the horror genre.

The Gift, out for a limited release on 20 December then wide in January 2001, is in many ways similar to *What Lies Beneath*. Like Zemeckis's film, *Final Destination* to some degree, and *Stir of Echoes*, *The Sixth Sense* and Neil Jordan's *In Dreams* the previous year, it features a protagonist who has somehow been granted the ability to see the invisible (ghosts, murders, future events) and has to accomplish a task (lay a soul to rest, save a life) despite their close relations' disbelief. Like *What Lies Beneath*, it is more akin to the thriller than the horror genre.

The Gift.

Cate Blanchett plays Annie Wilson, a fortune-teller in a small town in Georgia, who is asked to use her gift to help find a missing girl, Jessica King (Katie Holmes). Annie has a vision of Jessica being murdered and thrown in a pond, and her body is found at the place she indicates. It leads her to suspect the owner of the pond, Donnie Barksdale (Keanu Reeves), whose battered wife had asked Annie to read her cards.

Here again, more attention is given to the intricate relationships between the characters and the social repercussions of Annie's visions than to the ghosts she sees. But if the supernatural elements are similarly used more as a plot device than as the focus of the movie, they are much more integrated in the story and the general tone than in Zemeckis's film. The plot twists are predictable (invariably, Annie misinterprets her visions and suspects the wrong man, only to realise that the murderer is the one she had feelings for), but Raimi cleverly uses his small-town setting to create an eerie atmosphere which helps make Annie's visions seem like a natural part of the world she lives in.

A return of sorts to suspense and horror for Raimi, *The Gift* was also a clear departure from his previous genre outings. Far from the excesses of the *Evil Dead* series, the filmmaker's goal was to 'make the supernatural not as exciting and not as particularly frightening as I wanted. It was more about making it believable as a real thing that the audience could accept.'[24]

Raimi's efforts were not rewarded; critics were divided and *The Gift* was a commercial failure. Raimi went on to focus on the *Spider-Man* series and leave to others the task of directing his production company's genre features.

23 BBC Interview by James Mottram, http://www.bbc.co.uk/films/2000/10/18/harrison_ford_interview.shtml

24 'Sam Raimi opens *The Gift*, discovers suspense indiewood-style', Anthony Kaufman, *indieWIRE*, 9 January 2001, http://www.indiewire.com/people/int_Raimi_Sam_010116.html

Dead Funny

While high profile productions explored the line between horror and thriller, a handful of low-budget features came out that proudly claimed their belonging to the genre, while adding a hint of comedy to otherwise traditional scary movie plots.

Mike Mendez's *The Convent*, the story of a group of college kids who spend a night in a derelict boarding school haunted by demonic nuns, was a hit in every film festival it was screened at, from Sundance to the Brussels Festival of Fantastic Film, to FantasPorto in Portugal and Dead by Dawn in Edinburgh. A perfect midnight movie, it mixes gore, scares and silly jokes in an over-the-top, cartoonish blend reminiscent of *Evil Dead II*, Mendez's main inspiration. 'Watching that movie was kind of film school for me. I'm such a fan, humour and horror is the most natural mix, it's naturally where my mind goes,' the director says[25]. 'I was just being myself.' A heartfelt homage to splatter movies, *The Convent* takes its scary creatures seriously and jokes only at the expense of its selfish and libidinous victims, thereby avoiding any similarities with spoofs such as *Scary Movie*, released the same year. Adding to the eccentricity of the script, unusual camera angles and neon-light colours give the movie a unique visual style. The make-up design for the demons, particularly the main nun, is both scary and in keeping with the originality and colourfulness of the photography.

Mendez also had the brilliant idea to cast genre favourite Adrienne Barbeau (*Escape From New York* (1981), *Creepshow* (1982)) as nun-exterminator Christine. Looking tougher than ever as what the actress describes as 'the female version of Snake Plissken'[26], she steals the show from the moment she appears in the last act. Says Mendez: 'I don't know why, you have horror stars like Robert Englund and Tony Todd, but no one ever really gave any attention to Adrienne Barbeau. That was always weird to me. She's done great genre films and she's a great actress and she was married to John Carpenter, so it just seemed logical. The production company wanted to get Lynda Carter, who played Wonder Woman, or Linda Blair (*The Exorcist*, 1973), but I really insisted. She read it and really liked it and we've been friends ever since. She loved the experience and she loves that people still talk about it.'

The Convent was Mendez's second feature after 1997's low-budget thriller *Killers* (aka *Real Killers*). A lifelong horror fan, he was brought up by 'ultraconservative Catholic parents,' and after seeing *Halloween* at age six, was 'fascinated with that whole imagery, skulls and bats and all that. That was something my parents were very concerned about since they wanted me to be a good Catholic child. They didn't understand why I liked all these monsters and they still don't. That's where it began.'

Killers, selected for the Sundance Festival, gathered a lot of attention in the industry and opened doors for its 23-year-old director. 'I probably should have gone through those doors at the time, but instead I said yes to *The Convent*, which was not even a tenth of the size of the other movies that were being offered to me, because it was way more fun. The distributor of *Killers* was contractually obligated to make another movie and needed a horror movie; they just had a treatment and said I could do whatever I wanted.' Mendez developed the story with writer Chaton Anderson and was given eighteen days and $700,000 to shoot the movie. 'Even though the story's not mine, it was probably the most freedom and independence I ever had. It was all just a matter of doing it in the time and the budget.' The financial constraints meant

The Convent.

25 Interview with the author, San Diego, USA, July 2007.
26 Interview with Adrienne Barbeau, Uncle Creepy, *Dread Central*, 20 May 2005, http://www.dreadcentral.com/index.php?name=Interviews&req=showcontent&id=93

that many effects had to be improvised on set, including the demons' jerky moves and the bright green colour used for blood. 'We were experimenting as we were shooting, so some of it is kind of hokey. The weird insanity of the movie was very present on set, and I think that a lot of the insanity of making that movie found its way into the actual film itself. The blood is always changing colour; it's supposed to look like lava. We only had so much fluorescent paint and we had to keep watering it down because we were spreading so much of it. But I think the whole low-budget ineptitude of it adds an extra charm.' The filmmaker's energy and enthusiasm for the project, despite time and money limitations, certainly show through on screen and are amongst the movie's biggest assets.

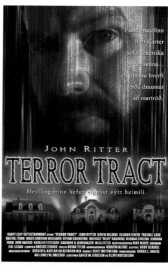

Despite being a success in every festival that screened it, *The Convent* was released directly on DVD in the States, further proof of the lack of faith distributors had in horror at the time. 'I think in France, Germany, Spain and Japan it got some sort of theatrical release. In the USA, Blockbuster didn't want to take the movie because of the opening.' Nevertheless, the movie has become a minor cult classic. 'The fact that people even know what this movie is to me is amazing. I used to believe that the further you get away from it the less people know what it is, but it seems to stay. People still enjoy it.'

Directors Lance W Dreesen and Clint Hutchison share a similar love for horror and unpretentious fun. Their first feature, *Terror Tract* (also known as *House on Terror Tract*), which premiered on American TV in October 2000, is an anthology movie whose segments are linked by an original story called *Make Me an Offer*, in which a real estate agent (John Ritter) shows a newlywed couple three houses in a suburban neighbourhood. But as it soon turns out, each of the properties has been the scene of some gruesome event, and finding a buyer is really a matter of life or death for the desperate agent.

Terror Tract. Cherry Falls.

Whether the story deals with real estate, a husband who catches his wife with her lover, a homicidal monkey or a teenager psychically linked to a serial killer, there's no shortage of blood and action. As with *The Convent*, the aim is to entertain and possibly shock with over-the-top, improbable scenarios rather than actually frighten or create creepy atmospheres, and a healthy dose of black humour makes its tone comparable to that of the *Tales from the Crypt* series. Unlike most anthology films, the wrap-around story is interesting, all three segments are comparably enjoyable, and the *Grand Guignol* ending, in which the whole neighbourhood goes insane, caps them off nicely.

Although *Terror Tract*, just like Mike Mendez's film, was a success in the festival circuit, it wasn't released theatrically in the United States. It would take Dreesen and Hutchison several years to go back behind the cameras, this time for two separate projects: *Big Bad Wolf* for the former in 2006, and *Conjurer* for the latter in 2007.

On a considerably bigger budget (a reported $14 million, against a mere $1 million for *Terror Tract*), *Cherry Falls* was another title that capitalised on the success of *Scream*. Using the same post-modern approach as Craven's hit, but mixing it with *American Pie* humour, Australian director Geoffrey Wright's Hollywood debut is a slasher movie with a twist: unlike Jason Vorhees or Michael Myers, whose victims are usually the least virtuous, this killer only targets virgins, which eventually leads the town's teens to organise a giant orgy to 'pop their cherries'. Despite a fair amount of gore and silly jokes, the blend doesn't really work here; the comedy bits aren't very funny and the scary scenes are too unoriginal to be frightening. Another horror title aimed at the non-horror crowd, *Cherry Falls* thankfully announced the end of the post-*Scream* self-conscious teenage slasher cycle.

Deep into the Woods. Versus.

27 The boy also murdered two young girls. In 1998, a 13-year-old boy killed his English teacher in Utsunomiya; two 14-year-olds stabbed an old lady to death in Tottori; and a 13-year-old boy knifed a classmate in Tokyo. On the subject, see 'Japan's Teenage Horrors', David Esnault, *Le Monde Diplomatique*, September 1999, http://mondediplo.com/1999/09/14japan

28 Interviewed by Tom Mes and Jasper Sharp, *Midnight Eye*, 4 September 2001, http://www. midnighteye.com/interviews/kinji_fukasaku.shtml

Foreign Frights

Outside the USA, horror was taken much more seriously.

Hit by a wave of recession following the 1999 introduction of the new Euro currency, Western Europe, unexpectedly led by France, reconciled with horror cinema after years – if not decades – of marginalisation of the genre.

Despite a few successes in the fifties (Henri-Georges Clouzot's *Diabolique* (*Les Diaboliques*, 1955), George Franju's *Eyes Without A Face* (*Les Yeux Sans Visage*, 1960) and seventies (Jean Rollin's vampire productions, including *The Nude Vampire* (*La Vampire Nue*, 1970) and *Lips of Blood* (*Lèvres de Sang*, 1975)), France had practically no horror tradition to speak of, and no producer in their right mind would have invested much in a genre title … until Lionel Delplanque's *Deep into the Woods* (*Promenons-Nous Dans Les Bois*) became the sleeper hit of the French summer. A retelling of Little Red Riding Hood, somewhere between *The Company of Wolves* (1984) and Agatha Christie's *And Then There Were None* (1939), this story of a group of comedians spending a gruesome night in an isolated castle after a performance is slow, atmospheric and at times surreal and poetic. Marketed as the French answer to *Scream*, the movie was actually closer to the works of Tim Burton and Dario Argento, Delplanque's main influences, and avoided both the jokes and traditional slasher structure adopted by Craven and his followers. If the result has flaws (the pacing is too slow, the characters highly unlikeable), Delplanque's intentions were nevertheless laudable. *Deep into the Woods* won a Silver Méliès at the Sitges Film Festival, and showed French filmmakers that local horror productions could be profitable. It opened on a couple of dozen screens in the US later that year.

Largely considered the birthplace of the genre, Germany's interest in horror movies almost disappeared in the decades that followed Robert Wiene's *The Cabinet of Dr Caligari* (*Das Cabinet des Dr Caligari*, 1920) and Murnau's *Nosferatu, eine Symphonie des Grauens* (1922). The success of writer/director Stefan Ruzowitzky's *Anatomy* (*Anatomie*, 2000) therefore came as a bit of a surprise. In this medical slasher/thriller, a student (Franka Potente) invited to an exclusive summer course at the University of Heidelberg discovers that the programme actually serves as a front for a secret society, the Anti-Hippocrates, which encourages its members to experiment on living human subjects to further their scientific knowledge. Evoking Germany's past through the history of the organisation (said to have known a golden age during the Nazi era) and the lead girl's family (her grandfather embraced the Anti-Hippocratic approach while her father, a 1968 demonstrator, rejected it), the movie touches upon generational, ethical and sociological issues, but fails to develop them further, instead favouring a rather pedestrian conspiracy plot. Nevertheless, *Anatomy* was a hit both in Germany and abroad, and was followed by a sequel in 2003.

Another great nation for horror, the United Kingdom, home of legendary production company Hammer, saw its genre production slow down and nearly disappear in the nineties. But in 2000, Simon Hunter's *Lighthouse* marked the first attempt at putting the country back on the horror map. A slasher movie (what else?) essentially set in and around the titular location, this low-budget and pretty unimaginative effort came out on DVD in the US in 2000 under the title *Dead Of Night*; it sat on a shelf in the UK until 2002, when it was given a small theatrical release.

In Japan, the J-Horror craze had waned and rather than long-haired ghosts, the genre successes of the year featured strong action components.

Versus, from newcomer Ryuhei Kitamura, sees a group of Yakuzas battle zombies in the Forest of Resurrection, where they have unwittingly buried their victims. Kitamura set out to avoid the clichés of Japanese horror and combined splatter with gangster film in a fast-paced succession of sword fights and visual gags which soon made *Versus* a cult favourite.

Kinji Fukasaku's *Battle Royale* (*Batoru rowaiaru*), based on a best-selling novel by Koushun Takami, was for months a subject of heated debate. Set in a near future where the government has adopted extreme measures to face juvenile delinquency and truancy, it follows forty-two ninth-grade students as they embark on what they believe is a school trip. In reality, they have been randomly selected for Battle Royale, a survival game on a deserted island where they will have three days to kill each other, or die all together at the end of the third day if more than one student is still alive. The survivor will be sent back into society, a living example of the lengths to which the authorities will go to discipline the youth.

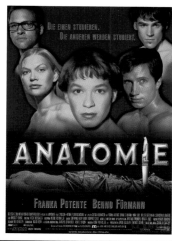

The movie focuses on Shuya (Tatsuya Fujiwara), a student who tries to survive without taking part in the massacre and has vowed to protect his friend Noriko (Aki Maeda). Around them, alliances are created and broken, old jealousies and flames lead to murder, friends betray each other. Gripping from its opening sequence, in which the students are brutally introduced to the rules of Battle Royale, the movie is driven by its characters and their relationships, and the human side of the story never gets lost in the action. Beyond the blood and mayhem, Fukasaku – who, as a teenager during WWII, worked in a factory which was a regular target for Allied bombings – delivers a movie both touching and deeply rooted in human nature; but as was to be expected, it is the on-screen deaths of its young protagonists that attracted the media's and national authorities' attention.

Uncompromisingly violent, *Battle Royale* was by its very nature bound to be the centre of controversy in Japan – the society it most directly criticises – and in the United States, a nation traumatised by the recent discovery, through the Columbine tragedy, of the level of rage, despair and destruction some of its students could be led to. Slapped with a severe R15 rating by the Japanese censor board, Fukasaku, who wanted his work to be seen by students the same age as those in the story, asked for a review. But before his request could be examined, the Parliament, shocked that the movie was allowed in theatres, questioned the validity of the board itself – a self-regulating authority whose members are selected by the industry – and considered banning the film. Youth crime had dramatically increased in Japan in the previous years; several incidents, including the 1997 murder of an 11-year-old by a 14-year-old boy who'd placed his victim's severed head outside the gates of his school[27], had shocked public opinion, and the parliament feared *Battle Royale* would push the youth to more acts of delinquency. Official protests only gave more publicity to the movie, which became such a hit that it was later re-released with enhanced special effects and additional footage.

Anatomy. Battle Royale.

Violence, however, was only instrumental in developing the real theme of the movie. Said Fukasaku in a 2001 interview with *Midnight Eye*[28]: 'The fact that adults lost confidence in themselves, that's what is shown in the film. Those adults worked very hard in the seventies in order to rebuild Japan … Of course there was a generation gap between the young and adults, but consistently adults were in control in terms of political stability and whatever was going on in the nation. But since the burst of the bubble economy, these same adults … were put in a very difficult position … and the children who have grown up and witnessed what happened to the adults, their anxiety became heightened as well.' This generation gap is further deepened by the country's educational system, for which the Battle Royale game was a thinly veiled metaphor. It's no coincidence that ninth-graders were chosen for this rite of passage, as it is from the end of the first nine grades that Japanese students start competing in national examinations to gain access to the higher grades and placement in the best schools. This competitive system naturally undermines team spirit and leads to self-centredness; its criticism is best reflected in the movie by the words one of the students shouts while shooting at his classmates: 'I want to win! I want to go to university!'

One of the biggest hits in the history of Japanese cinema and the winner of several awards in its home country, *Battle Royale* to this day still hasn't found a distributor in the US, due mostly to its controversial nature.

A largely inferior sequel, *Battle Royale II: Requiem* (*Batoru rowaiaru II: Chinkonka*), came out in Japan in 2003; directed by Fukasaku's son Kenta (who scripted both films), this none-too-subtle apology of terrorism (!), despite an increased body count, was quickly forgotten.

2001:

What is a *ghost?*

(Tagline for *The Devil's Backbone*, 2001)

2001 WAS NOT A VERY PROFITABLE YEAR FOR AMERICAN HORROR, WITH ONLY a handful of noteworthy productions, none of which reached the $100 million barrier at the box office. But the year which saw the beginning of a slow economic recession in the United States, following the bursting of the dot.com bubble, also marked the start of a change in the genre.

Teenage slashers, very much in vogue in the nineties and until then considered safe investments, generally failed to impress (Jamie Blanks' *Valentine*, starring *Buffy the Vampire Slayer* and *Angel* star David Boreanaz as a killer taking revenge on his old school bullies, grossed about $20 million theatrically on a budget of $10 million) or tanked completely – Stephen Carpenter's *Soul Survivors*, a clumsy cross between *Scream* and 1962's *Carnival of Souls*, cost $14 million but barely made $3 million back on its US theatrical run (sure, the movie opened a few days after 9/11, but its catastrophic opening weekend at $1,140,698 was enough indication that it wouldn't have been a hit under any circumstances).

The biggest success of the year, on the other hand, was an original and audacious co-production with France and Spain helmed by a relative unknown: *The Others*, from Spanish/Chilean director Alejandro Amenábar, which grossed more than $96 million during its 3-month run in the US.

The Year of the Ghost

Isle of Jersey, 1945. Grace Stewart (Nicole Kidman) lives with her two children in an isolated mansion, waiting for her husband to return from the war. Cut off from the rest of the world, she spends her days taking care of the kids, who suffer from a severe allergy to light. But when three servants arrive to work at the house, various supernatural events start disrupting the quiet, well-

ordered life of the Stewart family.

An old-school haunted house story, *The Others* mainly owes its success to Amenábar's ability to create the right atmosphere. The opening sequence, where Grace guides the servants through the mansion, brilliantly introduces the characters, the oppressive setting, and the discernible tension of the house's inhabitants. Grace comes across as authoritarian and inflexible, fearful and sad; her mansion is a dark and silent prison she and her children are unable to leave. Slow and quiet, *The Others* is a pure work of gothic horror, comparable to Jack Clayton's 1961 *The Innocents* and the tale that inspired it, Henry James's 1898 novella *The Turn of the Screw*.

Unlike those classics however, *The Others*' *Sixth Sense*-inspired ending makes the story less scary on second viewing; like in Tim Burton's *Beetlejuice* (1988), the haunted mansion is seen through the eyes of its ghosts. But this final shock is clever, consistent with the rest of the story, and introduced by a series of hints that viewers will enjoy spotting: the graves in the garden, the discussions about limbo, eternal pain and life after death, the fog, and so on.

Produced by Dimension Films, a company famous for its teen slashers and countless sequels (*Scream I, II* and *III* (1996, 1997, 2000), *Halloween H20* (1998), *The Faculty* (1998), *Hellraiser: Inferno* (2000)), *The Others* had Tom Cruise and business partner Paula Wagner acting as executive producers – in other words, warranties and advisors for the film and its director[29] – but Amenábar gained final cut by agreeing in exchange to sell Cruise and Wagner the remake rights to his 1997 thriller *Open Your Eyes* (*Abre Los Ojos*); the resulting movie, *Vanilla Sky*, would come out later in the year.

A critical and commercial success, *The Others* in many regards heralded the changes in horror production to come: real scares, more mature material, adult protagonists, and Hollywood's interest in foreign talents and sources. With the same elements, *The Ring* (2002) would soon make a deep mark on the genre.

If post-modern teenage stalkers in the *Scream* vein no longer ruled, the slasher genre,

29 'Interview with Alejandro Amenábar', Jeffrey M Anderson, *Combustible Celluloid*, 20 July 2001, http://www.combustiblecelluloid. com/interviews/amenabar.shtml

33

however, wasn't ready to die altogether. With Victor Salva's *Jeepers Creepers*, released under the radar on 31 August 2001, it would return in a new incarnation. Devoid of humour and self-reflection[30], slow and moody, this supernatural killer flick was as far from nineties horror as a slasher film could be, and soon became one of the sleeper hits of the year.

On their way home from college through a lonely stretch of countryside, brother and sister Darry (Justin Long) and Trish (Gina Philips) are nearly driven off the road by a beat-up truck. Soon afterwards, as they pass by an abandoned church, they see the truck driver dump what appear to be bodies wrapped in sheets down a pipe. As Darry, helped by his sister, tries to rescue the victims, he falls into the pit and finds himself in a cavern covered with hundreds of dead bodies. He manages to escape, but the incident has drawn the attention of the driver, a supernatural creature which goes hunting for 23 days every 23 years.

An old-fashioned creature feature, *Jeepers Creepers* starts off rather realistically, and the first 45 minutes, before the kids discover their stalker isn't human, have been unanimously praised as the strongest of the movie. Right from the start, Trish and Darry are believable as brother and sister; there's a real chemistry between the two actors, and their bond makes them instantly likeable. Except maybe for their much-criticised decision to go back to the church, their reactions all seem real; as Salva says in his DVD commentary: 'It was about time that we showed a film where, when a guy sees something traumatic, it really takes an emotional toll on him.' Philips's angry but terrified eyes and Long's frightened looks and apparent fragility make their characters all the more endearing.

Jeepers Creepers. Session 9.

Uncharacteristically, the scariest parts of the movie take place in daylight in an ordinary, unthreatening rural setting; once night falls and Darry and Trish first hear the bad news from psychic Jezelle at the coffee shop, the story turns supernatural and somewhat loses its nightmarish quality. The creature's first appearance, on the roof of the police car, is one of the last genuinely chilling images of the movie; and from the moment the Creeper is seen eating a severed head's tongue in front of an ad that reads 'Tastes damn good' – a tongue-in-cheek scene if there ever was one – it has shed most of its mystery. From that point on, the movie is a rather pedestrian succession of hide-and-seek sequences making for a few good shocks, but lacking the realism and eerie atmosphere of the first part. *Jeepers Creepers* nevertheless ends on an unusually downbeat note, a trait that certainly contributed to giving it a special place in the hearts of horror fans.

With the Creeper, it is clear that Salva's intention was to create a new classic monster, in the same league as Freddy, Jason or even the Creature from the Black Lagoon, the director's main reference. Salva commented in a 2003 BBC interview[31]: 'I think in the heart of every young horror fan is the desire to create his own creature'. Unfortunately, this is where *Jeepers Creepers* fails: its monster is too over-the-top, too fantastical by contrast with the beginning of the movie, and no good explanation is provided for its existence. Any information we get is given by Jezelle, who conveniently happens to have a psychic link with the killer, but is reluctant to disclose all relevant elements to the kids – a rather unsubtle storytelling trick which does little to make the Creeper seem more real.

A convicted child molester, Victor Salva was the object of much debate at the time of the release, and some concerned citizens called for the movie to be boycotted. Whether this confusion between the man's past actions and his value as an artist had an influence on the movie's box office performance is doubtful. In the end, *Jeepers Creepers* will only be remembered for what it is: a return to old-school horror, avoiding the jokes and clichés of the nineties *Scream* trend, and foreshadowing a comeback to serious cinematic frights.

Confirming the new wave of straight, edge-of-your-seat horror pictures, but on a much more modest budget, writer/director Brad Anderson's *Session 9* follows an asbestos elimination team working on an old, dilapidated mental institution. The place hides dark secrets, as do some of the men, and as the asylum reveals its mysteries, cracks start appearing in the workers' sanity.

Understated and character-driven, *Session 9* goes for dread and menace rather than gore and jump scares. Anderson's movie is a great example of psychological horror, a sub-genre in which 'the character's own thoughts, fears, guilt and emotional instability take over their physical world'[32]. The story's horrific elements take place almost entirely in the protagonists' heads; the tension comes from their interactions more than from outside events, and even the murders at the end are not shown on camera.

Inspired by the earlier classics *Don't Look Now* (1973) and *The Shining* (1980), Anderson intended his movie to be a reaction against the baroque, teen-oriented movies of the nineties: 'Good old-fashioned scary movies are harder to find these days. You couldn't have made *The Exorcist* today with that script and that kind of meticulous character development. Studios shy away from that. They want pretty teenagers being glib and impaling each other with barbecue tongs.'[33]

The Devil's Backbone.

Anderson's story of paranoia uses some of the genre's more traditional techniques in a brilliant sequence reminiscent of haunted house movies, in which the crew goes looking around the building for a missing team member. Full advantage is taken of the film's creepy location, but the most remarkable quality of this 20-minute montage is that it takes place largely in daylight, without any supernatural elements, and yet manages to be tense and disquieting.

Session 9's ending, unfortunately, doesn't offer the payoff this complex story called for. The final parallel between the asylum's history (told through the taped sessions of a doctor and his patient, a woman with multiple personality disorder) and the descent of team leader Gordon Fleming (Peter Mullan) into madness is weak, and doesn't give Fleming's climax of violence a satisfactory explanation.

Despite its flaws, *Session 9*, with its slow-building tension, its grown-up cast and its refusal to fall back on easy slasher tricks, was another step in the right direction. Horror was starting to be scary again.

Spanish Awakenings

2001 marked the beginning of a new era for Spanish horror. A nation known since the late sixties for its low-budget, gory and sexually explicit fright flicks, Spain had produced a handful of quality, higher profile genre films during the nineties (Alex de la Iglesia's *Day of the Beast* (*El Día de la Bestia*, 1995) Amenábar's *Open Your Eyes* (*Abre los Ojos*, 1997) and Jaume Balagueró's *The Nameless* (*Los sin Nombre*, 1999), but the true rebirth took place in the early 2000s, with the creation, on the one hand, of Fantastic Factory, and the release, on the other hand, of Mexican writer/director Guillermo Del Toro's masterpiece *The Devil's Backbone* (*El Espinazo del Diablo*).

Spanish distributor Julio Fernández first suggested to Brian Yuzna that he should move to Barcelona to produce movies with him in 1988, at the Sitges International Film Festival of Catalonia, a world-renowned event showcasing the best in horror and fantastic films. The *Re-Animator* producer, who at the time was busy developing his own projects to produce and direct, passed, and it took Fernández a decade to make him a second offer. By then the proposal was backed by the prospect of substantial subsidies from the Catalonian government's Finance Institute. Yuzna, who in those ten years had become one of America's most prolific and successful director-producers, submitted a business plan. The aim was to give Filmax – Fernández's distribution firm and Spain's fastest-expanding production company – a division entirely devoted to the financing, production and distribution of genre pictures, shot locally, but targeting an international audience.

According to Yuzna's plan, Fantastic Factory would produce three to four low-budget films a year with a mainly Spanish crew and an international cast, and a bigger, more ambitious movie every other year. In its six years of existence, the short-lived label ended up releasing nine titles,

30 With the exception of one line at the beginning of the film ('You know the part in horror movies when somebody does something really stupid, and everybody hates him for it? This is it.'), which Salva justifies by saying he used it 'because I wanted the audience to understand that my kids … have seen all the Freddy and Jason, they do live in the horror universe; they just don't think for a moment they could be part of it.' *Jeepers Creepers*, DVD audio commentary.

31 'Victor Salva, *Jeepers Creepers 2*', Nev Pierce, *BBC*, 21 August 2003, http://www.bbc.co.uk/films/2003/08/21/victor_salva_jeepers_creepers_2_interview.shtml

32 'Will you step into my parlor? A guide for horror lovers', *Enoch Pratt Free Library*, Baltimore, Maryland, http://www.prattlibrary.org/locations/fiction/index.aspx?id=3076&mark=psychological+horror#psychological_horror

33 *Session 9*, Brad Anderson website, http://www.bradandersonfilmmaker.com/sess.htm

four of which were helmed by Yuzna himself, and three by Spanish directors.

The division's first two features, Yuzna's *Faust: Love of the Damned*, a comic book adaptation starring Andrew Divoff and Jeffrey Combs, and Jack Sholder's *Arachnid*, a giant spider shocker with Alex Reid, opened in Spain in 2001 to disappointing reviews. Clearly, the young company was still trying to find its bearings, and Yuzna had to figure out the extent of the possibilities Spain offered. But with Stuart Gordon's *Dagon*, released locally in October 2001, Fantastic Factory struck critical gold.

Paul (Ezra Godden) and his girlfriend Barbara (Raquel Meroño) are on holiday on a yacht off the Spanish coast, when a storm forces them to head ashore to the unsettling village of Imboca. As they start looking for help, they soon realise that the unfriendly population of the little town worships a sea god called Dagon, and that their cult is slowly turning them into half-human, half-fish creatures …

Dagon.

Adapted from H P Lovecraft's short story *Dagon* (1917) and novella *The Shadow over Innsmouth* (1936), Gordon's film is dark yet wildly entertaining. Taking full advantage of his new location (transplanted from its original New England setting to Galicia, in the north west of Spain), the director captured the stories' atmosphere to perfection. The narrow streets, decaying houses, dark skies, pagan churches and mysterious inhabitants of Imboca (a play on words – 'boca' means 'mouth' in Spanish) are undeniably Lovecraftian; slowly revealing the town's unspeakable horrors, the photography and production design are two of *Dagon*'s best assets. British actor Ezra Godden is another important contributing factor to the movie's success; he brings humour to his part by playing it dead straight, thereby making his character almost instantly likeable. Gordon uses just the right amount of special effects: enough to progressively make the audience understand the horror of the villagers' physical degradations, but not too much, so we never really get accustomed to their looks. And in its daring, twisted ending, he hints at a world below the sea, populated with unknown creatures, but leaves it to the viewers to picture this new civilisation. *Dagon*'s goal is clearly to shock and amuse, and its final digressions on fate versus free will don't try to elevate it above pure entertainment; it is nonetheless a highly recommended treat for whoever loves the genre.

Gordon of course is well known to horror fans. Most famous for his directing debut *Re-Animator* (1985), the soft-spoken, affable Chicagoan has established himself over the years as one of the genre's most original voices, with movies as varied as *Dolls* (1987), *Fortress* (1993) or *The Pit and the Pendulum* (1991). *Dagon* was his fourth Lovecraft adaptation after *Re-Animator* (1985), *From Beyond* (1986) and *Castle Freak* (1995), all co-scripted by Dennis Paoli. Originally written in the mid-eighties, *Dagon* was rejected by Charles Band, with whom the filmmaker had a three-picture deal, after the success of *Re-Animator*; instead, the producer encouraged them to shoot *From Beyond*. After several unsuccessful attempts to get *Dagon* produced, the script was shelved, until Fantastic Factory came along. 'People didn't think that fish were scary,' Gordon recalls[34]. 'One of the heads of the studios actually said that to me, and I was thinking, I might just get a big fish head and put it on his desk … and then you tell me if it's not scary. We had people who said to us, make it about vampires and we'll make the movie tomorrow! But fish people? They just thought it was a stupid idea.' But the Factory producers knew better, and

34 Interview with the author, Brussels, Belgium, March 2004.

Spain offered the perfect setting for the story. As Yuzna said in an interview with *Fangoria*[35]: 'When Lovecraft wrote the story, it was more plausible, but today people are less likely to believe that there could really be such a totally deserted place anywhere in the US.' The movie was filmed on location in Pontevedra and Combarro in Galicia, a region of legends and superstitions, isolated from the rest of the country by mountains and dense forests. 'The thing with Galicia is that it's an unknown location for international audiences,' Yuzna continued, 'so it helps them suspend disbelief.'

The ending is arguably the most haunting sequence of the film. Surreal, downbeat and unexpected, it's a testament to Fantastic Factory's will to produce original stories that push boundaries. Gordon comments[36]: 'In the Lovecraft stories, that's the way it ends, where the main character realises that he's one of (the monsters) himself, which is a perfect ending. And a lot of the movies that I've made, that's what they're about, with the person realising that the monster is within them. That it's not something outside, it's part of you, and you have to be able to live with that.' Shot for $3,200,000, *Dagon*, after touring festivals throughout Europe and opening theatrically in Spain, came out directly on DVD in the States in July 2002.

Another excellent Spanish production which was only offered a limited release in the US is *The Devil's Backbone*. Set in an isolated orphanage at the end of the Spanish Civil War, it sees a group of children face their fears, first of the ghost of a young boy, Santi, who disappeared the night a bomb fell intact in the middle of the courtyard, then of a more physical threat, when caretaker Jacinto (played by Eduardo Noriega, of *Open Your Eyes* fame) attempts to take over the orphanage to steal the gold he believes is hidden within its walls.

'What is a ghost? A tragedy condemned to repeat itself time and again? An instant of pain, perhaps. Something dead which still seems to be alive. An emotion suspended in time. Like a blurred photograph. Like an insect trapped in amber.' With these lines, Del Toro closes what could well be the most poetic, chilling and thoughtful ghost story ever put on screen. Dark and atmospheric, this tale of loss, fear and bravery deals with the horror of war and its impact on children under cover of a supernatural story, by intertwining childhood fears and grown-up, real-life anxieties. Just like ghosts are trapped in time, humanity seems condemned to repeat its errors and go to war again and again, with devastating results. If at the beginning of the movie, the main threat for the children is a whispering apparition in a basement, the focus eventually changes to the caretaker's increasingly violent behaviour and his final attack on the schoolhouse. Forced to face their fears, the boys end up using them to survive, as they team up with the ghost to defeat Jacinto.

The Devil's Backbone.

Del Toro's ambition was to 'make it a really sad, nostalgic story about childhood – which in and of itself is a ghost – and about war. Every war contains so many ghosts that it is a perfect background for that story.'[37] This sadness permeates the movie, and is particularly apparent in Santi, the hollow-eyed, almost transparent 'boy who sighs'; his melancholy echoes the sad fate of the other innocents in the orphanage. Every character, from the strict governess to Jacinto's unfortunate girlfriend, has a tragedy of their own, and the ghost is little more than a catalyst, a reflection of their personal dramas.

Easily one of the best movies of the decade, *The Devil's Backbone* was extremely well received critically, with everyone from the *Guardian* and the BBC to the *Chicago Sun-Times* and *The Hollywood Reporter* singing its praises. But no matter how good they are, foreign-language films

35 Interviewed by Mike Hodges, 'Fear Today, Dagon Tomorrow', *Fangoria* 213, June 2002.

36 Interview with the author, Brussels, Belgium, March 2004.

37 'Real Backbone', Mark Salisbury, *Fangoria* 209, January 2001, p 30.

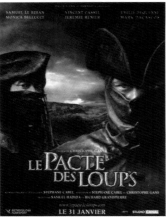

Brotherhood of the Wolf.

without any recognisable stars are a tough sell in the USA, and Sony Classics released Del Toro's movie on a maximum of 35 screens; in the UK, it opened in four cinemas. But despite its limited theatrical releases, this masterpiece went on to gain cult status among fans of the genre, and movie lovers in general.

France and England, Ready for More!

Like the previous year, France and England continued their slow (re)discovery of the genre. While France started the new millennium with mild supernatural movies and would be known in the following years for its hyper-violent realistic nightmares, England on the other hand began with a handful of slasher films, to later have its real successes with werewolves, zombies, aliens and underground creatures.

After the success of *Deep in the Woods* the previous year, France saw three high profile horror productions grace its screens in 2001. On a budget around $30 million, highly unusual for a genre movie in this country, *Brotherhood of the Wolf* (*Le Pacte des Loups*), from former Yuzna protégé Christophe Gans, was an international hit. Hugely popular in France, it also raked in nearly $11 million theatrically in the US, bringing its worldwide total to a stunning $70 million. A largely inferior film, Jean-Paul Salomé's *Belphegor: Phantom of the Louvre* (*Belphégor: Le Fantôme du Louvre*) was only allotted half of *Brotherhood of the Wolf*'s budget, and gained less than half of its success. Pitof's *Dark Portals: The Chronicles of Vidocq* (*Vidocq*), a supernatural detective story set in 19th century Paris, also mixed mild scares with big budget effects, and attracted over 1.8 million viewers to the cinemas. All three films boded well for the future of French horror.

Based on actual events, *Brotherhood of the Wolf* takes place in 1766, when Knight Grégoire de Fronsac (Samuel le Bihan) and his 'brother', Native American Mani (Mark Dacascos) are sent to the Gévaudan region to investigate a series of murders rumoured to be the work of a monstrous wolf. As Fronsac gets accustomed to the area and its inhabitants, he begins to realise that the beast may not be what it seems, and that a more sinister conspiracy may be responsible.

Brotherhood of the Wolf may not be a great film, but it is indisputably a surprising one. All at once historical drama, creature feature and action movie, it deals with contemporary themes – racism, class struggle, religious fanaticism – in a period setting, and while it may not do so subtly, it never preaches or forgets to be entertaining. A lifelong fan of Asian cinema (many Chinese and Japanese movies were first distributed in France through his label HK Video), co-writer and director Gans also manages to introduce martial arts in his fight sequences, and daring camera moves inspired by the likes of John Woo. Both were until then unheard of in a French movie, and both became immensely popular. As Dacascos declared in a 2002 interview with *Fangoria*[38], 'If you would have told somebody that this was the type of film you wanted to make, prior to actually doing it, they would have thought you were insane. But yet Christophe put all these crazy ideas together, mixed them up and came out with something pretty special.'

Unfortunately, what sets the movie apart is also its biggest imperfection. Gans, a movie aficionado if there ever was one, tried to cram so many genres, homages and influences into his story that he sometimes lost sight of its subject. *Brotherhood of the Wolf* starts off as a horror movie, with a prologue directly inspired by the horror classics and a few eerie shots of the beast and its master in the moonlight; continues in the vein of a detective story; turns midway into a love story; and ends up somewhere between period drama and kung-fu flick. Because of this lack of focus, fright fans may not have found what they were looking for; but the diversity of genres did enhance its mainstream appeal, and Gans's film sold over 5 million tickets in France.

After the pedestrian *Lighthouse*, England continued its slow revival with *The Hole*, a teenage horror story marketed as a post-*Scream* slasher, but actually more thriller than real slice'n'dice. Starting off as a classic love triangle in a private school – Martin (Daniel Brocklebank) loves Liz (Thora Birch) who loves Mike (Desmond Harrington) – the movie focuses on Liz, who's being interrogated by a police psychologist after three of her classmates were found dead in an old bomb shelter. She reveals that she and her unfortunate friends went down the shelter to avoid the school

38 'To Join the Brotherhood', Don Kaye, *Fangoria* 210, March 2002, p 41.

field trip, and found themselves locked in by Martin. The psychologist is ready to believe her, until she confronts the teenager again in the shelter and discovers a very different version of the facts.

Cleverly shot and featuring a bunch of excellent up-and-coming talents (including a pre-*Bend it like Beckham* Keira Knightley), Nick Hamm's *The Hole* had a lot going for it. Based on 17-year-old Guy Burt's 1993 novel *After the Hole*, its premise – a group of friends trapped in a confined space see their relationships break down under pressure – was excellent, and at least two other British underground frighteners, *The Bunker* (2001) and *The Descent* (2005), exploited the same idea. But in an effort to mirror the complexity of the book, the structure of the movie, alternating back and forth between the investigation and the events in the shelter, ruins the pacing and builds up to a final reveal that anyone who's ever watched a murder mystery could guess from the first couple of scenes. As a result, and probably also due to its deceiving slasher packaging, *The Hole* only made half its investment back during its theatrical run in its home country. In the US, it didn't come out until 2004, a few months after the release of Hamm's Hollywood thriller *Godsend*. Despite generally positive reviews, *The Hole* has since then practically lapsed into oblivion.

Japan Feels Lonely

With only a handful of J-horror titles released that year, Japan's interest in cursed videotapes and female ghosts crawling out of wells seemed to have nearly died. Aside from Norio Tsuruta's irredeemably boring *Scarecrow* (*Kakashi*, 2001), and Takashi Miike's ultraviolent manga adaptation *Ichi the Killer* (*Koroshiya 1*, 2001), the only notable genre production of the year was Kiyoshi Kurosawa's *Kairo* (released in the US in 2005 under the title *Pulse*.)

The Hole. Scarecrow. Ichi the Killer.

After the unexpected suicide of a young student, Kawashima (Haruhiko Kato), a young man taking his first steps into cyberspace, sees his computer play tricks on him and repeatedly invite him to 'meet a ghost'. As he investigates the problem, he realises that something much more sinister than a simple hacker is at play.

With his previous features, the poetic but hard to fathom *Cure* (1997) and *Charisma* (*Karisuma*, 1999), writer/director Kurosawa developed something of a cult reputation. While *Kairo* was his biggest success to date and arguably his most mainstream creation, it remained, like the rest of his work, slow, minimalist and enigmatic. The story is difficult to follow and some of the dialogue risible (to a girl who, spooked by the deaths of her friends, is afraid she'll be next, a fellow student says, 'Maybe while we're still alive they'll invent a drug to prevent death!'), but the movie does offer some haunting images, like the morphing shadow in the videogame arcade, and original metaphors between ghosts and web users. Like *Ring* or the

Ginger Snaps.

more recent *Phone* (*Pon*, 2002) and *One Missed Call* (*Chakushin ari*, 2003), *Kairo* shows a fear – or at the very least, distrust – of modern technology; in a country whose main exports are computers, electronic devices and cars, and which rose to economic superpower at the speed of light, leaving its population little time to adjust to the change, this anxiety may be less surprising than it seems. Scientific progress is usually antithetical to supernatural beliefs, but in the case of Japan, and to a lower degree, the Western world, the evolution happened so fast that it created new unknowns. After all, how many can claim to fully understand how a computer, the World Wide Web, or a mobile phone work? In 2000, while the movie was in production, the number of Internet users in Japan grew at the amazing rate of 74%, the ratio of surfers to the total population hitting 37.1%[39]. *Kairo* expresses Kurosawa's fear that under the pretext of bringing people together, new communication channels physically isolate them. Said the director[40]: 'I began to wonder what the closest feeling to experiencing death would be as a still living human. I couldn't help concluding that it would be like enduring eternity utterly alone. From there, the theme of loneliness emerged organically. Although it was not my original intention, this process gradually led me to incorporate the rampant loneliness of contemporary Japanese society as an integral element.' Kurosawa's message is front and centre in the movie; even the production design, with its grey, empty settings, is meant to reflect the characters' isolation. 'People don't really connect, you know,' one of them tells Kawashima. 'We all live our lives separately.'

'They don't call it the curse for nothing' (*Ginger Snaps*)

Isolation and evolution, although of very different natures, are also the themes of John Fawcett's *Ginger Snaps*, a Canadian teen werewolf film which caused quite a stir during its 2000-2001 festival run, winning several awards at the Malaga International Week of Fantastic Cinema, Best Canadian Feature at the Toronto International Film Festival, and later on, the first ever Saturn award for Best DVD release.

Teenage sisters Brigitte (Emily Perkins) and Ginger Fitzgerald (Katharine Isabelle) are outcasts, obsessed with death, and the best friends in the world. But their bond is tested when Ginger gets bitten by a beast on the night of her first period. She starts changing physically and mentally, suddenly becoming one of the school's most popular and attractive girls, as well as a powerful and hungry werewolf. Brigitte strives to save her sister from her aggressive urges, but Ginger fights her off …

'No one ever thinks chicks do shit like this. A girl can only be a slut, bitch, tease or the virgin next door,' says one of the eccentric sisters. Unlike most teen horror flicks, *Ginger Snaps* is not a movie *for* adolescents but *about* adolescents – teenage girls to be more specific – and its depiction of its young protagonists may not be realistic, but is certainly original. Every event it narrates can be seen either as simple entertainment or as a very thinly veiled metaphor for puberty and its effect on the body, mind, sexuality and relationships of the girls who experience it. For Ginger and Brigitte, menstruation is a curse, and the parallels with lycanthropy (blood, hair, pain) are underlined in a less-than-subtle way throughout the story.

The idea is not new. Besides being an obvious subtext in *Carrie* (1976), male equivalents *Teen Wolf* (1985) and *I Was a Teenage Werewolf* (1957), or *The Company of Wolves* (1984), to name a few, scholars have long considered anxieties relating to puberty and sexuality as an explanation for children's attraction to horror. Says author James Twitchell[41]: 'Horror monsters are every bit as anxious and confused about sex as their (teenage) audience. All of a sudden there is hair emerging in strange places, mysterious body fluids being secreted at unannounced times, breasts budding, voices cracking, and most important, those disturbing, exciting urges welling up inside.' What monster could represent those changes better than the werewolf? If we are to give credit to this supposal, Fawcett's movie did nothing but show explicitly what creature features had expressed unconsciously for decades. Needless to say, feminist film theorists have feasted on Ginger and Brigitte's story ever since its release.[42]

And if *Ginger Snaps* is not your typical teen flick, it is not a traditional werewolf film either.

39 Kristie Lu Stout, 'Japan Internet users up 74 percent', *CNN*, 24 April 2001, http://edition.cnn.com/2001/BUSINESS/asia/04/24/tokyo.netusersup/index.html
40 Quoted in '*Pulse* (2005)', *Rotten Tomatoes*, http://uk.rottentomatoes.com/m/1113170-pulse/about.php
41 James B Twitchell, *Dreadful Pleasures: An Anatomy of Modern Horror*, Oxford University Press, New York, 1985, p 68.
42 See for example Bianca Nielsen, '"Something's Wrong, Like More Than You Being Female": Transgressive Sexuality and Discourses of Reproduction in *Ginger Snaps*', *Thirdspace*, III, issue 2, March 2004, http://www.thirdspace.ca/articles/3_2_nielsen.htm. Nielsen further theorises that Brigitte kills her sister because 'she has become a grotesque representation of all that their community loathes about female sexuality. In this wider sense Ginger is killed because she has challenged her community's sexual taboos'.

'It's not the mythological creature born under the full moon,' Fawcett explained in the press book[43]. 'Rather, it's treated as a biological infection that grows from the inside out, through the blood stream.' Indeed, Ginger's transformation is closer to Jeff Goldblum's in Cronenberg's *The Fly* (1986) than to classic werewolf fare in that it is continuous and, it is suggested, irreversible. Instead of losing control of her body according to cycles of the moon, the teenager seems to be changing over several days, and her new state is permanently acquired. Unlike most lycanthrope stories, the movie is also more dramatic than scary, the ending sadder than horrific, the terror more psychological than overtly gory, and the humour darker than, say, *An American Werewolf in London* (1981).

Ginger Snaps opened theatrically in few countries, but was enough of a hit on DVD to justify a sequel and a prequel shot back-to-back and released in 2004. John Fawcett directed neither, but came back to the genre in 2005 with *The Dark*, and has in parallel established himself as a successful TV filmmaker.

The End of the World as We Know it

On 11 September 2001, millions of TV viewers witnessed a horror greater than anything that movies had presented. As the towers of the World Trade Centre collapsed, destroying in their fall America's perceived invulnerability, the way the Western world viewed horror cinema changed. Just as the Vietnam War had marked the end of the classic monsters' reign on the genre, so did 9/11 make the Blair Witch, the *Scream* killer and the Headless Horseman look harmless by comparison.

Thir13en Ghosts.

But if Hollywood put most projects on hold in the immediate aftermath of the terrorist attacks, it wasn't because studio executives were not sure how to top the images they'd seen broadcast *ad nauseam* on every news channel, or to ponder on ethical concerns, but because nerves had been rubbed so raw that any movie containing the thinnest point of comparison with the events threatened to further upset grieving audiences. Production slowed down, scripts and completed features were reappraised according to new standards. Studios were treading on eggshells; few horror movies made the cut. *Ginger Snaps*'s extremely limited New York City release notwithstanding, only two came out in the build-up to Halloween, against five the previous year. *Bones*, a mediocre revenge story starring rapper Snoop Dogg, tanked miserably; *Thir13en Ghosts* – yet another spectre story – on the other hand grossed twice its investment ($41 million on a $20 million budget), hinting that maybe, on-screen scares were exactly the sort of escapism audiences were looking for. As psychiatrist Dr Michael Brody stated on CNN a few days before Halloween that year[44], 'I think the nature of horror movies in general [follows] along a certain script. So like a roller coaster ride, it [gives] us some control. Hollywood … is … trying to look at the commercial possibilities and perhaps the reason that these rentals are so high for [movies like] *Die Hard* is as a nation we want to get mastery. We want to get control over what's happening.'

Thir13en Ghosts, from first-time director Steve Beck and Dark Castle producers Joel Silver, Robert Zemeckis and Gil Adler, and starring Embeth Davis and Matthew Lillard, was a silly and somewhat boring attempt at breathing life into William Castle's 1960 turkey of the same name. Despite Sean Hargreaves's gorgeous production design and stunningly frightening ghosts courtesy of the LA-based KNB effects production house, any suspense the script may have tried to create was annihilated by plot holes, scattershot editing, lame jokes and stereotypical characters. Audiences nevertheless embraced it as the only mainstream supernatural release of the season.

As the year drew to a close, fans, critics and studios couldn't help but acknowledge that the world as they knew it was gone, and that cinema would soon have to find a way to adapt to the changes. As *Fangoria* editor Tony Timpone stated in his November 2001 editorial[45], 'There used to be a time when we could tell our children that scenes of such mass destruction and terrifying evil could never happen to our country. America was too strong. That stuff only happens in the movies. Well, now we'll have to think of a new lie to tell them.'

43 *Ginger Snaps* online press book, http://www.ginger-snaps.com/presskit.htm

44 'CNN Morning News, Interview with Michael Brody and Andy Seiler', aired 27 October 2001, *CNN* transcript, http://transcripts.cnn.com/TRANSCRIPTS/0110/27/smn.22.html

45 'Horror Hits Home', Tony Timpone, *Fangoria* 208, November 2001, p 4.

2002:

'Before you die, you see the ring'

(Tagline for *The Ring*, 2002)

AS AMERICA MOURNED ITS DEAD AND THE WESTERN WORLD LEARNED TO cope with new fears, 2002 marked the beginning of a new era for horror cinema. The UK made a strong comeback to the genre; France and Spain continued their slow ascension. And if few independents made themselves noticed in the US, Hollywood on the other hand coughed out a couple of successful productions before hitting the jackpot in October with Gore Verbinski's remake of the Japanese hit *Ring* …

'Based on true events' (*The Mothman Prophecies*)

The first genre movie of the year, Mark Pellington's *The Mothman Prophecies,* followed *Washington Post* reporter John Klein (Richard Gere), who, two years after the death of his wife, somehow finds himself in Point Pleasant, a small West Virginian town whose inhabitants are having visions of a dark winged creature with red eyes, and premonitions of upcoming disasters.

Last in a series of films – *The Sixth Sense, The Gift, Final Destination, In Dreams, What Lies Beneath* to name a few – whose characters are afflicted by disturbing visions, *The Mothman Prophecies* is the only story to end with the disaster (the collapse of a bridge) the forewarnings pointed to. Despite the signs the villagers receive, no one eventually has any control over their destiny. This is probably why Sony/Screen Gems released this Christmas-set movie in January, the studios' traditional dumping ground for productions they don't have much faith in: a few months after 9/11, the emphasis on the characters' lack of control over their fate and inability to prevent the tragedy[46] inevitably brought back memories of towers crumbling and people jumping out of windows. This eerie, subtle and original take on the premonition sub-genre suffered from bad timing; *The Mothman Prophecies* barely recouped its investment during its

US theatrical run, grossing $35 million on an estimated budget of $32 million. The marketing campaign claimed – perhaps unwisely, given the mood of the time – that the movie was 'based on true events', a gimmick popularised in the seventies by *The Texas Chain Saw Massacre*'s pseudo-factual opening narrative and its vague similarity to the crimes of Ed Gein. As incredible as it may seem for such a supernatural story, the script of Pellington's film was indeed inspired by events that took place in Point Pleasant in 1966-67, as described by parapsychologist John A Keel in his 1975 book *The Mothman Prophecies*, which served as a basis for the movie. From late '66 to early '68, dozens of Mothman sightings were reported, and Keel himself asserts that he received several phone calls warning him of impending disasters. The terror culminated in the collapse of the Silver Bridge on 15 December 1967, in which over 40 people lost their lives. In his account of the events, Keel also described UFO activity observed around the same time, an aspect that screenwriter Richard Hatem chose to leave out.

Opening in the US on 22 February 2002, *Queen of the Damned* was another box-office disappointment, but the reasons for its failure were much more obvious than *The Mothman Prophecies*'. An adaptation of two of Anne Rice's novels: *The Vampire Lestat* (1985) and *Queen of the Damned* (1988), it followed the film of *Interview with the Vampire* (1994) and focused on Lestat, a character played by Tom Cruise in the first movie and this time given a lacklustre performance by Stuart Townsend. Leaving behind the period setting and sensuality of the first entry in the series, *Queen of the Damned*, the story of a vampire turned rock star, worked better as a long music video promoting the bands whose songs are used in the film than as an actual feature; obviously made for an audience of Goths and rebellious teens, it traded *Interview with the Vampire*'s mainstream appeal for cheap special effects and cheesy romanticism. In her last appearance on the big screen (she died in a plane crash shortly after production wrapped), singer Aaliyah, in the titular role, is both clumsy and fascinating; despite her lack of chemistry with Townsend's Lestat, she was hailed as the movie's only notable quality.

The Mothman Prophecies. Queen of the Damned.

Much more successful, at least commercially, Guillermo Del Toro's *Blade II*, the follow-up to Stephen Norrington's 1998 hit *Blade*, was released the following month. *Queen of the Damned* tried to combine vampirism with Goths and hard rockers, and similarly, the *Blade* saga attempted to inject new blood into the dying vampire genre by linking it to a popular subculture, in this case the rap/rave scene. Strictly speaking, despite a deceivingly traditional fright flick opening, Del Toro's movie was closer to comic-book actioner than pure horror, in accordance with the presumed interests of its teenage target audience. Indeed, its strengths lie more in fight sequences (choreographed by Chinese specialist Donnie Yen) and inventive special effects than

46 A theme very similar to 1999's *Arlington Road*, Pellington's previous film, in which the lead tries to persuade the FBI that his neighbour is a terrorist planning to blow up a building.

in scares or enrichment of the vampire lore.

In this sequel, half-vampire, half-human vampire hunter Blade forms an alliance with his sworn enemies when a new creature, the Reaper, appears that threatens both humans and the undead. Interestingly, this is the first movie of this book to present its monster as the result of a disease[47], a theme that will become increasingly popular throughout the decade. As one of the lead characters says: 'As you may know, vampirism is an arbovirus, one that's spread through the saliva of parasitic organisms. In this case, vampires are the vector. The virus replicates within the human bloodstream, evolving its host into an entirely new life-form.' Viruses would be used to justify the existence of zombies in both *Resident Evil* and *28 Days Later*, two of 2002's most successful productions, and would also be an underlying theme, in the form of a viral curse, in *The Ring*, the year's biggest hit. An obvious explanation for this sudden resurgence could be found in the news of the time, from the Anthrax attacks in the US to the foot-and-mouth and mad cow disease outbreaks in the UK, all starting or peaking in 2001, to the beginning of the SARS epidemic in Asia from November 2002 to July 2003, and later on, the Avian flu, from late 2003. In an increasingly crowded world, fears of spreading infections were bound to grow; combined with concerns over the effects of pollution and most importantly, the threat of bioterrorist attacks, these anxieties inevitably found an echo in pop culture, and horror movies offered a particularly appropriate outlet.

Often alternating between low-budgets and studio productions ('one for them, one for me,' as he likes to put it), Guillermo Del Toro seized the opportunity to play with a bigger train set and try his hand at new, innovative special effects, after the personal, controlled, low-key scares of *The Devil's Backbone*. The director's style and flair for visuals lent themselves perfectly to such a dark action piece. Unfortunately, as with the original *Blade*, *Blade II*'s main weakness is Wesley Snipes, whose stiff, dead serious interpretation fails to breathe any life into his character. It seems audiences nevertheless managed to identify with him, as the movie scared up a whopping $81 million in the United States.

Vampires and zombies weren't the only ones to return from the grave that year. Three of the eighties' most beloved killers also returned briefly, all offering equally disappointing sequels to their fans: *Jason X*, *Halloween: Resurrection* (oddly released in the middle of the summer), and *Hellraiser: Hellseeker*, coming out directly on DVD.

On the other hand, ghosts, so popular the previous year, made very few appearances. With the exception of *The Ring*, the only two American movies to feature them prominently, *Ghost Ship* and *Below*, didn't make much of an impact.

The story of a salvage crew discovering a ship abandoned forty years earlier under mysterious circumstances, Steve Beck's *Ghost Ship* should have benefited from its creepy setting, intriguing premise and a heart-stopping opening sequence that in itself justifies renting the DVD. But sadly, the film quickly sinks under the weight of its clichés, interchangeable characters and complete lack of tension and mystery. Furthermore, many of its scares were simply 'borrowed' from *The Shining*, from the beautiful woman who, when kissed by a crewmember, turns into a hideous ghost, to the little girl in a blue dress waiting at the end of the hallway. No wonder then that this bore-fest tanked at the box-office.

Released under the radar (pun intended) on less than 200 US screens, David Twohy's *Below* is a ghost story set in an American submarine during WW2. Although it featured a decent cast (led by Bruce Greenwood and *The Sixth Sense*'s Olivia Williams), an interesting premise and good production value, after a good start, it doesn't deliver on its promises. The story, like the characters, isn't original and strong enough to sustain interest; and there are so many false scares in the first half that when the real ones start later on, the audience no longer takes notice.

Blade II.

47 But obviously not the first to use or mention the theme; in the case of *Blade*, it was present from its comic-book days. The disease explanation for vampirism had also been seen in Richard Matheson's 1954 novel *I Am Legend*, and its adaptations, *The Last Man on Earth* (1964), *The Omega Man* (1971) and *I Am Legend* (2007).

Twohy's movie isn't bad, but it isn't very engaging either. As far as wartime underwater dramas go, Wolfgang Petersen's 1981 *Das Boot* has yet to be beaten, proving that in an environment as confined, dangerous and unpleasant as a submarine during an armed conflict, the real horror is not supernatural.

Even more disappointing, Robert Harmon's *They*, featuring a couple of young adults facing their childhood fears, gathered a maximum amount of unimaginative jump-scares in a minimum of time. Released in the States for November's Thanksgiving weekend, this turkey was another box-office disaster. As for William Malone's *Feardotcom*, opening in the late summer and starring genre favourites Jeffrey Combs and Udo Kier and *Blade* baddie Stephen Dorff in a story which sounded like a cross

Ghost Ship. They.

between *Pulse* (2001) and *Se7en* (1995), it deserved – and received – a fate worse than death, as its total theatrical gross in the US was less than a third of its budget. The film was a great disappointment for anyone who'd followed the director's career; with TV series episodes such as *Tales from the Crypt* (two episodes in 1994 and 1996) and *Freddy's Nightmares* (three episodes in 1989 and 1990) on his CV, Malone had already demonstrated his passion for the genre, and *House on Haunted Hill* (1999), his flawed but entertaining feature debut, had certainly shown promise.

Return of the Living Dead

Not all horror productions flopped. Of the year's biggest hits, two – one in the USA, one in the UK – were zombie movies, a sub-genre which would make a killing at the box office in the years

Resident Evil.

to come. Up until that point, the living dead had almost exclusively belonged to the world of low budget independent films, and had been marginalised and refused the attention bestowed upon vampires, werewolves and mad scientists in major features. The reasons for this lack of popularity amongst critics and general audiences are probably linked to the simplicity of the creature – the stupidest, least refined in the genre; a monster that doesn't speak or even think – and to its single-mindedness – *brains!* –, which make it better suited for splatter fests than elaborate dramas, and harder to reinvent and improve upon. Besides, in the absence of a great literary piece, the zombie didn't have the pedigree of Mr Hyde or the Frankenstein monster. The following movies, however, would put an end to this undead snobbishness …

British director Paul W S Anderson, of *Event Horizon* (1997) and *Mortal Kombat* (1995) fame, released his adaptation of Japanese company Capcom's hit videogame *Resident Evil* in March 2002. A prequel to the game, it followed Alice (Milla Jovovich) as she leads a team of soldiers into an underground research facility called the Hive whose controlling computer has turned homicidal and spread a highly contagious virus which killed (thus mixing two of the decade's favourite themes, technology gone wild and diseases wiping out the world's population, with a soupçon of genetic testing), then reanimated the scientists of the Hive. The crew has three hours to isolate the virus and prevent it from infecting the population of the nearby town, Raccoon City.

The videogame led its players through a mansion inhabited by flesh-eating creatures, and the movie depicts a military unit going down the halls of a technologically advanced facility to confront the living dead. Heavily inspired by the works of George A Romero (who was originally set to direct from his own screenplay, and had helmed a Japanese commercial for the second instalment in the game franchise in the mid-nineties) and Lucio Fulci, the game was intended to be as scary as it could be; the film on the other hand is primarily an action flick, with a very contemporary rock soundtrack (a sure sign that the audience is not expected to be frightened), fast editing and a clear tendency to make the dead more cartoonish than disgusting, with a level of gore miles under 'serious' zombie pictures. Nevertheless, Anderson injects a dose of suspense, hinting at the presence of the living dead rather than showing them in the first half of the story.

Although several adventure/fantasy games had seen film adaptation, for example *Lara Croft: Tomb Raider* (2001), *Mortal Kombat* (1995) and *Super Mario Bros* (1993), *Resident Evil* marked the first time a horror game was brought to the screen, an unsurprising fact given the newfound popularity of the genre. Indeed, like most productions, videogame-based movies only work commercially if they tally with a successful trend; *Lara Croft: Tomb Raider* for instance came out around the same time as *The Mummy Returns*, when audiences were showing a clear interest in adventure films. Anderson's zombie movie may have owed its success to its blend of faithfulness to the game and original additions to the storyline. Many elements were indeed borrowed from the original material (the basic story, of course, but also the undead dogs, the mutant, the map, the linearity of the plot, and the Romeroesque nature of the zombies, slow-paced, flesh-hungry and undefeatable unless shot in the head); others (the Red Queen – the super computer controlling the Hive – or the character of Alice, the strong and likeable zombie slayer) were invented to enrich the film's narrative and expand the *Resident Evil* universe, allowing the movie to stand on its own without alienating the fans of the game. Finding the right balance is traditionally what adaptations fail at; as Anderson stated in his keynote speech at the 2006 Hollywood and Games Summit[48], 'It's a minefield. And it's a minefield as a filmmaker you'd better learn to navigate.' The creative team designed their product to please both connoisseurs and novices. Said producer Jeremy Bolt in a 2002 *Fangoria* interview[49]: 'You don't have to have played the game at all to get something from this film.' In the end, only zombie fans were left out, but they represented such a tiny fraction of the potential demographic at the time that the filmmakers didn't feel the need to target them.

28 Days Later.

Best described as brainless fun, *Resident Evil* isn't a great film, or even an original one (amongst its best-known scenes is one where a soldier is cut into small pieces by a laser, a trick lifted from Vincenzo Natali's 1997 *Cube*), but it did drag zombies, for better or worse, into mainstream cinema. It grossed over $100 million worldwide, encouraging Hollywood to start work on dozens of horror game adaptations. The title also became a successful movie franchise. No surprise there: the closing sequence (which is very similar to scenes which open the 1962 film *Day of the Triffids*), in which Alice wakes up in a deserted laboratory and discovers a world devastated by the virus, was the perfect build-up to a sequel …

This sequel could well have been Danny Boyle's *28 Days Later*, released in the UK in November 2002 and in the US six months later, and which picks up pretty much where *Resident Evil* left off, only in a different setting. The movie starts with stunning views of a deserted London at the break of dawn, and a young man (Jim, played by Cillian Murphy) walking alone through some of the most iconic – and usually most crowded – places in the world. As he starts encountering survivors, he learns that the nation's population has been infected with the Rage virus, which turns them into mindless, indiscriminately aggressive creatures hungry for flesh and destruction. Only a handful amongst those he meets are still sane, and together they decide

48 Paul W S Anderson, 'Pressing the Right Buttons: How to Successfully Blend Game and Film', Hollywood and Games Summit, Beverly Hills, 2006; quoted on *Gamasutra*, 27 June 2006, http://www.gamasutra.com/php-bin/news_index.php?story=9875

49 'Girls, Guns and Ghouls', Mark Salisbury, *Fangoria* 211, April 2002, p 82.

to travel to a military base, from where a radio call claiming to have the answer to the epidemic is originating.

These first few scenes in an empty London were very likely the primary reason *28 Days Later* gathered the attention of the mainstream press. But there was much more to this post-apocalyptic story than met the eye. At first glance just another derivative entry into the living dead subgenre, Boyle's movie is tense, dark, smart and incredibly realistic, thanks to the believability of its premise (as in *Resident Evil*, a bio-weapon gets out of hand and spreads a deadly disease through the population – a sadly realistic threat in a time of bioterrorism and outbreaks), but also to its technical audacity. Indeed, shooting on digital video, a medium until then considered unworthy of feature films, gave the movie an instantly identifiable texture, and allowed Boyle to experiment at lower cost. Hence the film contains a myriad of elaborate shots through windows, fences or shiny drops of rain, an increasingly cold range of colours, and of course, the movements of the infected shot at a different frame rate, giving them speed and energy. Rather than distracting the audience from the plot, all of these filmic elements helped create a sense that the action takes place in a different version of the world, close to the one we know, but irrevocably altered.

28 Days Later.

The first part of the movie, by far the most thrilling, follows the classical zombie invasion scenario, but focuses on human relationships and the characters' reactions to the infected to a degree that hadn't quite been seen before. In this regard, *28 Days Later* elaborates on what was then known as Romero's trilogy of the dead, starting from the same proposition the American master used: that the zombie (or in this case, the infected) is the most human monster of all, a mere representation of ourselves, and that our reactions towards the dead are similar to the way we treat terrorists, criminals, or any other human threat. The second half of the film, where Jim and his group reach the military base, emphasises these aspects even more. The Major in charge keeps an infected chained to a wall outside the castle to 'learn about the disease' (in a scene inspired directly by Romero's *Day of the Dead* (1985)), and sees the situation as a direct continuation of what the world has always known: 'People killing people. Which is much what I saw in the four weeks before infection, and the four weeks before that, and before that, and as far back as I care to remember.' The Major's vision of the infected explained, the movie concentrates on the survivors, to the point where it nearly loses focus; the sick are less of a threat than the healthy, it tells us. Hardly an original message for anyone who has seen the gunmen at the end of *Night of the Living Dead* (1969), or the bikers of *Dawn of the Dead* (1978), it is also delivered in a way that doesn't seem plausible: why have all the remaining soldiers turned into sadistic, libidinous, trigger-happy individuals, while every civilian we've encountered is caring and selfless? And how could a whole battalion be defeated by one skinny, starved, half-naked man?

Technically speaking, as many have pointed out during the great Running Zombies vs Slow Zombies debate that followed the release of both this and the 2004 *Dawn of the Dead* remake, *28 Days Later* is not a zombie film, and its director was quick to disavow his living dead heritage. But beyond the fact that these flesh-eating creatures are still alive (much like the diseased of another Romero production, 1973's *The Crazies*), their behaviour, lack of motivation and even their appearance are incredibly similar to what we've seen in Romero's, Fulci's and Dan O'Bannon's works. The story follows the general structure of the sub-genre, and the scare tactics are clearly inspired by previous zombie flicks. Some scenes are even directly lifted from Romero's films: for instance, as has been pointed out, the chained soldier is a dead ringer for *Day of the Dead*'s Bub, and the supermarket scene echoes the sequence where the survivors of *Dawn of the Dead* go 'shopping' in the mall. Probably Boyle's attitude found its source in the marketing politics of Fox Searchlight (the studio that co-financed the film with British company DNA), which may have feared the zombie affiliation would confine it to a limited demographic. But viewers and critics were not fooled, and the living dead label didn't stop audiences from rushing to their local theatres. The movie grossed over £6 million during its run in the UK, and $45 million in the US, bringing the worldwide total to an impressive $82 million. Not bad for a picture which cost less than $9 million to make. 'It was successful here (in the UK), it was number one, but in the States it became a sort of phenomenon,' producer Andrew McDonald says[50]. 'It's the biggest success Danny's had in the States. It also had to do with where America was at that time. It was obviously post 9/11, and this general sense of paranoia contributed to its success.' Following this success, in September 2003, Fox Searchlight and DNA Films would announce going into business together as a joint venture.

For zombie fans, *28 Days Later* was exactly the fresh production this rotting sub-genre needed; for mainstream audiences, it acted as an introduction to the undead, tapping into the anxieties of the post-9/11 world. The dead were coming back to life in a big way.

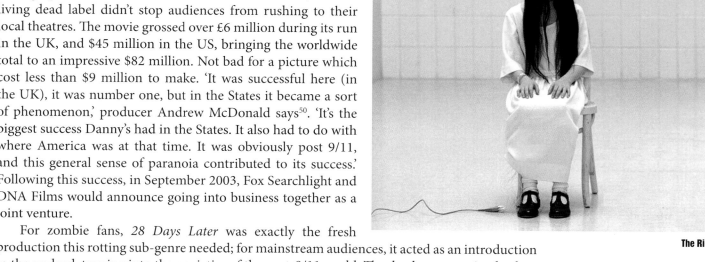

The Ring.

One *Ring* to Rule Them All

Just as Hideo Nakata's surprise hit *Ring* rekindled Japan's passion for ghosts and scary stories, so Gore Verbinski's $48 million remake *The Ring* sparked off a massive interest in all things horror throughout the world.

Korean-American producer Roy Lee is the man generally credited for bringing *Ring* (*Ringu*) to the attention of the studios, and launching Hollywood's J-horror remaking craze. According to legend, Lee discovered Nakata's film through one of the organisers of the Puchon International Film Festival (Korea's number one film festival, which has quickly become one of the world's most important meeting places in the industry), and sold the rights for over $1 million to Mark Sourian at DreamWorks. The reality is a bit more complex, as it is known that a *Ring* remake was in development earlier at Fine Line Features, a subsidiary of New Line, around the time Wes Craven was trying to set up a new version of *Kairo* with Miramax. When the project stalled with Fine Line, creative executive Mike Macari left the company to shop the remake around, and showed the movie to Lee, who eventually sold the rights to DreamWorks with his own name attached as a producer. No matter who originally came up with the idea of adapting J-horror to American tastes, it is Lee, with his company Vertigo Entertainment, who has since become the leader in the market, having served as a mediator between Asian producers and US studios for remakes of *Dark Water* (*Honogurai mizu no soko kara*), *Ju-on: The Grudge* and *Infernal Affairs* (*Mou gaan dou*). Eastern filmmakers trust him to come up with large sums of money for them without costing them a dime; and he has a talent for turning the films into high concept pitches for studio execs.

His deal for *Ring* secured, Lee signed *Scream 3* writer Ehren Kruger to pen the script and *Mousehunt* director Gore Verbinski (known today for his *Pirates of the Caribbean* trilogy) to helm. The pair decided to stay close to the original and retain its themes, basic storyline and main scares. Besides the obvious relocation of the events to the United States and the Americanisation of the characters' names (Sadako becoming Samara, for example), the main changes are found in the pacing, Western viewers being traditionally more impatient than Asians, and in the level of explanation given at the end of the film. Nakata's *Ring* left the situation unresolved and many questions open, but it was feared that US audiences, less accustomed to this perceived lack of logic, might feel disappointed or confused. This decision was the object of many debates between

50 Interview with the author, London, UK, October 2006.

The Ring.

the filmmakers, Verbinski and Kruger reportedly pushing for more abstraction, and Lee and DreamWorks asking them to go in the opposite direction. The result is an awkward compromise, an investigation story without an ending, where the last few scenes suggest that the protagonists have come to a satisfying conclusion but the clues they've found actually lead to more questions than there were to begin with. Where does the tape come from? Who was Samara? Who makes the phone call? And quite frankly, if her goal is to make her story known to the world, why not make it clearer in the video and end it with a message asking viewers to copy it?

The Ring's plot is weak and its characters hollow, but the shocks it delivers in the first and last act, before and at the end of the investigation, are highly effective; and the sight of Samara crawling out of the well is one of the most powerful and iconic horror images of the decade.

Critics were not always kind to Verbinski's remake. In the UK, the *Guardian* found it 'disappointing, losing most of the original's flavour, while retaining and amplifying what was muddled and unsatisfying about it in the first place'[51], while in the US, *Variety* called it a 'low-impact suspenser that sustains a certain mood but doesn't approach the full potential of its premise'[52] and *USA Today* also thought it stopped 'short of being truly effective'[53].

The Ring nonetheless managed the double feat of becoming one of the most successful horror films of the previous ten years, and one of the most successful remakes, with a total $128 million at the US box office. It received a sequel in 2005 and inspired Hollywood to produce a series of Asian horror 're-imaginings' that include, among many others, *The Grudge* (2004) and its 2006 sequel *The Grudge 2, Dark Water* (2005)*, One Missed Call* (2008), *The Eye* (2008), and *A Tale of Two Sisters,* aka *The Uninvited* (2008).

As surprising as it was, the success of *The Ring* wasn't exactly inexplicable. *The Sixth Sense* had whetted the audience's appetite for supernatural frights, light on gore, based on easily marketable high concepts: Lee's production was not only simple to sell, but also original and scary enough to bring something fresh to the genre, unlike most *Sixth Sense* wannabes. It also opened up a new market for mainstream horror: just as the success of J-horror rests on the shoulders of Japanese teenage girls, so are their American counterparts mostly popular with 15 year-old females. A genre traditionally considered the sole interest of adolescent boys suddenly revealed an ability to draw women into theatres, increasing its commercial appeal beyond DreamWorks's hopes.

This new target audience isn't the only reason behind Hollywood's love story with J-horror remakes. Studios, like most business enterprises, dream of finding sure-fire projects and are attracted to whatever comes close; this is why, following the logic according to which what has worked once should work again, any hit must be copied *ad nauseam*. New versions of Asian successes are therefore doubly interesting, since they have already been tested twice: they follow Verbinski's highly profitable *The Ring*, which, for what it's worth, has proved that these movies are transposable and interesting; and they've already proved financially viable in their home countries even though 99% of Americans have never heard of them. In other words, they have already been tried and showed their value, but to most, they'll still seem like original productions. As for the hundred dollar question – why remake them, and not just release them? – the answer is obvious: Western audiences, especially English-speaking, hate subtitles, are not used to dubbed films, find Asian movies too slow and boring, and put too great an emphasis on name actors and state-of-the-art special effects to be interested in low-budget Japanese productions. Also, without basic knowledge of the culture, many subtleties get lost in translation; and if some features follow the familiar three-act structure and move along at an acceptable pace, most can only be enjoyed by accustomed moviegoers. But then, shouldn't film studios and television networks realise that by turning every import into something cosy and familiar, they encourage their viewers' laziness? Yes, but they are crowd-pleasers, not teachers. Their goal is to make money, not to educate. Remaking foreign films certainly didn't start with *The Ring*, but they were until then a marginal phenomenon, usually limited to French comedies or the occasional Spanish drama.

With the horror genre beginning a new renaissance, *The Ring* arrived at the perfect moment.

51 Peter Bradshaw, *The Guardian*, 21 February 2003, http://film.guardian.co.uk/News_Story/Critic_Review/Guardian_review/0,,899357,00.html

52 Todd McCarthy, *Variety*, 3 October 2002, http://www.variety.com/review/VE1117918953.html?categoryid=31&cs=1

53 '*Ring* Has Hang-up or Two', Claudia Puig, *USA Today*, http://www.usatoday.com/life/movies/reviews/2002-10-17-the-ring_x.htm

As Roy Lee said in a 2005 interview with the International Edition of Japanese cultural magazine *Kateigaho*[54], 'the quality of Japanese movies has reached a level that is now competitive with the rest of the world. Also, mediators like me who can introduce Japanese films to Hollywood studios have appeared. These and a number of other factors all came together at just the right time, and Hollywood, which is always looking for interesting films, opened its doors wide.'

Big in Japan

The success of *The Ring* didn't stop at Asia's borders. It extended all the way back to the story's native country, where it made more money in two weeks than Nakata's *Ring* had in its whole theatrical run ($8.3 million against $6.6 million). The movie not only rekindled the audience's dwindling interest in national horror productions, but also encouraged filmmakers and producers to further explore the genre by dazzling them with the possibility of having their film distributed abroad, or the rights picked up for a remake. Some of them – Nakata included – would even get the rare (and dubious) honour of directing their own US versions …

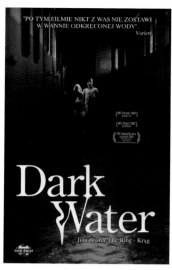

Dark Water.

Nakata himself would be the first to dive back into the J-Horror wave with *Dark Water*, another adaptation from a Kôji Suzuki story, about a mother, Yoshimi Matsubara, who moves into a flat with her six year-old daughter after her separation from her husband, and realises the place not only is prone to leaks and inundations, but is also haunted. Slow and character-driven, but with some genuinely creepy moments, *Dark Water* is as close to a social drama as horror movies will ever get.

Just like in *Ring*, the female protagonist deals with the spirit of a little girl, Mitsuko, victim of the negligence of her parents. In most Japanese films, vengeful spirits are the products of a disruption of traditional family structures – divorce, adultery, working mothers, child abuse – by modern society, a clear example of Japan's unease with its current evolution. In *Dark Water*, not only is the ghost the result of a separation, but the mother and child whose apartment is haunted also deal with the consequences of a divorce, the tough conciliation of family and work, the housing problem and the difficulty of finding a job. In a historically male-dominated society, where women stayed at home while the men fought at war, and where wives couldn't take part in any important decisions for their family or country, the large majority of *yurei* – ghosts in Japanese folklore – have always been female, as oppressed women were deemed more powerful in death and likely to take their revenge. Nowadays, women are given the opportunity to break away from their traditional roles, but their actions place them in equally hard situations, leading to the perpetuation of female apparitions, usually as Dead Wet Girls[55], the most popular form of ghost in the Japanese culture, who could be found in legends and tales long before the publication of Suzuki's *Ring*. Wetness is obviously a recurrent theme in *Dark Water*, and as Sadako died in a well, Mitsuko drowned in a water tank. Both spirits appear drenched, their long hair soaking wet. Seeping or stagnant water is often associated with sickness and decay in Japan, but as author David Kalat points out, the word 'wet' also has the second meaning of 'emotional'[56], which could lead to the interpretation that these wet ghosts are full of rage and sadness.

Interestingly, as suggested by the movie's ending, *Dark Water*'s ghost can also be read as a materialisation of Mrs Matsubara's mental breakdown, a pure creation of her overstressed mind, or the work of her husband, a powerful businessman who seeks custody of their child. This subtlety, and much of the movie's powerful social context, would be lost in the 2005 US remake by Brazilian director Walter Salles.

South Korea also jumped on the bandwagon. Japanese pop culture had been banned at the end of the Japanese occupation in 1945, and a system of quotas had been established to restrict film imports from other countries; but as this censorship was progressively abolished in the late eighties and throughout the nineties, Korean filmmakers were forced to learn to compete with international productions. Cheap and profitable, J- (or K- as it has been called) Horror found its place quickly in South Korea's film industry (the most obvious examples being *Whispering Corridors* (*Yeogo goedam*) in 1998 and *The Ring Virus* and *Memento Mori* (*Yeogo goedam II*) in

54 'Interview with Roy Lee, Matchmaker of the Macabre', Sumiyo Heianna, *Kateigaho International Edition*, Winter 2005, http://int. kateigaho.com/win05/horror-lee.html
55 The term was popularised by the NPR in 'Ghosts, Chills and *Dark Water* from Japan', Neda Ulaby, 11 July 2005, *National Public Radio*, http://www.npr.org/templates/story/story.php?storyId=4735733; but this author confesses she is ignorant of where it originated.
56 *J-Horror, The Definitive Guide to The Ring, The Grudge and Beyond*, David Kalat, Vertical, 2007, p 17.

1999), but if the genre blossomed thanks to the success of its Japanese counterpart, the country had its own tradition of long-haired ghosts, and developed a subtly different set of rules.

Still, separate tradition or not, Byeong-ki Ahn's *Phone* (*Pon*), released in its homeland in July 2002, was as obvious a dead ringer for *Ring* as one can get. The movie focuses on a woman who recently changed her mobile number and starts receiving odd calls; but complicates matters with a series of sub-plots and twists, leading to a final revelation reminiscent of that in *What Lies Beneath*. Once again, technological devices are linked to a ghost with long black hair (one common explanation for this persistent feature is that since women were traditionally expected to tie up their hair in neat ponytails, long flowing hair was a symbol of unruliness and rebellion.) *Phone* brought little to the genre, but was all the same a major success in its country.

The J-horror phenomenon spread outside of Japan and Korea with the Pang Brothers' *The Eye* (*Gin gwai*), a Hong Kong/UK/Singapore co-production. While some considered it a blend of *The Sixth Sense* and *The Mothman Prophecies*, this story of a young girl (Mun, played by singer Angelica Lee) who sees dead people after a corneal transplant is both scary and touching, and adds enough new elements to the mix to stand on its own.

Born in Hong Kong in 1965, twin brothers Oxide and Danny Pang started their careers in different areas of the film industry, Oxide directing short films and TV commercials in Thailand and Danny editing movies in Hong Kong. They united for the first time in 1999 for a dark thriller, *Bangkok Dangerous*. *The Eye*, their second feature, was shot partly in Thailand and partly in Hong Kong. Evidently, the brothers have been influenced by American cinema; from the opening titles to the CGI finale, many traits show that they have absorbed and integrated Western filmmaking tricks. Nevertheless, *The Eye* remains a distinctly Eastern production. Its pacing, alternating emotional scenes with ghost appearances, is closer to an Asian film, and the story is steeped in Thai and Chinese beliefs and cultural references, from the calligraphy room and the altar in the hall to the black figure which carries away the souls of the departed. As in most J-horror flicks, the lead is a woman, and most of the ghosts trapped in a loop and repeating their last moments are either females or children.

The Eye combines atmospheric chills and shock scenes, and excels at both. In the first category, the blurred images at the hospital and in the hallway outside Mun's apartment are simply chilling, and instantly help the audience understand the difficulties – and potential for the supernatural – of someone who has just regained her vision but doesn't yet understand everything she sees. The viewers are right there with Mun; they view a shape and suspect something's wrong, but they cannot identify the nature of the problem until it is right in front of their eyes. The scenes in the calligraphy room and in the elevator fall into the shock category; coming completely out of left field, they are incredibly effective. The tension falls somewhat in the second part, when Mun and her psychotherapist go to Thailand to learn about Ling, the girl who donated her cornea, and the story turns into an investigation *à la Ring*. But the end sequence, reminiscent of *The Mothman Prophecies* as it may be, is impressive; the movie ends with a literal bang.

The Eye grossed over $13.7 million in Hong Kong alone, and, very likely helped by the success of the *Ring* remake, was granted theatrical release in many countries throughout the world, including the US, UK, Italy and Spain. It was also remade twice: in India in 2005, under the title *Naina*, and in the States in 2008, through Tom Cruise's production company. It would also have two follow-ups, both directed by the Pang Brothers. In *The Eye 2* (2004), a pregnant woman (Shu Qi) starts seeing spirits after a suicide attempt; while *The Eye 10* (2005) tells of the ten ways ghosts

Phone. The Eye.

can be summoned. Neither sequel was as commercially or critically successful as the original, but both kept the quality level high and the ideas fresh, as the brothers cleverly chose to pick new protagonists and show different ways of encountering the dead. As of writing, *The Eye 3* is currently scheduled for release in 2009, directed by Hark Tsui.

Claustrophobic Horrors

2002 was a great year for horror in the United Kingdom, when no less than five major titles were released and made their mark on the genre.

Curiously, four of these films involved soldiers: *28 Days Later*, as we have seen, ended in a military retreat; *Dog Soldiers* pitted a squad against werewolves; *The Bunker* and *Deathwatch* depicted the horror of war

Dog Soldiers.

while introducing supernatural elements into typical wartime situations. Coincidence or sign of the times? Neil Marshall, writer and director of *Dog Soldiers*, wonders[57]: 'Who can say? It's like buses, isn't it? You wait for ages then five come along at once. Movie trends randomly appear and disappear just as fast. Since myself, Rob Green, Michael Bassett and Danny Boyle had never met, let alone heard of each other, it seems unlikely that we cottoned on to each other's ideas, and much more plausible that it was just a weird coincidence.' Maybe the involvement of UK troops in Afghanistan and the constant reminders of the war in the news struck the imaginations of the producers who financed the films and the distributors who released them around that time. Or maybe the soldiers-vs-supernatural sub-genre had simply been brewing under the surface for a long time. Whatever the case, the military would only be seen again in a handful of horror stories in the following years, including Korean import *R-Point* in 2004, and Joe Dante's controversial *Masters of Horror* television episode 'Homecoming' in 2005.

First out of the gates was *Dog Soldiers*, a one-night, one-location survival piece in which a group of soldiers on a routine exercise in the Scottish wilderness find themselves surrounded by werewolves, and take refuge in a deserted farmhouse. Avoiding all discussion on the nature and origins of the beasts outside (unlike previous lycanthropic efforts *Ginger Snaps* and *Brotherhood of the Wolf*), the movie focuses on the fight between the six men and the supernatural creatures. Nothing highly original there, but its lack of pretension and sense of fun, along with its non-stop action and the numerous twists it puts on the conventions of the genre, won *Dog Soldiers* a roaring ovation after its world premiere at the Brussels International Festival of Fantastic Film (as well as the Jury Award and the Audience Prize), and later, a cult following on both sides of the Atlantic. Released theatrically on its home turf on 10 May, Marshall's film opened to decent box-office (grossing £681,348 on its first weekend) and enthusiastic reviews. BBC critic Jamie Russell described it as 'the perfect Friday night movie … full of boisterous energy, some really disgusting moments, and some clever-clever genre in-jokes'[58]; the *Hollywood Reporter* called it 'well-made – though mindless – horror-mayhem film'[59]; while *Time Out* remarked that 'it may be barking, but this British underdog has teeth'[60]. Many saw a parallel between *Dog Soldiers* and *Night of the Living Dead*, a movie that to this day, Marshall hasn't seen. Instead, the filmmaker cites the influence of *The Evil Dead* (one of the soldiers is even called Bruce Campbell), *An American Werewolf in London*, various westerns, and the 1964 Michael Caine vehicle *Zulu*.

One trait *Dog Soldiers* has in common with Raimi's and Landis's classics is its humour, an element that Marshall says grew naturally from the characters and the outrageousness of the situation. 'I wanted to depict British squaddies as realistically as possible, and through my dad's stories and the research I did, I found that British soldiers have an incredibly sick and perverse sense of gallows humour that I really wanted to capture in the movie. Soldiers under fire often

57 Interview with the author, London, England, January 2008.

58 Jamie Russell, *BBC*, 9 May 2002, http://www.bbc.co.uk/films/2002/04/12/dog_soldiers_2002_review.shtml

59 Mark Adams, *The Hollywood Reporter*, 25 June 2002, http://www.hollywoodreporter.com/hr/search/article_display.jsp?vnu_content_id=1526383

60 TCh, *Time Out London*, 2002, http://www.timeout.com/film/reviews/65613/dog_soldiers.html

rely on humour to get them through. This story seemed like the ideal opportunity to integrate that. During the writing of the movie and throughout pre-production I had it in my mind that this was primarily going to be a scary movie, tempered by a few laughs, but once the cast came on board, that all changed. We knocked ideas back and forth and slowly introduced more and more sardonic character beats into the film. I think had I tried to make it purely scary, it would have back-fired and become laughable. But this way the audience is having too much fun to care about the budgetary restrictions. They appreciate that we clearly had our tongues firmly in our cheeks but never once undermined the horror.'

Dog Soldiers also shares a cartoonish approach to gore with *The Evil Dead* and *An American Werewolf in London*. In what could probably be the movie's most famous display of blood and guts, Sergeant Wells (Sean Pertwee) looks at his own intestines spilling on the floor and mutters, 'sausages'. This over-the-top, humorous quality is hardly realistic, and allowed the movie to gain a 15 certificate, at the time a prerequisite for a successful cinema run. 'There's a scene that I chose to cut that might have earned it an 18 cert,' Marshall recalls, 'but that's not why I cut it. I actually made every effort to earn the film an 18 cert but I guess because of the strong fantasy element to it, the BBFC gave it a 15 cert without asking me to make any cuts or changes. The scene that I cut out involves the character Spoon in his dying moments. One werewolf is holding him up against the wall by his throat while two others tear him in half below the waist, resulting in all his insides spilling out onto the floor. To achieve the shot, we cut a hole through the wall and had actor Darren Morfitt standing on the other side, with only his head, shoulders and arms through the hole. His fake body was then attached and filled with intestines, and on action, the werewolves rip him in half and his guts fall out. The reason I chose to cut the scene was because I felt the audience would not want to see Spoon in such a pitiful state. He'd fought tooth and nail to the last breath, hoping he'd give the werewolves the shits when they ate him. The effect was so gruesomely effective. I tried to put it on the DVD as an extra, but the BBFC said that to do this would certainly change the rating to an 18, so [distribution company] Pathé didn't want to do it.'

Dog Soldiers.

Born in Newcastle, North East England, in 1970, Marshall started his filmmaking career as an editor (namely on local director Bharat Nalluri's *Killing Time* (1998), which Marshall co-wrote) before directing an award-winning short called *Combat* (1999). Meanwhile it took him six years to set up *Dog Soldiers*, his first feature, which eventually found financing outside the UK. 'The UK industry turned their noses up at us. They weren't interested, even after the resurgence of horror in the US following the *Scream* movies at the end of the nineties. Financing ultimately came from several sources, including the Luxembourg Film Commission, but the bulk of it came from an Arkansas spinach magnate called David E Allen. He found the script and some artwork at the American Film Market in Los Angeles and decided to put his own money into the project.' To qualify for subsidies, the writer/director took his cast and crew to Petite-Suisse, Luxemburg. If Britain was about to experience a horror revival, it certainly was through no fault of its own.

Michael J Bassett's *Deathwatch* was similarly funded outside the UK, with German money and distribution presales; but Rob Green's *The Bunker*, released in September 2002 after being shelved for almost two years, is the only film in this group to have found financing in its home country, using the tax incentive system to attract private investors. Set at the German/Belgian border during World War II, *The Bunker* follows a group of German soldiers hidden in the titular location. Tired, strained and afraid, their relationships are already tense, when they start suspecting they are not alone in the tunnels.

Scary movies taking place in wartime are inherently difficult to make. More often than not, the horror of the conflict itself and the tension the troops are naturally subjected to are already so great that no supernatural evil can really add to their fright. This is why *The Bunker*, like *Below* (2002) and *Deathwatch*, leaves it up to the viewer to decide whether the location is haunted or the men have simply gone insane, thereby suggesting that war has terrible consequences for the psyches of those who fight it.

The idea is clever. The protagonists of *The Bunker* not only fear the American troops patrolling outside, but also the enemy inside, in their heads; crazy with guilt and mistrust, they have become strangers to themselves, they are afraid of each other and of their own reactions. Unfortunately, Green failed to translate this concept into visual terms. Very little happens; the characters, with a couple of exceptions, are interchangeable, and the setting, as realistic and convincing as it may be lacks variety. As for the evil itself, the lack of a clearly identifiable antagonist makes the story less engaging and tougher to follow. For a movie about jangling nerves and paranoia, *The Bunker* is oddly dull.

Different war, same nightmare: *Deathwatch* delivers a similar message, but is more appealing and visually stimulating than its predecessor. The story this time takes place in 1917, when a group of British soldiers, isolated from the rest of the regiment, reach the most forward German trench. It is nearly deserted; the only soldier they find is taken prisoner and warns them that there's an evil force at play in the trench. Strange things begin to happen, and the soldiers soon turn on each other.

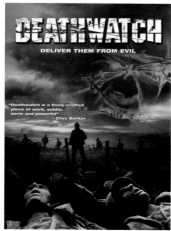

Although *Deathwatch* suffers from the same problem as *The Bunker* and *Below* (the rats, mud, rain, wounds, lack of comfort and war raging outside are much scarier than any supernatural being; and the limitations due to the location make for a somewhat tiresome experience), its gritty images and excellent performances make the constant confrontations between the soldiers more convincing, and its oppressive setting more real. Thankfully, writer/director Michael J Bassett made sure his actors looked very different from one another despite wearing the same uniforms and being covered in mud, and allowed them to move around the tunnels rather than sitting in the same place. He also took the action out of the trenches a couple of times, breaking the monotony of the environment, and a couple of graphic scenes (the death of Andy Serkis's character, for instance) spice up the action.

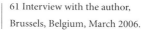

Deathwatch.

For all its advantages, *Deathwatch* is far from perfect. The basic storyline is easy to grasp, but the smaller developments are sometimes confusing. There aren't enough twists to keep interest at a peak throughout, and the viewers' efforts are rewarded by a predictable ending. As for the general message of the film – war can drive you insane – it is hardly revolutionary. Still, *Deathwatch* is a clever attempt at psychological horror, all the more noticeable for being part of the new wave of genre productions in the United Kingdom.

Bassett's career didn't follow the traditional film school path. A former assistant to a wildlife filmmaker and TV host, he considered becoming a vet before buying a video camera and starting directing shorts. 'It's not like in America, where being a filmmaker is part of the culture,' he says[61]. 'In the UK it's not a real career. After a while I got better at writing and directing; I sold some scripts and made a living doing that for a while and I would write very ambitious, big sci-fi expensive movies because that's what I wanted to make and wanted to see. Of course they never got made. So I figured out what it is that's gonna get made and what I liked. I liked horror and I thought I had a handle on how it could work. I wanted to make a movie in one location with a limited cast, and I was interested in World War I; I thought if I could bring the two horrors together I could make a movie which has an interesting thing to say and be a doable movie on a budget. So I wrote what was then called *No Man's Land* and later became *Deathwatch*.' Given Bassett's lack of directing experience, the producers asked him to shoot a short sequence from the script to prove his worth. The result must have pleased them, because a few months later he found himself filming in a trench in the middle of the Prague winter, for what turned out to be a gruelling shoot in the mud, the cold and the rain. *Deathwatch* was, in the filmmaker's terms, a 'moderate success', but it would take Bassett four years to get his next movie produced and released.

Like the three films above, *The Hole*, and many more, Welsh director Marc Evans's *My Little Eye* follows the breakdown of a small group of people under pressure in a confined location, where all try to figure out what is happening, only to realise the culprit is amongst them. If the formula is not new, each movie at least gives it a new twist; in Evans's story, the group members are contestants in a

61 Interview with the author, Brussels, Belgium, March 2006.

My Little Eye.

reality show broadcast on the Internet. Their challenge is to stay together in a house in the middle of nowhere for six months, but just as they are about to win, the organisers start spicing things up …

On this simple premise, Evans crafts a breathtaking game of cat-and-mouse, a fascinating and suspenseful film that takes full advantage of its low budget. Filmed at the height of *Big Brother* mania, Evans's thriller, a UK/USA/Canada/France co-production shot in Canada, is an obvious satire on the reality TV phenomenon and, to a degree, a critique of the Internet and its possible abuses. A touch of *The Blair Witch Project* is added to the mix, as the action is entirely seen through spy cameras placed inside the house, offering unusual angles full of dark corners from which killers could emerge at any time, keeping the viewers on their toes. Most of the soundtrack consists of noise effects and the occasional pop song the house's inhabitants are listening to. The location itself is suitably creepy and dark and contributes to the gloomy atmosphere the deeply contrasted photography creates. In such an environment, it is no surprise that the characters quarrel constantly, feel depressed and fantasise about their return to the world. Surprisingly perhaps, we know very little about them; no one speaks about their previous lives or the people they've left behind.

Too dark for a real mainstream success, *My Little Eye* nevertheless grossed nearly £840,000 on its opening weekend in the UK in October 2002, and had largely paid back its £2 million investment by the end of the month, taking £2,566,742.

And in the Rest of Europe …

While Britain's production was in full throttle, the rest of Europe – represented by the now usual suspects, Spain and France – made do with two minor features, *Darkness* and *Bloody Mallory*.

Jaume Balagueró's *Darkness*, produced by Fantastic Factory, came out in Spain in October 2002. Basically a haunted house story, it follows a family of Americans as they move into a house in the Spanish countryside. As always, strange things start to happen, and their relationships deteriorate rapidly. Could it be their problems are linked to the history of their new home?

This summary doesn't sound very fresh, and Balagueró must have been aware of it. Instead of concentrating on the house and its supernatural inhabitants, the writer/director added countless wild camera moves and little plot twists to confuse matters and give the illusion that something more complex than ghosts was at play. Unfortunately, none of these tricks work. The film starts off as a drama, with the emphasis placed on the feelings and interactions between the members of the family, but the characters somehow remain two-dimensional and unlikeable. When the horror begins, Balagueró falls back on irritating shaky cameras, cuts to black accompanied by screams, and the threadbare trick of the shadow whooshing past in the foreground, used not once, not twice, but a stunning three times. The actors' performances do little to help; the father (Iain Glen) ends up simply caricaturing Jack Nicholson in *The Shining*. Armed with the best intentions, Balagueró nevertheless failed to deliver something new and exciting. He would however return to give ghosts a much more satisfying treatment in *Fragile* a few years later.

Meanwhile in France, newcomer Julien Magnat released *Bloody Mallory*, a horror actioner in which a young woman, Mallory (Olivia Bonamy) embarks on a crusade against the forces of evil after discovering on her wedding night that she's married a demon, and that she has no choice but to kill him. The groom dies cursing her, and she surrounds herself with a team whose colourful members include a transvestite and a mute telepath.

Featuring a strong female lead, *Bloody Mallory* contains an improbable mix of influences ranging from *Buffy The Vampire Slayer* and *The Exorcist* to Japanese manga and *Lara Croft: Tomb Raider*. In equal parts supernatural thriller and action, Magnat's film targeted a wider audience than the traditional 100,000 moviegoers French horror films tend to attract in their homeland; but this supernatural melting pot, irreverent and silly, didn't have enough bite to leave a real mark on the genre. Still, Magnat aimed in the right direction, and his work, like Gans's, prefigured the attraction horror would soon hold for local filmmakers.

Bloody Mallory.

Masters of Horror

Just as scary movies started blossoming again in the US and abroad, director of *The Convent* (2000) Mike Mendez, and author of *The Dead Hate the Living* (2000) Dave Parker, unleashed *Masters of Horror*, a made-for-TV documentary about the greatest filmmakers working in the genre. Hosted by actor Bruce Campbell, the 90-minute Showtime special included interviews with the likes of Wes Craven, John Carpenter and George Romero, and offered a full overview of horror in the past three decades. 'I was in-between films and wondering what I was going to do when just by luck, someone told me that a subdivision of Universal wanted to make a DVD about the greatest horror directors,' Mendez recalls[62]. 'I said I think I know something about that, and it became my mission to make the greatest DVD ever. Now the company released their first two DVDs in that series and they bombed so badly that Universal cancelled the line, but thankfully I cared so much, and I had so many great interviews, that I said I could turn it into a TV special. They said that was great and we sold it to Showtime. It was a dream come true to work with all my heroes, and I was really surprised that everyone agreed to do it. It really got the term "Masters of Horror" started and it was a very big hit for Showtime. I'm very proud of it; I only wish it was available on DVD.'

By the end of 2003, filmmakers were more conscious of their horror heritage and promising box office returns, along with some interesting projects in the works, showed a rekindled enthusiasm for all things scary around the world. It seemed that the genre was finally moving in a new and exciting direction.

62 Interview with the author, San Diego, USA, July 2007.

2003:

'You want Scary? This is Scary.'

(Tagline for *The Texas Chainsaw Massacre*, 2003)

IF 2002 SHOWED THE FIRST SIGNS OF A RESURGENCE OF INTEREST IN HORROR amongst filmgoers worldwide, 2003 was truly the year of the revival, and a great time for scary movie fans. Big budget productions were challenged by daring and increasingly violent independent films, which found a kind of mainstream recognition unseen since *The Blair Witch Project*. Horror productions abounded all around the world; a couple of slasher legends made a much anticipated comeback; and at the end of the year, the hit remake of a classic would set off yet another new trend …

Overall, the level of gore and graphic murders found in the year's most successful productions was significantly higher than it had been at any point in the past decade. Clearly, this trend answered a need, and its cause may be found in the international climate of the time.

While the situation in Afghanistan, after the invasion launched in October 2001 by the US and the UK, was far from stabilised, US troops being stuck in the middle of a political and social muddle in a country where suicide bombers and rebel fighters posed a constant threat, the American government declared war against Saddam Hussein's Iraq in March. This time, the invasion was not approved by the UN Security Council, and the United States' disdain for international law antagonised several European countries – among which France – and instantly affected the perception of the nation around the globe. From then on, America was no longer seen as a defender of democracy and a protector of the weak, but instead received the image of a self-appointed leader of the world, an almighty, contemptuous tyrant who refused to abide by the rules. That US soldiers died abroad and that the government no longer provided reassurance was bad enough, but the lack of footage from the war made the public's imagination go wild. The Pentagon and the White House imposed a blackout on images of coffins returning from the war, of American POWs, or of anything showing troops hurt or in danger. But some pictures leaked, further piquing the people's curiosity, the most infamous and gruesome being a four-minute clip showing the decapitation of Wall Street Journal reporter Daniel Pearl in February 2002, which circulated for a while on the Internet. As director Eli Roth recalls[63], 'Everybody felt like we were not getting the truth. Everybody thought about those horrible things going on, it was on everybody's mind. You were thinking about torture and all those things. You were thinking about what would happen if you were Daniel Pearl. Violent images are a safe way to work through that fear. We know they're fake, so we don't feel threatened. We all felt like it could all fall apart any time. It's the first time in the US that we thought like that. Before that, we were the ones who were feeding the world.'

With a strong censorship on real-life events, Americans turned to movies to exorcise the scary thoughts that kept popping up inside their heads.

Big Productions, Little Impact

January being the studios' traditional dumping ground for genre movies they have lost faith in, the year started with a mediocre production whose unexpected success could only be attributed to the audience's newfound thirst for horror. With a budget of just over $12 million, Jonathan Liebesman's *Darkness Falls*, which takes place in a village cursed by a crone known as the Tooth Fairy, managed to take in more than $32 million on 2,837 screens. But this cliché-ridden and silly take on childhood terrors and fear of the dark, filled with cheap jump-scares and hollow characters, scored low with critics despite some good special effects and interesting creature designs, and it would take its first-time helmer three years to get another feature-directing gig (*The Texas Chainsaw Massacre: the Beginning* (2006), which did little to gain him the fans' trust).

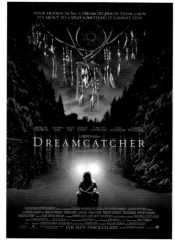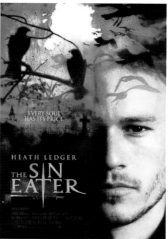

Darkness Falls. Dreamcatcher. Sin Eater.

Dreamcatcher, a sci-fi/horror hybrid from director Lawrence Kasdan, who co-wrote this Stephen King adaptation with William Goldman, wasn't quite as lucky commercially. Opening in March to poor reviews, it barely made back half its investment during its US release. This story of four friends whose hunting trip in Maine is disrupted by the arrival of a sick stranger deals with psychic abilities (once again), mind control, body snatchers, and an alien invasion. The acting is decent and the snow-covered scenery stunning, but *Dreamcatcher* suffers from its length (136 minutes) and only sustains interest in its first half, until the first creatures appear on screen and turn what seemed like an intriguing premise into what Roger Ebert rightfully described as 'a monster movie of stunning awfulness'[64], and a mishmash of old science fiction clichés.

Sin Eater (aka *The Order*), from director Brian Helgeland with Heath Ledger and Shannyn Sossamon, the team behind *A Knight's Tale* (2001), was another massive miss. It cost Twentieth Century Fox an estimated $38 million and didn't even make $8 million back during its US release. This theological thriller about a priest investigating the heretical rite of sin eating – absolving the dying by literally swallowing their sins – sacrificed chills for dull theoretical conversations on the meaning of life, truth and faith. In a time where cases of paedophilia within the clergy are pounced upon by the media, the only way to picture a priest who would be likeable to a widely atheist crowd is to make him rebellious and close to losing his faith: in other words, to reduce him to a stereotype. Similarly, the Church is invariably depicted as corrupt, and its members are always greedy and mischievous. But if these clichés might please non-believers (while of course alienating Christians), the same viewers can only be disturbed by the fact that these movies presuppose the existence of God to justify the supernatural events they describe: if Heaven and

63 Interview with the author, Los Angeles, USA, January 2008.
64 Roger Ebert, Chicago Sun Times, 22 March 2003, http://rogerebert.suntimes.com/apps/pbcs.dll/article?AID=/20030322/REVIEWS/303220302/1023

Hell are human inventions, why bother trying to be absolved at all? No wonder this low, incoherent and needlessly complicated borefest failed to find an audience.

Less typical was Glen Morgan's effort to update 1971 thriller[65] *Willard*, about a young misfit who discovers he has a psychic connection with the rats in the basement of his mother's house, and who uses these new 'friends' to take revenge on his tormentors. Produced by Morgan and *Final Destination* partner Wong for New Line Cinema, and starring an amusingly over-the-top Crispin Glover as the titular loser, this remake was a dark, stylish and old-fashioned chiller revolving more around the quirky personality of its protagonist than around the rats themselves. Glover's Willard is weak and unable to stand up for himself; viewers don't really know whether to sympathise with him or despise and fear him until the *Grand Guignol* finale, although some traits – the way he treats the dog and the cat, his growing hatred for his peers – indicate that the latter might be more appropriate. Eventually, in what could be the movie's most memorable scene, the outcast turns into an all-out villain, and Glover's performance becomes an almost perfect recreation of Dwight Frye's Renfield. Said Morgan[66], 'We got started just before 11 September … For us, the theme of *Willard* was, don't become what you hate. It's really apropos of the time.' Unfortunately, as timely as it may have seemed to its makers, this fascinating and unconventional story was a resounding flop.

The same year, Morgan and Wong's previous feature received a disappointing sequel. In *Final Destination 2*, from actor/stuntman-turned-director David R Ellis, young Kimberly Corman saves herself and a few others from a car crash which should have cost them their lives; but as was to be expected, Death starts getting back at them one by one. Decidedly less fresh than the original, this follow-up, penned by the future writers-directors of *The Butterfly Effect* (2004), Eric Bress and J Mackye Gruber, compensated for its lack of smarts with a much higher degree of gore and a series of impressive, elaborate death scenes which had audiences cheering and wincing in unison. Much like in the slashers of the olden days, these bloody pay-offs are the only amusing part of the movie, and if this may be enough to give gorehounds a good time, the story isn't half as clever as the first film, and is hardly worth a repeat.

Featuring a group of characters unrelated to the brother and sister of the original (here, a busload of cheerleaders and football players, unlikeable from the start, are stalked by the Creeper on the last night of its feeding cycle), *Jeepers Creepers 2* only has the Creeper in common with the original – in other words, *Jeepers Creepers*'s weakest element. While Salva's first entry in the series relied on atmosphere, two believable protagonists and the mystery surrounding the nature of the killer, his sequel on the other hand shows the monster in the opening scene, slays several people in the first act and revolves around self-centered, homophobic, racist kids no viewer in their right mind would want to identify with. Repetitive and schlocky, the new movie simply upped the body count and creature effects, forgetting all about character development and storyline. Even the original's beautiful photography is not matched here, the fields around the bus being as brightly lit as a sports arena on a game night. Like *Final Destination 2*, *Jeepers Creepers 2* reduced an interesting and well executed concept to slasher level. A second sequel is nevertheless set for a 2009 release.

Speaking of slashers, two horror icons made a comeback in the long-awaited face-off *Freddy vs Jason*, released in August 2003 in the US. The concept was the stuff fan dreams are made of: a WWE-type showdown between two genre legends, both teen killers, both unstoppable. The two franchises belonging to the same company, New Line executives realised early on that they could be turned into one highly profitable movie. But it wasn't until 1994 and the release of *Jason Goes to Hell*, which ends with Jason's hockey mask being pulled into the ground by Freddy's trademark claw, that New Line, along with *Friday the 13th* producer Sean S Cunningham, began development on the title.

Final Destination 2. Jeepers Creepers 2. OPPOSITE: Willard.

65 The 1971 original was based on a novel by Stephen Gilbert, and followed the next year by a sequel, Ben, most famous today for Michael Jackson's interpretation of the eponymous song.

66 'A scary classic remade: Mouse Hunt meets Psycho', Elvis Mitchell, The New York Times, 16 March 2003, http://query.nytimes.com/gst/fullpage.html?res=9E07E4D7143EF935A25750C0A9659C8B63&sec=&spon=&pagewanted=all

As similar as the two franchises may have seemed, the challenges were obvious: the movie had to satisfy die-hard fans as well as novices; Freddy and Jason had to share the spotlight in equal measure to please everyone; the two killers had to be brought into the same world (Freddy stalks the youth of Elm Street in their dreams; Jason's victims are real-world kids at Camp Crystal Lake); and while the film had to feature a group of teenagers caught between the monsters, the focus had to be on the titular characters. A reported eighteen drafts from twelve different writers (including *The Crow*'s David J Schow and *Star Trek* writer Ronald D Moore) would be necessary to bring the two series together into a coherent story, and the resulting film is clearly the product of many compromises. In addition to all these difficulties, internal dissensions within the production team further complicated the matter, as Cunningham explained to writer Peter M Bracke[67]: 'With [Cyrus Voris and Ethan Reiff …], we turned in a draft that I thought was pretty successful. But [New Line President of Production] Michael De Luca just flat-out hated it. Then *Scream* opened and it was like, it's a brand new ball game now. We can't do the same old stuff. So De Luca basically just threw it all away.' The executive was later replaced, but not before he hired Damian Shannon and Mark Swift, the writers who would eventually be credited for the script.

Freddy Vs Jason.

The final screenplay was based on a reasonably simple concept (Freddy Krueger sends Jason Vorhees to Elm Street to rekindle the fear he needs to come back to life; but when Jason starts killing all of Freddy's children, Krueger steps in to stop him), but mixed in so many elements and influences that the movie is hard to follow. In an effort to maximise action and scares, the writers made the story jump too fast from scene to scene and introduce too many ideas and characters without leaving viewers the time to digest what they have seen, or giving them the chance to anticipate the killers' next appearances. Director Ronny Yu (*The Bride with White Hair* (*Bai fa mo nu zhuan*, 1993), *Bride of Chucky* (1998)) did his best to make sense of this muddle, but the end result is somewhat of a mess. Character development, as is too often the case, gave way to a series of stereotypes (the virginal final girl, the pothead, the slut), and the dialogue ended up consisting mainly of puns and one-liners.

Still, a couple of scenes stand out. The climactic fight, when the teenagers finally leave the screen to the two iconic villains, is as close as could be to the face-off fans anticipated. But both killers being immortal, no satisfying answer could be brought to the age-old question, 'In a fight between those two, who would win?' Another good moment takes place at the hospital, where children are lying in a coma after abusing a dream-suppressing pill – an undeniably creepy thought.

Born and raised in Hong Kong, Yu's passion for movies was sparked at a young age, under unusual circumstances. 'I had polio,' Yu recalls[68], 'when I was a little boy, I wanted to play soccer and fight but couldn't so I got to be by myself all the time. My father would take me to the theatre, because he loved Hollywood movies, so every day at 10am he would drop me in a theatre, then at lunchtime he would come and pick me up, then at 2pm we would go to another theatre and I'd watch another movie. So I got to watch all the movies, action movies, horror, sexy movies … That experience got stuck in my mind because the moment I was in the theatre, I'd forget I had polio. And for those two hours I would feel so good.' After a management and communications degree, Yu embarked on his first filmmaking adventures as a writer, producer and director in his hometown. Lacking formal training, he picked up the technicalities on the job. 'My cameraman would ask me questions like, what lens do you want? But I didn't know anything! But what was good was that I'd watched so many movies and read so many comic books that in my mind, it's all visual. I'd say, "I don't care, you pick, I just want to do this much and you pick the lens!" I also learned a lot from my editors.' The success of his 1993 fantasy epic *The Bride With White Hair*, and

67 Quoted in *Crystal Lake Memories – The Complete History of Friday the 13th*, Peter M Bracke, Titan Books, 2005, p 270.
68 Interview with the author, Brussels, Belgium, March 2004.

its sequel the same year, caught the attention of Hollywood; but it wasn't until 1998 that he accepted a studio offer for another bride, the *Bride of Chucky*, which breathed new life into the dying *Child's Play* series. *Freddy vs Jason* would be his third – and to date, last – US feature, after the 2001 thriller *The 51st State*.

'In America I work on mainstream studio movies,' he explains. 'They finance the whole thing and they hire you, so you have to follow their system. As a director sometimes it's not easy because you don't have that much control and you don't have the final cut. So I need to pick my battles. If you fight all the time, you get so tired. Sometimes you have to give in to make them feel comfortable and then you can go and suggest your way. Making movies in Hollywood is spending 60% of your energy on politics. Hong Kong is different, the investments are so small that you have more control; you do whatever you want as long as you don't spend too much money. Just like independent movies.' Yu's slasher films were no exception to the studio control rule, and the filmmaker remembers being told early on, for both *Bride of Chucky* and *Freddy vs Jason*, that his features would be part of a larger ensemble and therefore have to follow some rules. 'They said they were slasher movies, so people had a series of expectations I should meet. I said OK and followed the rules, but then I put in little things that are more personal and different. But since I follow the rules they don't see when I slide in something a little bit different. Then everybody wins. And especially in fantastic movies the audience expects you to use some imagination.'

Gothika.

By their very nature, 'versus' films have to please fans with divergent opinions on the nature and the ending of the story, and require the agreement of more producers; Yu found himself caught in the middle of this battle, much like the teenagers of the story between Krueger and Vorhees. Still, *Freddy vs Jason* was a hit, opening at $36 million and grossing over $82 million at the US box-office. It also whetted the fans' appetite for movie face-offs, and a sequel has been part of New Line's projects ever since. Several comic books also reprised the idea, from *Army of Darkness vs Re-Animator* (Dark Horse, 2006) to the more recent *Freddy vs Jason vs Ash* (Wildstorm/DC, 2007-2008), based on an unproduced movie script. For all its shortcomings, *Freddy vs Jason* remains a brilliant concept, and one that fans wish will someday receive a more satisfying execution.

Last of these studio-backed disappointments, *Gothika*, from French actor-turned-director Mathieu Kassovitz (*Hate* (*La Haine*, 1995), *The Crimson Rivers* (*Les Rivières Pourpres*, 2000)), made a small profit, but gathered a long line of bad reviews. With a theme reminiscent of Neil Jordan's *In Dreams* (1999) – here, a psychiatrist (Halle Berry) is arrested for the murder of her husband and locked up in the mental facility she used to work in, where she starts being haunted by the ghost of a young girl – Kassovitz's first English-language feature is an honest, if formulaic, effort, featuring an excellent performance by Berry and disquietingly dark locations. Unfortunately, this new production from Dark Castle, a company decidedly more interested in flashy special effects and name actors than in solid screenplays, simply wasn't very scary.

A Seventies Revival

The true resurrection of horror didn't come through big budget productions, but with a series of independent movies which dared to deliver real scares and which were embraced by fans and mainstream audiences alike, thanks in large part to the audacity of a small distribution company called Lionsgate.

'At that time, we were growing,' Lionsgate's Senior Vice-President of Acquisitions Eda Kowan recalls[69]. 'We started as an art house distributor at the end of the nineties; *American Psycho* in 2000 was a big release for us. So we knew we couldn't compete with studios on the same films, we knew we needed to find films that they would shy away from, and that would define Lionsgate. We released movies like *Irréversible* (2002) because we thought they deserved a theatrical release, but we knew we couldn't rate it or cut it, so we didn't release it thinking it'd make a gazillion dollars at the box office. That's a guiding principle for us: we release what we're

69 Interview with the author, San Diego, USA, July 2007.

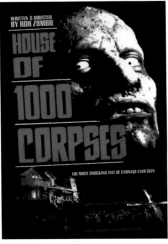

House of 1000 Corpses.

really passionate about.'

The first Lionsgate release to cause a stir in the horror world was rock star Rob Zombie's *House of 1000 Corpses*, a movie abandoned by all the majors involved in its production or release. 'Rob made the film for Universal in 2000, but [once the picture was finished], they thought it was way too edgy for them,' Kowan explains. After the MPAA slapped the movie with an NC-17 rating, the director re-cut it to secure an R, bringing its runtime down to 89 minutes. 'MGM then acquired the film, and for whatever reason, internally, I don't even know if the deal had been signed but Rob and certain executives had a difference of opinion. There's a story that words were exchanged at a party and the next thing Rob knew, MGM refused to release it.' According to Zombie himself[70], the cause of the breakdown had been a joke he made in a TV interview, where he observed that Universal had dropped the film because they found it 'morally objectionable', but MGM 'apparently have no morals; they're happy with some blood.' The studio, which claimed no deal had been confirmed or made official at the time, allegedly stopped all contact with the filmmaker the next day. Kowan continues, 'We found out that the movie was available again and we'd always thought it was an awesome film, so we approached him. It is an edgy film; looking at it you would see why Universal wouldn't release it …'

'Edgy' doesn't even start to describe Zombie's film; that Universal financed it in the first place is a freak of nature. Narrating the journey of four friends abducted by a family of deranged murderers on the night before Halloween, *House of 1000 Corpses* is a movie made by a horror fan, for horror fans; visually stunning, it stars several seventies underground icons (Karen Black, Bill Moseley, Sid Haig) and uses genre imagery extensively. Halloween, sideshow creatures, clowns, a funhouse and a very hot psychotic babe, with strong overtones of *The Texas Chain Saw Massacre* and a rocking soundtrack: everything seemed destined to please scary movie aficionados; unfortunately, the screenplay got lost on the way. With a storyline reduced to its barest ingredients, underdeveloped characters, a loud soundtrack and flashy images thrown randomly in the mix, *House of 1000 Corpses* is the missing link between Grindhouse cinema and MTV, an exercise in style filled with colourful monsters, profanity and skinned flesh. But if Zombie's writing skills needed some refining, his heart was in the right place. And while critics panned the picture, the horror community embraced the filmmaker as a saviour of the genre, and turned a movie which a year before wouldn't have had a chance at a theatrical release, into a small success.

Zombie himself was instrumental in the promotion of the movie. Says Kowan, 'Whatever happened between him and the studios, we didn't want to change the film; we just wanted to work with Rob and get the film out to the widest audience possible. For months at every concert he ran a trailer or footage, he was tireless. He's a huge part of why that film opened to the success it was. We opened it originally on just under 600 screens, and it made headlines everywhere. To the public it was as if the movie was coming out of nowhere, while in the industry of course everyone knew, there were stories left and right. To his credit he got behind it 150% and played a huge part in the film working. It was a great collaboration. We're not a studio, and that film was very important to us. We gave it a huge amount of focus.'

Sold as 'the movie some never wanted you to see', an obvious reference to its rejection by the studios, *House of 1000 Corpses* grossed $12 million in the US and over $16 million worldwide, bringing its total theatrical performance to nearly $30 million. The characters of the insane Firefly family became popular enough to be turned into a line of toys, courtesy of NECA, and to star in Zombie's next film, *The Devil's Rejects*, in 2005. 'We always knew that the horror audience never went away,' Kowan adds. 'There were so many bad films in the late '80s that they started being more selective of what they were screening, but they never went away.'

House of 1000 Corpses was also the first in a series of throwbacks to the movies of the seventies, a decade where independent horror blossomed and favoured realistic frights over supernatural scares. With titles such as *Last House on the Left* (1972), *Deliverance* (1972), *The Hills Have Eyes* (1977) and *The Texas Chain Saw Massacre* (1974), they often depicted in graphic, humourless and sometimes crude ways the fate of city dwellers forced to survive unexpected attacks in an unfamiliar environment (usually the countryside). Jerky camera moves and

70 'Rob Zombie Says Joke Derailed Corpses Deal With MGM', *VH1 News*, 23 July 2002, http://www.vh1.com/news/articles/1456217/20020723/zombie_rob.jhtml

grainy cinematography were introduced, gore and nudity became trademarks of the genre; influenced by the events of their time – the Vietnam war, the Watergate scandal, the sexual revolution – seventies filmmakers were keen to show the dark side of Flower Power. Their movies didn't just scare: they disturbed, disgusted, provoked and caused controversy.

NYU graduate and former PA to David Lynch Eli Roth was equally eager to shock and intrigue. His first feature as a writer/director, *Cabin Fever*, the story of five college students who catch a flesh-eating virus while spending a week in a cabin in the woods, was intended as an homage to the seventies and early eighties movies he grew up loving, with direct references to *Last House on the Left* (the song), *Dawn of the Dead* (the screwdriver gag), *The Evil Dead* or *The Texas Chain Saw Massacre*. The film featured a few unforgettable moments of gore – the infamous leg-shaving scene being the highlight – but there was more to it than blood, nudity and striking special effects. In place of the usual cookie-cutter teenagers, Roth made a point to write characters who felt real, were immediately distinguishable, and weren't all meant to be liked by the audience, a trait some were afraid would mean viewers wouldn't sympathise with them. Says Roth[71]: 'I remember the distributors telling me, "We're not worried about the violence, we're worried that your characters swear so much and they're unlikeable." I said to them, "I hate to break it to you, but 'fuck' is no longer a swearword. Teens use it every other word. That's how people talk."' The filmmaker cleverly made their behaviour the centre of the story: the way they antagonise the locals (like in the movies that inspired him, Roth exploits the city/country divide) and abandon each other as soon as the disease hits, is in effect scarier than the virus itself. More than a group of kids facing an invisible killer, *Cabin Fever* is about selfishness, fear and the breakdown of relationships. In that context, no wonder the nicest girl dies the nastiest death. And if the middle segment worked perfectly as a straight horror flick, Roth gave the rest of the film an original tone, from teen sex comedy in the first reel to gross-out humour in the third act, with moments of Lynchian surrealism (the pancake kid, the hospital bunny).

Cabin Fever.

This mix of gore, realism and fun was exactly what the market was looking for at that moment: a daring movie, written and directed by a true fan, but not disturbing enough that it wasn't accessible to a larger audience. Besides, although Roth had imagined the story nearly ten years earlier when he caught a similar disease during a stay in Iceland, viruses had become a very timely issue by the time of the release, with the SARS crisis in Asia and Canada making headlines around the world from late 2002 to mid-2003.

Screened in the Midnight Madness section of the Toronto Film Festival in September 2002, *Cabin Fever* became the object of a bidding war between distribution companies. Says Kowan, 'We'd read the script and met with Eli Roth in Cannes a year and a half before, so we were really well aware of it. It got into Midnight Madness, and it was available. It was unusual in that traditionally all the films that are available are shown the first week, and the second week people start to leave, but *Cabin Fever* didn't screen before the second Thursday. It was an industry screening, not a public screening. It brought the house down. We walked out of there thinking, this is something for us, we know how to market this. It was horror but it had a sense of humour; it's so over-the-top in some scenes that instead of a jump you're getting nervous laughter. Brilliant.' Although traditional genre distributors like New Line and Dimension were interested, Roth and his producers decided to sign the deal with Lionsgate, at the time known as a small arthouse company. As the director recalls, 'this was the first festival post 9/11, there weren't so many movies being made and we were lucky enough to have this bidding war. The reason we went with Lionsgate in that they committed to spending $12 million in prints and advertising. It was a huge deal for them.'

In the absence of stars on whom to build up a marketing campaign, media attention focused on Roth, who was more than willing to play the game and become a very vocal advocate of the genre. 'I felt like nobody was sticking up for the genre,' the filmmaker recalls. 'I wanted to be like Quentin Tarantino, the way he became the movie geek authority of seventies movies, I wanted to do that for horror movies. Horror at the time was still a dirty word and there was

71 Interview with the author, Los Angeles, USA, January 2008.

nobody saying, I love these movies, this is what I want to do, unapologetically. Everyone else at the time was using horror as a stepping stone for their career. But I thought, I love these movies, this is not a stepping stone, this is too important for me. I was on every single horror website, I knew where the horror fans were and there was nobody supporting the genre as openly as I did.'

Word of mouth built up quickly, online and on the festival circuit, and *Cabin Fever* became the sleeper hit of the fall, opening doors to the next horror productions and turning Roth, who had spent almost ten years trying to finance his first movie, into an overnight success. '*House of 1000 Corpses* paved the way for *Cabin Fever*, there's no question,' he acknowledges. 'With *House of 1000 Corpses*, Lionsgate was cautious; they put a million dollars into it and put it out on 600 screens and it did very well for them. So when they got *Cabin Fever*, they knew there was an audience for R-rated horror films and they released it on 2,000 screens.' Raking up $21 million theatrically on a $1.5 million budget, 'it became their highest grossing movie of the year; it out-grossed seven of their other movies combined.'

Although it wouldn't come out in the US until June 2005, French production *High Tension* (*Haute Tension,* aka *Switchblade Romance* in the UK), from director Alexandre Aja, was also picked up by Lionsgate at the 2003 Toronto Film Festival, three months after its release in France. The very linear story of two students (played by Cécile de France and Maïwenn) on a study break when a homicidal truck driver (Philippe Nahon) attacks the countryside house they're staying in one night and abducts one of them, it is famous for both the degree of suspense Aja builds in its first half, and its absurd climactic reveal. After introducing two likeable characters and placing them in an ordinary, realistic situation, the writer/director puts them through hell, and if the synopsis itself would hardly revolutionise the genre, Aja's mastery, and the movie's sheer brutality and relentlessness, made *High Tension* an instant cult classic. As many critics pointed out, it certainly lived up to its title! Unfortunately, rather than sticking throughout to the wonderful simplicity the plot had demonstrated until then, the filmmakers decided to sacrifice it for a trendy, see-how-clever-we-are twist ending, as incoherent as it was unnecessary, and allegedly suggested by co-producer Luc Besson. Still, horror reviewers and fans – many of whom watched the movie on imported DVDs, in its original, un-subtitled French version – saw in this nasty little slasher one of the best entries in the genre in recent history.

High Tension.

After an average performance in its home country (110,000 viewers – about the same amount as for any noteworthy local genre production), *High Tension* received a small release a year later in the UK, and opened in the US mid-2005. Several scenes had to be re-cut to obtain an R-rating from the MPAA, and to avoid being limited to arthouse theatres, the opening was dubbed in English, the idea being that the lead girl would still be French, but would be spending time with an American girl and her family. Says Kowan, 'Alex Aja as a filmmaker is so good, there's almost no dialogue and it's so visceral that you forget that it's in a foreign language. We wanted the broadest audience possible to see this film. That's why we dubbed it for the first thirty minutes. We didn't want it to be perceived as a foreign film, we wanted people to see it just as a horror film. And if you release it as an NC-17, you're limiting your screens right away because the chains won't show it. From an economical standpoint it wouldn't make sense, you're spending so much money for a wide release, between 15 and 20 million dollars. It's so competitive too, because you may only have one weekend to get an audience and if the film doesn't perform at a certain level, it's very hard to hold those screens for a second weekend, when there's another wide release.' Thanks to these changes, *High Tension* opened nationwide on 1,323 screens.

Alexandre Aja and creative partner Grégory Levasseur (here credited as co-writer and art director) became friends at a very young age, when they discovered their common passion for horror movies. 'We were ten when we met,' Aja recalls[72]. 'I was reading a French magazine called *Mad Movies*, and Greg asked me if I'd seen the movie on the cover. From that moment on we were always together.' Adds Levasseur[73]: 'We started out with make-up effects with latex and fake blood, we took pictures and sent them to magazines … Then we started writing horror and sci-fi screenplays, we were about fourteen. We learned a lot from there, understanding little by little how it works and what makes a

Wrong Turn.

screenplay interesting. We finally shot a short film when we were seventeen.' The son of director Alexandre Arcady and film critic Marie-Jo Jouan, Aja grew up in a movie-friendly environment, and spent days learning about the filmmaking process on his father's sets, which he admits helped him enormously when he finally ended up in the director's chair. 'I learned so much that when I first found myself directing a crew on a film set, I didn't feel as scared and uncomfortable as I would have been otherwise. It also allowed me to move faster, and I didn't have to go to film school.' The short, *Over The Rainbow*, was chosen as the official selection of the Cannes Film Festival in 1997, and Aja and Levasseur were offered the opportunity to film their first feature. Says Aja: 'We were nineteen, and it turned out to be a complete disaster. We had a choice between two scripts: one was a first draft of *High Tension*: one night, two girls, an isolated house; the other was *Furia*, and that's what we chose to make. It was a sci-fi movie, and maybe we shouldn't have strayed too far from horror.' Despite being selected in several festivals, *Furia* was soon forgotten, and it would take them four years to release their second film, which would put Aja at the top of *Fangoria*'s 25th anniversary list of the '13 Rising Talents who Promise to Keep Us Terrified for the Next 25 Years'[74].

Unlike other filmmaking duos, Aja and Levasseur never shared directing credits. 'I see myself as a co-director,' Levasseur explains; 'we're shooting everything together. Alex is the actual director because it makes it so much easier to just have one person giving instructions on the set, but we have to agree on everything. We have the same vision, but it makes things easier to have one person who makes the final decision. We always write together, which makes directing together easier; we're both behind the computer and Alex types. If we don't agree on something on set, we discuss it on the side, between us, not in front of the crew. But it hardly ever happens anyway.'

Lionsgate wasn't the only studio to release seventies-inspired survivals. Rob Schmidt's *Wrong Turn*, distributed by Twentieth Century Fox, told the same story as Wes Craven's *The Hills Have Eyes* (1977) – a family of hideous-looking cannibals living in a remote area stalks a group of people whose car broke down on a nearby road – only the killers were West Virginia inbreds instead of New Mexico mutants. With an extra hint of *Deliverance* (to which one of the characters makes an explicit reference) and, of course, *The Texas Chain Saw Massacre*, the movie was, as its director told the BBC at the time[75], intended as 'a simple, really scary horror film with several moments of graphic horror,' like 'in the seventies and eighties, before the genre got diluted by self-referential humour and winks at the audience.'

Dead serious, and more classical and unified in tone and pace than *House of 1000 Corpses*, *Wrong Turn* grossed $15 million theatrically in its home country, a true accomplishment considering its relative lack of originality, mixed reviews, late May release (against *Finding Nemo*!)

72 Interview with the author, Ouarzazate, Morocco, August 2005.
73 Interview with the author, Ouarzazate, Morocco, August 2005.
74 'The New Future of Fear', *Fangoria* 234, July 2004. This entry by Caroline Vié.
75 Rob Schmidt interviewed by Anwar Brett, *BBC*, June 2003, http://www.bbc.co.uk/films/2003/06/19/rob_schmidt_wrong_turn_interview.shtml

The Texas Chain Saw Massacre.

and a promotional campaign reduced to a minimum, due to the MPAA's concerns that the trailers and TV ads were 'too intense'. Faced with the rating board's repeated rejections of their advertisements, Fox backed down and chose to limit their promotion. Said Schmidt in a 2003 interview for Arrow in the Head[76]: '[The studio fears they will] get attacked by politicians and media folks for promoting violence. I heard they might be taking their logo off of the prints because they don't want a backlash. Our theatrical trailer got kicked back something like 21 times by the MPAA … It will be an easy shot for the anti-violence in media lobby to go after the film and Fox has a whole slate of movies they're trying to get ratings on. They can't be regarded as gore merchants or the MPAA will give them a hard time on all their other products.' As violent (or 'intense') as *Wrong Turn* may have been considered at the time, it was still tame by comparison with the R-rated *Saw*s and *Hostel*s of the following years. But a change of mentality was slowly starting to take place …

'Nothing cuts like the original!' (*The Texas Chain Saw Massacre* 1974)

While *Wrong Turn*, *Cabin Fever* and *House of 1000 Corpses* were all considered successes, their popularity was still limited to a certain audience demographic. It's no wonder that the movie that would bring survivalist horror into the mainstream was a remake of the 1974 masterpiece which inspired every single one of these productions: *The Texas Chain Saw Massacre*.

The announcement of this project by producer Michael Bay, at the time also rumoured to direct, was not met with enthusiasm. The Internet backlash which immediately followed made it one of the most talked about productions in Hollywood, months before its release. The eventual appointment of commercial and music video director Marcus Nispel at the helm did little to appease the fans, who claimed that a $9.2 million New Line production could never come close to the original.

In a way, they were right. The bleakness, energy and stylish direction of Hooper's classic could simply never be matched. Known the world over as one of the most shockingly gory movies ever made, it actually showed very little, and traded cheap tricks and fake blood for cleverly placed cameras and sound effects, turning its micro-budget into an advantage. The grainy cinematography gave it a touch of authenticity, and allowed no distance between the viewer and the events on the screen. The experience was raw and immediate, and all the more powerful since it reflected the social turmoil of the mid-seventies: the deterioration of the family as a basis for social order, the battle between age groups, and the Flower Power revolution. Would it survive, and what would be left of it? Nispel, Bay and screenwriter Scott Kosar happily decided to leave all those qualities out of their remake, and to turn *The Texas Chain Saw Massacre* into a blood-drenched slasher.

Very little was known about Leatherface in the original, yet he was still very much the focus of the movie. In Nispel's version, it's the opposite: we see him at length, hear about his childhood, learn his real name, but he's only just one of the many colourful maniacs Erin and her friends meet on their journey through the Texas countryside. Instead, the most interesting protagonist is final girl Erin, impeccably played by Jessica Biel: a noteworthy choice, but this emphasis on her character – a typical slasher feature – made her death highly unlikely in the eyes of the audience, who assumes from the start that she'll get away unharmed. Original director of photography Daniel Pearl reprised his duty, but with very different results: the remake looks good … too good.

Yet Nispel's take on *The Texas Chain Saw Massacre* is undeniably entertaining, a word which

76 'The Arrow interviews … Rob Schmidt!', *Arrow in the Head*, May 2003, http://www.joblo.com/arrow/interview84.htm

would perhaps not have been associated with Hooper's version. It may not stand comparison to the original, but judged on its own merits, it isn't a bad film. It is simply different. Slicker, glossier; more classical in tone and structure and therefore more accessible to a wide audience; more fun than shocking; and no less original than, say, *Wrong Turn*. Bay and fellow producer Mike Fleiss's challenge was audacious, but it paid off. Helped by a strong marketing campaign, an already identifiable name and a carefully chosen release date (17 October), *The Texas Chainsaw Massacre* opened on 3,016 screens and raked in over $28 million in its first weekend, with a total US theatrical gross of $80 million by the end of the year.

Naturally, a tidal wave of remakes of horror classics would soon ensue, sweeping away any attempts at original productions. To Hollywood execs, the idea is simple (or shall we say simplistic?): if a movie was successful once, it'll work a second time. Those who haven't seen or heard of the first version will be attracted by the brilliance of the concept, just like audiences before them who flocked to theatres to see the original. This theory of course ignores the fact that what pulled in viewers in the first place may have had nothing to do with the title or the basic storyline. Success may come from an array of different factors; the director and cast, quality of the picture or its timeliness being the main ones. In that case, studios will probably rely on the second group, those who are familiar with the original, and for whom, as film critic Dave White pointed out[77], the remake is the equivalent of comfort food. As White wrote: 'In this genuinely frightening decade when you can watch real people get their real heads really cut off online, the narratives have retreated into a now-comparatively safe past. Leatherface is as warm and familiar a presence as Rosemary Clooney singing a lullaby to Bing Crosby in *White Christmas*.' The idea isn't new; sequels, and the never-ending series of Dracula and Frankenstein adaptations worked on the same principle. Remakes simply take it that extra step further.

May.

Off the Beaten Track

A handful of independent and offbeat genre movies gained special places, if not at the box office, at least in the fans' hearts that year. First to seduce them was *May*, from director Lucky McKee, starring Angela Bettis in the titular role.

May is a sweet but lonely girl, isolated since childhood by an excessive imagination and a lazy eye. Desperate to break out of her shell, she decides one day to approach a boy she's developed a crush on. When he ends up rejecting her after a couple of disastrous dates, she turns her attention to her lesbian colleague, but this new relationship isn't any more satisfying …

Slow and character-driven, *May* was as different as could be from the likes of *Cabin Fever* and *House of 1000 Corpses*. A mix between romantic comedy, drama and horror, it worked mostly thanks to McKee's visual flair and to Bettis's performance, turning a frail oddball into an endearing character the audience could relate to. 'I think every being alive understands loneliness; everyone's been an outcast at some point in their lives,' says Bettis[78]. 'That's the part that people respond to. I don't really see *May* as a horror movie; it's more like a romance that goes all wrong. It was very touching for people.'

A tough movie to sell, *May* received a limited US release from Lionsgate in June 2003, but found reasonable success and a great cult following on DVD. '*May* screened at Sundance,' Kowan recalls, 'and we thought it was great and played really well to the audience. We fell in love with the film and thought it deserved a theatrical release, even though we didn't know what kind. A movie like *Cabin Fever* plays wide; we would screen it to a recruited audience and they'd love it, while *May* is more caviar for horror fans. It's more personal, less high concept. You couldn't give the movie a one liner and people would know what it's about.' Nevertheless, those who saw *May* responded strongly to it; its lead actress became an instant sensation in the horror world, and both she and McKee made it to the aforementioned *Fangoria* list of hopes. 'I've been an actor

77 'I Spit on Your Horror Remakes, Sequels', Dave White, *MSNBC*, 25 October 2005, http://www.msnbc. msn.com/id/9805698

78 Interview with the author, Sitges, Spain, October 2007.

for 16 years and I've never been pigeonholed. I did theatre, I played all kinds of stuff. Then I did *May* and ever since then, all the offers I get are horror. I have to do different things, otherwise as an actor you end up feeling like there's this black hole you're getting sucked in …' Touching without being cute, and brilliantly acted, directed and photographed, *May* – and its lead – certainly deserved to become cult favourites.

Born in California in 1975, McKee shot his first short film, a retelling of *A Nightmare on Elm Street*, when he was twelve years old. An imaginative and isolated child, much like the character of May, he grew up writing and drawing comic books, until he realised filmmaking would be a more suitable path for him. During his studies at USC, the aspiring director made several short films, including a first version of *May* ('about a girl who kept body parts in her closet,' according to Bettis) and also developed a script for a feature version. After graduating in 1997, McKee directed his first movie over two four-day weekends, the very low budget zombie story *All Cheerleaders Must Die* (2001), which to this day has yet to find distribution. A former classmate, Marius Balchunas, who had in the meantime created his own production company, then remembered the script of *May* he'd read while in college, and offered McKee a deal to make the film.

Of *May*, which ended up costing an estimated $500,000, the writer/director says[79]: 'We just tried to do something from the heart, you know? Something personal, and not try to cut any corners. Make a full swing and try to make a mark. People come up to me; it's amazing the emotional response that it has on them. Film is communication and the movie is about loneliness, so it kind of lets other people know, "Yeah, I feel lonely too." It is just something to relate to.'

Bubba Ho-Tep.

Equally built around its characters despite a premise at first sight close to a superhero comic book, Don Coscarelli's *Bubba Ho-Tep*, starring Bruce Campbell and Ossie Davis, was a big festival hit around the world. Opening theatrically in September on a small platform release, it was successful enough in the cities where it played (Seattle, New York, Los Angeles) to see its allotted screens grow to 25 nationwide by early December. It grossed a total of $2 million in US theatres, and another $6 million on DVD, thanks to MGM's backing of a disc filled with extra features, whose centrepiece was an audio track where Campbell commented on the movie in character.

Adapted from a 1994 novella by Joe R Lansdale, *Bubba Ho-Tep* follows the adventures of Sebastian Haff (Campbell), an ageing Elvis impersonator who claims to be the real Elvis, as he and fellow retirement home resident Jack (Davis), who believes he is John F Kennedy, fight an ancient Egyptian mummy who appears at night in the halls of their nursing home. Given the weirdness of its synopsis, many simply expected a full-on battle between supernatural forces and a larger-than-life rock star. But behind this kitschy, bizarre and, let's face it, downright silly premise lies a story with a real heart and three-dimensional characters, a subtle and touching fable about old age, mortality, regrets and redemption. While the movie remains ambiguous as to whether Sebastian Haff is indeed the King, it is easy to read his mummy-battling quest as a metaphor for anything – friendship, pastime – that would bring back some of the joy, sense of purpose and excitement of youth to a senior citizen who feels useless, tired and abandoned. Coscarelli doesn't sugar-coat his depiction of oldness; his Elvis is sick, decrepit, abandoned by his family, and treated with condescendence by visitors and patronising nurses alike. Yet he and his fellow retirees are instantly likeable, and their fragility makes the movie more thrilling, since

79 'An Are You Going Exclusive Interview', Christopher P Garetano, *Icons of Fright*, December 2005, http://www.iconsoffright.com/IV_LuckyAYG.htm

Dead End

you know they might die, and touching, because you genuinely care about them, and know that even if they stayed alive, the lives they would go back to would never be satisfying.

To this human drama, Coscarelli adds a fair dose of supernatural scares and a touch of humour, cleverly used to stress the absurdity of the characters' adventure and the sadness of their condition, but never at the expense of Haff/Elvis or Jack/JFK. The performances are great all around, and if the critics saw Campbell's impersonation as the highlight of the film, Davis's black Kennedy also deserved some credit. Finally, the soundtrack, reminiscent of Elvis's music without ever using any of his melodies, reflected the movie's perfect blend of emotion and total coolness. Hail to the King!

A sequel, entitled *Bubba Nosferatu*, had been rumoured to be in the works since *Bubba Ho-Tep*'s DVD release, and in 2005, Coscarelli gave the audience a glimpse at what he envisioned[80]: 'We decided against *Bubba Sasquatch*, I couldn't talk anybody into it. We did a lot of touring in film festivals; Bruce Campbell would ask every audience to vote whether it should be *Bubba Nosferatu* or *Bubba Sasquatch* and *Nosferatu* always won. We have a pretty cool storyline planned out; the goal is to have more young Elvis. There will still be some old Elvis in it but in the previous movie, maybe 20% was young Elvis; I think it's gonna be more evenly split in this. Bruce really liked playing the young Elvis with his entourage of boys, these sorts of mafia guys,

80 Interview with the author, Turin, Italy, November 2005.

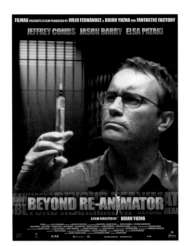

Beyond Re-Animator.

and I think there's a lot of opportunities for them to get into mischief. It could be a lot of fun.' But at the end of 2007, Campbell publicly announced he would not reprise his role, and the project seems to have been abandoned. Whether a sequel ever sees the light of day or gets lost in development hell, *Bubba Ho-Tep* will remain an oddity in the horror world and in Hollywood.

More conventional but no less entertaining, French writers-directors Jean-Baptiste Andréa and Fabrice Canepa's *Dead End* made the best of its tiny budget with this story of a family on their way to grandma's house on Christmas Eve, stuck on a never-ending stretch of road, terrorised by a mysterious lady in white and a black car. Linear to the extreme and featuring a very limited number of characters, *Dead End* is an exercise in fright with a touch of dark humour; a thinly veiled homage to the works of David Lynch wrapped in a script worthy of the best *Twilight Zone* episodes. Although the scares are aplenty and evenly spaced, the movie relies mainly on its eerie atmosphere and on the impeccable performances of its cast. Ray Wise (*Twin Peaks* (1990-1991), *Jeepers Creepers 2* (2003)) and Lin Shaye (*A Nightmare on Elm Street* (1984), *Snakes on a Plane* (2006)) are perfect in the roles of parents on the brink of a nervous breakdown; only Mick Cain, playing their rebellious, obnoxious teenage son, is an obvious miscast, if only because he looks a good five years too old for the part.

The only major flaw in the film is the *Carnival of Souls*-esque ending, which was predictable and pedestrian and disappointed fans and critics alike; but thankfully, the 80 minutes that lead up to it were perhaps enough fun for them to forgive this final imperfection. As co-director Andréa explains[81]: 'The movie isn't about its ending. *Dead End* is about how this family goes to pieces in this extreme situation. We knew some people would guess the ending but thought it didn't really matter because it wasn't what the movie was about anyway. It probably was a mistake because the people who guessed felt frustrated because they would have liked to be proven wrong. At one point we thought about not putting it in the movie and leave it open but then we would have been frustrated as screenwriters; it's such an easy solution to leave things open and not answer to any question … The last image, with the note Ray Wise wrote, also changes the way you interpret the story. The two realities cannot be conciliated and you have to make your own choice. People took the ending too seriously; all we wanted was to have fun with the fact that we had the freedom to put these two realities together.'

Dead End went on to win awards in several festivals, including the 2003 Brussels International Festival of Fantastic Films, Cinénygma in Luxemburg, Fantasia in Montreal, and the San Sebastian Horror Festival; it was released theatrically in the UK in December 2003, and went straight to DVD in the US, through Lionsgate, late in 2004.

The road that led Canepa and Andréa to this success, however, was almost as long and eventful as the one the characters find themselves on in the movie. 'I'd been a screenwriter for six years,' Andréa recalls, 'and had my mind set on someday directing what I'd written. I was working with Fabrice, but we couldn't find anyone interested in financing one of our projects in France. Their only interest was in social dramas, or silly comedies. At some point we decided to write something that wouldn't cost too much, and to write it in English so we could try to sell it abroad. At first we sent the script to a few production companies here in France, but they never replied. We finally handed it to James Huth, who eventually became our producer, and he sent it to a friend in the US. So all of a sudden, in three months' time, we had all the funding in place.' The idea for *Dead End* came from a desire to work within the horror genre, and was inspired by a local ghost story. 'The hitchhiker story – a car driver takes a hitchhiker on a dark and deserted road and the hitchhiker disappears without a trace – made a big impression on me; it's an international myth you can find everywhere in the world in slightly different forms. Sometimes the hitchhiker is evil; sometimes it is good and warns you against a danger. The version that traumatised me as a kid was the one that takes place in the South East of France; it's called La Torne and I imagined it as a woman dressed in white.' Production took place in LA, in a stretch of road on Franklin Canyon, just off Sunset Boulevard, with an American crew; post-production was mostly done in Paris.

Dead End is to this day Canepa's only feature film credit. Andréa moved away from the

81 Interview with the author, Paris, France, July 2004.

genre for his second picture, *Big Nothing* (2006), starring David Schwimmer, but wrote Huth's third directorial outing, *Hellphone* (2007), and is planning his return to horror.

The Dead Walk!

Following the success of *28 Days Later* in the UK, and *Resident Evil* in the US, zombie features started surfacing around the world. If the living dead had never really left the screens – zombies always have rabid followers, ready to watch the oddest, most obscure titles – the movies they starred in hadn't really been widely shown to festival audiences and mainstream theatres since the mid-nineties; the last one to make a lasting impression being probably Michele Soavi's 1994 *Dellamorte Dellamore* (*Cemetery Man*), a France/Germany/Italy co-production which was granted limited US release in 1996. But despite the exposure this year's pictures would receive, with theatrical releases in their home countries and at least limited runs in the US, they would all fail to impress, commercially or critically.

Beyond Re-Animator was undoubtedly the most highly anticipated of the four notable zombie movies released in 2003. Announced in the early days of Fantastic Factory, but the object of rumour since the release of the first sequel to 1985's *Re-Animator*, *Bride of Re-Animator* (1990), *Beyond Re-Animator* was directed by Brian Yuzna, who'd produced the first and directed the second entry in the series, and filmed in Spain. The title reflected the filmmaker's ambition to expand the universe created in H P Lovecraft's 1922 short story, taking the action from the grounds of the Miskatonic University and Dr West's house to a Massachusetts prison where the scientist is serving time and looking for ways to capture the soul.

Unfortunately, much like West's patients, *Re-Animator* came back to life without its soul. The sheer madness of the first movie is artificially recreated, and if the result is entertaining, it really isn't quite as fresh and new as the original. As Yuzna himself explained in a 2003 *Fangoria* interview[82]: 'I always said from the beginning that the hardest thing was to find the tone … The first movie's tone was unexpected, and it's not unexpected anymore. It won't seem as outrageous as the first one.' Jeffrey Combs does a brilliant job reprising the role which gave him instant horror recognition almost twenty years earlier; as the obsessed scientist, he looked more than ever determined and confident in the importance of his research. Replacing Bruce Abbott's Dan Cain as West's partner in crime, is Jason Barry who, like his predecessor, is both likeable and bland. The rest of the cast on the other hand range from just bad to downright laughable, Elsa Pataky being easily the worst of the lot. The special effects, by Screaming Mad George (who also handled them for *Bride of Re-Animator*) and Pedro de Diego, are convincing and inventive; but they are the focus of the third act, while the first film relied much more on the craziness of the situation. Fun but forgettable, *Beyond Re-Animator* was released by Filmax on 171 screens in Spain, but went to DVD in the US after a TV premiere on the Sci-Fi Channel and a short festival run.

Una de Zombis. Undead.

Also from Spain, Miguel Ángel Lamata's *Una de Zombis*, a low budget gangster/living dead movie starring local superstar Santiago Segura, was screened at the Sitges Film Festival and received a limited release later in the year, then was quickly forgotten.

On the other side of the globe, Australian writers/directors Michael Spierig and Peter Spierig clearly wanted to be the next Peter Jackson, and their debut feature *Undead*, set in a little village whose inhabitants are turned into zombies by a meteorite shower, constantly fluctuates between *Braindead* and *Bad Taste*, only minus Jackson's talent. The story is unnecessarily complicated and the characters underdeveloped, but the filmmakers desperately try to make up for the script's shortcomings with an overdose of one-liners, thick splatstick humour, ugly blue-filter photography, slow motion, odd camera moves and guitar riffs. As a result, *Undead* is completely devoid of lightness and subtlety. Although advance word was positive since its Fantasporto screening (go figure), reviews were understandably terrible, and the general mediocrity of the movie was reflected in his poor theatrical results, both in Australia and during its limited release in the US.

Undead. House of the Dead.

Videogame adaptation *House of the Dead*, from German director Uwe Boll, also suffered from an excess of loud music and frantic editing. But while *Undead* used those tricks to try and appeal to genre fans, Boll seemed to only have gamers in mind, and used the barely-there plot (a group of friends take a boat to an island for a rave, only to find the place deserted and infested with zombies) to recreate the videogame experience, going so far as to randomly insert images from the game into the film, or shooting action scenes from the point of view of a character, as in a shoot'em'up first person game. Whereas Paul W Anderson expanded the world of *Resident Evil* and turned it into a real feature, all the while staying faithful to the story's origins, Boll chose to make his movie feel like the original Sega game but modified its setting and its characters. Adding to the paucity of the plot and the hysterical direction, the actors' performances are worthy of a student film, and are out of place in a $7 million production. *House of the Dead* was Boll's eighth film as director, and was widely criticised and lambasted by genre fans. Still, the joke was on them, as *House of the Dead* made its money back and then some; in the US only, it grossed over $10 million during its theatrical release in October. Says the filmmaker[83]: 'I started [my career in the US] with *Sanctimony* (2000), which was a serial murder thriller; then I did *Blackwoods* (2002), a ghost story, and *Heart of America* (2003), about school violence, so my first three films [in America] were completely different. Then came *House of the Dead*, and it made a lot of money worldwide. It showed that [videogame] movies have an audience; people are interested in them.' Boll would spend the next four years adapting games for the big screen, with increasing budgets and decreasing success; but would find more success in cheaper productions from 2008, including that year's outrageous gore comedy *Postal* and the nasty serial killer flick *Seed*.

Asia Strikes Back

83 Interview with the author, Brussels, Belgium, March 2005.

While the horror revival reached a peak in the United States, Japan and South Korea enjoyed a new height in the J-horror craze, each country boasting at least one major success in the first half of the year.

Takashi Shimizu's *Ju-On: The Grudge*, a theatrical release which followed two made-for-TV *Ju-On* movies (both in 2000) and two three-minute stories in the TV anthology *School Ghost Story G* (*Gakkou No Kaidan G*, 1998), is a collection of short episodes revolving around a house where a murder happened, and which has since become cursed. The segments are linked together by the house, which kills anyone who enters and turns its victims into ghosts, but also by certain events and characters (the sister who visits the house at the end of the second episode is the lead character in the third one, for example).

Like most vengeful spirits in Japan, the ghosts encountered in the house are the results of a grudge, a stain left on a place where some horrible wrongdoing was committed; this curse infects anyone who comes in contact with it, perpetuating the cycle of death and destruction. The concept of viral contamination is recurrent in J-horror (Sadako's video from *Ring* is another example), perhaps as a subconscious reminder that in an overcrowded society, the flaws and problems of one affect many. As a consequence, there is no resolution possible to the grudge, no exorcism, no cure: the curse cannot be lifted and will keep spreading, unless people stop visiting the cursed house or watching the *Ring* video. Other popular J-horror themes to be found in Shimizu's movie include ghosts using modern technology (phones, CCTV, TV sets, photos), long hair, and an anchor in social realities: the issue of health care for the ageing population, in a country where providing for parents and grandparents used to be an essential part of one's duties, is evoked in the first segment; Kayako and Toshio, the first victims of the house, were killed by their husband and father; and rarely, if at all, does the film feature a traditional, united family (Kazumi and Katsuya are childless, Hitomi is a career woman, etc.)

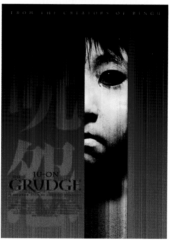

Ju-On: The Grudge.

The stories told in *Ju-On: The Grudge* are extremely simple. Their links and chronological logic may be harder to follow, but each individual episode tells of an encounter with the ghost and a death in a reasonably straightforward way. More than anything else, it is Shimizu's direction, his sense of timing and his admirable use of sound effects that make the movie scary. And while most J-horror productions keep their ghosts as hidden as possible, *Ju-On: The Grudge*'s apparitions become increasingly present and visible as the movie progresses; says Shimizu[84]: 'All the Japanese neo-horror moviemakers try to obscure the image of the ghosts and hide them. That's been one of their main strategies. But I don't want to do the same thing as them. I want to show the ghosts as much as possible, even though I know some people might laugh. Actually, at the first screening of *Ju-On: The Grudge* someone laughed during the film and told me afterwards, "it was very funny!" But someone else told them, "don't laugh at something so scary!" The reactions have been personal and diverse. And that's the kind of reaction I want.'

The strategy paid off; *Ju-On: The Grudge* is considered one of the scariest horror movies in recent history, both in Asia and in the Western world. A sequel would come out the same year; shortly afterwards, Shimizu would be offered the opportunity to remake his film for an American studio, and then to add a follow-up to this remake. A second Japanese sequel is expected in 2009. In the US, *Ju-On: The Grudge* would get a limited theatrical release then come out on DVD, through Lionsgate.

Born in Maebashi City in 1972, Takashi Shimizu started his career as an assistant director, while studying film production at the Tokyo Film School. One of his teachers, *Kairo* director Kiyoshi Kurosawa, noticed a short film he'd made in his class and introduced him to a producer at Kansai TV, who was working on the aforementioned anthology *School Ghost Story G*. The two segments Shimizu would write and direct for the movie, and which would become the basis of the *Ju-On* series, were then seen by *Ring* and *Dark Water* producer Taka Ichise, who helped him finance a longer version of the story. The result, V-cinema production *Ju-On*, would be cut in half and released in two parts. Finally, the unexpected success of the videos would inspire

84 'Ju-On Director Interview', Patrick Macias, *Japattack*, 26 July 2003, http://www.japattack.com/main/?q=node/72

Battlefield Baseball. A Tale of Two Sisters.

Shimizu to write and direct a theatrical feature, known in Japan as *Ju-On 3* and to Westerners as *Ju-On: The Grudge*.

Derived from the *Versus* wave, *Battlefield Baseball* (*Jigoku kôshien*), from *Versus* screenwriter Yudai Yamaguchi, couldn't be further from the *Ring* wave. Combining martial arts, high school and humour with a hint of baseball in an overly complicated plot, this genre-bending splatstick action comedy starred *Versus* actors Tak Sakaguchi and Hideo Sakaki, and gained a cult reputation in the West even before it was seen outside Japan. But given the mixed criticism it received after its Cannes premiere, it would take over two years before a DVD company picked it up for distribution in the US.

South Korean psychological horror film *A Tale of Two Sisters* (*Hongryeon Janghwa*), from writer/director Ji-Woon Kim, based on an old local folktale, was extremely well received by international critics. Revolving around two sisters who return home to their father and abusive stepmother after a stay in a mental institution, the story is pretty much impossible to summarise without giving away some key revelations. While reviewers emphasised the oppressive and claustrophobic atmosphere Ji-Woon Kim instils, the scares he cleverly places throughout the movie and the depth of description of the characters' psyches, they forgot to point out that for the average Western audience member, watching *A Tale of Two Sisters* is an incredibly trying experience. Long, seemingly incoherent and very confusing, the mystery unfolds slowly until the final explanation, revealed through so many flashbacks that full understanding requires repeated viewings. The characters behave in unnatural and erratic ways, and while the movie features a couple of typical J-horror scenes involving ghosts and long hair, the emphasis is clearly placed on the unspoken drama that took place before the events of the film, one of the girls' descent into madness and schizophrenia, and the consequent breakdown of the family. Still, despite its overly complicated plot and the subtlety of its scares, Korean audiences – predominantly female: an unsurprising fact, given the themes of the story, and J-horror's popularity with teenage girls – turned out massively to the theatres, making the movie one of the most popular of the year in the country.

Meet the Locals

While Australia unleashed its *Undead* zombies upon the world, New Zealand would make itself noticed with a ghost story, *The Locals*, from writer/director Greg Page.

New Zealand doesn't have a long history in the horror genre. Aside from Peter Jackson's work on *Bad Taste* and *Braindead* and the occasional chiller (David Blyth's 1984 *Death Warmed Up*, Scott Reynolds's 1997 *The Ugly*, Glenn Standring's 2000 *Irrefutable Truth about Demons*), few horror films have been produced in the country, and fewer yet are known about abroad. In that regard, that the New Zealand Film Commission backed Page's *The Locals*, and sent him to festivals around the world to promote it, was an event in itself.

The story of two friends, Grant (John Barker) and Paul (Dwayne Cameron), who get stuck on a countryside road when their car breaks down on their way to a weekend of surfing, Page's film isn't particularly scary or original, but it builds up an eerie atmosphere and takes full advantage of its location, thanks to its beautifully stylised cinematography. While it may not satisfy gorehounds (although they might be pleased to see some old-fashioned, *Evil Dead*-like stop-motion animation in a couple of scenes), and despite the simplicity of its plot, there is an undeniable freshness and innocence to this tale of friendship between two likeable, believable characters. 'I'm a horror geek,' the filmmaker explains[85], 'I love blood and guts and brains and the original few drafts of the script were very gory. But the more I developed the script the more the story of the two guys came to the top, and in the end, I lessened off on the gore to make sure the actual characters story was strong, because otherwise it would have lost some of its heart.'

85 Interview with the author, Brussels, Belgium, March 2004.

Auckland-based filmmaker Greg Page made his first mark on the local movie industry with his award-winning 1995 claymation series *Decaff*, before becoming one of New Zealand's most sought-after music video and commercial directors. The idea for *The Locals*, his first feature, came to him as he was driving one night on the back roads of the North Island. 'The area just below Auckland is very foggy and spooky and there's been a lot of history in the land, land battles and stuff. It was like two in the morning, and these three kids were standing on the side of the road hitchhiking, and they were just staring at me, turning really slowly to watch me go past, as if they were in slow motion. It was really scary.' Once the script was completed, Page started looking for financing. 'It was also hard to make the Film Commission believe in me,' he recalls, 'and believe that they could make a genre film that wasn't packed with New Zealand identity. Here the story could be anywhere. It was a hard call for them to put money in a film that wouldn't have a New Zealand stamp all over it.' Shooting for six weeks at the end of the winter, the filmmaker was lucky enough to have many experienced crew members on board. 'Half the crew who shot my film had just finished shooting *Lord of the Rings*, and it had been such a hard shoot, so tiring and so huge that when they came onto my set, they were really happy to be on a small film. I had an amazing crew, an amazing technical support, beautiful locations … That's the advantage of shooting in New Zealand.'

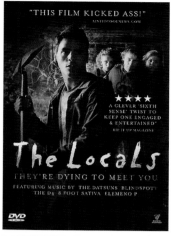

Releasing his movie in his home country, on the other hand, proved difficult. 'People in New Zealand don't go and see local productions because they've been disappointed by so many films in the past, they just don't bother.' *The Locals* came out on 22 screens and grossed just under NZ$ 50,000; it went straight to DVD in most overseas territories.

The year was relatively quiet for European filmmakers, and with the exception of Stefan Rozowitsky's painfully dull *Anatomy 2* (*Anatomie 2*), from Germany, it is France which, once again, was the centre of attention, as in addition to Aja's *High Tension*, a little film called *Maléfique* gathered some surprisingly positive reviews locally and abroad when released in May 2003.

The Locals. Malefique.

Set in a penitentiary, *Maléfique* follows convict Carrère (Gérald Laroche) and his cellmates Lassalle (Philippe Laudenbach), Marcus (Clovis Cornillac) and Daisy (Dimitri Rataud), who find an old journal hidden in the walls of their cell. The four inmates soon understand the book deals with black magic and could help them escape. But there might be more to it than they initially realise …

Shot for €1 million, a small budget even by France's standards, Valette's first feature, taking place almost entirely within four walls with the same four characters, was a brilliant example of resourceful filmmaking. Suspenseful and original, this story of entrapment, physical and psychological, remains focused on its strong characters, a trait which places it in a league above mere gore fests and supernatural adventures. Says Valette[86]: '[French production and distribution company] Canal + wanted to develop a series of low budget genre films, and *Maléfique* was in their first batch [along with 2002's *Bloody Mallory*]. We started developing the film before *Brotherhood of the Wolf* came out, but we shot it much later, because making the script interesting and adapted to its budget took a long time. They left me almost complete artistic freedom; I'd insisted early on that there wasn't enough money to boss me around. Otherwise there's no point making these kinds of films …' Despite a small arthouse release, *Maléfique* attracted a similar number of viewers to bigger genre productions. Still, it would take Valette several years to go back behind the camera, with 2007's J-horror remake *One Missed Call*.

86 Email interview with the author, January 2008.

2004:

'Ever felt like you were surrounded by zombies?'

(Tagline for *Shaun of the Dead*, 2004)

AS THE WORLD FULLY DIGESTED THE AFTERSHOCKS OF 9/11 AND DISCOVERED the horrors of the wars in Iraq and Afghanistan, audiences everywhere would see their appetite for on-screen scares and violence increase in 2004. Faced with increasingly disquieting international news, they found comfort in the thought that what happened to movie characters was still much worse than what could happen to them.

If the 2003 launch of the Iraq invasion and the subsequent media censoring had been eye-openers for many, 2004 would be for all a year of disillusions. Early in the year, reports of torture, rape and possible homicide of Iraqi prisoners in Abu Ghraib by American soldiers, with the possible involvement of official authorities, were made public, leading to several convictions and demotions. Photographic evidence was published in several major magazines, newspapers and TV channels across the world, causing an international uproar. The outrage was soon followed by accounts of cruel and inhumane methods of interrogation and treatment of prisoners at the Guantanamo Bay detention camp in Cuba, which were reported to the media by soldiers, FBI agents and non-governmental organisations. Both scandals would have a long-lasting impact on the United States' image abroad and on the collective conscience of US citizens. As Senator Norm Coleman was quoted saying, it was simply 'not what you'd expect from Americans'[87].

Meanwhile, the hunt for Weapons of Mass Destruction in Iraq, led by the CIA since 2003 and used by the US government as the legal justification for the war, was still fruitless, and in October 2004, the Iraq Survey Group officially reported that Saddam Hussein did not possess illicit WMDs at the time of the invasion. Had the government lied? And just when it looked like things couldn't possibly get worse, public enemy number one, Osama Bin Laden, released a video on Al Jazeera on 29 October, days before the US presidential election (and Halloween! The Bin Laden mask is, after all, one of the most popular in recent history), threatening further attacks against the United States and criticising George W Bush's response to 9/11.

In addition to the human generated destruction of life, Mother Nature herself claimed her share of victims that year, with hurricanes Ivan and Jeanne killing respectively 89 in the Caribbean and the US, and 3,036 in Haiti and its surroundings. Worst of all, the Boxing Day Tsunami, one of the deadliest natural disasters in history, killed over 225,000 people in eleven countries, including Indonesia and Thailand.

Between terrorists and tidal waves, the events of the year gave the world an increased awareness that death really could occur anywhere, at any time, without any warning or justification. Could scary movies really top the horrors seen on CNN and in newspapers? The big genre successes of 2004 would include three zombie pictures, a J-horror remake, and a torture flick (surprised?) from two Australian newcomers …

Year of the Dead

Following the development in cinematic zombies started with *Resident Evil* and *28 Days Later*, 2004 would see the release of several high-profile zombie movies, which would receive praise from the critics and excellent box office results. While in the nineties, a budget over $5 million was unimaginable for an undead picture, Zack Snyder's remake of George Romero's 1978 *Dawn of the Dead*, released on 19 March in the US, was made for more than $30 million ($28 million is the official budget, but according to rumours, it actually cost $10 to 15 million more), nearly $27 million of which was made back during its opening weekend. Impressive numbers, not only for a living dead flick, but also for the remake of a sequel.

Dawn of the Dead (1978). Dawn of the Dead (2004).

The project wasn't however met with great enthusiasm. As had been the case with the remake of *The Texas Chain Saw Massacre*, online forums were inundated with angry comments as soon as the project was announced. The original film had a huge following, and horror audiences have a tendency to behave very protectively of their favourite monsters, zombies being possibly the most popular of them all. To make matters worse, Romero himself, whose advice had not been asked by the producers, was very vocal in his opposition to the remake, stating that it could not possibly be a good idea.

One person, however, who never doubted the movie's potential despite being a fan of the seventies classic, was screenwriter James Gunn, who'd started his career writing and directing *Tromeo and Juliet* (1996) for infamous New York-based independent company Troma, and was at the time perhaps best known for his 2002 big screen adaptation of *Scooby Doo*. '[Producer] Eric Newman and I had been friends for a long time,' Gunn recalls[88], 'and he would call me a lot to try to get me to write different projects. I would always pass. And then one day he called me and said he could buy the rights to *Dawn of the Dead* and he'd do it if I wrote it. I immediately saw the potential for a remake. I'm generally not interested in remakes, they just tell stories that have already been told, but I saw the possibility of being able to tell the story of people in a mall during a zombie apocalypse and making it a different story from the original *Dawn of the Dead*.'

87 'Weekly Review', Roger D Hodge, *Harper's Magazine*, 18 May 2004, http://www.harpers.org/archive/2004/05/WeeklyReview2004-05-18

88 Interview with the author, Los Angeles, USA, January 2008.

Dawn of the Dead.

And a different story it is. Keeping only the basics – a zombie invasion, a group of strangers regrouping and barricading themselves in a shopping mall – this new version is more action-orientated, fun and exciting than Romero's film. A commercial director, Snyder brings an undeniable energy to the story and turns the classic's slow, brooding atmosphere into an equally dark but faster-paced, relentless piece. The opening scene, where a little girl attacks the lead character (Sarah Polley) and her husband, and the news montage of the credits, are enough to stress the difference between the two films. As the director told *Fangoria*[89], 'We've put some steroids into it.' A re-imagining in the best sense of the term, this update exploits its premise to the fullest and builds a new storyline around it, adding fresh ideas and new characters, the way the best remakes did in the eighties. David Cronenberg's *The Fly* (1986) and John Carpenter's *The Thing* (1982) were both cited as references by the makers of the new *Dawn of the Dead*.

The new *Dawn of the Dead* also disposes of Romero's heavy criticism of consumerism. While the 1978 movie established a parallel between the zombies and real-life shoppers wandering aimlessly down the halls of shopping arcades, the remake concentrates mainly on the living: their relationships, their struggles and even their religious beliefs. This shift of focus could be a sign of the times. Though it may well be the most basic creature of the horror bestiary, the zombie is also the closest to humans, and the most contagious of all, since a simple bite can turn any of us into one of them. Therefore it lends itself well to metaphors of all sorts, and Romero himself exploited this aspect in every one of his films to date to comment on aspects of our society. If with *Dawn of the Dead*, the Godfather of the genre was concerned about the growing materialism of the late seventies, today's filmmakers are influenced by international events, and examine the reactions of ordinary citizens faced with unusual threats. The living dead can then become a representation of Osama Bin Laden's terrorists, Saddam Hussein's troops, or the local shooter on campus. No surprise then that Gunn readily describes Snyder's movie as a cross between action, horror and war. 'I thought a lot of it was like a war film when I was writing it,' he explains. 'I studied all that military history, battles with a small group of people surrounded by a huge army, and some of them survived and some of them lived for quite a while. And basically it was the same concept for *Dawn of the Dead*.'

Gunn was the first name Newman brought on board, and the producers only started looking for a director once a draft had been completed that they were satisfied with. Says Gunn: 'The first person we talked to was David R Ellis, a good action director. I pushed really hard for Eli Roth because I liked *Cabin Fever* a lot, but the studio didn't okay it because they didn't think that *Cabin Fever* was a big enough deal. It was finished, but it hadn't come out yet. And then Zack came along, and when I heard that a commercial director who'd never directed a feature was going to do it, I was kind of bummed out, because here we had a guy, Eli, who had directed a feature, who the studio wouldn't say yes to, but they say yes to a guy who'd only done commercials. I thought his commercials were fine, visually and everything, but I still didn't know. Then I met him, and I loved him. I knew he was a smart guy and he wouldn't hold back [on the gore and violence]. I was very happy at that point.' Snyder was the perfect choice, and he would confirm his ability to turn improbable concepts into hits a few years later with 2007's Greek war movie *300*.

The screenwriter remembers enjoying a high degree of artistic freedom on the remake, but having to leave out a few scenes for budgetary reasons. 'In the original draft there were animals coming back to life as well. In the beginning when there's the big overhead shot of the woman running from her husband and all that crazy stuff is happening, she's running away and then she looks down and she sees that little bird that's been cut in two or is half squashed and yet it's alive; it was this horrible thing magnifying the sickness of everything and how it goes down to the lowest level. It did add a little more humour, too. The thing with the dog going back and forth between the two buildings was different [in the original script]; it used to be that there was a pet store in the mall and they trained the dogs.'

Surprisingly, the aspect of the movie that caused the biggest discussion was the fact that rather than shuffling, like Romero's creations, the zombies could run and jump. The running-

89 'New trip to the Maul', Michael Rowe, *Fangoria* 230, March 2004, p 22.

vs-shambling argument, initiated by *28 Days Later*, quickly grew out of proportion and became one of the most debated issues in recent horror movie history.

'The outcry was really stupid,' Gunn comments. 'I think there's a place in the world for slow zombies and running zombies. I get a lot of people telling me about how I revolutionised the horror genre by making zombies run, which to me is sort of pathetic, like that's my thing. The reason that zombies run is that I wrote that first scene with the little girl in it, and the little girl is at the end of the hall, and I thought, it'd be scary if she ran down the hall. I wrote the script in order, as it happens, and so since I'd made her run, I made other zombies run. *28 Days Later* hadn't come out yet at the time I was writing, I think I was in the process of writing it when it came out in England.' Thanks to this minor change in their nature, the zombies appeared much more dangerous and could pose a real threat not only in large groups, but also individually. Purists – and Romero, defending his bread and butter – argued that the living dead would see their ankles and tendons snap if they attempted to run, and that Danny Boyle's infected could move quicker because they were still alive. Fortunately for Gunn and Snyder, most viewers didn't bother looking for too much logic in reanimated corpses, and embraced the new film for its sense of fun and inventiveness.

'Fun' is also an adequate description of Edgar Wright's *Shaun of the Dead*, a British production which caused quite a stir on both sides of the Atlantic during its 2004 release. Described as a zom-rom-com (for zombie romantic comedy), Wright's movie was as far from the chills and gore of *Dawn of the Dead* as any living dead flick could get.

Following thirty-something salesman Shaun (Simon Pegg), his best friend Ed (Nick Frost) and his ex-girlfriend Lizzie (Kate Ashfield) as they flee to take refuge in a pub during a zombie invasion, the story focuses on these protagonists – their reactions, their relationships and the impact of these supernatural events on their lives – more than the creatures they fight, or the way they fight them. The first twenty minutes of the film introduce the characters in a succession

Dead Meat.

of everyday scenes worthy of a TV comedy-drama (indeed, the inspiration for the film came from an episode of the TV comedy *Spaced* (1999), written by and starring Pegg, and directed by Wright), and the only zombies we get a glimpse at are still living: Shaun, shambling out of bed yawning; a group of people walking aimlessly down the street … Shaun is so caught up in his problems that when he finds the first signs of a real zombie invasion, he fails to notice them, and when he and Ed encounter their first living dead, they mistake him for a drunk. There lies the genius of *Shaun of the Dead*: rather than spoofing the genre, piling up the gore and winking at the audience, it establishes a very life-like situation with realistic characters, and keeps the focus on its anti-heroes once the supernatural begins.

Wright's fascination for the human side of his story is such that he even manages to give his living dead a certain depth, a sadness unseen in most post-*Night of the Living Dead* movies. Said Wright in a 2004 MCN interview[90]: 'That's part of why we didn't make a farce, because with farcical zombie movies, you never get any personality. The great thing about the old George Romero films is that every now and again you get a scene where you see, like, a zombie mother dragging around a plastic doll, obviously having some kind of remembrance of the daughter she once had.' Just like Romero, Wright uses his creatures as metaphors; here, they represent the loneliness, disconnection and loss of identity of big city dwellers. 'Zombies are just like us, working on instinct,' Simon Pegg explained in the same article. 'There are other concerns represented in film now; if [in the fifties] it was automation and the atomic bomb, now it's about having the enemy within, a kind of viral paranoia that reflects fears of terrorism … In our film, [zombies] stand in for apathy, and urban living, and becoming an anonymous automaton in a collective, where you don't have any identity other than as a member of a gang.'

Romero's work was also a great source of inspiration for the director's style, the soundtrack and the nature of the creatures in *Shaun of the Dead*, and the movie references *Night of the Living Dead* ('We're coming to get you, Barbara') and *Dawn of the Dead* (Foree Electrics, the store where Shaun is employed, is a nod to actor Ken Foree) several times. Romero himself was so pleased with the homage that he invited Pegg and Wright to cameo in his 2005 film *Land of the Dead*.

Shaun of the Dead, however, isn't perfect. As clever and original as it may be, the movie sometimes suffers from its mix of genres: it is never really scary or touching, despite some great moments (Shaun's stepfather telling him how he would have liked his stepson to love him, Shaun's mother getting bitten), and if you're not a fan of the filmmaker's particular brand of humour, there's little left in the story to keep you excited to the end credits. Thankfully for Wright and Pegg, both audiences and critics identified with Shaun and Ed, and the movie was a minor commercial success. As *Chicago Sun Times* reviewer Roger Ebert, generally not a big genre fan, commented[91]: 'Good thing the movie is about more than zombies. I am by now more or less exhausted by the cinematic possibilities of killing them. I've seen thousands of zombies die, and they're awfully easy to kill, unless you get a critical mass that piles on all at once. George

90 'MCN Interview: *Shaun of the Dead*', Andrea Gronvall, Movie City News, 13 September 2004, http://moviecitynews.com/Interviews/shaun_dead.html

91 '*Shaun of the Dead*', Roger Ebert, *Chicago Sun Times*, 24 September 2004, http://rogerebert.suntimes.com/apps/pbcs.dll/article?AID=/20040924/REVIEWS/40913006/1023

Romero … was essentially devising video game targets before there were video games: they pop up, one after another, and you shoot them, or bang them on the head with a cricket bat. It's more fun sitting in the dark eating peanuts.'

Western Europe was obviously the place to be for the living dead at the turn of the millennium, as another movie came out in 2004, this time from Ireland, that featured flesh-eating zombies. *Dead Meat*, from first-time director Conor McMahon, tells the story of a young couple isolated in the countryside (by far the most dangerous place in Irish or British movies in the 2000s …) and surrounded by a group of attackers stricken by a very peculiar form of mad cow disease. Fun, bloody and highly referential, this super-cheap production funded through the Irish Film Board dealt in a very direct (if goofy) way with the anxieties derived from the bovine spongiform encephalopathy epidemic that had affected the United Kingdom since the mid-nineties, and caused the destruction of millions of animals and the deaths of over 170 people who had acquired a variant of the disease. The threat reached a peak in 2001, when the Food and Agriculture Organisation of the United Nations advised consumers to be wary of potentially contagious beef meat, prodding many to turn to vegetarianism or to boycott fast-food restaurants. Mad cow disease is to this day a major source of concern, especially in the United Kingdom, the nation most widely affected by the disease. Says McMahon, 'When I started writing, *28 Days Later* and *Shaun of the Dead* hadn't come out yet, and I hadn't seen a decent zombie flick for a good ten years. Shows you how long it takes to get a movie made … I thought of the mad cow disease because there's been a few cases in Ireland, and I found it oddly fitting to mix it with the living dead. A bit like in Romero's *The Crazies*. I had all those things on my mind at the same time, and they all ended up in the same script.'[92]

Germany added its own riff on the living dead theme with *Night of the Living Dorks* (*Die Nacht der Lebenden Loser*), from writer/director Mathias Dinter. Unlike *Shaun of the Dead* and *Dead Meat*, *Night of the Living Dorks* is primarily a teenage comedy with zombies thrown in for good measure; silly and often aiming below the belt, it was nevertheless a sign of the great popularity of the sub-genre, and was filled with little in-jokes for scary movie fans. Dinter describes himself as a real horror buff, and the decision to give the scares a backseat came both from personal taste and commercial considerations, *Night of the Living Dorks* having cost about $4 million to make. 'I was very comfortable with the mix of horror and comedy,' Dinter explained, 'Because if I had to choose one direction, I wouldn't be able to. Comedy is just commercially a good thing to do in Germany but horror you can hardly ever do. I like making horror movies because you know, it's just fun, the genre is fun. And the mix was a time travel back to when I was 15. In Germany the audience isn't that big; if a film is big in Germany it means it has a million viewers out of 80 million Germans. If you cut that down to the people who actually like horror movies that's an audience of 100,000 people; it isn't commercially viable. There is definitely a subculture in Germany, with guys like Olaf Ittenbach who do these films that go direct to DVD, but that's a whole different thing. I'm not in that loop so I wouldn't know if it's profitable.'[93]

US writer/director Matthew Leutwyler's *Dead and Breakfast* was yet another example of how well zombies and comedy mixed. This story of a group of friends who stop for bed and breakfast on their way to a wedding and get attacked by the locals, possessed by an evil spirit, once again includes many nods to genre classics and keeps its tongue firmly in cheek. Well paced, well acted (with genre favourites John Carradine, Jeremy Sisto and Gina Philips in the starring roles) and amusing at times, it is unfortunately killed by its own cleverness, as its in-jokes, winks and country songs (!) get tiresome quickly. The silliness culminates in a Michael Jackson *Thriller*-esque dance sequence involving the possessed town residents. Shot for an estimated $500,000, this direct-to-DVD release toured festivals around the world for nearly two years, and is better seen with a large audience or a group of gore-loving friends.

Night of the Living Dorks. Dead and Breakfast. Resident Evil: Apocalypse.

Finally, *Resident Evil: Apocalypse* curiously distanced itself from the creatures the first instalment of the saga did so much to popularise. Much closer to the videogame in its structure, characters and themes (Jill Valentine and Carlos Olivera both appear in the Capcom version; and the superhero-like mutated powers of Alice and of the Nemesis are common gaming

92 Interview with the author, London, UK, August 2004.
93 Interview with the author, San Sebastian, Spain, October 2004.

elements), this sequel targeted game players and teenagers and focused more on the action components of the franchise than on the horrific. Directed by first-time helmer Alexander Witt and penned by original writer/director Paul W Anderson, *Resident Evil: Apocalypse* was another hit for the series, with a $23 million opening in the US in September 2004.

'Do you have a grudge?' (*The Grudge*)

With the success of Gore Verbinski's 2002 remake of Hideo Nakata's *Ring*, producer Roy Lee had become the man of the hour for Hollywood studios, and Lee himself was convinced J-horror remakes were guaranteed box-office gold. In 2003, when Take Ichise visited the US to seek financing for a series of low-budget films to be shot in Japan, Lee seized this opportunity to organise a screening of *Ju-On: The Grudge* for a group of potential investors. The screening went down a storm, and *The Evil Dead*'s Sam Raimi ended up buying the rights for his brand new production company Ghost House Pictures, for a mere $250,000. Still admired by genre fans for his horror background, but with the added clout and financial credibility of a blockbuster filmmaker since *Spider-Man*, Raimi intended to use Ghost House to produce a series of low-budget scary movies, and *Ju-On: The Grudge* seemed like the perfect starting point. Impressed with Takashi Shimizu's directing skills, he hired him to helm the remake, making this the fifth time – after *Ju-On 1* and *2* and *Ju-On: The Grudge 1* and *2* – Shimizu tackled the *Grudge* series.

The Grudge, as the new version was called, retained the same basic story as *Ju-On: The Grudge*, and mixed in a few elements from the video movies. Despite Raimi's wish to clarify the storyline and iron out any illogicality, the script remained ambiguous, edited in non-chronological order, and on the whole, was so close to the original that it offered very few surprises to anyone familiar with the 2003 Japanese hit. To avoid having to relocate the action and transpose it into another culture (could a long-haired American woman be as scary?), it was decided the film would take place in Japan, with a couple of US exchange students, including *Buffy the Vampire Slayer*'s Sarah Michelle Gellar as the social worker who covers for the missing nurse, in the lead roles. This unusual choice allowed writer Stephen Susco to add a new challenge for the heroes: not only do they have to escape the curse, but they also have to understand its logic in a country where customs and traditions seem illogical and unfamiliar to them. A similar confusion reigned on the set: shooting in Japan with a Japanese crew and many Japanese actors, but for an American studio and American producers, Shimizu had to adapt his working methods and find a middle ground to satisfy everyone. For example, while he claims that his American stars were friendly and unassuming, he admits having had a hard time with the hours they could work. 'In Japan actors and actresses can work all day. As long as we put them in a taxi and they get home safely after working, that's fine. But American actors have only a certain amount of hours they can work in a day, then that's it. It was really hard for me to work around that with those actors, actresses, and crews.'[94]

An experiment in culture shock, *The Grudge* could have gone horribly wrong, but in the expert hands of Raimi and Shimizu, it turned out to be a huge hit, its $110 million US gross placing it just under *The Ring* in the most successful remakes of all time. Reviewers however were not convinced, and many criticised the movie for its lack of character development and its unnecessarily complicated storyline. Setting the action in Japan didn't solve all of *The Grudge*'s problems: while Asian viewers like their films to have a certain degree of mystery and don't bother to look for logic behind every single event, Western audiences don't tend to appreciate unexplained twists, plot holes and open endings. *The Grudge* certainly offers a few good scares, but with its constant time-jumps and apparent lack of coherence, it is still too confusing a film to be considered a classic. The Japanese ghost story is decidedly reluctant to fit into the traditional Hollywood thriller mould.

Resident Evil: Apocalypse. The Grudge.

94 'Takashi Shimizu: Director of *The Grudge*', Staci Layne Wilson, *Horror. com*, 10 May 2004, http://www.horror. com/php/article-605-1.html

Hits and Misses

Alongside the zombie and Asian trends, US studios, aware of the popularity of horror but reluctant to target directly what they still saw as a limited audience, churned out a series of bastardised productions, mixing mild scares or horror themes with thriller (David Koepp's *Secret Window*, starring Johnny Depp and adapted from a Stephen King novella; *Godsend*, from Nick Hamm, with Robert De Niro in one of his worst on-screen appearances), adventure (Stephen Sommers's *Van Helsing*, in which Hugh Jackman, in the titular role, battles monsters from the classic Universal horror films of the 1930s) or action (David S Goyer's *Blade: Trinity*, easily the worst in the series). The results were varied: if *Secret Window* grossed over $47 million during its US theatrical release, *Blade: Trinity* and *Van Helsing* had more trouble paying back their massive investments (an estimated $65 million and $160 million, respectively) during their cinema run in the States, but scored big internationally; and *Godsend* tanked.

Seed of Chucky. Van Helsing.

Two major studio subsidiaries however released a couple of pure genre flicks, made on a budget, and aimed at a specialised audience: *Seed of Chucky*, from Universal's Rogue Pictures, and *Anacondas: The Hunt for the Blood Orchid*, from Sony's Screen Gems.

In *Seed of Chucky*, written and directed by first-time helmer and Chucky creator Don Mancini, who had scripted the four previous films in the series, the killer doll helps his plastic wife Tiffany to transplant her soul into the body of actress Jennifer Tilly (who has provided the voice for Tiffany in the *Chucky* films since *Bride of Chucky* in 1998). This done, the demonic doll impregnates the actress with his seed to give their doll child Glen (or Glenda) a body to incarnate in. Sounds tasteless? It is. While the special effects, especially those involving the puppets, are top-notch, and the photography is as glossy and beautiful as in Ronny Yu's *Bride of Chucky*, *Seed of Chucky* pushes the self-reflective jokes that made *Bride of Chucky* a success beyond the limits of absurdity in a *mise-en-abyme* (with several actors playing themselves) not seen since *New Nightmare*. The new addition to the family, the pants-wetting, gender-confused

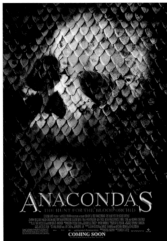

Glen, doesn't bring much to the family dynamics, and the jokes involving him simply aren't funny; too clever for its own good, the movie fails both as a Hollywood satire and as a comedy of manners. A direct consequence of the box office success of *Freddy vs Jason*, *Seed of Chucky* was about as artistically satisfying as the long-awaited showdown. Horror fans are always happy to see their favourite villains on the big screen, but one can only wish the movies they star in had more meat on their bones.

Anacondas: The Hunt for the Blood Orchid, a sequel to the 1997 Jennifer Lopez vehicle *Anaconda*, didn't seem promising. A silly giant snake story with a mid-range budget ($25 million), a TV director (Dwight H Little) and no stars to speak of, *Anacondas: The Hunt for the Blood Orchid* was a recipe for disaster. But thanks to its action-packed direction, lack of pretention and decent special effects, it turned out to be pure B-movie delight. With a cast of hot girls, bad guys with foreign accents, and tough action heroes, Little's flick doesn't take itself too seriously, but unlike *Seed of Chucky* or *Dead and Breakfast*, never winks at the camera.

Aware of its B-status, it quickly piles up the gore and ratchets up tension from the moment the protagonists leave on their quest for the Blood Orchid, a flower rumoured to be the botanical equivalent of the legendary fountain of youth. Not to everyone's taste, as evidenced by the abysmal reviews it received upon release, but fans of cheesy scares and silly fun will be more than satisfied.

**Anacondas: The Hunt for the Blood Orchid.
Exorcist: The Beginning.**

'God is not here' (*Exorcist: The Beginning*)

2004 saw the release of two prequels to William Friedkin's 1973 shocker *The Exorcist*: Renny Harlin's *Exorcist: The Beginning* and Paul Schrader's *Dominion: A Prequel to The Exorcist*. Both films are more worthy of attention for the events that surround their making, than for their intrinsic qualities.

The Exorcist had already been followed by two sequels: *Exorcist II: The Heretic*, by John Boorman, in 1977 and *The Exorcist III*, by Blatty himself in 1990. Both featured the character of Regan (Linda Blair), the possessed girl of the original movie. Schrader's film was meant to be a prequel focusing on Father Merrin, the priest played by Max Von Sydow in the first film. After living through traumatising events during World War II, Father Merrin takes a break from the Church to conduct archaeological excavations in British-administered East Africa, where he digs out what appears to be a pagan church dedicated to an unidentified demon. Producing company Morgan Creek hired John Frankenheimer (*French Connection II*, *Ronin*) to helm and Liam Neeson to star. Unfortunately, Frankenheimer ended up leaving the project (coincidentally, a month before he passed away) and Neeson left shortly after. Paul Schrader (writer of *Taxi Driver* and director of the excellent *Autofocus*) was appointed to replace Frankenheimer, with actor Stellan Skarsgård (*Good Will Hunting*, *Deep Blue Sea*) taking the lead. The script was penned by William Wisher (*Terminator 2: Judgement Day*, *Judge Dredd*) and Caleb Carr. Says Schrader, 'When I started working on the movie, they already had a screenplay, some of the cast [Gabriel Mann and Billy Crawford] and some of the sets in place. But when I read the script, there was something there I related to, and I knew I could make it my own. I rewrote parts of it that I found too long or too repetitive; for instance the demon and Merrin had ten pages of dialogue towards the end. I also added a few extra scenes and reworked the relationships between Merrin and a few other characters.'[95]

This, unfortunately, would only be the beginning of the production's troubles. The shoot went smoothly and everyone on set seemed happy with the results … until Schrader screened a rough cut to studio executives. Slow and character-driven, Schrader's prequel simply wasn't a horror film. A Calvinist-turned-Episcopalian whose parents considered watching movies a sin and who once contemplated a career in the clergy, the filmmaker was interested in aspects of the story that had little to do with spinning heads and projectile-vomiting; instead, he chose to

95 Interview with the author,
Brussels, Belgium, March 2005.

focus on the theological and cultural aspects of his subject matter. *Dominion: Prequel to the Exorcist*, as the film ended up being called, deals with such issues as faith and guilt through Merrin's path to redemption, and the culture shock and evils of colonialism with the clashes between British forces and local tribes. 'My goal was to stay as far as I could from Friedkin's film. I've put in little references to it, like the white face that you could see in *The Exorcist*'s subliminal shots, or the fact that the demon is an African version of Pazuzu. But my intention was clearly to distance

myself from Friedkin's work,' the director explains. Interesting as this exploration of the human mind may have been, Morgan Creek and Warner Bros simply refused to release Schrader's film, as they thought it offered audiences very little – if anything – of what they would expect from an *Exorcist* movie. For what may well have been the first time in history, they discarded the entire feature, less than 10% of the material shot eventually finding its way into the new version, and hired director Renny Harlin (*A Nightmare on Elm Street 4: The Dream Master*, *Die Hard 2*) to create a brand new movie with for the most part the same cast and the same locations, but a rewritten screenplay.

If Schrader made a horror movie without any horror, Harlin delivered an action film without any action. One might have expected the man behind such thrill-packed hits as *Cliffhanger* and *Deep Blue Sea* to insert explosions and wild chases, but the Finnish director showed great restraint. Trouble is, he also forgot to fill his movie with something – anything – else. Harlin throws some blood here and there for good measure, but doesn't bother trying to create any suspense, develop characters, or heaven forbid, add any depth to the story. *Exorcist: The Beginning* is as painfully long and badly paced as *Dominion: Prequel to the Exorcist*, a boring and pedestrian production which doesn't even have its predecessor's excuse of pursuing higher aspirations.

Satisfied by Harlin's more conventional approach, Warner Bros released *Exorcist: The Beginning* in August 2004. Critics were not kind. The BBC observed that 'even the simplest shocks are screwed up'[96], while the *Los Angeles Times* called it a 'perfectly mediocre film'[97]. *Dominion: Prequel to the Exorcist* received a limited opening on 110 screens nearly a year later, after positive reactions from the European press at its world premiere at the Brussels International Festival of Fantastic Films. Reviewers were slightly kinder to Schrader's movie, possibly because of its history, but as many pointed out, both versions merely emphasised the fact that over thirty years after its original release, Friedkin's *The Exorcist* remained an impossible act to follow.

'Warning: Shocking, horrific, controversial' (*Murder-Set-Pieces*)

2004 was the year graphic violence blossomed, and torture became a genre of its own. As observed, blood and guts had been on an upward curve in cinema for the previous few years, and this trend also affected non-horror movies, as the debates around the hyper-violence of Mel

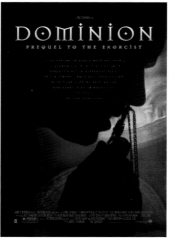

Dominion.

96 New Pierce, *BBC*, 28 October 2004, http://www.bbc.co.uk/films/2004/10/18/the_exorcist_the_beginning_2004_review.shtml
97 Kevin Crust, Los Angeles Times, 21 August 2004, http://www.calendarlive.com/movies/reviews/cl-et-crust21aug21,2,5709811.story

Gibson's *The Passion of the Christ* in February 2004 clearly showed. Just when it seemed movies couldn't get more violent, a couple of features came out that further pushed the boundaries, and seemed to have no other goal than to shock and disgust their audience.

The Hillside Strangler, from writer/director Chuck Parello, tells the real-life story of Kenneth Bianchi and Angelo Buono, two serial rapists and killers collectively known as the Hillside Strangler in the late 1970s. Dark, realistic and brutal, the movie received a one-theatre release in New York in October 2004, and went straight to DVD everywhere else.

Murder-Set-Pieces, by Nick Palumbo, is to this day known as one of the nastiest, most mean-spirited pieces of celluloid ever made, and was, from its first showing, the object of passionate debates and full-on hatred. Says Palumbo: 'Fear is the primal instinct that we can all relate to. For me, a film that mirrors the nightly news in America is the ultimate example of horrific. I wanted to create what people read and hear about on a daily basis in America: murder, rape and dehumanisation. I wanted to show people what violence in America is really like, and to also show the horrible problem in the States of how parents do not take care of their children … I'm a visceral person in the extreme, and I wanted to assault the viewer with imagery never before seen in a 35mm motion picture.' A direct descendant of *Maniac* (1980) and *Henry, Portrait of a Serial Killer* (1986), two films considered cult classics despite their gruesome content, this rape-and-murder story seen from the point of view of the killer may not be everyone's cup of tea, but it is hard, in retrospect, to understand what the fuss was all about.

Murder-Set-Pieces.

Trying to view *Murder-Set-Pieces* objectively today is nearly impossible. Reportedly inspected on set by the police, turned down for processing by no less than three colour labs, and eventually banned in the UK, it doesn't quite live up to its reputation. Sure, it is graphic and exploitative, but it isn't nearly as shocking as the rumour wants you to believe. An *American Psycho* without the depth, ambiguity and character development of the 2000 Bret Easton Ellis adaptation, Palumbo's movie is filled with gratuitous sex and violence, but its notoriety for being the closest thing to snuff is hardly deserved. At the very least, its photography, production value and actors (among which are Gunnar Hansen, Cerina Vincent and Tony Todd) are good, and while it is mainly notable for its nudity and brutal murders, since it doesn't try to create anticipation, suspense, or identification with the victims, it isn't significantly nastier or grittier than *The Hillside Strangler* or *H6: Diary of a Serial Killer* (*H6: Diario de un Asesino*, 2005).

So why was this movie the focus of so much negative attention? Palumbo believes the answer is in the film itself. 'People, especially Americans, cannot handle the truth. Magazines like *Fangoria* and *Rue Morgue* can pretend that the concept of a Freddy Krueger is not that of a child molester, and we can make a hero out of him because he is so over the top, and therefore unrealistic. I made a very simple, but very pure horror film, and they cannot separate the artist from his art. A lot of people in Hollywood have labelled me an anti-Semite, a Neo-Nazi, a misogynist, and so on. It's untrue, it's asinine in the extreme and it has cost me work.' Another reason for this hatred could be found in the fact that unlike other directors who would have quietly accepted the lack of media coverage and let their film sink into oblivion, Palumbo chose to use it to his advantage in interviews and on specialised message boards. His alleged forum spamming and his insistence on having his film covered in the media guaranteed him a level of publicity that similarly 'shocking' movies have rarely achieved, but also added fuel to the *Murder-Set-Pieces* fire.

As for the BBFC (British Board of Film Classification), the reasons for its rejection were clear: the Board feared the mix of sex and violence presented in the movie might arouse and excite some viewers more than disturb them. *Murder-Set-Pieces* was last banned in the UK in February 2008[98], with the following justification:

'Under the heading of "Rejects", the Guidelines identify as of particular concern "graphic rape or torture", "portrayals of children in a sexualised or abusive context" and "sex accompanied by non-consensual pain, injury or humiliation".

'The Board's position that scenes of violence with the potential to trigger sexual arousal may encourage a harmful association between violence and sexual gratification is reflected in research and consistent with public opinion. It is the Board's carefully considered view that to issue a certificate to *Murder-Set-Pieces*, even if statutorily confined to adults, would involve risk of harm within the terms of the Video Recordings Act 1984, would be inconsistent with the Board's Guidelines, and would be unacceptable to the public.

'The Board considered whether the issue could be dealt with through cuts. However, given that unacceptable content features throughout, and that what remains is essentially preparatory and set-up material for the unacceptable scenes, cuts are not a viable option in this case and the work is therefore refused a classification.'[99]

Interestingly, the last paragraph defines pretty accurately what would soon become known as torture porn …

In the US, *Murder-Set-Pieces* is available on DVD in a truncated, R-rated version, from Lionsgate.

Saw.

'Let the games begin!' (*Saw*)

Not every filmmaker in this new wave intended to use hyper-violence to shock and disgust. Newcomers James Wan and Leigh Whannell took the box-office by storm with their worldwide success *Saw*, a graphic yet undeniably clever and entertaining crowd-pleaser, which would soon become the first instalment in the single most profitable horror franchise of the 2000s.

The basic set-up of *Saw* was simple. Two men (played by Whannell and Cary Elwes) wake up chained to opposite corners of what appears to be a disused washroom, with a corpse lying between them, a gun and a microcassette player in the dead man's hands. The tapes they find give them instructions, and let them know that if one doesn't kill the other within the next eight hours, he and his family will be murdered. Around these events, writer/director Wan and writing partner Whannell crafted a captivating thriller, and gave birth to a new horror icon, on a par with the Jasons and Freddies of the eighties: the Jigsaw killer, a man whose motivations and *modus operandi* are original yet (more or less) realistic, and whose fascinating personality will be further developed with subsequent sequels. Alongside the basic plotline, the movie follows the police investigation and the kidnapping of one of the prisoners' family; but the bathroom scenes are certainly where most of the tension is concentrated, and they constitute the most memorable part of the story, along with the flashbacks revealing previous traps conceived by Jigsaw. If *Murder-Set-Pieces* aimed to show what went through a serial killer's head, *Saw* on the other hand stayed on the side of the victims, as Whannell explained in a 2004 interview with *Fangoria*[100]: 'What we wanted was to be with these guys throughout the entire film. We wanted the audience to feel what the characters were feeling, so that by the time the film ends, you want to get out of that room as badly as they do.' With a final twist that no one saw coming, this exercise in smart low-budget filmmaking only had one notable flaw: Cary Elwes's ridiculously over-the-top performance as the family man caught in Jigsaw's trap, over-articulating every word, moving his eyebrows in all directions and making each single line sound ominous or pathetic.

The story behind the making of *Saw* is almost as fascinating as the movie itself. 'I met Leigh

98 As of April 2008.

99 BBFC Decision, 27 February 2008, *BBFC*, Reference AVV245696, http:// www.bbfc.org.uk/website/Classified. nsf/0/C459C3DC24C72664802573FC 005EB482?OpenDocument

100 'Saw cuts deep', Sarah Walker, *Fangoria* 236, September 2004, p 46.

101 Email interview with the author, April 2008.

Saw.

(Whannell) at the university we attended,' James Wan recalls[101]. 'We were both there to study media arts. Most of the people in the course were mature-aged students, and since Leigh and I were in the few that were fresh out of high school, we shared a lot of things in common and became good friends. We knew we wanted to make a super-low-budget movie that we could finance with our hard-earned money, so the idea had to be small and doable. But we wanted to come up with something that was cool and high-concept even with no money.' Knowing they could never afford A-list actors, Wan and Whannell had to come up with a script which would be clever enough to attract attention. 'I called Leigh up one day and said, "Listen, I don't quite know what I have here, but see if you like it. The whole movie takes place in a bathroom, there are two people chained to the opposite sides of the room, and lying in between them is a dead body. In the corpse's hands are a gun and a tape recorder. Our two guys realise that they're put in this predicament to kill each other and all the while, someone is watching them. You think this voyeur is the villain of the movie, but at the end … the dead body gets up off the floor and walks out!" After I finished pitching that, I was expecting Leigh to blow it off, but he really loved the concept and thought we might have something here. So he went off for an entire year to write the first draft, and brought in all the serial killer element of Jigsaw and the traps.'

With the screenplay completed, Wan decided to shoot a scene to give potential investors a glimpse at the tone of the feature, and prove them he would be able to helm despite his limited experience behind the camera. The seven-minute short showed Whannell struggling against the jaw trap which actress Shawnee Smith eventually found herself in, and sparked the interest of several studios, including Lionsgate, which ended up distributing it. Says Eda Kowan: 'It was amazing. We asked, is there a script? We read it overnight, loved it, and that was it. The film was made for little over a million dollars with an eighteen-day shoot, and they were racing to submit it to Sundance.' The cut shown at Sundance, the world-renowned independent film festival, was an NC-17 version, which was later re-edited to obtain an R rating for the general release. 'One of the producers even carried the print with them on a plane to the screening. It played there and it was unbelievable. I don't think we'd even seen the film with the final sound and in its final cut, and certainly not on a big screen. It was like a rock concert. It played through the roof.' A test screening organised soon afterwards confirmed the excellent reception the film received from the Sundance audience. 'It's rare for a horror film,' Kowan says. 'You're recruiting to see how broadly the film will play, so your recruit is not just the core demo. It scored unbelievable so we tested it again just to make sure. It also screened at Toronto and people were yelling at the screen, "don't open the door"!'

Saw opened wide in the USA in October 2004, just in time for Halloween, and its great popularity with festival and test audiences was reflected by the box-office results. Wan's film grossed over $18 million in its first weekend, and ended up earning more than $55 million in US theatres. 'I think people fell in love with it for a bunch of reasons,' the director explains. 'It was different to the norm. I think the biggest factor was that we gave the audience a dark and twisted horror thriller that was intelligent. Most horror movies don't put any effort into the script at all. Leigh and I wanted to make a smart whodunit movie that was set in the horror genre. There is a misconception that *Saw* is popular due to its traps and games, but I honestly believe that people loved the first *Saw* for the twists and turns of the screenplay and the shocking ending.'

Choose Life

As well as the wave of violence which was prevalent in independent horror offerings, a handful of intriguing and varied features could also be found.

Mick Garris's *Riding the Bullet*, adapted, as is often the case with Garris, from a Stephen King story, tells the nostalgic and touching tale of a young man learning to deal with loss and his own mortality. After a failed suicide attempt, horror-obsessed art student Alan Parker (Jonathan Jackson) embarks on a one-night hitchhiking trip through the countryside to visit his mother, who has just suffered a stroke. He is soon picked up by a mysterious man who offers him a life-altering choice …

King's original story was no more than 35 pages long, so Garris, who also wrote the screenplay, had plenty of space to elaborate and make it his own. As a result, *Riding the Bullet* is the filmmaker's most personal work. 'When I first read the short story, I was going through a lot of things,' Garris recalls[102]. 'I had lost my brother several years earlier, and my father just a year or two before I read it, and so I was in a particularly tender spot, and it just made me think about the theme of this story. To most people I think it's just a simple little ghost story, but to me, that theme of appreciating what you got when you got it and it will always be yours struck me as particularly potent.' The writer/director added many personal ideas to the plot, including Alan's suicide attempt, his passion for the romantic imagery of death, and his break-up with his girlfriend. 'I wanted [Alan] to realise on his long journey home that death isn't beautiful, it's ominous and threatening. When you're 21 you don't expect to be confronted by mortality and maybe there should be a little more thought. Yes, your twenties are a time when you should be able to just have fun and grow and have a good time but you don't want to wait until too late to express your emotions to the people who mean something to you.' To underline his message, Garris decided to transpose the story to the late sixties, a time when 'our society had to make similar life-or-death choices.' Garris holds fast to his theme; even the soundtrack, which includes tracks by The Zombies, The Strawberry Alarm Clock and The Youngbloods, reflects the message which he wanted to convey. Unfortunately, it seems that his producers saw things differently. Convinced that fans of the author would expect more

Riding the Bullet.

scares than tears, they insisted the filmmaker insert a certain amount of frightful elements into the script. As a result, *Riding the Bullet* is an uneasy mix of horror and drama, the result of obvious compromises: although the notion of loss is an underlying thread throughout, the film can at times feel somewhat disjointed, as if ideas had been thrown together and didn't all blend; one could easily lose sight of the plot between flash-backs, visiting spirits and real-life, contemporary events.

Riding the Bullet may not be perfect, but it is a movie with an unusually big heart. 'From an audience standpoint it's a Stephen King movie,' Garris concludes, 'but it taps into things that I think all of us share and that are also so specific to my own life. It's the movie that's closest to my heart in everything I've done, the one I feel the most personally and artistically attached to.'

It's a very different type of emotion that writer/director Robert Parigi's first effort *Love Object* depicts. The story of Kenneth (Desmond Harrington), a shy, insecure copywriter who starts to live out his fantasies about co-worker Lisa (Melissa Sagemiller) with a sex doll, this tale of obsession starts out as an intriguing drama, as the young man establishes his 'relationship' with his rubber darling and increasing creepiness ensues. Much like Lucky McKee's *May*, *Love Object* focuses on a loner whose isolation and inability to communicate lead them to homicide, and develops slowly from romantic comedy/drama to horror. Unlike *May* however, Parigi's film keeps an objective perspective and sacrifices poetry for cold realism. But the movie loses much of its appeal in its second act, once the young man unsurprisingly kidnaps his co-worker, and

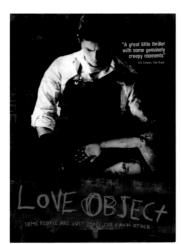

Love Object. Open Water.

ends with an unnecessary final twist which doesn't bring much to the story. Despite winning a handful of festival awards, notably at France's Fantastic'Arts in Gérardmer, *Love Object* failed to draw much attention and came out straight to DVD in the summer.

May's lead, Angela Bettis, starred in Tobe Hooper's *Toolbox Murders*, as a young woman moving with her husband into a run-down apartment building in Hollywood, and discovering that her neighbours are being massacred one after the other. This traditional slasher, as simple as it was linear, was hailed by the specialised press as Hooper's best movie since *The Texas Chain Saw Massacre* (which, as some hurriedly pointed out, wasn't saying much). Suspenseful, atmospheric, claustrophobic (almost all of the film takes place in the apartment building) and featuring great performances from Bettis, Sheri Moon and Juliet Landau, *Toolbox Murders* was a remake of Dennis Donnelly's 1978 eponymous hack'n'slash, but only shared the title and the most basic plot elements with its predecessor. Sadly, Hooper's return to form only received a limited release in the US and a few festival bookings before appearing on DVD in 2005.

It nevertheless allowed two up-and-coming screenwriters to be discovered by the genre press: Adam Gierasch and Jace Anderson, who had already collaborated with Hooper on his previous feature, *Crocodile* (2000). Two lifelong horror fans who specialise in dark, gory, scary stories with hints of other genres (mostly comedy and *film noir*), they would, in the years to follow, add Hooper's *Mortuary* (2005)to their credits, as well as Dario Argento's *Mother of Tears* (*La terza madre*, 2007) – the final film in his cult Three Mothers trilogy, preceded by *Suspira* (1977) and *Inferno* (1980) – and *Autopsy* (2008), Gierasch's directing debut.

Open Water, from writer/director Chris Kentis, tells the story of a couple who get left behind in the middle of the ocean on their scuba-diving vacation in the Caribbean. Based on true events, as the tagline itself makes clear, this raw and visceral movie was presented as the lovechild of *Jaws* (1975) and *The Blair Witch Project* (1999), since the entire film was filmed on handheld camera, with very little music, to give it a realistic feel. Like *The Blair Witch Project*, the result left some bored and unimpressed, made a few others sick, and terrified the rest. This micro-budget production (figures vary, but the consensus is between $130,000 and $400,000) was bought for $2.5 million by Lionsgate after its screening at the Sundance Film Festival, and raked in over $30 million over the course of its summer/fall cinematic run in the States. Slow, minimalist, but ultimately conveying an increasing sense of isolation, despair and fear, *Open Water* would be followed years later by a series of films, from *[Rec]* (2007) to *Cloverfield* (2008), which would use the same tricks.

Return of the Curse

That Canada's most successful horror production in recent history, *Ginger Snaps*, would receive a sequel seemed pretty natural; but in 2004, it wasn't one, but two *Ginger Snaps* movies that opened.

Ginger Snaps: Unleashed, from director Brett Sullivan, picked up where the first film ended, with Brigitte running away from home following Ginger's death. Now a lycanthrope herself, she tries to avoid the transformation by injecting herself with monkshood; but when she collapses in the street, the police assume that she is taking illegal drugs, and so she is sent to rehab. If *Ginger Snaps* showed the werewolf as a metaphor for puberty and blooming sexuality, its sequel goes further by exploring themes such as teenage depression, drug use and suicide, and presents the 'curse' of the first instalment as a disease. Darker and more serious than the original, *Ginger Snaps: Unleashed* manages to find its own tone and introduce new and interesting characters, while retaining the originality and freshness of the first film. A worthy sequel and a success of its own, it also featured some great creature effects, courtesy of Gregory Nicotero and Howard Berger's KNB EFX.

Set in the 19th century, Grant Harvey's *Ginger Snaps Back: the Beginning* sees the Fitzgerald sisters, ancestors of the first two films' Ginger and Brigitte, take refuge in a trading fort besieged by werewolves. A prequel to the other two films, this period piece took a more traditional approach to the myth, and while it remains a suspenseful, beautifully shot and atmospheric adventure movie, it loses much of its predecessors' bite and subtext. Adequately described as 'Canadian Gothic' by one reviewer[103], this peculiar fairy tale did have at least one theme in common with the original: the sisters' struggle to find their place in a predominantly male society. The only two girls in the fort, Ginger and Brigitte appear more equal than in the contemporary stories, as actress Emily Perkins explains[104]: 'At the time women were very oppressed by the patriarchal culture, but they had close friendships where they would hold hands in public and sleep in the same bed and no one would call them a lesbian because such things were not considered then. They managed to find this space where they were equal. I think that's what we did in the third movie: they're not being defined in terms of their looks or the power they wield.' An unusual ending to an unusual franchise, *Ginger Snaps Back: the Beginning* toured festivals, then appeared straight on DVD in most countries.

Ginger Snaps: Unleashed. Ginger Snaps Back: The Beginning.

Europe

In addition to the zombie movies already examined, Europe continued to produce its share of horror features. Italy made a quick comeback with *The Card Player* (*Il Cartaio*), a disappointing serial killer flick from horror maestro Dario Argento, and *Three Faces of Terror* (*I Tre Volti del Terrore*), a fun and unpretentious anthology movie by effects artist Sergio Stivaletti. France's only genre title was *Saint-Ange* (*House of Voices*), from writer/director Pascal Laugier, a traditional mystery set in an abandoned orphanage. Spain saw the releases of *Blood Red* (*Rojo Sangre*), by Christian Molina, the amusing story of an actor-turned-murderer, written by and starring genre icon Paul Naschy; and a couple of Filmax productions: *The Machinist* (*El Maquinista*) and *The Werewolf Manhunt* (*Romasanta*). Germany, finally, would see the release of *Tears of Kali*.

Produced by Filmax and shot in and around Barcelona, *The Machinist*, from *Session 9* director Brad Anderson, starred Christian Bale, then best known for his turn as the buffed-up killer in *American Psycho* (2000). The film gained much publicity as Bale starved himself into a human skeleton, losing a reported 62 pounds before regaining the weight and an additional 40 pounds for his role in *Batman Begins* (2005). As emaciated insomniac Trevor Reznik, an industrial machinist whose life slowly turns into a paranoiac's daydream through his lack of sleep, Bale is shockingly skinny, but his appearance, far from a simple gimmick, serves the story and contributes to the actor's haunting and touching performance, one of the best of his career. The dark and monochromatic photography, inspired by the scientific observation that sleep-deprived patients lose the ability to see bright colours, allows viewers to look at the world through Reznik's eyes and gives the film an eerie, nightmarish quality. This is further enhanced by the use of Barcelona doubling for Los Angeles, making the character's environment never entirely identifiable or familiar. The intrigue itself is nothing special, the final revelation already having been seen in many films, although the plot, from writer Scott Kosar, unveils in a suspenseful way; it's the atmosphere and the strong performances the entire cast deliver that carry *The Machinist* and make it a movie that lives beyond its plot twists and its lead actor's commitment to the role.

Paco Plaza's *The Werewolf Manhunt*, written by Elena Serra and Alberto Marini, is set in the mid-nineteenth century in a village whose inhabitants disappear one after the other, and the survivors start to believe that a werewolf may be hiding in the surrounding forest. The film is based on the true story of Manuel Romasanta (played by Julian Sands), a travelling salesman accused of murdering thirteen people and using their body fat to make soap, and who avoided capital punishment by claiming at his trial that the devil had turned him into a wolf-man.

103 Mariko McDonald, *Film Threat*, 13 July 2004, http://www.filmthreat. com/index.php?section=reviews&I d=6242

104 Interview with the author, Brussels, Belgium, March 2005.

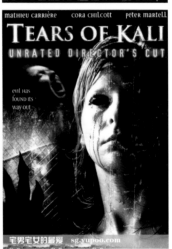

The Machinist. The Werewolf Manhunt.
Tears of Kali.

Gorgeously photographed and featuring some great effects, Plaza's third feature (after *OT: la Película* and *The Second Name* (both 2002)) gave its supernatural elements a back seat, focusing instead on creating a dark atmosphere reminiscent of the gothic chills of the old Hammer movies, and establishing the historical and scientific context of the story. The film mixes fact and fiction, and mostly follows the investigation of Romasanta's lover Barbara (Elsa Pataky). Adopting the point of view of the murderer, the film keeps the audience open to the possibility that the serial killer is indeed a werewolf and even includes an original and beautiful transformation scene. Clever and moody, *The Werewolf Manhunt* received a modest opening in Spain and came out direct to DVD around the globe.

On 11 March 2004, Spain experienced a true-life nightmare of its own, when a group of Islamic extremists launched a coordinated series of bombings in the Madrid underground, killing 191 and injuring nearly 2,000 people. In the aftermath of the attacks, massive demonstrations were organised throughout Spain and around the world to protest against the war in Iraq. Several countries, including France, consequently raised the level of their national security alert, thereby contributing to the general anxiety of the population.

While, as *Night of the Living Dorks* director Mathias Dinter pointed out, Germany doesn't produce many mainstream horror movies, it does have a thriving underground scene. Following the example of filmmaking pioneers Jörg Buttgereit (*Nekromantik* (1987)) and Andreas Schnaas (*Violent Shit* (1989)), others such as Olaf Ittenbach (*Legion of the Dead* (2001)) have since the late eighties tested the patience of the censors with micro-budget productions filled with graphic violence and nudity and usually dealing with taboo subjects such as necrophilia or torture. Often amateurish and purely exploitative, few are worthy of much attention, and fewer still manage to be seen outside Germany. Andreas Marschall's *Tears of Kali* was one of those lucky few. An anthology film relating the fates of three survivors of a homicidal sect, the movie starts with a scene in which a woman cuts off her own eyelids, leading unsuspecting viewers to believe that this will be another feature aimed solely at gore-minded fans. But even though *Tears of Kali* requires a strong stomach at times, it is the cleverness of each set piece that puts it above the average underground horror production. While the heavy atmosphere, supported by dark and grainy photography, contributes as much as the gore to the creation of a general feeling of discomfort, each segment ends with a little twist that shows the power of what the former members of the cult have unleashed. Interviewed in 2006, Marschall said[105]: 'I was interested in the way some representatives of the so-called New Age, eager to improve the human being by positive thinking, longing for harmony, suppress their shadow and their dark sides, until these shadows come back from behind as demons. This is not only known in esotericism, but also in politics, if you look at radical do-gooders, who only want the best but become dangerous fanatics.' Unfortunately, although it deals with a topical subject, the film never goes beyond the simplest aspects of its ghost story and only gives the vaguest explanations of the origins of the sect, the ghosts, or the reason these cult members have so far escaped their fate; by the end of the film, the mystery remains intact. Despite these shortcomings, *Tears of Kali* is a surprisingly smart and effective little shocker which, although not appealing to everyone, is guaranteed to please hardcore horror fans while avoiding the pitfalls of purely gratuitous gore.

'Ring ... Ring ... Ring ...' (*One Missed Call*)

In January 2004, Japan saw the release of yet another *Ring* rip-off: *One Missed Call*, in which students die after receiving a phone call from their own number during which they hear themselves die. Obviously inspired by *Ring*, this new entry in the killer technology sub-genre was directed by Japanese shockmeister Takashi Miike (*Audition, Ichi the Killer*) and was a very traditional and sedate movie for a filmmaker best known for his scenes of carnage and torture. *One Missed Call* follows the *Ring* formula to the letter and brings very little that is new to the genre; it also lacks the atmosphere and well-timed shocks of its predecessors. These flaws didn't stop it from being a major hit in its home country or from spawning two sequels

105 'Running-Wild Interview', Jens Pohl, *Running-Wild.net*, January 2006, http://www.running-wild. net/releases/interview_andreas-marschall_01-2006.html

and a TV series, proof of the ongoing popularity of J-horror, and of the resourcefulness of its producers, who always find quick ways to capitalise on every success.

The same year, Miike contributed a segment to the horror anthology *Three... Extremes* (*Saam gaang yi*) (decidedly a fashionable sub-genre that year), along with directors Fruit Chan and Chan-wook Park (*Oldboy* (2003), *Sympathy for Mr Vengeance* (*Boksuneun naui geot*, 2002)). As the title makes clear, this acclaimed collaboration between South Korea, Japan and Hong Kong – each country being represented by a different filmmaker – gathers three outrageous, disturbing shorts whose main purpose is to make viewers squirm in their seats, and is a sequel of sorts to *Three* (*Saam gaang*, 2002), a South Korea/Thailand/Hong Kong co-production later released in the United States as *Three ... Extremes II*, to capitalise on the second film's success. Fruit Chan's segment, 'Dumplings', deals with two taboos: abortion and cannibalism, and asks the question, 'How far would a woman go to keep her youthful looks?' By turns shocking and fascinating, it is by far the most accomplished of the three, but also the one with the most predictable conclusion. Chan later released a 90-minute version of his film, which was screened in festivals around the world and collected awards and rave reviews along the way. Chan-wook Park's 'Cut' examines how far a man would go to protect his wife, and is perhaps the most classic, but also the most tense of the three segments. 'Cut' shows a more Westernised sensibility in its theme and approach than Chan's and Miike's pieces, and has been compared to *Saw*. Miike's psychological contribution, 'Box', the weakest section of the film, seems to be asking, how unintelligible can one's film be? For this visually stunning segment, Miike exchanged his trademark taste for blood for a touch of poetry, and if the plot could have benefited from a greater coherence, its fragmented storyline gives it a dream-like quality that makes it unique, but tough to follow. Together, the three segments of *Three ... Extremes* are brilliant exercises in style, somewhat lacking in substance, but certainly achieving their goal: to intrigue and surprise their audience.

South Korea contributed to the soldiers-vs-supernatural sub-genre with Su-chang Kong's *R-Point*, a ghost story set during the Vietnam War, when South Korea joined the United States in the fight against communism. When the country's Vietnam headquarters receives a distress call from a platoon which had been presumed killed six months earlier, nine soldiers are sent on a rescue mission to the island of R-Point, 'where those who have blood on their hands will not return'. Far from the clichés of K-horror, *R-Point* is not centred around the revelation of an ancient grudge, does not deal with social issues, and features a majority of male ghosts and victims (although the main spirit is, in the end, a more traditional long-haired female). Going for atmospheric frights more than

One Missed Call. Three ... Extremes. R-Point.

jump-scares or gore, it does offer a few chilling scenes – the ghost patrol, the discovery of the radio – but despite its excellent premise, fails to maintain tension or offer a real crescendo in its scares. The ghostly nature of the patrol calling for help is understood early on, so there is no real mystery surrounding the soldiers' situation; and the protagonists themselves aren't developed, distinguishable or likeable enough to make the viewers care for them. Still, *R-Point* was a breath of fresh air, and local audiences embraced it as such. A big hit in its home country, it received a limited release in the US in 2006 – a rare feat indeed for a South Korean movie – and amazingly enough, has so far managed to avoid receiving the remake treatment, even though its topical nature could make it the perfect candidate for an American adaptation.

2005:

"Oh yes. There will be blood."

(Tagline for *Saw II*, 2005)

ANOTHER YEAR MARKED BY VIOLENCE, BOTH IN WORLD EVENTS AND IN movies, 2005 began with George W Bush's inauguration, on 20 January, for his second term as President of the United States. With the situation in Iraq still unstable – the number of US casualties reaching 2,000 in October – a series of suicide bombings perpetrated by Islamist militants on 7 July hit a bus and three trains in the London Underground, killing 56 and injuring over 700. A failed attack followed a couple of weeks later, on 21 July, when an attempt was made to blow up three trains and one bus in London. In this instance, only the detonators went off, and no one was injured.

Further tension between the Muslim and Western communities would result from the publication on 30 September 2005 in a Danish newspaper of twelve editorial cartoons, most of which showed the prophet Muhammad, to illustrate an issue on Islamic terrorism; demonstrations, flag burnings, death threats and attempted destruction of embassies followed the original publication and the reprinting of the drawings in dozens of outlets around the world. Then in October and November, France was shaken by a series of riots, burnings of cars and public buildings, and violent incidents between the police and youths from the *banlieues* in the Paris suburbs and various parts of the country. President Jacques Chirac declared a state of emergency on day 12 of the 20-day unrest.

In America however, the most devastating events of the year did not have religious or social origins. Hurricane Katrina, one of the deadliest in American history, struck Florida and New Orleans in late August, killing more than 1,800 and leaving thousands homeless. In September, Hurricane Rita hit Texas and Louisiana as well as the Gulf of Mexico, causing over 100 direct or indirect deaths. Hurricane Stan caused flooding and mudslides in Southern Mexico and Central America, leaving over 1,000 dead in October. The same month, Southern Florida, Mexico and Cuba were affected by Hurricane Wilma, directly responsible for 23 deaths. A few

96

additional lives were claimed by smaller hurricanes and tropical storms all over the continent. The economic consequences were disastrous, and so were the political repercussions in the United States, as the Bush administration was harshly criticised for its slow and uncoordinated response to the flooding in New Orleans. Already shaken by the realisation that the war in Iraq had led to an unstable situation and that the media were being controlled, the US population started to lose their trust in the security that the government was supposed to offer them.

A troubled year for the international community, 2005 saw an increasing number of horror productions of a generally good level of quality come out in theatres and on DVD, especially in the United States and in Western Europe. Remakes, zombie movies and hyper-violence were once again the main trends.

The Ring Two.

'It begins again' (*The Ring Two*)

Following the success of *The Grudge* and *Dawn of the Dead* in 2004, Hollywood started a systematic plundering of both Asian hits and old American classics, adapting them to what they assumed were the tastes of the new generation with generally disastrous results. Manufactured to please a very young and supposedly undiscerning audience, they almost always lost the edge of the originals and replaced any fresh ideas with PG-13 scares.

The Ring Two, released in March, wasn't a remake *per se*, but a sequel to Verbinski's 2002 update of Hideo Nakata's *Ring*. Directed by Nakata himself, this follow-up wisely stayed away from the universally decried *Ring 2* (*Ringu 2*, 1999), although both have the young son at the centre of their plot. Here, when the journalist of the first film, Rachel Keller (played by Naomi Watts), and her son Aidan (David Dorfman) move from Seattle to Oregon to forget the horrors of the cursed videotape, Keller realises Samara has followed them and is trying to come back to life by possessing Aidan. On this rather unimaginative concept, Nakata piles up plot holes, clichés, un-frightening shocks and incongruities, turning the story into an incoherent mess. In this regard, *The Ring Two* is an excellent example of the differences between American and Asian sensibilities. At first, hiring a Japanese director must have looked like a great idea[106]: who better than Nakata knows what made *Ring* so terrifying? Western directors too often seem to believe that the greatness of J-horror lies in its most obvious components – long-haired ghosts and grudges – and forget that more than the spirits themselves, it is the way they are introduced to the audience that makes them scary: the slow building of tension, the familiar environments and social issues on which they thrive, and the amazing sound effects surrounding their apparitions. But just as US filmmakers don't fully understand Asian films, Asian directors don't necessarily grasp what makes US audiences tick, or the degree of logic required in a Hollywood production. The Japanese are not as concerned with the plausibility of the plot and concentrate more on the themes and atmosphere; Americans need their movies to have at least an air of coherence and lead to an understandable conclusion. The computer-generated deer Rachel and Aidan encounter on the road, in a sequence meant to recall *The Ring*'s horses, might have been creepy in an Asian film, but here, they were obvious CGI and oddly out of place in the context of a traditional Hollywood film. But maybe Nakata isn't to blame. Perhaps it is more likely that DreamWorks executives, anxious to match the elements of the remake and of the original, instructed writer Ehren Kruger to add surreal scenes to recall the previous successes' style, misunderstanding their intrinsic logic.

The Ring Two cost $60 million to make and grossed around $75 million in US theatres, a

106 Commercials director Noam Murro was originally slated to direct, but dropped out, and *Donnie Darko* helmer Richard Kelly was for a while rumoured to take over.

decent profit, but slightly under the expectations of its producers, who were hoping to top the numbers of the remake.

It was only a matter of time before Nakata's other Japanese hit, *Dark Water*, received the Hollywood treatment. Award-winning director Walter Salles's remake opened in July in the US and the UK to mixed critics and disappointing box-office. Starring Jennifer Connelly and Tim Roth, the story was basically the same as the original, with the action transposed to New York City, in an apartment building so dreadfully ugly that it's hard to sympathise with the mother and child who decide to live there: after all, if they freely picked that place, they brought their troubles upon themselves! Gloomy and slow-paced, *Dark Water* focused on the social aspects of its story – the nasty divorce, the housing situation, the problems faced by a single mother – but unlike Nakata's original film, it fails to reconcile these issues with the supernatural side of the plot. The ghost is little more than a detail, a traditional spirit whose appearance is highly predictable and less dramatic than the building's bad plumbing system. Interestingly, the ending parallels *The Ring Two*: both movies emphasise the relationship between mother and child, and both feature a spirit trying to take the place of the kid and steal their mother's affection. *Dark Water* didn't recoup its $30 million investment with its US theatre run, leading some to think the J-Horror craze had ended.

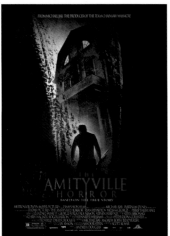

Dark Water. The Amityville Horror.

Three American classics were remade the same year, with results ranging from unnecessary (*The Amityville Horror*) to downright offensive (*The Fog*). Despite the fans' online protests every time a new title was announced, each one of these updates was eventually profitable, one of them even recovering its cost three times over in US theatres alone.

The remake of *The Amityville Horror* adds very little to the 1979 version, unless one takes into account the dozens of computer-generated effects which litter the film. Based on Jay Anson's 1977 book as well as Stuart Rosenberg's picture, and, like the other two sources also claimed, 'based on actual events', Scott Kosar's script followed the basic plot of the original: a young couple (Melissa George and Ryan Reynolds) buy the home of their dreams, only to find it is haunted by the spirits of the previous inhabitants, a family murdered in the house by one of its members. Director Andrew Douglas adds countless little shocks and ghostly apparitions, but forgets to create any tension or atmosphere: a shame for a filmmaker who claims to have drawn inspiration from Stanley Kubrick's *The Shining* and *Ring*. Bland but watchable, this Michael Bay production could have been an improvement upon the first film, which was itself a rather unimpressive effort, had it not chosen to go down the CGI and cheap scares route. Nevertheless, Douglas's *The Amityville Horror* was a hit ($64 million in US theatres on an $18 million budget), possibly for the same reason the original grossed $80 million in 1979: both were released at times of economic instability, when audiences could easily relate to the problems – destruction of property, possible financial disaster for the family – the protagonists faced. As Stephen King wrote about the original: 'I found myself wondering not if the Lutz clan would get out alive but if they had adequate homeowner's insurance … The main reason that people went to see it, I think, is that *The Amityville Horror* … is really a financial demolition derby.'[107]

Jaume Collet-Serra's *House of Wax*, remake of the 1953 Vincent Price classic, played it as safe as *The Amityville Horror* did, with poorer creative and commercial results. Replacing Price and his grown-up co-stars by the now typical bunch of good-looking twenty-somethings (Elisha Cuthbert and Chad Michael Murray leading the ensemble), and preferring flashy special effects to moody atmosphere, this uninspired update was mostly noted for the presence of media darling Paris Hilton in the cast, a bad omen if there ever was one. Released in May, it raked in $32 million in US theatres, $2 million more than its reported investment.

107 *Danse Macabre*, Stephen King, Hodder, 1981, p 170.
108 However, one key scene, set in flashback on the soon-to-be-ghostly ship, was cut and without this, the whole reason for the ghostly invasion is rendered incomprehensible. The scene can be found in the DVD extras.
109 'Interview: Rupert Wainwright, *The Fog*', Tom Charity, *Lovefilm*, 2005, http://www.lovefilm.co.uk/ features/detail.html?section_ name=interview&editorial_id=2635

As bad as *House of Wax* may have been, it paled in comparison with the atrocity that was Rupert Wainwright's *The Fog*, a real insult to contemporary moviegoers in general and horror fans in particular. Wainwright updated John Carpenter's distinctive electronic score with a hip pop rock soundtrack, changed the main characters into a bunch of personality-challenged pretty young things, and replaced the eerie and unfolding mystery with predictable, formulaic scares and bad computer-generated effects. The remake also tried to spell out every detail of the plot, making sure that the very immature audience it targeted would not be confused by the subtleties of the action[108]. With a budget eighteen times superior to the first film (inflation not taken into account), this hideous rehash still managed to be profitable, grossing over $29 million at the US box-office. As an excuse for the lack of energy and blandness of his PG-13 offence, Wainwright explained[109]: 'I think a lot of us did some re-examining after the Columbine high school shooting. In *Stigmata* we had a scene of Patricia slashing her wrists, and she shoved the knife right through the wrist. I remember at the time we were editing there was a news story about a girl in high school in England slashing her arms, and I looked at this scene and thought if one girl does that because of this movie it's not worth it. So I cut that voluntarily – toned it down. I think life imitates art much more than the other way round.' Too bad the filmmaker didn't take into account the hordes of despairing Carpenter fans who may well have contemplated murder or suicide watching his movie.

Big Budget = PG-13

While indies tried to exorcise the fear of a nation through extreme images, executives preferred, like Rupert Wainwright, to play it safe. Graphic violence was steadily on the rise in independent films, but nearly all the genre pictures produced by majors in 2005 were, like *The Fog*, rated PG-13. Hollywood had finally started backing pure horror features (and not supernatural thrillers, or action flicks such as *Van Helsing*), but their aim was to hit the widest possible target audience. The rating fit the style of a handful of productions (*The Exorcism of Emily Rose*, *The Skeleton Key*), but others (*Cursed*, *Boogeyman*) felt watered down.

Making a movie accessible to the largest demographic makes perfect sense for very big budget productions, when a high number of tickets must be sold to recoup the investment,

House of Wax. The Fog.

but the following films were made for comparably small amounts of money. Created in 1984 to allow the MPAA to warn parents that some material might be unsuitable for their children without having to slap the movie with an R, the PG-13 label was born after PG films such as *Dragonslayer* (1981), *Poltergeist* (1982) and *Indiana Jones and the Temple of Doom* (1984), filled with explicit violence (although of a fantastical nature), sparked fierce debates amongst parental organisations. But while ratings should be nothing more than an indication of the content of the movie, and not a comment on the quality of the picture or a goal filmmakers should strive to achieve, 'PG-13 horror' has been, since the early 2000s, synonymous with 'mindless

moneymaker' in the eyes of genre fans. The reason behind this is simple: instead of giving their story the amount of R-rated material it requires (for instance, a slasher or a zombie pic would generally need to be more explicit than a ghost film), producers often aim to tailor their plot to obtain a specific rating. This business-minded approach traditionally leads filmmakers to make their work follow a pre-established format and perpetuate stereotypes that studios assume constitute the basis for easy box-office success. In other words, if some movies are PG-13 by nature, others are PG-13 for pure economic considerations, and it's against this second category that horror fans rebel.

In the first category though, Iain Softley's *The Skeleton Key*, an old-fashioned gothic haunted house tale, is the perfect example of a story that didn't need any gore and violence to work. Set in New Orleans, it follows a private caregiver Caroline Ellis (Kate Hudson) who takes a job in an old mansion whose owner has been paralysed by a stroke. Caroline soon starts uncovering the dark past of the house, and suspects that the invalid man's wife has put a spell on him. With a good cast, beautiful sets and a strong screenplay by Ehren Kruger, featuring a coherent and surprising twist ending, *The Skeleton Key* could have become a classic, had it not been for its flat, by-the-numbers direction. Where a traditional, atmospheric approach, *à la The Others* (2001) or *The Innocents* (1961), would have been required, Softley shoots his film like a slasher, with unnecessary violin crescendos and jump-scares. Both the setting and the hoodoo-voodoo elements are also sadly underexploited; the house itself, a gorgeous plantation home, could have been used as a more predominant part of the story. With all these shortcomings, *The Skeleton Key* feels like a missed opportunity; a good and simple little story killed by its director's uninspired treatment.

The Exorcism of Emily Rose was another example of adequate PG-13 material. Spooky and intelligent, it features several creepy scenes of possession and plenty of supernatural shocks, without needing any gore to be effective.

Since William Friedkin unleashed the ultimate exorcism movie upon the world in 1973, demonic possessions have not been popular subjects in film, most likely because few filmmakers dared run the risk of seeing their movie compared to a timeless classic. Wainwright's *Stigmata* and Steven E de Souza's 2000 made-for-TV *Possessed*, starring Timothy Dalton, were amongst the few exceptions: neither was

The Skeleton Key. The Exorcism of Emily Rose.

110 *The Exorcism of Emily Rose* was only loosely based on the Anneliese Michel case; another movie, Hans-Christian Schmid's *Requiem*, came out a few months later and claimed to follow the facts closely. Despite winning some awards, this drama never received a wide release outside its home country, Germany.

very well received; and the *Exorcist* sequels/prequels themselves were never considered great successes. The curse of *The Exorcist*, however, ended with Scott Derrickson's *The Exorcism of Emily Rose*, a true story which cost a mere $20 million and returned $75 million in the States, 30 of which was reaped on its mid-September opening. Basing his film on the case of Anneliese Michel[110], a German teenager who died in 1976 after being the object of a church-approved ritual to free her from the demons that allegedly had taken hold of her, Derrickson and co-writer Paul Harris Boardman cleverly chose to structure their story around the trial of the priest who performed the exorcism and was accused of letting the young woman die. Anchoring the horrors of the possession in the cold reality of a courtroom not only gave the scary scenes a more dramatic tone, like a constant reminder that the events described actually happened, but it also invited viewers to question their own beliefs and their interpretation of the notion of freedom of religion. Would they have declared the priest guilty for attempting to save the girl with methods in accordance with his religion? The issue is at the core of the movie, giving it a depth until then unseen in a sub-genre notorious for its projectile vomiting and crucifix masturbations. Said Derrickson in a 2005 interview[111]: 'The movie is intended to stretch and provoke everyone who sees it, including Christians, including believers. It did that to me. That's one of the reasons why I thought it was a worthwhile story. When we got into the making of the movie, I thought, there is a way to construct this thing so that there's just no easy wrapping this movie up for anyone.' Despite horror fans' traditional dislike of all things religious, *The Exorcism of Emily Rose*'s mild, sophisticated chills struck a chord with the audience, prompting investors and observers to comment that PG-13 horror was far more profitable, and that R-rated horror was 'dead'. Its success however was surpassed a month later by the R-rated *Saw II*, and scary movies with stronger content were once again in demand.

Geoffrey Sax's *White Noise* starred Michael Keaton as Jonathan Rivers, a man trying to communicate with his recently deceased spouse through EVP (Electronic Voice Phenomenon, or voices in static). An intriguing idea based on a concept not often exploited in fiction, Keaton's return to the genre never tried very hard to frighten and ends up as an awkward mix of supernatural love story and cheap jump-scares, as if neither Sax nor writer Niall Johnson had been able to figure out what threat this white noise could possibly present. Mildly entertaining despite its lack of ingenuity, *White Noise* managed to gross over five times its $10 million budget during its January/February run in the US, and was followed in 2007 by an abysmal sequel, Patrick Lussier's *White Noise 2: The Light*, starring Nathan Fillion.

Unlike *The Skeleton Key*, *The Exorcism of Emily Rose* and possibly *White Noise*, *The Cave* is the kind of movie that could have benefited from a darker tone and more gruesome deaths. But would pursuing an R-rating really have helped this ridiculous underground creature feature to rise about its complete mediocrity? More action/adventure than real scary movie, Bruce Hunt's film is filled with clichés and incoherencies (the monsters in the cave have adapted to their environment and developed giant wings that scrape walls and ceilings when they fly), poorly edited, and instantly forgettable.

In the same vein as the terrible *They* (2002) and *Darkness Falls*, Stephen T Kay's *Boogeyman*, produced by Sam Raimi's Ghost House Pictures, was a ridiculous muddle of stereotypes, improbable situations and bad acting, and adequately described as 'aimed firmly at the teen market … light on gore and populated by pretty nobodies … A humourless trudge through haunted house clichés, it's unlikely to scare anyone old enough to get past the box office'[112]. Predictable and dull, it was nothing we hadn't seen a hundred times, but still managed to be a hit, nearly returning its $20 million investment on its opening weekend. A direct-to-DVD sequel came out in early 2008.

Cursed was the obvious result of studio meddling and ratings considerations. This werewolf story set in the glamorous world of TV and PR in Hollywood, starring Christina Ricci and Joshua Jackson, should have marked the celebrated return of genre legend Wes Craven, five years after his last entry in the *Scream* series. Instead, the movie mostly drew the attention of the press through its difficult production history, as Dimension, unhappy with Kevin Williamson's script,

White Noise. The Cave. Boogeyman.

111 '*The Exorcism of Emily Rose*: Scott Derrickson, Paul Harris Boardman, Laura Linney, Jennifer Carpenter', Steven D Greydanus, *Decent Films Guide*, 2005, http://www.decentfilms.com/sections/articles/emilyrose.html
112 *Boogeyman* Review, Paul Arendt, *BBC*, 28 February 2005, http://www.bbc.co.uk/films/2005/02/22/boogeyman_2005_review.shtml

Cursed.

ordered a reshoot of a large portion of the film, forcing Craven to recast some major roles. The company later re-cut the movie to obtain a lower rating than the R Craven was contractually asked to deliver. Consequently, *Cursed* feels like a truncated feature, with a few great ideas left undeveloped (an exploration of the lycanthrope myth, a whodunit to find the beast, an homage to Universal's *The Wolf Man* with the fortune teller of the opening scene), odd jokes thrown in at inappropriate moments, a post-modern outlook years after it went out of fashion, the world's ugliest werewolf transformation (all achieved through CGI) and worst of all, a complete lack of tension. Craven later admitted[113]: 'I'm very disappointed with *Cursed* … [It] was basically taken away from us and cut to PG-13 and ruined. It was two years of very difficult work and almost 100 days of shooting of various versions. Then at the very end, it was chopped up as the studio thought they could make more with a PG-13 movie, and trashed it. We were writing while we were shooting. It wasn't ready to film. We rewrote, recast and had two major reshoots … After a while, I regretted it was called *Cursed* because it was cursed … I thought it was completely disrespectful, and it hurt them too, and it was like they shot themselves in the foot with a shotgun.'

Thankfully, Craven would make a return to form a few months later with *Red Eye*, a thriller with Cillian Murphy and Rachel McAdams. 'It's important for me while I have this opportunity to do other things, to do them,' Craven commented at the time[114]. 'And when they least expect it I'll come back and scare the pants off people. I've been doing horror for thirty-five years and I just feel like if I did any more right now I'd be repeating myself. The script of *Red Eye* came along at the right time, it was unplanned, I hadn't heard about it but I thought for years about making a thriller someday and there it was.'

The only notable R-rated big budget production that wasn't a remake that year, John Polson's *Hide and Seek*, probably owed its rating to the dark nature of its themes rather than to an excess of graphic violence. When his wife commits suicide, Dr David Callaway (Robert De Niro) and his daughter Emily (Dakota Fanning) move to the countryside to leave their painful past behind. But when the troubled little girl finds herself a new imaginary friend, spooky things start to happen that make her father wonder if her new companion exists only in her head. Tame and shamelessly derivative, Polson's film is the latest in a line of *The Sixth Sense*-inspired movies built entirely around an incoherent and disappointing twist ending. Needless to say, the critics did not appreciate it; but as is often the case, no number of negative reviews could stop it from becoming a minor commercial success and it grossed $51 million – $21 million more than its reported cost – during its US theatrical release.

113 Interview with the *New York Post*, quoted in 'Wes Craven Disappointed with *Cursed*', 2005, *Movies Online*, http://www.moviesonline.ca/movienews_3495.html
114 Interview with the author, Brussels, Belgium, October 2005.

'The dead shall inherit the earth' (*Land of the Dead*)

The success of Zack Snyder's *Dawn of the Dead* not only encouraged studios to invest in more remakes, it also underlined once again the popularity of the zombie sub-genre. In a time of controversial wars and nearly apocalyptic natural disasters, the living dead, a perfect allegory for the human condition, would still be the creature of choice.

This is not to say, however, that every zombie movie would be a self-important, politically charged, message piece, although a few, as will be seen later, did fall into this category. Dave Gebroe's *Zombie Honeymoon* for instance was a simple love story between a young bride and her groom who dies under strange circumstances during their honeymoon and comes back to life moments later as a flesh-eating but still enamoured ghoul. This cute, character-driven low-budget drama, reminiscent of Yuzna's *Return of the Living Dead 3* (1993) minus the extreme gore, was at once touching, sweet and tragic. Inspired by a real-life event – the death of Gebroe's brother-in-law – the movie is the result of influences ranging from the obvious: *Night of the Living Dead* (1969) and Lucio Fulci's *Zombie Flesh Eaters* (*Zombi 2*, 1979), to the more unusual: Michelangelo Antonioni's and John Cassavetes's films. Financed independently, it was championed by Larry Fessenden and John Landis, who both saw a rough cut of the feature and allowed Gebroe to use their names to raise the money needed to complete the picture. Landis even gave the young director a quote to use in his promotion: 'The first truly romantic flesh-eating corpse movie.' *Zombie Honeymoon* toured festivals in 2005 and 2006, before getting a DVD release in the US in February 2006.

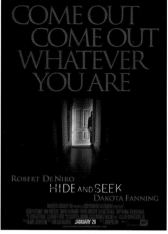

Ireland/UK co-production *Boy Eats Girl*, directed by Stephen Bradley and starring Samantha Mumba and David Leon, was also, to a degree, a zombie love story, with an added touch of comedy. Nominated for five Irish Film and Television Awards, it came out in its home country in September, but wouldn't get a DVD release in the US until January 2008.

Tobe Hooper's *Mortuary*, about a single mother (Denise Crosby) and her kids (Dan Byrd and Stephanie Patton) who move into a funeral home in a small Californian town and realise that the place hides some dark secrets, only offered some very mild scares, despite a great setting and an intriguing beginning.

Jeremy Kasten's *All Souls Day: Dia de los Muertos* takes a very literal approach to the holiday, turning it into a real *dia de los muertos* as the dead rise in a cursed Mexican town and attack a couple of Americans stranded in the wrong place at the wrong time. 'Knowingly tacky'[115], as one critic accurately described it, Kasten's movie may have flaws, most of which are linked to its low budget and cheesy screenplay, but it remains an amusing and silly little zombie flick, made with obvious love, enthusiasm and fondness for the genre.

Red Eye. Hide and Seek. Zombie Honeymoon.

Which is more than could be said of *Day of the Dead 2: Contagium*, a sequel in name only to the Romero classic, and which could well be the cheapest-looking, stupidest entry in a sub-genre that has seen its share of turkeys. Directed by Ana Clavell and James Glenn Dudelson (although it's hard to believe two people were needed to create this dud), *Day of the Dead 2: Contagium* was produced by Taurus Entertainment, the distributor which owned the rights to *Day of the Dead*, but none of the cast or crew members of the original were involved. So bad it's funny, it was universally ridiculed by the horror community, shocked that such an atrocity could have been committed under the name of this popular series of films.

George Romero himself returned in 2005 with his long-awaited fourth entry in his living

115 Scott Weinberg, *DVD Talk*, 17 January 2006, http://www.dvdtalk.com/reviews/19708/all-souls-day-dia-de-los-muertos

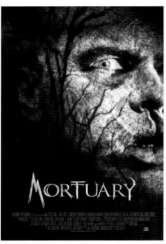

Boy Eats Girl. Mortuary. All Souls Day.

dead saga. But while the aforementioned films purely meant to entertain and shock, Romero's *Land of the Dead* was a bleaker, more seriously ambitious attempt at political satire. Shot on a much bigger budget (an estimated $17 million) than the previous ones and produced by Universal, it marked the first time the filmmaker was contractually bound to deliver an R-rated cut of a zombie film for theatrical release (the earlier films had been released unrated), a fact which, combined with the unusual scope of the project, caused something of a stir amongst diehard fans, even though a director's cut was later released on DVD and the studio let Romero have the freedom to make the movie he'd envisioned.

Set years after the beginning of the plague, *Land of the Dead* depicts a world where zombies have been left to roam deserted towns and landscapes, evolving and developing a new consciousness, while the living find refuge in walled-off cities, where the wealthy live in tall buildings to protect themselves against the chaos of the streets. In this stratified society, the dead want to break into the city, the poor want access to the skyscrapers, and the rich are ruled by evil capitalist Kaufman (Dennis Hopper). Romero uses this new division of society as a not-too-subtle metaphor for the class struggle between the haves and the have-nots, and perhaps more specifically, for the situation of illegal immigrants in post-9/11 America; Hopper's bad guy is intended as a barely hidden caricature of George W Bush himself. The writer/director also further explores the underlying themes of the three previous films: racism, sexism and consumerism. 'I wrote the first draft of this film right before 9/11,' he declared at the time of the release[116]. 'Literally I sent it out to studios three days before 9/11. Everybody then wanted to make friendly little lollipop movies, so I had to stick it on the shelf for a while. Then after the invasion, I took it off the shelf and I said, "Gee, this is even more interesting now!" To make it sort of address this new normal … So I was a little fast and loose with some of the referencing, you know the post-9/11 stuff in it. But I think it makes it a little stronger.'

Dawn of the Dead and *Day of the Dead* introduced the idea of zombies as the most human monsters in contemporary cinema; *Land of the Dead* takes this concept a step further, by inviting the audience to root for the dead against the decadent and greedy living. The creatures have started to think and use tools and weapons, an evolution initiated by Bub, the lab rat from *Day of the Dead* (though of course the speaking dead of *The Return of the Living Dead* had shown the way in 1985); led by Big Daddy (the undead saviour of the oppressed, played by Eugene Clark), they make for the first time the conscious decision to invade the city and take back what used to belong to them, in a Marxist revolution/Fall of the Roman Empire-type of climax. An intriguing – if contradictory – idea, the thinking zombie is the very reason *Land of the Dead* doesn't quite work as a horror movie. Lost in his social commentary, Romero seems to have lost sight of the fact that once the dead only target the bad guys, and there is no one alive to sympathise with, they are no longer a source of dread and horror. Simply put, *Land of the Dead* is not scary. Sure, there are good special effects and action scenes aplenty, but the creeping terror which pervaded *Night of the Living Dead* and its sequels is completely absent here. Also

116 'George Romero talks about *Land of the Dead*', Rebecca Murray, *About.com*, June 2005, http://movies. about.com/od/landofthedead/a/ deadgr062105.htm

disturbing is the fact that with its zombies and rebels causing explosions and attacking the population all over the city, all for the greater good, Romero isn't far from suggesting terrorism and civil wars could be adequate responses to difficult political situations.

Land of the Dead made over $20 million at the US box-office: not a giant hit, but still more than any of Romero's previous zombie films. Would it mean that the goremeister would seek a bigger budget for his sequel? The answer, three years later, would surprise many.

The Boys are Back in Town

George Romero and Wes Craven were not the only praised filmmakers to make a comeback that year. Created by Mick Garris, a director-driven TV show titled *Masters of Horror* premiered in the second half of 2005 on Showtime in America. For its first season, the series comprised thirteen 60-minute episodes, each directed by a master of the genre. The rules were simple: every mini-feature had to be shot in Vancouver (with one exception, Takashi Miike's *Imprint*, filmed in Tokyo), in ten days, with largely the same crew and on the same limited budget, without constraints or censorship on the content. The format – and the opportunity to work outside the usual Hollywood boundaries – attracted many great names, and season one saw Stuart Gordon, Don Coscarelli, John Landis, Joe Dante, Dario Argento, Lucky McKee, John McNaughton, Tobe Hooper, William Malone, Larry Cohen, John Carpenter and Takashi Miike join Garris. The choice was based 'partially [on] relationships, partially on personal taste and partially on who the financiers would approve,' Garris, the master of the Masters, explains[117].

'For years I wanted to do an anthology series,' he continues. 'Most of these directors are friends of mine and we've been friends for a long time. John Landis and I tried to get an anthology series going, Clive Barker and I almost had one going at HBO but it was just a more general idea then.' The concept became more accurate once Garris started organising regular dinners for

Land of the Dead. Masters of Horror: Imprint.

117 Interview with the author, Turin, Italy, November 2005.

105

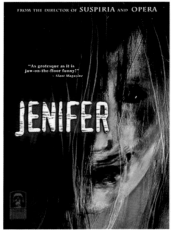

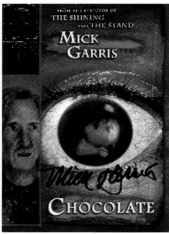

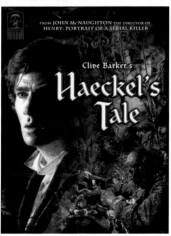

Masters of Horror episodes: Jenifer, Chocolate, Deer Woman, Haeckel's Tale, and Dreams in the Witch-House.

his filmmaker pals. 'We were spending time together and having fun together in social events every couple of months or so, then the idea sort of crystallised that these are the people who should be doing it. Since we were jokingly calling ourselves the masters of horror,' – a name Guillermo Del Toro is credited for – 'it just seemed right to give voice to the people who really know this stuff and haven't really had the chance recently to show what they're really capable of doing at their best.'

With horror movies breaking records at the box-office, the timing could not have been better. Landis adds, 'What happened was that at the third dinner Mick said, "Would you guys, if I could get the money, would you do a film together?" And everyone said sure, but he said we had to commit to him because that's how he would get the money. So we agreed. And he got the money so fast, everyone was surprised!'

Garris signed with distribution company IDT (which at the time owned Anchor Bay Entertainment) and cable network Showtime, as they both guaranteed total freedom to the filmmakers, a brave decision considering the outrage and controversy that followed singer Janet Jackson's 'wardrobe malfunction' at the Super Bowl halftime show in February 2004. Showtime did however later decide not to air Miike's *Imprint*, a particularly intense episode dealing with torture and abortion, but the film was released uncut on DVD.

The greatest consequence of the absence of studio process was undoubtedly the amazing variety of the shows, which ranged from comedy (Landis's *Deer Woman*) to sex and gore (Argento's *Jenifer*), supernatural thriller (Garris's *Chocolate*) to pure slasher (Coscarelli's *Incident On and Off a Mountain Road*), post-apocalyptic (Hooper's *Dance of the Dead*) to period horror (McNaughton's *Haeckel's Tale*). Says Garris: 'Each of these guys has their own vision and we encourage that. On shows like *Tales from the Crypt*, they wanted them all to have the same signature; we wanted the opposite of that. That's why all of them seem very personal, whether it's just a personal style, or a different theme. We really encouraged that; we told everyone from the outset all we want is smart and scary. So you get different levels and layers and approaches and I think that's the biggest success we've had with the show.'

As a result, fans and online critics didn't necessarily agree on which episodes were the best of the series. The only film that was shown to critics was the first one to air, Coscarelli's *Incident On and Off a Mountain Road*, and the reviews were positive. A successful blend of slasher and survival based on a short story by *Bubba Ho-tep* author Joe R Lansdale, it follows the confrontation between a young woman (played by Bree Turner) and a killer called Moonface (John DeSantis). 'I'd heard roughly what the other episodes were about,' Coscarelli recalls[118], 'and I don't think that story-wise I had a competition there because it seemed like their stories were very different from anything that I was doing. But there was no question that I was curious to know what [the others] were doing, especially once I started to see the resources we would have and how the others were going to solve the problems that I was going through. Actually once I started shooting I was more like, good luck to them! It was difficult, [especially since mine] was more ambitious physically, it required chasing and running in lots of shots. The other episodes used more dialogue, it's cheaper and easier.'

Dario Argento's *Jenifer*, about a police officer (Steven Weber) who saves a disfigured woman (Carrie Fleming) and slowly falls under her spell, was another fan favourite. Based on a story published in *Creepy Comics*, it was the only episode to have been the object of a few cuts. 'I had

to leave out some images, but not too much,' Argento says. 'Not like in my other films where people would cut fifteen minutes out. What's missing is the close-up of Jenifer giving oral sex and biting a man's penis off.'[119]

Garris's *Chocolate*, in which a man starts experiencing sensations felt by a woman he's never met, as in a telepathic spell, is probably the strangest of the lot. Somewhere between thriller, murder mystery and romance, the episode, based on Garris's own short story, was inspired by 'a dream I had once where I experienced what it was like to murder someone and it was as brutal as in the film, it was a knife murder and I felt the blood running down my arms as the lead character describes ... It was also shortly after I met the woman who became my wife and it deepened me. That's how that story came to be, the story of a guy who experiences a woman from the inside out and is embarrassed at his shallowness in contrast with her depth.'

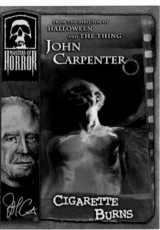

Masters of Horror: Homecoming. Masters of Horror: Cigarette Burns.

But the most controversial of all was Joe Dante's *Homecoming*, another example of the living dead being used as social satire, in which US soldiers who died in the war come back to vote against the president's re-election. Sacrificing scares, character development and even storyline to follow its political agenda, the film was praised by some for its courage, and criticised by others for its self-importance, its lack of subtlety, and sometimes even for its poor taste. 'The zombie genre is a fairly disreputable one and I didn't want this to seem like we were exploiting the people who have died,' Dante explains[120]. 'We wanted to be respectful as much as possible and to be on the side of the soldiers who were doing their jobs even though it's I think wrong. And maybe they thought wrong but what are you going to do? They draft you, you go out there and they give you a gun, are you going to say you don't want to shoot anybody? So we went overboard to try and make the zombies have some dignity.' No matter what one might think of the quality and relevance of *Homecoming*, its very existence exemplified the degree to which the horror movies, voluntarily or not, reflect the concerns of the time they were made. 'There's politics in all (these episodes),' Dante continues. 'George Romero's *Night of the Living Dead* was

118 Interview with the author, Turin, Italy, November 2005

119 Interview with the author, Turin, Italy, November 2005. The missing footage can be found in the extra features of the DVD.

120 Interview with the author, Turin, Italy, November 2005.

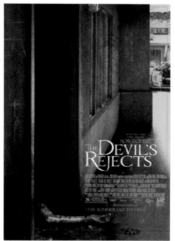

The Devil's Rejects.

made during Vietnam and it's impossible to watch the movie and not feel that. I think that's true of every era, every story; all had an underpinning of the anxieties of the age. The Cuban missile crisis may have been worse than this age but considering the things that have happened in the past five years nobody really feels safe anywhere and I think that's one of the reasons why horror movies are so popular.'

Season one of *Masters of Horror* was a success and a second batch of thirteen episodes was soon in the works.

Tales of Murder, Mayhem and Revenge

Not quite a Master yet, but hailed as one of the genre's new hopes, Rob Zombie continued his love song to seventies filmmaking and his exploration of the dark side of rural America with *The Devil's Rejects*, a sequel to 2003's *House of 1000 Corpses*. Produced and distributed by Lionsgate for a reported $7 million, *The Devil's Rejects* follows the murderous Firefly family as they escape the siege of their home and are chased by Sheriff Wydell, whose brother was killed by the family in the first film.

Less cartoonish than *House of 1000 Corpses*, *The Devil's Rejects* is closer to a road movie or a western than to horror, but is on the whole a much more accomplished film. If Zombie used his first movie to experiment with camera moves, editing, colour and sound, and ended up with a 90-minute music video, his sequel on the other hand is restrained, linear, and powerful. With a southern rock soundtrack and snappy, quotable dialogue which unlike *House of 1000 Corpses*'s, doesn't come down to a succession of one-liners, *The Devil's Rejects* has a realistic feel that the writer/director's previous movie lacked, yet keeps a certain sense of humour and an awareness of its B movie roots.

The main element that divided critics and viewers alike was the level of graphic violence on display. The movie follows the Firefly gang as they abduct, torture, humiliate and eventually kill a group of innocents in a motel, and the realism of the situation, coupled with the fact that the killers are the most developed and interesting characters, shocked and disgusted many. *Empire* critic Kim Newman wrote[121]: 'It's uncomfortably the work of someone who thinks mass murder is cool and has no feeling for regular humans, but makes room for actors who were in all Zombie's favourite '70s horrors and recreates the exploitation vibe of the decade in sticky style.' Indeed, while Zombie fights the notion that *The Devil's Rejects* conveyed a message or took sides[122], there is little doubt that it is the villains he is enamoured with, and everything from their repartee to the slow-motion flashbacks of the end sequence shows that he expects the viewers to feel for them. No surprise then if this amorality antagonised a large segment of the audience: few could sympathise with such loathsome anti-heroes. Still, *The Devil's Rejects* marked a giant step forward in Zombie's screenwriting and directing prowess, and even critic Roger Ebert, traditionally not a big fan of 'murder, mayhem and revenge', as the tagline put it, gave it three stars, stating that 'a kind of heedless zeal transforms its horrors … There is actually some good writing and acting going on here, if you can step back from the material enough to see it.'[123] Offensive or not, the very fact that a

Saw II.

seventies-style exploitation film could get so much attention was an accomplishment in itself, and horror crowds praised its maker for his uncompromising vision. As a reader wrote to *Fangoria*[124], 'Thank God for Rob Zombie … for giving us true fans what we've been waiting to see for some time now. Let's try and think of some original horror – and get rid of all the PG-13 bullcrap!'

Released in the middle of the US summer, *The Devil's Rejects* recouped its cost over its opening weekend, debuting at number eight at the box office, and grossed an additional $10 million by the end of its theatrical run: a decent performance, but not the hit its investors had come to expect after *House of 1000 Corpses*. The relative failure of Zombie's film, combined with the success of *The Exorcism of Emily Rose*, led some observers to believe that enthusiasm for R-rated horror had already waned.

But *Saw II*'s $31 million opening, a few days before Halloween, would once again prove that adult scares would not go out of fashion so easily. Directed by Darren Lynn Bousman and written by Bousman and Leigh Whannell, this second instalment revolves around shady detective Eric Matthews (Donnie Wahlberg), who must save a group of people – including his own son – from the shelter where Jigsaw (Tobin Bell) has imprisoned them, before they die from the effects of a nerve gas.

Nowhere near as inventive as the original, *Saw II* fleshes out the character of Jigsaw and attempts to add twists and surprises, but concentrates on such uncharismatic protagonists that the movie's main appeal ends up being the gruesome traps the prisoners must face to find the antidote to the gas. Upping the gore and body count, like most horror sequels tend to do, Bousman's first contribution to the series is entertaining, but lacks the suspense and mystery of James Wan's creation. Still, developing the cancer-ridden killer's motivations and Amanda's backstory were interesting moves the next sequels would also build on. 'For me, [*Saw II*] wasn't so much the continuation of the story, but more about the character of Jigsaw we had created,' Wan, who remained involved in a supervising capacity, says of this follow-up[125]. 'I felt like

121 Kim Newman, *Empire*, 2005, http://www.empireonline.com/ reviews/ReviewComplete. asp?FID=11276

122 'I don't really want to say anything because I like leaving movies up to everyone's interpretation. I don't really like being force-fed anyone's ideas on anything, ever': 'Interview: Rob Zombie', Carlo Cavagna, *About Film*, August 2005, http://www.aboutfilm.com/features/ devilsrejects/zombie.htm

123 Roger Ebert, *Chicago Sun-Times*, 22 July 2005, http://rogerebert. suntimes.com/apps/pbcs.dll/ article?AID=/20050721/REVIEWS/ 50712001/1023

124 Anthony DiFilippo in 'Postal Zone', *Fangoria* 247, October 2005, p 10.

125 Email interview with the author, April 2005.

Satan's Little Helper.

we had come up with a really interesting and flawed villain and that the sequels should be an exploration of this character.'

Horror aficionados flocked to theatres for *Saw II* that October, but another Halloween treat awaited those who stayed at home. Jeff Lieberman's *Satan's Little Helper*, his first genre feature since the 1981 slasher *Just Before Dawn*, tells the story of 9-year-old Douglas Whooly (Alexander Brickel) who dresses up on Halloween as the eponymous character from fictional videogame *Satan's Little Helper*, and meets a man dressed as Satan burying a body in a front yard. Thinking the murderer is only pretending, the kid invites him home to play …

A subtle and wonderfully subversive comment on the influence of fiction on children's perception of the world and on the power and dangers of Halloween, *Satan's Little Helper* is as much a black comedy as it is a horror film. While some of its simplest scenes are genuinely disturbing and there is a real sense of suspense throughout, it's the cynical way Lieberman confronts the child's innocent naivety with the killer's actions that really stands out. Set in a typical American town and filmed with an old-fashioned approach which makes it seem almost dateless, the action could take place anywhere and the fact that many of the murders occur in daylight and in plain sight, in a peaceful and familiar setting, makes the writer/director's message all the more chilling. In a post-9/11, post-Columbine America, where each neighbour could be a homicidal maniac and every house hide a terrorist, Halloween may appear to be a hazardous institution; but if at first Lieberman's tale seems to confirm this notion, it also stresses the importance of the holiday. 'I always say that 364 days in the year, most people wear costumes,' the filmmaker explains[126], 'and only one day are they not in costumes, and that's on Halloween. They allow themselves one day a year to show who they really are, and they can't lie. People are always so quick to try and cancel Halloween, they're always saying, don't trick or treat, you're selling kids the devil, all that sort of nonsense; as far as I'm concerned, I'm absolutely positively sure that there is no guy with a tail or whatever the hell they try to force-feed you about the

126 Interview with the author, Brussels, Belgium, March 2005.

devil. The more they say you can't have Halloween, the more I want to endorse my kids to make Halloween the biggest deal. When I was a kid, it was smaller than Valentine's Day as far as popularity and importance; but now, as far as money that's being spent, it's second only to Christmas. I just want to live long enough to see it become number one. And it will, it's human nature; people feel liberated on Halloween.'

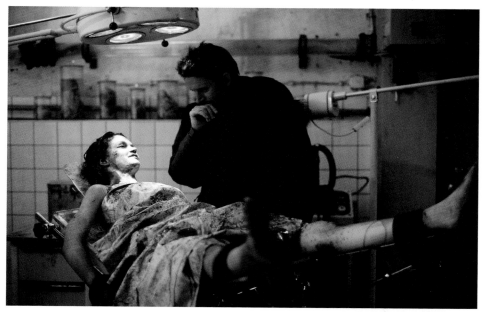

Symbolising both the danger and fun of the holiday, Joshua Annex is brilliant as the silent Satan Man, but if his performance is convincing, credit must also be given to his amazing mask, which emphasises the comical and scary aspects of his character. 'I knew that the irony of the movie had to also come from the mask,' Lieberman says. 'The mask was going to represent the whole movie; he has a big grin and yet he's not grinning. Depending on what he's doing he has all these different expressions.' The only downside is that the movie takes a more conventional turn in its last ten minutes and ends almost like a traditional slasher.

Surprisingly few horror movies have managed to capture the spirit of Halloween. As funny, irreverent and chilling as the holiday itself, *Satan's Little Helper* is the best and wittiest homage any nostalgic trick-or-treater could ask for.

'Face your deepest fear' (*The Descent*)

Just like its United States counterpart, European horror kept growing steadily, especially in the United Kingdom where no less than four (or five including Irish zom-com *Boy Eats Girl*) features would leave their mark on the genre …

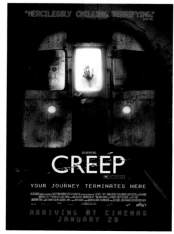

Creep.

First out was newcomer Christopher Smith's *Creep*, about a girl (Franka Potente) trapped at night in the London Underground system and chased by a mysterious killer. Starting off as a thrilling ride through familiar locations, the first half of the film exploits Londoners' traditional distrust for their transport system with its deserted, dimly lit stations, aggressive commuters and useless security officers. But the intrigue and atmosphere soon give way to a more classic slasher structure once the lead girl finds herself in the creature's lair and from that point on, *Creep* not only abandons all hope for a logical explanation, but also bases its chills on gruesomeness and jumps only. It works – the movie does deliver a few scares – but the general impression is that Smith didn't take full advantage of the setting and premise of his story.

Underground dwellers could also be found in Neil Marshall's *The Descent*, in which six girls on a spelunking trip in the Appalachian Mountains get themselves lost in an as-yet unexplored cave system, and discover they are not alone.

Starring relative unknowns (Shauna McDonald, Natalie Mendoza, Saskia Mulder, Nora-Jane Noone, MyAnna Buring and Alex Reid) as the 'six chicks with picks', *The Descent* is one of those rare horror movies that almost everyone, critics and audience members alike, appreciated. Exploiting to the full the scariest aspects of the story's unusual location, Marshall played both on the viewers' fear of the dark and on their claustrophobia, the scene where one of the girls gets stuck in a narrow tunnel ranking amongst the most nerve-racking in recent genre history. 'I remember when I was ten years old I went on a school trip in a mine,' Marshall recalls[127]. 'We all gathered together and the guide said, I want you to turn all your torches off, and for the first time in my life I experienced pitch black. It's not like when you're at home and the lights

127 Interview with the author, Brussels, Belgium, March 2006.

are off but you have street light coming in or the stars or whatever; it's pitch black. You can move your hand in front of your face and you can't see anything. It made me cling to my torch; out in the world it is just a torch but in there it's your whole life.' To recreate this experience and give a sense of the darkness of the environment, the director asked Director of Photography Sam McCurdy to only light the screen with the torches and flares the characters carry with them down the cave, and this technique certainly enhances the horror and isolation of the lost spelunkers' situation.

The gore is plentiful and the special effects, courtesy of Special Makeup Effects Designer Paul Hyett, are convincing, but more than the violence or the storyline, it's the entirely female cast which garnered the most attention. 'Part of the idea was to make this horror movie more accessible to women, having made a very masculine movie with *Dog Soldiers*, even having the word "soldiers" in the title was enough to put women off seeing that movie; and yet, it didn't make the film any less accessible or acceptable to men. A lot of people didn't even think about it, or question it until after the film was over. Others did pick up on it right away and immediately began to read things into it: the whole film is anti-male, or anti-female, a feminist doctrine about a journey into the subconscious, or even a journey through the female body, or that it's about death and re-birth and so on. I love the idea that people chose to analyse the movie and take meaning from it, and I'm fascinated by some of the theories they come up with. I think it brought so much attention simply because it was unusual and unexpected in the genre, which just goes to show how little some people think or know about genre film-making. It's been breaking down social barriers, examining important issues, and generally pushing the envelope of cinema since cinema began. As such it seems surprising that making an all-female action horror movie in 2005 should be such a big deal …'[128]

The Descent.

With glowing reviews and excellent advance word, *The Descent* seemed set to become a major hit but fate – and a handful of suicide-bombers – had decided otherwise. 'We'd had a premiere and party for *The Descent* on the night of 6 July,' Marshall explains. 'I awoke the next morning to find London in chaos, and several of my friends unaccounted for. As it turned out everyone was fine, but for a while one of the actors was missing in King's Cross (near where the bombs had exploded on the Underground system), and my editor had taken the tube directly ahead of one of the trains that blew up. That was the closest call. Throughout the day news filtered in that the bus that blew up had had a poster for my film emblazoned on its side, and that the only thing remaining was Jamie Graham's quote from Total Film: 'Outright terror!' Several newspapers and TV crew latched onto this as being significant in some way. One news channel even reported that it was somehow in bad taste that the poster had been there at all! As if we'd stuck it on the bus after it blew up or something. It was insane, and certainly not the kind of publicity we needed the day before the film opened. The following day, 8 July, people were still being pulled out of the mangled wreckage of the tube trains, both the living and the dead. With people really trapped underground, literally beneath their feet, the cinema-going public were in no mood to go and see a harrowing film about people being trapped underground. *The Descent* did a fraction of the business it was expected to do that weekend.' Exorcising one's fears through a work of fiction is one thing; showing scary scenes that remind viewers directly of close real-life horrors is another entirely.

128 Interview with the author, London, UK, May 2008.

Still, Marshall's movie was a minor success in the UK, and performed extremely well on DVD. In the United States, Lionsgate released it over a year later. 'The reason for the vast difference between the UK opening and the US opening is simple: *The Cave*. We knew we had a degree of competition from this rival cave-based horror movie, and we also knew it had a much bigger budget than we did. What we didn't know at the time was how bad it actually was, but hey. In the UK, we worked hard and fast and managed to get *The Descent* into cinemas several months ahead of *The Cave*. In the US, Lionsgate had only recently come on board and couldn't possibly get their promotional campaign together in time, so they wanted to put as much distance as possible between us and *The Cave*, which had opened in both the UK and US in August 2005. Lionsgate screened the movie for the first time in the US at Sundance in January 2006. Following the buzz from that event, I attended the annual Comic-Con in San Diego in July to do several days of press and publicity before the film opened across the US on 4 August.' Lionsgate also decided, with Marshall's agreement, to trim the ending of the movie for its theatrical release, after it tested higher without the added bleakness of the last few seconds of the original cut.

Grossing over $26 million in US theatres and an estimated $60 million worldwide, *The Descent* would be followed by a sequel directed by editor Jon Harris in 2009, and opened the doors of Hollywood to Neil Marshall. Hailed as the saviour of British horror or, as one *Fangoria* cover had it[129], 'horror's new hope', the writer/director would soon explore another genre with his third feature, the post-apocalyptic action thriller *Doomsday*. Needless to say, Marshall was happy that the poster and its tagline ('Survive this!') didn't appear on any London buses when it came out in 2008 ...

Another filmmaker who had appeared on the horror radar with a werewolf movie made his comeback the same year. Canadian director John Fawcett's new movie *The Dark*, coincidentally the same title under which *The Descent* had originally been developed, was filmed in the UK in the summer of 2004, and starred Maria Bello and Sean Bean as a couple whose daughter vanishes on the beach during their stay in Wales. Another girl shows up in her place and tells them she's been dead for decades.

Based on ancient Welsh legends and on a 1994 novel, *Sheep*, by Simon Maginn, *The Dark* starts off as an atmospheric chiller set in gorgeous coastal landscapes, but its plot, heavy on spooky mythology, quickly becomes muddled, and the resolution is unrewarding. Fawcett offers some interesting scenes, like the flashback to a group suicide from a cliff, but between the confusing twists, silly final act and *The Ring*-like scares (with sheep instead of horses), viewers are likely to lose interest fast.

The Descent. The Last Horror Movie.

The same could be said about Julian Richards's *The Last Horror Movie*, which, once the novelty of the concept – a serial killer films and comments on his crimes, and distributes the tapes through a video rental store – wears off, becomes somewhat tedious. As graphic and coldly realistic as, say, *Murder-Set-Pieces*, Richards's film is nevertheless clever – although not as clever as the similarly themed 1992 Belgian black comedy *Man Bites Dog* (*C'est Arrivé Près de Chez Vous*) – and relies heavily on the charisma of its lead, Kevin Howarth. Unlike *Murder-Set-Pieces*, *The Last Horror Movie* didn't have much trouble getting released after a successful festival run, and even won several awards, including the Jury Prize for Best UK Feature at the 2003 Raindance Film Festival, the Critics' Award at the 2004 Fantasporto, and the Best Actor and Best Feature awards at the 2004 New York City Horror Film Festival. But ironically for a film which contains a strong commentary on the link between on-screen and real-life violence,

The Ordeal.

it was later pulled by its UK distributor Tartan Video after a teenage murderer cited it as an influence when tried in 2007.

'What's the worst that could happen?' (*The Ordeal*)

Belgian cinema is better known for its social realism than for its horror movies – *Man Bites Dog* (1992) or *Rabid Grannies* (*Les Mémés Cannibales*, 1988) being amongst the few exceptions – but first-time director Fabrice du Welz managed the seemingly impossible task of getting a genre flick financed in his home country. *The Ordeal* (*Calvaire*) revolves around Marc Stevens (Laurent Lucas), an itinerant singer trapped on Christmas Eve in the house of deranged innkeeper Bartel (Jackie Berroyer), who slowly convinces himself that Stevens is actually his estranged wife. The plot puts an unusual twist on the traditional (and decidedly popular) stranded-in-the-countryside subgenre, and the tone of the movie, between reality and dream, horror and black comedy, is as strange and surreal as the storyline. Obvious influences include *The Texas Chain Saw Massacre* (1974), *Straw Dogs* (1971) or *Deliverance* (1972), but du Welz adds his own brand of dark humour and a cold, dream-like quality which contrast strongly with the realism of Hooper, Peckinpah or Boorman's films.

With no real suspense or resolution to speak of, *The Ordeal* mostly relies on its offbeat secondary characters, its stunning cinematography and its surreal atmosphere. 'I grew up watching Italian, American and British horror movies,' du Welz explains[130], 'and I always thought my first film would be horror. But I wanted to experiment, use the clichés of the genre and twist them in another direction. I didn't allow myself to use music for example, because most horror movies rely so much on their soundtrack. I wanted to have an unpleasant passive victim and a more interesting psychopath the audience could like. I also wanted to shoot in an area I knew well, the Belgian Ardennes, while most of the time French-speaking genre directors tend to be influenced by American movies for the setting. I tried to play with the rules of the genre and

130 Interview with the author, Brussels, Belgium, April 2005.

bend them in an unusual way, but in a familiar environment.'

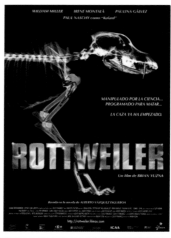

The Ordeal premiered in Cannes in May 2004, but it would take nearly a year to be released in Belgium. Too arty for the horror crowd and too disturbing for arthouse theatres, this genre-bending mix of survival, exploitation and dark comedy was as hard to market as it was to categorise. 'The structure of the whole film is peculiar. I quickly realised that this was a problem for some people; if you're expecting a classic three-act story you're going to be disappointed, and many criticised the ending, saying it lacked pay-off of some sort. But my goal was to convey feelings. The first ten minutes of the film look like a low-budget handicam TV reality show; the exposition sequence is very long and it all goes downhill from there, you slowly get into Bartel's head. And the movie's look, the colours, the lighting emphasize this progression: Bartel's house is lit like in a Clint Eastwood movie, with no source of light inside the house. By contrast the ending is more abstract, less saturated; the landscapes are more present and impressive.'

The Ordeal enjoyed a certain cult recognition and writer/director du Welz would go on to film a second, bigger-budget feature, Vinyan, in 2008.

Fantastic Factory Strikes Back

While 2005 was an exceptionally good year for horror productions in the United Kingdom and Belgium, Spain, through Filmax's Fantastic Factory, delivered three films of unequal quality.

Released in its home country in June, Brian Yuzna's *Rottweiler* is without a doubt the worst of the lot. Strangely paced and utterly absurd, this odd story of a half-robot, half-dog creature unfortunately marked a low in Yuzna's directing career.

Luis de la Madrid's *The Nun* (*La Monja*) was an equally silly, but slightly more entertaining effort. Focusing on a dead nun who seeks revenge on the school girls who drowned her, this ghost story may not be scary or very well-written, but it is an amusing and, like all Fantastic Factory productions, beautifully shot little film. 'The story started as a little joke that circulated in the Filmax office; in the international department somebody one day started talking about a killer nun,' de la Madrid says[131]. 'People found it interesting and funny and elaborated on it as a joke. They asked Jaume Balagueró (*Darkness* (2002)) to develop a story based on the killer nun. The basic idea was that some girls in a high school had killed a nun and that the nun was coming back twenty years later to take revenge. Even the international buyers liked the idea, so they asked Manu Díez to write the script which was the one that was given to me to read.' Filmed in English with British and Spanish actors, *The Nun* was from its conception intended for an international market, and would indeed be released in the US on DVD six months after its Spanish premiere, by Filmax partner Lionsgate.

Balagueró himself was back in the director's chair that year for *Fragile* (*Frágiles*), another ghost story this time set in a children's hospital, where the little patients are terrorised by the spirit of a 'mechanical girl'. Starring Calista Flockhart (*Ally Mc Beal*) as the brave and caring nurse who faces the ghost with the children, an unusual but excellent casting choice, *Fragile* is old-school horror, filled with tension and anticipation in an atmospheric setting. The movie offers good chills throughout, but the highlight is the ghost itself, whose terrifying appearance and

Rottweiler. The Nun.

131 Interview with the author, San Sebastian, Spain, November 2005.

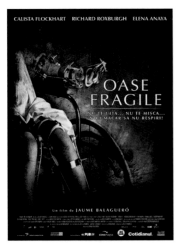

Fragile. Wolf Creek.

jerky gait qualified the movie for a specially created Scariest Ghost Award at the 2006 Brussels International Festival of Fantastic Film. *Fragile* also won prizes in Gérardmer, and received the Goya for Best Special Effects. 'The idea for the movie came from a photo,' Balagueró recalls[132]. 'I was helping a friend to clear the attic after his grandfather's death. His grandfather was a doctor and we found a medical print of a little girl with the disease the film talks about, the glass-bone disease. The pictures showed a little girl with her body full of metallic orthopaedic pieces. It was really shocking. It was also very sad, and I wanted to make it an emotional ghost story, a ghost tale about living people more than dead people.' Touching and spooky, *Fragile* is unfortunately almost unseen outside of Spain.

Australian Blood

From Australia, *Wolf Creek*, a hyper-realistic survival from first-time director Greg McLean, made the horror community sit up and take notice.

Based on the Backpacker Murders case of the early nineties[133], *Wolf Creek* tells the story of three friends who embark on a trip through the Australian desert to explore the meteor site of Wolf Creek. After the visit, the car refuses to start and they find themselves stranded in the middle of the night. They have no choice but to accept the help of a jovial outbacker, Mick (John Jarratt), who happens to be driving his tow truck through the isolated area. Once at Mick's place, they fall asleep by the fire. When they wake up, they have been separated, tied up and gagged, with no one around to hear them scream.

Much has been written about the graphic violence – some would say the nastiness – of *Wolf Creek*, but much like *The Devil's Rejects*, it's really the realism with which this violence is shown that upsets and disturbs. The quasi absence of music, as in *The Texas Chain Saw Massacre*, and the use of digital cameras, as in *The Blair Witch Project*, suppress the detachment that extraneous soundtracks and slick photography usually create between the viewer and the events unfolding on the screen; but more original is the fact that the movie is split in two very distinctive parts: up to the moment the protagonists fall asleep, the first forty-five minutes work as a road movie, slow and entertaining, while after that point the mood switches to that of the most graphic and uncompromising horror film. This two-act structure is further stressed by Will Gibson's beautiful and deeply contrasted photography: clear and bright for the landscapes of the first half, dark and bleak for the cramped, almost claustrophobic close-ups of the second. Thanks to this division, the characters seem more real, less one-dimensional, which makes it all the more surprising and painful when things finally get ugly. More than the stylish direction, the excellent performances, especially from Jarratt, or the gorgeous landscapes and cinematography, it's this ingenuous way that sympathy is built which gives the drama a context that sets *Wolf Creek* apart from mere exploitation fare.

Not everyone agreed though, and if once again, horror fans embraced the film for the thrill ride it offered, critics were less enthusiastic; Roger Ebert – who had granted Zombie's *The Devil's Rejects* three stars –gave it zero, saying: 'There is a line and this movie crosses it. I don't know where the line is, but it's way north of *Wolf Creek*. There is a role for violence in film, but what the hell is the purpose of this sadistic celebration of pain and cruelty?'[134]

Premiering at Sundance in January 2005, *Wolf Creek* was bought by the Weinstein Company and generated much hype in the festival circuit before its release in the UK, Australia and the USA in the last quarter of the year. Opening in the US two days before Christmas, the worst possible time for such a harsh genre movie, it still managed to gross a little under $5 million in its first three days: quite a feat, considering it only cost about $1 million to make.

Hungry Spirits

2004 had already seen Asia's enthusiasm for local horror diminish somewhat, and this downward trend continued in 2005. A handful of pure J-horror productions, with curses and long-haired

132 Interview with the author, Brussels, Belgium, March 2006.
133 In September 1992 a decaying corpse was found in the Belango State Forest in New South Wales, and this precipitated a hunt for a serial killer as more bodies of missing backpackers were discovered over the next year. Ivan Milat was eventually arrested and charged for the killings in July 1996.
134 Roger Ebert, *Chicago Sun-Times*, 23 December 2005, http://rogerebert.suntimes.com/apps/pbcs.dll/article?AID=/20051222/REVIEWS/51220004/1023

ghosts, graced the screens in Korea (Dong-Bin Kim's *Redeye* (*Redeu-ai*), a ghost story set in a train, remarkable only by its introduction of a killer wig) and Hong Kong (the Pang Brothers' *The Eye 10* (*Gin gwai 10*), a teenage-friendly follow-up to *The Eye* and *The Eye 2*, about the ten ways in which ghosts can be encountered).

More original was Paul Spurrier's *P* (also known as *The Possessed*), a Thai film worthy of attention not only for its quality, but also for being helmed by a British director.

When country girl Dau (Suangporn Jaturaphut) leaves for Bangkok to earn money for her family, she finds herself working as a go-go dancer and learns to deal with the harsh reality of her new life through the magic skills her grandmother taught her to use. But her power soon gets out of control, and an organ-eating entity starts possessing her.

Mixing social drama with supernatural scares, *P* (named after the Thai name given to ghosts) works both as a realistic and touching description of life in a Bangkok brothel and as a scary movie, and the two elements are naturally integrated into each other, the horror scenes giving the film a darker tone without ever distracting from the very real situation at hand. 'In Thailand the spirit world and the actual world are entwined,' says Spurrier[135], a former child actor who fell in love with the country during an assignment as a cameraman on a BBC documentary. 'It is absolutely true that there are hexes and curses, and I know more than one foreigner who had a disagreement with a local and became convinced after a series of disasters that they were cursed. So whilst for a Western audience the film is bizarre and fantastic, you could say that for a Thai audience it's almost a reality show.' The director even recalls encountering girls who had resorted to magic, much like his fictional lead does. 'I walked into a bar and spoke to a girl and I asked her how it was going and she said, "Well, our last month was really dreadful, I had no customers, no money, couldn't send any money home, but now it's great! I went back to the country and saw the witch doctor and he gave me some spells and this month we've had thirty customers!" This is not at all uncommon, and I found it fascinating that in Thailand this belief, this mythology, belief in the spirit world is so much a part of their lives that it's part of the life in bars as well, to find the customers, use the magic to make yourself look pretty and give you confidence … I thought, what a wonderful way to tie the two things that interested me, the spiritualism in this environment where you'd least be expecting to find it.'

Faster paced and easier to follow for a Western audience than most local productions, *P* certainly benefited from its director's knowledge of European and American filmmaking, despite being shot entirely in Thai, with a Thai cast and crew. But its difficult subject matter earned Spurrier a lot of negative attention from organisations and individuals who claimed the movie could harm Thailand's reputation. This might explain why distribution has to this day proved impossible to secure in most countries. 'The reality is that nobody that I showed it to in Thailand has been offended by it,' the director says; 'I showed it at one of the go-go bars and had positive reactions. One girl burst into tears and said she couldn't watch it because it was the story of her life; another wanted to have a copy to send to her mother to show her where she worked and let her know what she does. It didn't offend anybody and they all thought it was real. I think that if you ask most British people anyway what they know about Thailand, they would say good food, lovely beaches and prostitutes and sex. My film at least makes them understand the reality of that. You don't deal with problems by just brushing them under the carpet and saying they don't exist.'

The Eye 10. P. Marebito.

Finally, in Japan, *The Grudge* director Takashi Shimizu broke away from the dead wet girl mould with *The Stranger from Afar* (*Marebito*), in which cult filmmaker and occasional actor Shinya Tsukamoto stars as a cameraman obsessed with death, who one day brings home a strange girl he found in the underground. More intriguing than scary, Shimizu's first venture into psychological horror territory is slow and silent, except for Tsukamoto's voice over and bits of vaguely pretentious dialogue. Hardly the crowd pleaser, *The Stranger from Afar* nevertheless won awards in Brussels and at the Los Angeles Screamfest, and added some long-awaited range to the director's filmography.

135 Interview with the author, London, UK, August 2005.

2006:

'Welcome to your worst nightmare.'

(Tagline for *Hostel*, 2006)

2006 WAS A RELATIVELY QUIET YEAR ON THE SOCIO-POLITICAL FRONT, DURING which the international community tended its wounds (the year started with anti-war protests, continued with Donald Rumsfeld's resignation and ended with the deaths of Augusto Pinochet and Saddam Hussein). It also marked a peak for horror, both for the amount and quality of the features released, and for the numbers they drew at the box-office. After the surprise success of low-budget gritty productions such as *Saw*, the studios jumped on the bandwagon, backing real genre pictures – no supernatural thrillers this time! – and even aping the independents with big budget B-movie hybrids such as *Snakes on a Plane*. Once again, it would be a movie year dominated by high-profile remakes and R-rated violence.

'The lucky ones die first'

Following the box-office shocks of *The Amityville Horror* in 2005 or *Dawn of the Dead* the year before, the trend for 2006 oscillated towards R-rated pictures, both for remakes and for general horror productions, studio-backed or independent. With a couple of exceptions, milder, PG-13 scares were now reserved for ghost stories like *The Grudge 2* or *An American Haunting*. Had hardcore genre fans won their fight? For a fleeting moment, it may have seemed as though victory was near.

One sign of this change, and one of the best and most profitable movies of the year ($41 million in the US, against a $14 million cost) was Alexandre Aja's grisly remake of Wes Craven's 1977 *The Hills Have Eyes*, produced by Craven himself and funded by Fox Searchlight, the speciality film division of Twentieth Century Fox.

Much like the original, *The Hills Have Eyes* takes place in the New Mexico desert, where a

family travelling to California gets stranded and attacked by a group of backcountry mutants.

Aja's update is an impressive improvement on Craven's film. Bigger, faster and more suspenseful and explicit, this survival tale revolves around carefully constructed characters viewers can actually root for, and is beautifully photographed by *High Tension*'s director of photography Maxime Alexandre. The first half of the film, gritty and at times upsetting – the attack on the RV is especially hard to stomach – sets the scene for the payback which comes in the second half, a more entertaining yet equally gruesome adventure which shows a real progression in the remaining characters' personalities. Besides developing the protagonists, Aja and writing partner Grégory Levasseur stuck relatively close to the 1977 version for the storyline and major plot twists, but added a backstory for the mutants. 'We were huge fans of the original,' Aja explains[136], 'so we knew we weren't going to go too far from it, we had to respect the movie's spirit. We wanted to keep its savage, realistic aspect but at the same time add a story that involved the tests that the US army conducted in the forties and fifties in the New Mexico desert – the armed forces conducted about 350 atmospheric tests, each time asking the people to leave the area, but not always making sure that they'd all gone … That is how we wanted to explain why the region was deserted and where the mutant family comes from. It allowed us to tell a larger, more epic story elaborating on the original material. The original had a budget of $250,000; we have a real budget and we can achieve so much more.'

The financial limitations faced by Craven in the seventies may be precisely what made *The Hills Have Eyes* the perfect candidate for a successful remake, as it left space for improvement and development. But it is another, less necessary redux that allowed producers Craven, Peter Locke and Marianne Maddalena to secure financing: 'I got all the rights back on the original when *The Texas Chainsaw Massacre* was announced for Michael Bay's company,' Locke recalls[137]. 'I tried to get [*The Hills Have Eyes*] going, but no one was interested. Then *The Texas Chainsaw Massacre* did $100 million at the box office, and everybody wanted to make *The Hills Have Eyes*: I got two

The Hills Have Eyes.

136 Interview with the author, Ouarzazate, Morocco, August 2005.
137 Interview with the author, Ouarzazate, Morocco, August 2005.

offers and [the agency] William Morris became involved and I got another offer immediately.'

According to the producers, hiring the director was a no-brainer, Aja's *High Tension* and his enthusiasm for the project being largely sufficient to convince them that he'd be the perfect choice. As for the French filmmaker, starting to work outside of his home country, with a US studio, seemed like a natural evolution. 'Most of the movies [Greg and I] loved were American,' says the filmmaker, 'so of course directing a movie for an American company is a dream come true, but it wasn't planned from the start. France has many advantages, including the fact that a director always has final cut, but it's also very hard to make a genre movie in France. French movies are financed by TV channels, and they only buy prime-time programmes: no R, no NC-17. It's a lot easier to make genre films in the US.'

If *High Tension* had introduced Alexandre Aja to horror fans the world over, *The Hills Have Eyes*, a mainstream hit, established the filmmaker as a force to be reckoned with in the genre. His next feature, *Mirrors*, loosely based on the 2003 Korean film *Into the Mirror* (*Geoul sokeuro*), would be one of the most anticipated movies of 2008.

Writer/director Glen Morgan and producer James Wong, the duo behind *Final Destination*, took a similar approach to their remake of *Black Christmas*, with less fortunate results. Staying close to the storyline of the 1974 original, Morgan also decided to give more information on the killer's backstory, but this

Black Christmas. 2001 Maniacs. The Omen.
OPPOSITE: The Wicker Man.

addition doesn't make him scarier, or the suspense more intense. In the end, Morgan and Wong brought nothing new to the table and Bob Clark's classic, a film which practically invented the slasher sub-genre, remains the only *Black Christmas* that scary movie fans will ever need to see.

First-time director Tim Sullivan's *2001 Maniacs*, a remake of Herschell Gordon Lewis's pioneering gorefest *Two Thousand Maniacs!* (1964), starring Robert Englund and Lin Shaye, was an equally bloody but much goofier effort. Voluntarily dumb and over-the-top, this silly Southern cannibal story is strangely entertaining despite its ridiculous plot and bad acting, and seems to have been put on celluloid only to be enjoyed in the company of a group of friends and a few bottles of beer. The first movie to be produced by Raw Nerve, the company Eli Roth created with partners Scott Spiegel and Boaz Yakin, *2001 Maniacs* initially attracted attention thanks to Roth's involvement, but soon made a name for itself on the festival circuit. It was released directly on DVD in the US in June 2006.

The final R-rated remake of the year was John Moore's *The Omen*, which may well be the most unnecessary update of the decade. Rushed to meet its gimmicky release date, 6 June 2006 (or 6/6/06), this flat, by-the-numbers (pun intended) repetition of Richard Donner's timeless 1976 original is tasteless and painfully boring, its only 'innovation' being to replace the adult couple played by Gregory Peck and Lee Remick with the hipper and younger Liev Schreiber and Julia Stiles as the parents of a child who turns out to be the Antichrist. Lord, have mercy on their souls.

Just as pointless was Neil LaBute's redux of *The Wicker Man*. Starring a misguided Nicolas Cage as a policeman investigating the case of a missing girl on an isolated island, this farce leaves out the eeriness and religious comment that made the 1973 version a cult classic, and stumbles from ridiculous to downright idiotic, the scene in which Cage runs around in a bear suit leaving most critics and viewers puzzled.

Also PG-13 (not a drop of blood in sight, even on the dead bodies), Simon West's remake of *When a Stranger Calls* hardly revolutionised the genre, but is still an interesting effort, using all the tricks in the book to get some jumps out of its tired premise – a young girl alone in a house, receiving phone calls from an increasingly menacing stranger – and

Pulse.

unlike *Scream* and its post-modern followers in the nineties, playing its scares dead seriously. Filled with clichés (the good old shower curtain scene is a prime example), it is nevertheless sufficiently well-crafted to work at times, thanks notably to the fact that West chose to stretch the first twenty minutes of Fred Walton's 1979 original over more than an hour, keeping the killer in the shadows as long as possible. By the end of the film, the stranger turns out to be a regular human being, another reminder that in the 2000s, your neighbour or colleague could well be more dangerous than any supernatural stalker.

Asian horror, of course, wouldn't go untouched. Jim Sonzero's *Pulse*, a dreadful and incoherent adaptation of Kiyoshi Kurosawa's 2001 *Kairo*, was originally meant to be directed by Wes Craven, who had campaigned for Miramax to buy the rights for him back in 2001, before *The Ring* made a killing at the box-office. The production was repeatedly greenlit then interrupted by the Weinsteins, and Craven was eventually pulled off and replaced with Sonzero, whose credits mostly consisted of music videos. The result was the disastrous mess which opened theatrically in the US in August 2006.

The Grudge 2, Takashi Shimizu's sequel to his remake of the 2003 Japanese hit, marked the director's sixth incursion inside the *Ju-On* house. The most linear of the series, it follows the formula established by the films to the letter, but its J-horror shocks have grown stale and each appearance of the blue-lit kid and long-haired skinny female are now met with laughter more than screams. *The Grudge 2* grossed less than $40 million in the US, a failure compared to the $110 million of the first redux. With the low results of *Dark Water* the previous year, Roy Lee's Midas touch reputation was quickly declining.

'Sit back. Relax. Enjoy the fright.' (*Snakes on a Plane*)

Besides remakes of previous hits, Hollywood invested in an array of nearly original movies (the list includes a sequel, a prequel and a videogame adaptation), most of which were rated R. With three notable PG-13 exceptions – *The Return*, *An American Haunting* and *The Covenant* – these productions showed a real desire on the studios'[138] part to step up their game and capitalise on the success of smaller and more daring releases, but their most commendable efforts were rarely rewarded.

Starring Sarah Michelle Gellar as Joanna Mills, a sales rep going back to her native Texas where she grew up having visions and unexplained episodes of self-mutilation, Asif Kapadia's *The Return* offered few surprises. While its theme – the impact of violent events on a person's life – is certainly interesting, it gets lost in a muddled and unbelievably slow intrigue, which, added to the movie's lacklustre direction and photography, makes even the cast's generally good performances go unnoticed. A commercial disappointment, *The Return* further suffered from its bad timing: released a few years earlier, during the pre-*The Ring* wave of protagonist-with-supernatural-gift thrillers, it might have found a wider audience.

Also PG-13, Courtney Solomon's *An American Haunting*, an old-fashioned demonic possession tale set in the early 19th century and inspired by the legend of the Bell witch, didn't do too well either at the box-office. Suffering from comparison with the much scarier *The Exorcism of Emily Rose*, and much closer to Friedkin's *The Exorcist*, Solomon's film is an old-school period piece, gorgeously shot and with a great cast, but not original or frightening enough despite its oppressive atmosphere and a surprising conclusion. 'I based the script on Brent Monahan's 2000 book *The Bell Witch: An American Haunting*,' Solomon explains[139], 'because I liked the explanation that he gave. A poltergeist seemed more believable; others think the house had been built on ancient Indian burial ground, or that Betsy Bell had been possessed by a demon, but that's been seen hundreds of times in horror movies. I did a lot of research on the subject before I wrote the script.'

Renny Harlin's *The Covenant*, about four descendants of old New England families who must use their supernatural powers to defend their bloodline, was the last PG-13 film of the year and was obviously aimed at a very young audience. Slick and crowded with pretty faces and flashy special effects, this warlocks-meet-*The OC* story wasn't as frightful as *The Craft* (1996) or as clever and fun as *Buffy the Vampire Slayer*. Its vacuous characters, soap-like dialogue, rock soundtrack and asinine storyline may have seduced a handful of pre-teens, but didn't fool anybody else, and *The Covenant* only just recouped its reported $22 million investment in the US.

French director Christophe Gans's *Silent Hill*, based on the eponymous Konami video game, suffered from the traditional problems of game adaptations: a woolly plot and hollow protagonists. Visually stunning, this story of a mother looking for her lost daughter in the abandoned town of Silent Hill introduces an extraordinary world populated with weird and creepy creatures, but lacks atmosphere, tension or anticipation, and doesn't offer enough twists and turns to keep viewers interested. Impressive armless freaks and faceless nurses pop up randomly, and their appearance is so flatly portrayed that even the characters who face them don't seem too disturbed. An original and satisfying explanation is eventually given, but so rapidly and un-climactically that few will take notice. At 125 minutes, it's

The Grudge 2. The Return. An American Haunting. The Covenant.

138 We'll include subsidiaries of majors, such as Rogue Pictures or Fox Searchlight, in the 'studio' category.
139 Interview with the author, Brussels, Belgium, March 2006.

also much too long. Inventive and gorgeous but ultimately dull, *Silent Hill* was nevertheless a success, with a total lifetime gross of nearly $100 million, twice its initial cost.

The second sequel to Wong and Morgan's *Final Destination*, written and directed by the original duo, once again ups the gore, but completely forgets to tell a story or introduce interesting characters between the deaths. Its only appeal seems to be the way the teenagers are killed off, and *Final Destination 3* is pure splatter, pointless and nowhere near as entertaining as the first two films. Even its opening scene, a rollercoaster disaster, doesn't have the impact – quite literally – of the plane crash and the car collision which opened the previous films. Yet it was a big enough commercial success to warrant the production of a fourth entry in the series, due in 2009.

The Texas Chainsaw Massacre: The Beginning, from director Jonathan Liebesman, is, as its name suggests, a prequel to the events

Silent Hill. The Texas Chainsaw Massacre: The Beginning.

described in the 2003 remake, and closely follows the structure of the 1974 original. Bloody but not in the least bit suspenseful (especially since this is a prequel, we know from the start how the story will end), *The Texas Chainsaw Massacre: The Beginning* is, like *Final Destination 3*, built around the kills, and its protagonists, Sheriff Winston (Lew Temple) included, severely lack charisma. Besides, Liebesman's film makes the same mistake as Tobe Hooper's own 1986 sequel: by revealing the face under the mask, they show Leatherface's human side and weaken him as an unstoppable, legendary killer.

David R Ellis's *Snakes on a Plane* was a real oddity, and an ultimate indicator that Hollywood was desperate to surf the indie horror wave. *Freddy vs Jason* director Ronny Yu was initially set to direct, and his enthusiasm reflected to perfection the movie's trashy appeal: 'The second they told me the storyline I said I wanted to do this movie. It's about a plane on the way from Honolulu to Los Angeles, and when they're halfway, 500 poisonous snakes get released, and the first person to be killed is the pilot. As the audience, I say how the hell can they get out of the situation? I'd like to see it! So I said I want to do that. Hopefully we'll start shooting soon.'[140]

A true B-movie with the kind of high concept title you usually find in the bargain bin of the local video store, but with a $33 million budget and an A-list star in the person of master of cool Samuel L Jackson in the lead, *Snakes on a Plane* was produced by New Line Cinema, the company behind *Willard* (2003), *Blade* (1998) and *Freddy vs Jason* (2003). It

140 Interview with the author, Brussels, Belgium, March 2004.

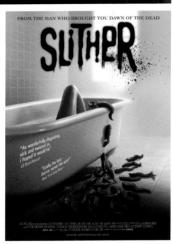

generated an unprecedented Internet buzz months before its release; most of the hoopla was based on its title, so that when the producers announced they were planning on changing it to *Pacific Flight 121* in March 2006[141], Jackson himself pleaded in favour of retaining the original. While principal photography had wrapped in September 2005, New Line, in an atypical move, ordered some reshoots in March to build on the project's online reputation and add some R-rated scenes to the then-PG-13 feature. Horror buffs were pleased to hear the news, and judging from the hype on the web, it seemed the filmmakers had a major hit on their hands.

But when the movie opened in August, they were in for a disappointment. Its $15 million opening was largely under the $20 to 30 million they had anticipated, and the production fell to the number six slot at the box-office in its second week. Still, *Snakes on a Plane* did exactly what it said on the tin: fast-paced and highly entertaining, it offered all the jump-scares, horrible deaths, gratuitous nudity and one-liners one could have hoped for. But this summer blockbuster with B-movie aspirations suffered from the very different expectations its dual nature had brought forth: Saturday night audiences found it too silly, gruesome or small-scale to be interested, while those who'd wished for Z-level schlock thought it was too slick and were rebuffed by the use of CGI. Proof that no big budget flick can rely solely on a 'cult' vibe, and that blogs and websites are by no means evidence of the thoughts of mainstream moviegoers, *Snakes on a Plane* will hopefully be judged on its own merits as the buzz fades away, and will be remembered as the fun and unpretentious nature-runs-amok show it really is.

Legless creatures of a different kind could be found in *Slither*, James Gunn's first feature film directing credit. Witty and in equal parts funny and horrifying, this story of a small town whose inhabitants are attacked one by one by hideous slugs from space is a loving homage to the eighties alien invasion and zombie films the writer/director grew up watching. Inspired by the works of David Cronenberg, Peter Jackson, John Carpenter, Fred Dekker and Frank Henenlotter, Gunn

Snakes on a Plane. Slither.

141 New Line loves flight number titles; the attentive reader will remember that *Final Destination* was initially called *Flight 180* …

125

wears his influences on his sleeve (a banner in a bar even advertises 'Henenlotter's Saddle Lodge Deer Cheer') and if the filmmaker throws comedy into the mix, his jokes aren't meant to poke fun at the classics, but come from the outrageousness of the situations the film describes, like a *Re-Animator* or a *Braindead*, and from the protagonists, around which the movie completely revolves. 'When you take the violence and grossness as far as *Slither* does, the whole thing is so over-the-top you have to laugh,' says Gunn[142]. 'People laugh at being scared and people laugh at being grossed out. That, and the movie is filled with a bunch of fun characters: some who are funny and know they're funny, like Bill Pardy, played by Nathan Fillion, and some who are hilarious and have no idea they are, like Jack MacReady, played by Gregg Henry.' Fillion, Henry

Slither.

Elizabeth Banks and Michael Rooker form a group of colourful, likeable rednecks, and if Henry's one-liners sometimes sound artificial, the love triangle between Banks's Starla Grant, Rooker's Grant Grant and Fillion's Bill Pardy adds humour and depth to the story.

A throwback to a sub-genre which hadn't been exploited for years, *Slither* could have been a difficult project to finance, had it not been for Gunn's can't-do-no-wrong reputation after *Scooby-Doo* (2002) and *Dawn of the Dead*. 'It also has a very unusual structure,' the filmmaker continues, 'it changes protagonists throughout the film, from Nathan Fillion's character, to Elizabeth Banks' character, to Michael Rooker's character, to Tania Saulnier's character, and back again. People weren't used to seeing that in a genre script. Nor were they used to seeing the emphasis on humour and character the movie has. But in the end, Universal and Gold Circle backed all of these oddities and let me film the script the way I wrote it.'

Critics loved the movie: *Variety* described it as 'gleefully nasty and ingeniously twisted,'[143] while *Empire Magazine* stressed the fact that it 'did both its genre parents proud.'[144] Unfortunately audiences didn't seem to agree, and *Slither* grossed less than $4 million in its early April opening, starting out at number eight then quickly falling out of the top ten. Darker than *Shaun of the Dead*, the only successful horror-comedy in recent history, and released at a time when scary movies tended to be realistic and serious, *Slither* simply didn't come out at the right moment. Says Gunn: 'It's a mix between horror and comedy but it's also a black comedy, and black comedies don't do well. It also has an independent type of humour to it, which is unusual to mix with those things and it's also a gross-out film, so it wasn't very commercial. It's like I perfectly set out to make a movie that wouldn't make money and would be a cool film. I'm really happy with it though, it could have gone much worse. Just the fact that it got such good reviews was great. When you make three number one movies in a row, people think you have the Midas touch, but I never thought it would be a big hit, I always knew it was a bit too weird. It was a big success with the horror fans, but it's a small community; people who go see movies are not the horror fanatics, they're people going out for dates on Friday night …'[145] A horror comedy made by a film geek for film geeks, *Slither*, despite being a crushing box-office disappointment, heralded the arrival of a promising director.

The same year, United Artists released the product of its collaboration with another genre-friendly filmmaker, Lucky McKee. *The Woods*, about an all-girl school where students start vanishing one after the other, was the *May* director's first studio picture, and turned out to be a nightmarish experience for him. The movie was caught in a series of mergers, bankruptcies and partnerships, which resulted in United Artists becoming part of the Sony empire in April 2005. Says friend and *May* star Angela Bettis[146]: 'The video regime changed, and the project got shelved.

142 Email interview with the author, September 2005.
143 Joe Leydon, *Variety*, 19 March 2006, http://www.variety.com/review/VE1117929975.html?categoryId=31&cs=1
144 James Dyer, *Empire*, 2006, http://www.empireonline.com/reviews/ReviewComplete.asp?FID=133047
145 Interview with the author, Los Angeles, USA, March.
146 Interview with the author, Sitges, Spain, October 2007.

United Artists supported the picture and they were so gung-ho about it; they loved *May*, they said he could do whatever he wanted. In the middle of it the regime changed, and the new people didn't know what this was and how to market it. Eventually they put it out on DVD.'

Filmed in gorgeous, deep dark colours and recreating the oppressive world of a private school in the sixties, *The Woods* is part-*Carrie*, part-*Evil Dead*, part ghost story, and all original. Atmospheric, character-driven and featuring an excellent cast led by the beautiful Agnes Bruckner and supported by genre favourite Bruce Campbell, McKee's film is permeated by an underlying tension and an increasing sense of dread, although there aren't quite enough genuine scares to keep this drama moving, and the witchcraft theme isn't exploited to its fullest. Still, *The Woods* is an old-fashioned and moody tale which should have deserved to be seen in theatres.

Finally, Dimension produced *Feast*, a creature feature in the vein of *From Dusk Till Dawn* (1996), from first time director John Gulager, son of actor Clu Gulager (mainly known to horror fans for his turn in *The Return of the Living Dead* (1985)). Gulager's film was the product of Ben Affleck and Matt Damon's *Project Greenlight III* (2005), a television reality show following the making of a movie, in this case *Feast*. The result is gory and silly, but tries by all means available to give its viewers a good time.

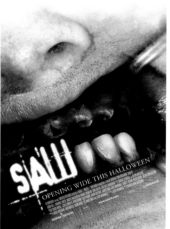

Saw III.

'Suffering? You haven't seen anything yet.' (Jigsaw in *Saw III*)

In 2006, movie violence reached its peak. The result of a long evolution, from the gory deaths of *Final Destination* (2000) to the inventive traps of *Saw* (2004), this trend was largely analysed as a consequence of the tensions in world affairs and the declining economy. Graphic violence wasn't confined to horror films: Mel Gibson's *Apocalypto* featured scenes of human sacrifice and was criticised for its bloody depiction of pre-Columbian America, and even James Bond bled and was tortured in *Casino Royale*. Furthermore, various non-genre pictures dealt directly with

contemporary issues; titles such as *V for Vendetta* and *United 93* dealt with terrorism with varying degrees of realism; *24*, one of the most popular series on television, examined whether torturing a terrorist was legitimate to avoid another 9/11. *An Inconvenient Truth* attempted to scare its viewers with a different kind of threat, environmental this time; *Why We Fight*, out for a limited release in January, examined America's war policy over the past century; and *The Blood of my Brother*, released in the summer, documented life in Iraq from the point of view of the locals. Clearly, real horrors were on everyone's mind, and genre movies, as always, offered the most immediate outlet for the world's fears.

'If it's Halloween, it must be *Saw*', the tagline for *Saw III* proclaimed. And indeed, for the third year in a row, the end of October was dominated by Jigsaw and his apprentice Amanda, who this time abduct a doctor and force her to keep the cancer-ridden killer alive while another victim finishes his tests. Directed, like the second instalment, by Darren Lynn Bousman, *Saw III* again put the emphasis on the inventiveness and bloodiness of the kills, on Jigsaw's personality, and on several twists in the story, but was considerably more entertaining than Bousman's second entry into the increasingly *Grand Guignol* series. Despite abysmal reviews, the movie was hugely successful, grossing $33 million – more than three times its reported budget – in its first weekend, and over $80 million in US theatres by the end of the year. Like the previous years, advertising for the film included the 'Halloween Blood Drive', inviting fans and members of the press to give blood to the American Red Cross. In addition to this unusual marketing stunt, Lionsgate sold limited edition prints of the poster, for which a vial of actor Tobin Bell's blood had been mixed with the red ink, and offered all proceeds to the Red Cross.

Hostel.

But for all the gore *Saw III* had on display, it's Eli Roth's *Hostel*, released in January, which was for better or worse the focus of most attention. The movie follows two Americans (played by Jay Hernandez and Derek Richardson) on a backpacking trip around Europe looking for girls, drugs and excitement. The two are lured, along with the Icelander (Eythor Gudjonsson) they meet on the way, to a hostel in Slovakia. Unbeknownst to them, the place belongs to an organisation which provides rich businessmen with young victims to torture and kill.

The first part of the film takes place in Amsterdam and describes the trio's adventures in coffee shops and whorehouses. The second half, set in Slovakia, is all about the hostel and the fate that awaits the three friends. 'The first half is sex and the second half is violence, and they parallel each other,' Roth explains[147]. 'The slaughterhouse parallels the brothel. It's this same idea of paying to do whatever you want with somebody. It's a film that's really about exploitation. It's not an exploitation movie, it's a movie about exploitation, and it's about the things that human beings do to each other for pleasure and to what degrees, how far human beings would go to satisfy their own sick urges.' Still, the first part of the film is light-hearted and introduces the protagonists as fun-loving and likeable, if seriously sex-crazed, college boys. But the tone shifts as soon as they reach Slovakia. Parties and flirts no longer seem innocent and as people start disappearing, it quickly becomes obvious that something very wrong is happening.

The problem with *Hostel* is that naturally, anyone who has heard the basic premise of the film has a pretty clear idea what is happening and can easily guess how the story is going to end for most of the characters. And since the movie doesn't leave much mystery or build much tension, the main interest of the second half is to see how far Roth will go in his depiction of

147 Interview with the author,
Prague, Czech Republic, April 2005.

Hostel.

the horrors the three men will have to endure. There are glimpses of brilliance – the new girls in the bedroom waiting for Paxton when he comes back, the landmark seen on the cell phone picture – which hint at a more suspenseful third act, but they are few and far between, and since the audience knows what happened to Paxton's pals long before he does, the climax is fairly predictable.

This is not to say that *Hostel* isn't clever, or that the torture scenes are its only highlights, far from it. Not only does Roth take the time to introduce well-written characters, develop their story and place them in a realistic and believable situation, but the themes he deals with make his movie extremely timely. Sure, the plot is supposedly based on true events[148], but more pertinent yet were the obvious parallels between *Hostel* and real-life atrocities that the Western world was only too familiar with, from Kana (Jennifer Lim)'s burnt face recalling the blowtorch torture Saddam Hussein's troops used against Iraqi dissidents[149], to the image of Josh (Derek Richardson) hooded, stripped to his underwear and tied to a chair directly mirroring photographs from Abu Ghraib published by the US media a couple of years earlier. 'Nothing scares me more than these Al-Qaeda videos that you see on the Internet with people getting decapitated,' Roth revealed on the set of the movie. 'I was sitting there and thinking, what if you're in a room and someone's going to kill you and no matter how much money you offer them or no matter what combination of words or sentences you say, they're going to do it? Your life is over and it's all because of whatever circumstances you wound up in this horrible place. That terrifies me, and it's part of real life, it's out there and everybody's seen it; it's a very public thing now.' The movie shows the journey of American boys flying to a foreign country and getting tortured and killed: the link with a certain war situation was obvious.

Combined with the success of Roth's *Cabin Fever* (2003) and the popularity of the *Saw* series, the seasonable nature of *Hostel*'s subject matter must have, consciously or not, been recognised by its investors, and the filmmaker managed to secure financing easily. 'I wrote the

148 'It was based on true events that are happening in Thailand, where families would sell a member of their families to organised crime and American and European businessmen travelling there would pay $10,000 to walk into a room and shoot them in the head. I was researching to do a documentary and I quickly realised that the closer I got to the subject matter, the more endangered I was; you can never get anyone to talk about it and if you did you'd get killed.' Eli Roth, interview with the author, Prague, Czech Republic, April 2005.

149 A very graphic video of these events appeared online in June 2004, on the website of the AEI, American Enterprise Institute for Public Policy Research, as an answer to the photographic evidence of the Abu Ghraib excesses.

first draft and showed it to [Raw Nerve producing partners] Boaz and Scott and [producers] Mike Fleiss and Chris Briggs, and they loved it. I got on a plane to Prague, I figured out the budget, I met the crew; two weeks later we had the money with different companies fighting to finance it and Sony's Screen Gems picked it up for world distribution. It's truly an independent film and it got worldwide distribution before we even started shooting, which is incredible; it's very comfortable shooting and knowing your film's going to come out. It will be one of the only movies that'll be written, produced, shot, edited, completely finished and released in theatres within a year.' *Hostel* also struck a chord with the audience. It opened at number one, beating *The Chronicles of Narnia*, with nearly $20 million in its first three days, and ended up grossing $47 million in American theatres – quite an accomplishment for such a gruesome, $4.5 million picture.

But its success didn't please everybody. A series of articles from various critics soon appeared online and in print, criticising this new wave of films, including *Hostel, Wolf Creek, The Devil's Rejects* and *Saw*, that David Edelstein of the *New York Magazine*[150] described as 'torture porn', or, as some later wrote, 'gorno'. The implication of the term is that movies such as Roth's are structurally similar to pornography, articulated around the money shots (in this case the torture), the scenes in-between being little more than useless filler, and that the only satisfaction they offer viewers is the sadomasochistic pleasure of seeing innocents get mutilated or killed.

This reduction of the sub-genre to a mere variation of pornography is insulting both to the filmmakers and to their audience, and shows a gross misunderstanding of the appeal of movies such as *Hostel* and *Saw*. While there might be a small minority of people who do get excited by cinematic violence – passive sadism is nothing new – the large majority was simply enjoying the rollercoaster ride of the gross-out thrills these extreme features offer; a ride which, in the context of post-9/11 America, was a more appropriate vent to the public's fears than the subtle supernatural chills of, say, *The Others*. Stephen King famously wrote that horror 'feeds the alligators of the mind'[151], and if these alligators won't be satisfied with more elaborate scares, why not resort to cheaper means? What matters first and foremost is the release.

Describing these movies as torture porn not only ignores the complexity of Jigsaw's personality, the development of *Hostel*'s protagonists or the excellent performances of its cast, it also implies that they glorify violence, when their messages are entirely different. *Saw*, particularly through the character of Amanda, makes viewers question the killer's methods and motivations and ultimately incites them to value life. *Hostel* examines one of the most blatant deviances of modern society: the objectification of women in particular and human beings in general. Nothing good comes out of the violence seen, and as the sequel would soon prove, even Paxton's life would be irremediably damaged by his actions.

Still, 'people were threatened by the success of *Hostel*; it was too real for them,' says Roth, who quickly became the poster boy for movie violence and the focus of most attacks. 'Even the *Saw* films still had this element of fantasy. But a lot of people who saw *Hostel* at number one were really upset about it, they didn't understand it. I'm not making films that are going to please everybody; if you put that level of violence in *Hostel*, you know it's going to upset people. You've got to be willing to put yourself out there.'

Roth was only the latest in a long series of filmmakers, from Herschell Gordon Lewis to Wes Craven, reviled for pushing the boundaries of what can be put on screen. 'Horror movies are all about exploring that dark territory of things nobody wants to think about,' the writer/director observes[152]. 'How can you do that and have restrictions and make it safe and clean? The whole thing with horror movies is to show what people are afraid of!'

Other directors had been singled out over the past couple of years for their violent yet

Hostel.

150 'Now Playing at Your Local Multiplex: Torture Porn', David Edelstein, *New York Magazine*, 28 January 2006, http://nymag.com/movies/features/15622

151 Edelstein himself used the quote in several articles.

152 Interview with the author, Los Angeles, USA, January 2008.

153 '*Hostel* Director Wants No-Limit Horror', Josh Horowitz, *MTV*, 28 March 2007, http://www.mtv.com/movies/news/articles/1555691/story.jhtml

successful work, and *Total Film* critic Alan Jones grouped them under the moniker 'Splat Pack' in a 2006 article. The Pack included Roth, Neil Marshall, Greg McLean, James Wan, Leigh Whannell, Darren Bousman, Rob Zombie and Alexandre Aja: an odd assortment of filmmakers who reportedly had in common a love for, in Roth's words,[153] 'really bloody, violent, disgusting, sick movies.'

The link between these filmmakers wasn't necessarily easy to see and while some, like Roth, embraced it, others shrugged and pointed out that the directors (and writer, in Whannell's case) weren't the same age or at the same stage in their careers, weren't all planning to keep making horror films, and didn't even all know each other. Still, the term stuck, and even *Time* magazine devoted an article to the newly created community[154]. 'Alan Jones clearly understood the need of those who read and write about movies to quantify and categorise things into more easily digestible chunks,' Marshall explains[155]. 'People generally prefer details to be broken down into simple facts, figures, lists, and in this case, categories. Like music and fashion, the film industry follows movements, trends and patterns, and categorisation such as the French New Wave or the Movie Brats is an easy way of identifying those shifts in taste.' The shift Jones identified with the Splat Pack was a direct consequence of both the difficult climate in international relations and the evolution of movie techniques. The mid-2000s saw 'a wave of ultra-gory, R-rated horror movies seeking to revisit the more gritty, hard edged and bloody cinema of the late seventies and early eighties,' Marshall continues. 'Back then, such films were usually low-budget, with a few notable exceptions, quite often Italian, and released in flea-pit cinemas or straight to video, still in its infancy at that time – and before the Video Nasty fiasco, in the UK at least. At the start of the new millennium, after a decade in which horror movies were not so popular or mainstream, and in which the CGI revolution changed the way blood, guts and gore were depicted and sanitised on screen, a new generation of horror filmmakers figured it was time to re-invent the kind of visceral thrills that got them into horror movies in the first place. Only now, we could do it with decent production values and target a much broader and more accepting audience. It was time to splash the screen red with blood again!'

Turistas.

If the term designated a group of writers and directors, it was really a temporary movement that it referred to, as most of the Splat Pack members have left or are considering leaving the genre, at least for a while. 'Horror needs to continue reinventing itself and surprising audiences or else it will go stale and dry up,' Marshall adds. 'A lot of the films that have followed this trend have concentrated so much on the gore, they've sacrificed story, plot and character along the way. Who knows what the next trend will be?'

Besides *Saw III* and *Hostel*, one more realistically graphic feature would make waves in 2006. *Turistas* (*Paradise Lost* in the UK), produced by Fox Atomic, directed by John Stockwell (*Blue Crush*, 2002) and starring Josh Duhamel and Melissa George, focused on a group of American and British backpackers in Brazil, who end up getting abducted by traffickers in human organs. Sound familiar? Developed around the same time as *Hostel* but released nearly a year later, in December 2006, *Turistas* shared more than a couple of passing similarities with Eli Roth's European cautionary tale. Set in a sunnier and more exotic location, with more innocent and likeable protagonists, Stockwell's film is also divided in two parts: a vacation in paradise, with music, drinks and girls, followed by a slow descent into hell, with screaming victims getting slowly tortured. Yet it is lighter, less gloomy and gory, more suspenseful and adventure-orientated, and its underlying theme, although linked to *Hostel*'s, varies slightly: if Roth's movie could be seen as a direct consequence of terrorism and the war in Iraq, *Turistas* seems to comment on

154 'The Splat Pack', Rebecca Winters Keegan, *Time*, 22 October 2006, http://www.time.com/time/magazine/article/0,9171,1549299,00.html
155 Interview with the author, London, UK, May 2008.

The Gravedancers.

America's behaviour towards developing nations, as the lead organ-harvesting surgeon claims to be treating tourists the way they treat Brazil: 'The whole history of our country is you taking from us: our land, our sugar, our gold, and even our bodies for sex or for our insides … but I have found a way to give back.'

But whatever the motivations of their killers, the message of both films was clear: outside their borders, US citizens were not safe. Attacked in their homes by Islamic fundamentalists, targeted by rebels in Iraq, scorned (or so they thought) by European nations, led by France, who refused to join the revealingly named War on Terror – the Freedom Fries movement in 2003 showing how strongly they reacted to France's rejection – Americans felt a natural distrust of foreign territories. But even though it tapped into this widespread sentiment, *Turistas*, released three weeks before Christmas and perceived as an exact copy of *Hostel*, was a flop, taking under $4 million when it opened in the US.

'Unrest in peace' (*The Gravedancers*)

While big companies had taken over the hyper-violence trend (*Saw III*, *Hostel* and *Turistas* were directly or indirectly produced by Lionsgate, Sony's Screen Gems and Fox Atomic), independent filmmakers went back to supernatural frights with a series of very different, generally excellent, and uniformly R-rated features.

Mike Mendez's *The Gravedancers*, about a couple and their former college friend who are haunted by the ghosts of three murderers after a night of drunken fun in a cemetery, was part of Eight Films to Die For (aka Horrorfest), an annual film festival organised by Courtney Solomon's distribution company After Dark Films, and launched in 2006. Darker and much more serious in tone than Mendez's previous feature *The Convent* (2000), this atmospheric and old-fashioned story, with its *Haunted Mansion*-inspired spirits, showed a true will to send chills down its viewers' spines.

'I wanted to make *Gravedancers* pretty much right after *The Convent*, but it's been a very difficult journey,' Mendez explains[156]. 'Nobody in Hollywood knew what to make of *The Convent*, so I wanted to make a movie that could satisfy myself, my friends, but also be a little bit more accessible and a little bit more mainstream, but not some sell-out bullshit. I fell in love with *The Gravedancers* because it was creepy and supernatural and showed a lot of stuff that I didn't get to do in *The Convent* or in *Killers* (1996). It also has a fun, *Evil Dead* element and by the end it gets kind of crazy.'

Despite the success of his second movie, the filmmaker still had trouble securing financing for his project. 'We started shopping it to studios, but they didn't seem very interested because *The Sixth Sense* was very popular and they all wanted happy ghost movies. Finally we hooked up with Madonna's company, Maverick; they had a deal with Fox and we were going to do it with Fox for $15 million, and then it all turned out to be completely untrue. Maverick was supposed to pay for it but in reality they didn't have any money and Fox didn't want anything to do with it once the money was gone. We found another company who said they would make it for $10 million but they sat on it for two years; it took them all that time to realise we were never going to get a big star in it. So we finally made it for $2.5 million, just because I was tired of waiting and just needed to make this movie. But while when we were trying to get it made no one wanted violent ghost movies, when we were trying to sell they were all like, we don't want ghosts, we want *Saw*! So no one wanted to buy it.' Not only was the torture wave an obstacle, but Mendez claims even the genre's popularity made things more difficult. 'The boom of horror was nothing but bad for me, because now suddenly everybody was making horror movies. All of a sudden the floodgates opened and you couldn't sell your movie because everybody was looking for a distributor. It was just hard to get anything out there.'

Subject Two.

After Dark's Horrorfest arrived at the right time, and Mendez was glad to join the selection, which also included Spanish director Nacho Cerdà's Russian-set Filmax production *The Abandoned* (later to receive a separate theatrical release). 'The Eight Films to Die For is a real unique concept where for one weekend, eight horror movies would play, much like a horror festival, but at your local multiplex all over the US,' continued Mendez. 'It was great, because it allowed the film to play nationally and it was sold out each time it played. It was a hit; audiences jumped and screamed. The hardest thing was that it was just for four days. But it was very successful for the time it was in theatres and it did very well on DVD.'

While Mendez scared audiences with his grim grinning ghosts, independent filmmaker Philip Chidel updated the Frankenstein myth with *Subject Two*, in which a mad scientist (Dean Stapleton) repeatedly kills and reanimates his guinea pig, a young medical student named Adam (Christian Oliver). Made for under $25,000 and shot in just sixteen days in Aspen, Colorado, Chidel's film is a great example of a low budget exploited to the fullest thanks to the filmmaker's resourcefulness and creativity. Building his plot around the few elements he knew wouldn't cost him much – a cabin in the woods, a snowmobile – and a very simple concept, the writer/director avoided repeating himself with the constant cycle of death and resurrection by adding philosophical observations about life and death, with humour and playfulness, and was careful to avoid heavy religious discussions and boring medical speech. The relationship between the doctor and his subject is at the core of the story, and its evolution, from their first dialogue to the final twist, is what truly sets the movie apart.

156 Interview with the author, San Diego, USA, July 2007.

'I knew I could use the cabin, and I started thinking about the kind of character who could live in such an isolated place,' Chidel explains[157]. 'The snow reminded me of the final scene in *Frankenstein*, when the monster disappears, and it made me realise that in the novel, when the monster comes to life, the scientist rejects it right away. But what if he hadn't? That was the starting point for the story, and it completely changed the dynamics between the characters.'

Premiering at Sundance in January 2006, *Subject Two* enjoyed a brief festival run during which it received the Best Film Award at the London Sci-Fi Film Festival, before getting a direct-to-DVD release.

Also set in the mountains but with a different beast entirely, *Abominable*, from first-time director Ryan Schifrin, mixed Bigfoot with *Rear Window* in this story of a man (Matt Mc Coy) crippled after a climbing accident, who sees the legendary Abominable Snowman through the window of his cabin in the woods and must convince the people around him of the monster's presence before they all get killed.

Abominable.

Unpretentious and fun, *Abominable* strikes a perfect balance between humour and chills thanks to its tongue-in-cheek approach to the material, both serious and highly aware of its B-movie status. These qualities are reflected in the creature itself, silly-looking yet menacing, and which Schifrin does not hesitate to put in the spotlight in several scenes. 'As much as I love horror movies, when you get right down to it, I don't enjoy making people feel bad,' the filmmaker explains[158]. 'And that's quite a conundrum, when the reason people go to horror movies is to feel scared. [But] I can't bring myself to send people home feeling like crap after they've watched a movie. The term "rollercoaster ride" is what I try to aim for instead. When you're on a rollercoaster as it is going up and up, you get that pit of fear in your stomach, that anticipation and suspense, and then there's the drop – a thrill and burst of adrenalin – and after it's over you find yourself laughing and having had a lot of fun. Which is really what is most important to me: the fun factor. When you have Bigfoot bite a man's face off, it's silly and funny and gross but hopefully, more than anything, the emotion that overrides it all is fun. It's all a very fine line to walk, because too much cheese will clog your arteries, and too much seriousness will become pretentious, so like any recipe you have to have just enough of the right ingredients. You have to trust your instincts as you walk this line because it's all a matter of having good taste and it's easy to trip up.'

With its mythological monster and light-hearted tone, *Abominable* could not have been further from the likes of *Hostel* and *Saw*, which seemed to be all that horror fans were craving. 'There are always fads in genres that are hot but if you are reactive, and try to jump on the bandwagon, by the time you get your movie out there you'll have missed the boat,' says Schifrin. 'So while I enjoyed J-Horror or torture movies as a viewer, I had no desire to tell those kinds of stories. I love monsters, and I just focused on making something that I would really enjoy watching. And for me, those old monster movies are timeless classics, I never get tired of watching them. As my first film, I chose to do an old-fashioned horror movie for a few reasons. In order to not let our low budget be a hindrance to story, I decided to do a limited location, all-takes-place-in-one-room story. One of my favourite Hitchcock films is *Rear Window*. I decided that to combine that with an old-school monster would be a great dramatic device. The *Twilight Zone* episode where William Shatner sees the monster on the wing of the plane is another favourite of mine, and another great example of a limited location story. I also was experimenting with shot composition, for example trying to sustain shots for as long as possible without cutting, and using camera movement and subject movement to keep the shot going, especially in the first half of the movie. This style is a more old-school approach, where a lot of things today are all about fast cuts and short attention spans.'

157 Interview with the author, Brussels, Belgium, March 2006.
158 Email interview with the author, June 2008.

With a great cast (including cameos from genre legends Jeffrey Combs and Lance Henriksen), a good level of gore and an excellent score, courtesy of the director's father, legendary composer Lalo Schifrin, *Abominable* proved the man-in-a-suit sub-genre still had some good years ahead. 'After the movie was finished,' producer Theresa Eastman recalls[159], 'we showed it to distributors, and it just so happened that the Sci-Fi Channel had a hole in their schedule – one of their movies was not quite ready – and they needed to acquire a film to fill that slot. So they obtained the television rights for a period of time, and we went with Anchor Bay for DVD. Both

companies have been fantastic to work with.' After a limited theatrical release, it premiered on Sci-Fi in May 2006 and quickly became one of the channel's top-rated feature films. It eventually came out on DVD in October 2006.

Ti West's *The Roost* is comparable to *Abominable*, in that its young director built a suspenseful adventure around a preposterous supernatural enemy and gave his movie an old-fashioned flavour. Introduced by a horror host (Tom Noonan), like the late night TV shows of the fifties, *The Roost* follows four friends whose car breaks down on their way to a wedding, and who get attacked by deadly bats in the isolated farmhouse where they find refuge. Filmed in two weeks on a shoestring budget on the border between Delaware and Pennsylvania, the movie relies on sound effects more than music, and much of its retro charm comes from its simplicity and its grainy, moody images. 'I don't see *The Roost* as a nostalgic movie,' says first-time director Ti West[160], fresh out of NYU at the time of the shoot. 'But I grew up with old movies, so I was definitely influenced by them. My main goal was to make sure that the acting and directing were as realistic and plain as possible, otherwise the rest of the movie is so strange and crazy that I would have run the risk of turning it into a parody. I gave it a dark and grainy look, to make it look like the movies I grew up with. We shot on film, on Super 16, instead of digital; that's actually where 80% of the budget went! We didn't have much light so we used everything we could find, like the torches the actors were holding.' Slow, silly, but also inventive and fun, *The Roost* toured festivals around the world before being distributed on DVD in the UK (through the FrightFest label) and the US. Since then West has directed several other low-budget features, including *Cabin Fever 2: Spring Fever* (2008), the sequel to Eli Roth's 2003 hit, and *The House of the Devil*, set for a 2009 release.

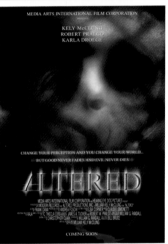

The Roost. Altered.

The countryside must have been a hazardous place to stay in 2006, as Eduardo Sánchez's *Altered* showed yet another kind of wilderness danger: aliens. The *Blair Witch Project* co-director's first feature since his 1999 megahit, *Altered* followed four men seeking revenge against the aliens who'd abducted them years ago and killed one of their friends. Set over the course of one night with a limited cast, Sanchez's second effort is slicker than the first, but relies on the same low-key intensity and slow-building dread, with (somewhat ridiculous) little green men interspersed here and there. A decent and engaging little flick, *Altered* sadly went practically unnoticed for its December DVD release.

Unsurprisingly, Dave Payne's *Reeker* also took place in the middle of nowhere. The story of a group of friends stranded (2006 was certainly a bad year to drive outside the city) in an eerie deserted oasis, Payne's movie may not be very original – there's very little that hasn't been seen a hundred times in its synopsis or its clichéd final twist – but it still manages to be entertaining and suspenseful, thanks to better-than-average characters, excellent special effects, beautiful

159 Email interview with the author, June 2008.

160 Interview with the author, London, UK, August 2005.

Reeker. See No Evil.

photography and a few good gags and clever ideas, like having a blind man amongst the main protagonists. As its title suggests, *Reeker* may also well be the first horror movie to revolve around the highly un-cinematic sense of smell without resorting to odorama or similar gimmicks. 'I wanted to make a movie about a smelly monster,' Payne explains[161]. 'With that in mind, I wanted to make a slasher film; I wanted to see young people get killed one by one, so it was always about a group of people somewhere isolated who would get killed. I wanted it to be a monster movie too, something a little bit supernatural and mysterious, with a ghost-like creature. It was hard to come up with a new and original creature. I just figured that we could just make it Death itself, and that's where the twist of the movie comes from. The whole challenge was to make the smell of the creature appear on screen. I always like to have some kind of challenge, even on the Roger Corman [productions I started out with], when I only got twelve days to shoot. I had to figure out how to make a movie about a smell actually scary.'

Starring Michael Ironside, Derek Richardson and Payne's wife Tina Illman, *Reeker* was pretty well received by critics and fans, and even enjoyed a decent-sized (103 screens) theatrical release in the UK.

The final independent film of the year, former porn director Gregory Dark's *See No Evil*, produced by the World Wrestling Entertainment and Lionsgate, starred wrestling champ Kane as an unstoppable killer stalking a group of delinquents in a rundown hotel. A pedestrian slasher with a good level of gore but no characters to root for and no real surprises, this amusing but unoriginal effort managed to gross over $15 million in the US, despite some pretty bad reviews.

161 Interview with the author, Brussels, Belgium, March 2006.

Televised Nightmares

2006 wasn't only a good year for horror on the big screen and on DVD; it was also a great time for the genre on TV, with at least two anthology series and a made-for-TV feature worth mentioning.

Masters of Horror enjoyed a second series, following the same principles as the first: same budget, same time to shoot, same freedom for the directors. Greenlit before the first series even aired on Showtime ('the fans showed such great enthusiasm,' Garris explains[162], 'they pre-ordered the episodes or subscribed to the channel before the show started, so the producers knew we couldn't lose.'), the new season saw the return of

several Masters who'd enjoyed working on the first season – John Carpenter, Stuart Gordon, Joe Dante, John Landis, Tobe Hooper, Dario Argento and Mick Garris – and attracted a few new recruits: Brad Anderson, Ernest Dickerson, Tom Holland, Peter Medak, Rob Schmidt and Norio Tsoruta.

'The directors who took part in the series last year saw that it was possible to work within the constraints,' Garris continues, 'and they've become more ambitious this year. We had much more second unit work! They also realised they could really do whatever they wanted and deal with serious issues, and that made them more adventurous.' Following Joe Dante's *Homecoming*, which openly criticised the war in Iraq, some of the filmmakers chose to tackle society subjects. Carpenter's *Pro-Life* dealt with abortion, Schmidt's *Right to Die* talked about euthanasia, while Medak's *The Washingtonians* had a strong anti-governmental propaganda subtext; yet this time none of them sacrificed entertainment value for their socio-political message. 'No one's trying to force-feed anything on the viewers,' Garris says. 'Funnily, when we shot *Pro-Life*, we gave it another name, *Like Father Like Son*, to make sure it wouldn't scare off actors and so that we could secure locations. But it's not a political film, it's a real monster movie! And Ron Perlman's character, the anti-abortion militant, is actually likeable.'

More ambitious, but on the whole less satisfying than the first series, the second featured a few brilliant episodes. Stuart Gordon's *The Black Cat*, inspired by the eponymous Edgar Allan Poe story and starring Jeffrey Combs as the legendary author, is widely considered the best film of the show. Twisted and chilling, this Gothic tale of insanity, scripted by *Re-Animator* writer and frequent Gordon collaborator Dennis Paoli, is certainly the most mature, touching and complex entry in the series. John Landis's *Family*, a dark comedy about a homicidal maniac named Harold (George Wendt) who from the outside seems like the perfect neighbour, was a hilarious illustration of America's current fear of the man next door. The tone of this satire is established by its wonderful opening shot travelling through Harold's picture-perfect house to the basement, where he is giving an acid bath to the latest addition to his imaginary family; and much of the episode's success is due to Wendt's amazing performance. Last but not least, Mick Garris's *Valerie on the Stairs*, based on a story by Clive Barker, dealt, like *Chocolate*, with themes of isolation and loneliness, but also with the thin line between fiction and reality, sanity and madness. 'The hero creates an impossible love story with the perfect woman, who desperately needs him but whom he can't have,' Garris comments. 'It's the opposite of *Chocolate*, where she doesn't need him and rejects him, when he could have given her more than she could ever have hoped for.'

The same year, Garris would direct Stephen King's *Desperation* for a 130-minute TV special on ABC. In some regards an easier, more visual story to adapt to the screen than the average

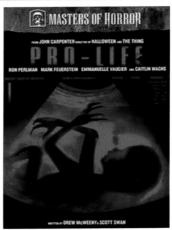

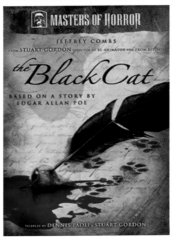

Masters of Horror: Family. Masters of Horror: Pro-Life. Masters of Horror: The Black Cat.

162 Interview with the author, Turin, Italy, November 2006.

King novel, *Desperation* follows a couple arrested on a desert road by a mysterious cop (Ron Perlman), who sends them to jail in a strangely empty city. Exploiting its Arizonian environment to the fullest, and with a brilliant cast led by an extremely creepy Perlman, Garris's film doesn't waste time getting into the action and keeps the pace up throughout.

'I thought of adapting it for the first time when we were shooting *The Shining* in Colorado,' Garris says. 'At the time we wanted to work with a studio. We signed with New Line in 1998, but *Scream* was out around that time, and no one really wanted to produce a serious, scary horror movie. The market wasn't ready and [New Line chairman] Bob Shaye dropped the project while we were in pre-production. Eventually we decided to approach the main TV channels; ABC passed, then when NBC and CBS showed interest, they changed their mind and decided to produce it. But the channel had changed a lot since *The Shining*; Disney bought it and it's no longer a place where a horror director can find the support he needs …' From pre-production battles with the producers to fires on the set, the making of *Desperation* was no picnic; but the worst hardship was the release date chosen by ABC: 23 May 2006, the night of the *American Idol* finale, one of the highest-rated shows in television history … The movie divided the few horror buffs who tuned in, and the reactions ranged from 'better than the book' to 'worst Stephen King adaptation ever'. As for the best-selling author himself, he declared on his website that Garris had produced 'an extraordinary piece of work'[163], and that *Desperation* was 'probably the best TV movie to be made from (his) work'[164].

Another Stephen King book, *Nightmares and Dreamscapes*, also made its way to the small screen in 2006, in the shape of an anthology mini-series of eight episodes directed by the likes of Rob Bowman (*The X-Files*) and Brian Henson (son of Jim Henson, creator of the Muppets). While the quality of the TNT show was generally pretty high, some episodes suffer from the inherent problems of a short story adaptation, and their endings feel somewhat rushed, with no satisfying resolution. On the other hand, Mikael Salomon's *The End of the Whole Mess*, the video diary of a genius who unwillingly destroys the human race, is the best film in this collection, well-acted, full of surprises and undeniably engaging.

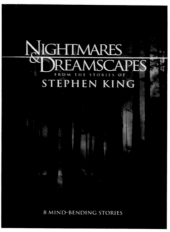

Desperation. Nightmares and Dreamscapes.

Forces of Nature

In the UK and Ireland, six horror movies came out in 2006, and all received a good amount of attention in the genre community.

Severance, from *Creep* director Christopher Smith, was probably the most successful. The story of a group of employees of a multi-national weapons company stranded in the Hungarian countryside during a team-building weekend, this slasher/survival – whose title echoes *Deliverance* – avoids the traditional cast of pretty teenagers, and much like *Hostel* or *Turistas*, takes the time to properly introduce its future victims and make them distinguishable from one another before sending them to the meat-grinder. The first forty-five minutes are spent setting

163 *StephenKing.com*, 23 February 2005, http://www.stephenking.com/pages/news/archive.php
164 *StephenKing.com*, 18 May 2006, http://www.stephenking.com/pages/news/archive.php

up the unpleasant situation in which the team – an insecure boss, a pothead, the token American and four other members of the European Sales division of the company – find themselves lost in an isolated, rundown cabin in the middle of the woods, with no other company than each other and no means to leave, since their bus driver won't venture anywhere close to where they are staying. Despite a few incidents, the tone is more humorous than ominous, until they realise they might not be alone. The second act, in which a mysterious presence picks them off one by one, is by far the best part, with an oppressive atmosphere, a few great gags (including a death seen through the eyes of a severed head), and the movie's most realistically gruesome scene, when a team member loses his foot in a bear trap. The killers remain unidentified until the last act of the film, unfortunately disappointing and un-climactic, the only downside of this otherwise greatly entertaining little flick. Between this and *Hostel*, holidays in Eastern Europe

were looking decidedly unappealing … 'We needed somewhere that a group of people could convincingly be lost for days,' writer James Moran says[165]. 'In the UK, you're never that far from a town. It also had to have experienced war quite recently, due to the weapons company plot, and be somewhere that the characters might not know what country they've wandered into. Looking on the map, there was a nice, large area where Hungary, Serbia and Romania all intersected, which was perfect. Lots of countryside to get lost in.'

Strangely perhaps, *Severance* was widely sold as a horror comedy ('as witty as *Shaun of the Dead*, as scary as *The Descent*', said the tagline), especially in the United States, where the success of *The Office* on television and *Shaun of the Dead* at the cinema had made British humour very popular, with *The Descent* adding further clout to UK-originated horror. But if Smith's film has its funny moments, it is essentially a creepy, gory movie including some nasty deaths and dealing with timely issues (after all, the heroes are weapon dealers fighting off a bunch of Eastern European terrorists), and anyone looking for a *Shaun of the Dead*-like dose of absurd humour would feel let down. 'I call it a horror with some funny bits,' Moran explains. 'I understand why marketing wanted to link it to a recent, great movie, but I don't think that sells it accurately. I wanted it to be a full-on, strong horror when the story kicks in, and the first half was a bit of a stealth bomb, having some fun and laughs to soften the audience up so they don't think it's going to go quite as dark as it does.'

Severance.

Much funnier was Jake West's sci-fi/horror comedy *Evil Aliens*, in which the crew of a TV show investigating paranormal events find themselves confronted with way-too-real evidence of life from another planet. Self-referential, gory, schlocky and over-the-top in every way, West's movie seems specifically made for genre festivals and midnight screenings. The perfect feature for a double bill with *Braindead* or *Bad Taste*, *Evil Aliens* is cheap and often voluntarily dumb, but will stop at nothing to make genre-loving audiences laugh (the alien-harvesting scene is a fine example), and succeeds exactly where more polished and ambitious productions like *Undead* (2003) failed.

165 Email interview with the author, June 2008.

Evil Aliens. Isolation.

If Jake West's *Evil Aliens* could be described as 'aliens in a farmhouse', then Irish director Billy O'Brien's *Isolation* was clearly *Alien* on a farm. Set entirely in one location, over a couple of nights, with a small group of actors, this dead serious entry pitted its heroes against the strangest foe ever encountered in any straight horror movie: mutated cows. As silly as the concept may have sounded, O'Brien managed to deliver a claustrophobic, tense and extremely seasonable feature. 'I grew up on a farm,' the filmmaker says[166], 'and I used to help my dad with the farming and the cattle and so on. I was recounting to somebody in London a particularly nasty calving experience, and because the people I was speaking to grew up in London they hadn't been near a farm, and they were shocked. I thought that was interesting. I put it away in the back of my mind and then about a year later I thought, what if there was a monster inside a cow? That's where it came from. My previous film was a short, *The Tale of the Rat that Wrote*, and it was all about animal testing. The first half of the script was easy to write, but then I started researching because I realised I'd have to keep it realistic. When I started researching genetics it fitted perfectly, because I could keep it almost real.' Even the look of the monsters was the object of much attention and careful study, to make sure the farm and its inhabitants would look as real as possible. 'I hired someone to research the creatures on a more visual level. People still have *Babe* in mind, or pretty Irish farms, so I got a scrapbook of photographs of cow diseases and abandoned farms, some horrific genetic experiments gone wrong in America. I didn't want the designs to look like Giger.' As a result, *Isolation* incorporated various themes and issues which had made headlines around the world in the past few years: mad cow disease, very prominent in Ireland, with four reported human cases by the end of 2006, but also the concerns over genetically modified food and the genetic enhancement of livestock, resulting in the current trend towards organic food.

With amazing creature effects, courtesy of British SFX practitioner Bob Keen (*Hellraiser* (1987), *Dog Soldiers* (2002)), and a highly realistic feel despite the outrageousness of its synopsis, O'Brien's first feature is an excellent little chiller, its only flaw being that it may be too long. *Isolation*

166 Interview with the author, Brussels, Belgium, March 2006.

won a Silver Méliès, as well as awards at the Austin Fantastic Fest, the Gérardmer Film Festival and the LA Screamfest.

If it wasn't obvious enough that the countryside was a place of terror in the British Isles that year, two movies, *Wild Country* and *Wilderness*, were even named after the environment they took place in. Relatively scarce in the eighties and nineties, the man-lost-in-nature sub-genre was back with a vengeance in the United States and in Europe, where low-budget filmmakers seemed constantly inspired by the great outdoors[167]. 'I think it's based on mankind's instinctive fear of the forest primeval,' Neil Marshall, whose first two movies were set outside the city, explains. 'A lot of urbanites are genuinely ill at ease in the countryside. I think a lot of people, especially among contemporary cinema audiences, feel the same way. How many of them actually spend time in the wilderness? It's as alien an environment to them as any far off world could be.' A more pragmatic factor might also have to be taken into consideration. 'It's cheaper to go down to the woods and shoot a movie *au naturel*, than build sets or pay through the nose for inner city locations. Producers are always on the look-out for material they can pull off cheaply and effectively. Survival horror has a successful track record at the box office, so if a script ticks the right boxes – scary old forest, rickety old cabin, bunch of nubile teenagers, mad mutant axe murderer – then it stands a much better chance of getting made than a script with hundreds of CGI mutants attacking a skyscraper in downtown Manhattan.'

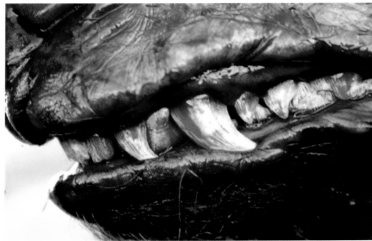

Wild Country. Wildnerness.

Wild Country, from Scottish director Craig Strachan, could have been pitched as *Dog Soldiers* seen by Ken Loach. The story of a group of Glasgow teenagers hunted by a beast in the Highlands, it focuses heavily on the relationships between the five youths and on the character of Kelly Ann, a girl who recently had to give up her newborn baby for adoption. These elements give the otherwise classically-structured plot a freshness and a realism teen-centric horror movies often lack. Strachan also chose to avoid traditional werewolf lore for his Bob Keen-engineered creature. 'I knew right from the start that I didn't want to use the usual imagery: no silver bullet, no full moon,' the director says[168]. 'I avoided the cliché of the full moon behind the cloud and the howling wolf. I also wanted to avoid the transformation scene, because we didn't have the budget, and because *An American Werewolf in London* already had the best one.' As the wolf, mostly filmed in close-ups in the dark, can hardly be seen, *Wild Country* relies more on its young cast and its isolated location, from castle ruins to thick forests, to create mood and thrills. Without being particularly scary or original, Strachan's film had enough going for itself to receive some good reviews when it was released in Scottish theatres in February 2006.

Shot in Northern Ireland, British director Michael Bassett's *Wilderness* takes place on a deserted island, where inmates from a young offenders institution are sent for a survival game, only to realise they are the targets of a very real hunter. Another movie where relationships evolve and break down under pressure in an isolated environment, *Wilderness*, as its title indicates, uses its setting to the fullest ('It was hard work,' Bassett recalls[169], 'because it was forests and rivers and mountains, climbing and running and kicking, so you're tired all day.') but also introduces an unfamiliar type of protagonist: aggressive, violent, despicable offenders. The idea might seem absurd – who would care what happens to them? – but it works nevertheless, and after a while the characters become so real that likeable or not, their fate becomes interesting. 'You have to have some sense of honesty to the characters you're creating,' Bassett explains. 'I

167 Asian horror on the other hand seems entirely city-centric.
168 Interview with the author, London, UK, August 2005.
169 Interview with the author, Brussels, Belgium, March 2006.

Broken.

still think my characters are too soft; I've been to offenders' institutes for research purposes and they're not nice people, they're not sympathetic in any way. You can't put them literally on to the screen because [the audience] would wish them dead immediately, I think. But with this you see the essence of who they are.' The emphasis is clearly put on the offenders' reactions to the events more than on uncovering the hunter's identity. 'I knew I wanted them to know who the killer is halfway through the movie so it's not a big revelation at the end; it's not what it's about and it's not what's interesting. I get it out of the way pretty fast because then they start blaming each other, that's the interesting thing.' Starring Sean Pertwee (*Dog Soldiers*) and Alex Reid (*The Descent*) as the two unfortunate supervisors, this gory survival was met with mixed reviews yet received a small theatrical release in its home country.

Adam Mason's *Broken*, again set in the middle of the woods, could have been classified as torture porn by the critics, had its budget and distribution been large enough to draw their attention. The story of Hope (Nadja Brand), a woman struggling for forty days to survive a kidnapping, it opens with another victim unstitching a hole in her stomach to retrieve a razorblade before being shot in the head, and then moving on to Hope's awakening, buried alive in a coffin. 'The beginning is pure exploitation cinema,' Mason, who co-directed with writing partner Simon Boyes, confesses[170]. 'That girl with her tits hanging out and her guts bursting out from her stomach, that's designed so that a buyer in whatever country sees it and thinks, we can sell this to those horror kids. That first half hour is all gore, and really pretty much gore for the sake of gore.' But if the beginning comes across as another *Saw* wannabe, *Broken* soon shifts to a darker, harsher, more realistic tone, and a slower pace. 'The [rest of the movie] is much more grown-up. I want to make films that show my view of the world, that is that it's full of utter psychos who want to screw you over and rape your wife and cut her head off. The real world is cruel and uncompromising and doesn't care about you or me, and I want to reflect that.' Whether viewers will enjoy the director's vision is a matter of personal taste, but there is no denying that Mason's third feature (but the first to be valued by the genre

170 Email interview with the author, November 2006.

community … and the filmmaker himself) is a pitch-black, uncompromising, mean-spirited, yet compelling and competently made effort.

'*Broken* was made out of total rage,' Mason continues. 'Rage at my impotence within the British film industry. It amuses me that horror is becoming a bit of a buzz word over here, thanks to Neil Marshall and Christopher Smith I guess. Those guys have helped it for people like me. But really the state of the UK film industry sickens me. It's really pathetic. We're directly competing with the USA, so it's kind of like if you tried to open a burger bar in Oxford Street next to McDonalds. You know you're going to go bust even if your burgers are amazing …' The writer/director channelled his frustration into the shoot, which proved to be as harrowing as its on-screen result. 'It was brutal. Make no mistake about that. There were no *lattes* on set, put it that way. [Lead actress and producer Nadja and I] both suffered a lot making it, emotionally, physically and financially. [And we had] no budget. Like Eli Roth's monthly Starbucks bill, probably.'

Somehow, these harsh working conditions, combined with Mason's will to prove himself outside the system, may well have been the source of this movie's strength and originality. The antithesis of glossy Hollywood horror, *Broken* will not please everyone, but it stands as a testimony to what a gifted and determined filmmaker can accomplish with a limited cast and crew, and no budget to speak of.

'You'll never feel safe in your home again' (*Them*)

The year also saw some quality productions come out of France, Spain, and even Sweden, where a little film called *Frostbite* (*Frostbiten*) was one of the first horror features to see the light of day (pun intended) in the country.

Frostbite.

From first-time director Anders Banke, *Frostbite* follows Annika (Petra Nielsen) and her daughter Saga (Grete Havnesköld) as they move at the beginning of the winter to a little town in Lapland, where the population slowly gets turned into vampires, a month away from the first rays of sun. Entertaining, full of great special effects and playing with the genre's clichés, *Frostbite* built on the specificities of its location, but suffered from its structure, divided between the parallel adventures of the mother and her daughter, and from its tone, at times too light and teenager-friendly.

'We totally lack the tradition of making fantastic films,' producer Magnus Paulsson says[171]. 'We have a small film industry that puts out about 20-25 features per year. Out of them, maybe four or five make it internationally, and it is usually heavy dramas, police movies or silly comedies. It took a long time to convince people that it is possible to do something like *Frostbite* here in Sweden. There have been some attempts at making horror here, but nothing really worked out. Hopefully people now realise that it is possible and we will see more fun films coming out. They have realised that in our neighbouring countries Denmark and Norway, so I think we can look forward to some cool features in the near future that use the cool (and sometimes very cold) landscapes here.'

This unusual production was screened in festivals around the world, and received the Best Film Award at Fantasporto. Says Banke[172]: 'What's really pleasing to us is that it's getting a theatrical release in many countries. The thing is, there are quite a number of low-budget vampire films churned out each year, most of them not very good. But as *Frostbite* is Swedish, and has an exotic and unusual setting, I think it makes the film stand out from the crowd. Also, ironically, since it is in Swedish, it's considered an arthouse film in English-speaking territories, and both our UK/US distributors are well-known and respected arthouse specialists. So, we've made a "quality" film! Maybe it won't do as much business as if it had been shot in English, who knows,

171 Email interview with the author, October 2006.

172 Email interview with the author, October 2006.

but for most territories it simply doesn't matter. Even though I despise dubbing, I'm actually looking forward to seeing *Frostbite* dubbed into Spanish, German and Russian. I think it'll be a very surreal experience!'

In Spain, 2006 was the year the last Fantastic Factory production, Brian Yuzna's *Beneath Still Waters* (2005), adapted from a novel by Matthew J Costello, came out on DVD. One of the Factory's most ambitious pictures, with underwater scenes and multiple locations, this tale of an ancient evil brewing in a town flooded by the construction of a dam may have been too much to handle for the Filmax subdivision. The photography is, as always, gorgeous and the beginning of the movie is convincing enough, but the disastrous international cast, cramped sets and rushed third act leave an impression of low production value. Clearly out of its depth, Fantastic Factory closed its gates indefinitely at the end of the production. 'At the beginning it was really a lot of fun,' Yuzna said of his Spanish experience in a 2006 interview[173], 'because we were doing something new and it was very successful. But [success] changed the nature of the company. The decision-making got to be bureaucratic and there was less risk-taking. Eventually there wasn't really anybody in the ownership of the company that were genre people … They quit being quite so supportive of the more commercial or exploitative elements and I think that the last few pictures reflected that. Those pictures didn't have the support the first ones had so there was never a chance to fix the stuff that didn't work with reshoots.'

The Abandoned. Them.

But even without its horror subdivision, Filmax would continue to produce and distribute genre features, and their success would grow quickly. Nacho Cerdà's *The Abandoned* (2006) was soon followed by an anthology TV series, *Six Films to Keep You Awake* (*Películas Para No Dormir*, 2005-2006), which could be seen as the Spanish answer to *Masters of Horror*. With episodes directed by Álex de la Iglesia, Jaume Balagueró, Paco Plaza, Enrique Urbizu, Narciso Ibáñez Serrador and Mateo Gil, the show was inspired by Serrador's own *Historias Para no Dormir* which ran from 1965, and gathered the hottest talents in the country for six very different 70-minute films. The best – Balagueró's *To Let* (*Para Entrar A Vivir*), Plaza's *A Christmas Tale* (*Cuento de Navidad*) and de la Iglesia's *The Baby's Room* (*La Habitación del Niño*) – were shown in horror festivals, and all were later released on DVD, Lionsgate picking up distribution rights in the US.

Meanwhile, France continued its wave of hyper-real horror with two new productions: *Satan* (*Sheitan*) and *Them* (*Ils*).

Kim Shapiron's *Satan* centres around a bunch of young Parisians who, after a night out, follow a girl they've met in a club to her family's countryside house. The film takes more than an hour to set up the scene and familiarise the viewers with the characters, but whether the audience is supposed to get attached to these misogynistic and aggressive drunkards is hard to tell. Little happens during this introduction, but the last act, when the deranged clan which welcomed them inside their home reveals their real intentions, is pure *Grand Guignol*. Oddly paced, crude and eventually unrewarding, *Satan* nevertheless features a fascinating performance by Vincent Cassel as the unavoidable country hillbilly.

Them, from first-time directors Xavier Palud and David Moreau, is a linear and classical home invasion story in which a French couple is attacked at night in their isolated home in Romania by an invisible enemy. With a dark photography, absence of sub-plots, minimum amount of blood

173 Quoted in 'Brian Yuzna, *Beneath Still Waters* interview', Daniel Robert Epstein, *UnderGround Online*, 2006, http://www.ugo.com/ugo/html/article/?id=17380

and emphasis on sound effects rather than music, Moreau and Palud keep things as simple and realistic as possible, insisting in the opening and again before the end credits that the script was based on true events. To add to the realness and tension, the camera stays with the frightened couple throughout, revealing only what they see. 'We thought it'd be the best way to scare people,' Moreau explains[174], 'and that was our only goal. We wanted the audience to follow the story with the characters, and understand what's going on at the same time as the characters.' The nature of the assailant therefore remains unknown until the ending, a fact that the film's PR milked for all its worth, even though its divulgence

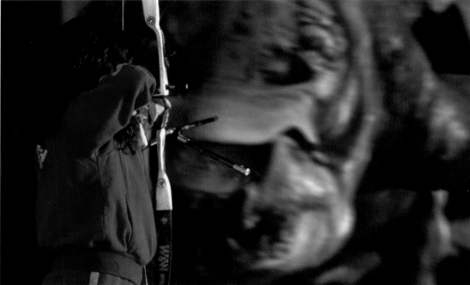

is rather anticlimactic. 'We wanted to avoid anything that had to do with evil or ghosts,' Palud says[175]. 'We thought that choosing villains who weren't evil, who weren't bad but were the result of external circumstances was more disturbing than yet another boogeyman.' This efficient, if slightly too long despite its 77 minute runtime, little film was well received in France and abroad, and allowed its writing-directing duo to have their first meetings with Hollywood studios.

Creature Feature

Although Asia took a break from long-haired ghosts in 2006, the continent didn't forget about horror altogether. South Korean director Joon-ho Bong's *The Host* (*Gwoemul*) may have been the only notable genre picture to come out, but it marked a clear departure from the scary movies of the previous years. A move forward or a throwback to the era of the monster movie (*kaiju*, as they are known to the fans)? In any case, this story of a family fighting to survive and stay together when a monster emerges from the Han River did not go unnoticed. With impressive visual effects, strong characters, a beautifully designed monster and gorgeous cinematography, *The Host* stunned both South Korea, where it became the highest-grossing local movie up to that point, and the rest of the world, where thanks to the buzz generated by its Cannes premiere, it received a theatrical release in late 2006/early 2007 in several countries, including the UK, Australia and the United States.

The Host.

While its subject matter may have seemed silly, *The Host* included elements of political satire. Inspired by a 2000 incident where a member of the US military working in Seoul dumped a large quantity of toxins down the drain, triggering a wave of anti-American sentiment amongst South Koreans, the movie begins with a scene in which a US scientist orders his assistant to get rid of bottles of formaldehyde in a similar fashion. It then depicts local authorities as indifferent, corrupt and propagating lies, claiming that the monster is the host of a deadly virus, and ends with environmental demonstrators protesting the use by the government of a hazardous chemical weapon to eliminate the creature. 'There are lots of elements of satire here,' Bong commented in a 2007 interview[176]. 'I think it's because we have a lead protagonist family who are weak and powerless. I sometimes wonder if, for the weak and the powerless, democracy might not be such a huge help … In regards to the Korean society or some other countries, I wonder how much the system really protects the weak … Our family is going on this long journey, but no one helps them at all. That becomes the focal point of the satire. Even though our military dictatorship is over and it's more democratic than the past, there's always this sort of thing remaining there, especially for the lower class.'

The Host won numerous prizes, including Best International Film at the Saturn Awards, Best Film at the Asian Film Awards, and Best Special Effects in Sitges.

174 Interview with the author, Brussels, Belgium, April 2008.
175 Interview with the author, Brussels, Belgium, April 2008.
176 'The Host: Monstrous political satire', Steve Biodrowski, *Hollywood Gothique*, 8 March 2007, http://hollywoodgothique.bravejournal.com/entry/24485

2007:

'It's not a remake. It's not a sequel. And it's not based on a Japanese one.'

(Tagline for *Hatchet*, 2007)

WHILE THE US GOVERNMENT KEPT SENDING TROOPS TO IRAQ, A NATION still torn by suicide bombings and other terrorist attacks, America also experienced a deeply traumatic event at home when on 16 April, Seung-hui Cho, a 23-year-old student from the Virginia Polytechnic Institute and State University (Virginia Tech) went on a shooting rampage in his school, killing thirty-two and injuring twenty-three before committing suicide. The event is recorded as the deadliest school shooting in US history, and reignited the gun control debate.

The year was also difficult for the United Kingdom. Still stunned by the high profile disappearance on 3 May of three-year-old Madeleine McCann during a family holiday in Portugal, the country was also shocked by the discovery (and thankfully, disablement) of two car bombs outside a crowded nightclub near Piccadilly Circus in central London on 29 June, and by the explosion of another car bomb at Glasgow International Airport the following day, where five were injured. If these events weren't enough, a strain of bird flu, potentially deadly to humans, was found in a turkey farm in Suffolk, and an outbreak of foot-and-mouth disease in Surrey caused the destruction of all livestock in the contaminated area in August.

2007 was also the year horror was declared dead by both the *LA Times* and the *NY Times*, after the consecutive underperformances of *Grindhouse*, *28 Weeks Later* and *Hostel: Part II*. An adaptation of Stephen King's *1408* then made a killing at the box office over the summer, prompting observers to claim that the R-rated horror trend had come to an end. R-rated productions *Saw IV* and *30 Days of Night* became big successes around Halloween, yet 2007 remained, in the critics' minds, the time that the popularity of the genre declined, and horror was no longer a sure-fire way to return and multiply an investment. From November 2007 to mid-February 2008, Hollywood was rocked by the longest strike by the Writers Guild of America in history. This halted TV and film production and cost the industry an estimated $1.5 billion.

But never mind strikes and box-office results, some excellent features were released over the course of the year, and independents as well as studios released some great R-rated, grown-up films made to please scary movie fans. From torture flicks to eighties slashers, supernatural villains to zombies, every horror buff could find a little something to their liking.

More Gore in Store

If *Hostel* and the *Saw* series had been embraced by the horror community and, to some degree, mainstream audiences, in the previous years, 2007 wouldn't be so kind to what was now widely known as 'torture' films, and some of the blame can be laid at the door of one movie: Roland Joffé's *Captivity*, starring Elisha Cuthbert.

Captivity.

Tailored by its producer, After Dark Films, to surf the hyper-violence wave, *Captivity* – the story, as its title subtly suggests, of a female model captured by a bunch of potential torturers – caught the public's attention in a big way in March, when dozens of particularly disturbing billboards appeared in Los Angeles and New York. These were described by the Internet Movie Database as follows: the advertising took the form of 'multi-panelled posters. The first panel was labelled "Abduction", featuring actress Elisha Cuthbert appearing petrified, her mouth covered by a black gloved hand. The second panel was labelled "Confinement" and showed Cuthbert behind a chain-link fence with a bloody thumb poking through. The third was labelled "Torture" and featured Cuthbert on her back, her face hidden within a white cast and with red tubes going up her nose. The fourth panel was labelled "Termination" and featured what appeared to be a limp body hanging over a table.'[177] The posters caused such uproar that After Dark Films and Lionsgate, who released the movie theatrically, decided to take them down immediately, and executives from both companies passed the buck on to each other. As it turned out, the advertisements had been rejected by the MPAA, who customarily reviews promotional materials

177 'Trivia for *Captivity*', *Imdb*, http://
www.imdb.com/title/tt0374563/trivia

Captivity.

178 'MPAA Suspends Rating of After Dark Films' *Captivity*', MPAA Press Release, 29 March 2007, quoted in *Remove the Rating*, 30 March 2007, http://removetherating.blogspot.com/2007/03/updatempaa-press-release.html

179 'BC's Top 10 Best and Worst List of 2007!', Brad Miska, *Bloody-Disgusting*, 29 December 2007, http://www.bloody-disgusting.com/news/10782

180 Interview with the author, Los Angeles, USA, January 2008.

181 'Shades of Ugliness: An Issue of Humanity', David Poland, The Hot Button, 4 June 2007, http://www.thehotbutton.com/today/hot.button/2007_thb/070604_monhtml

182 Interview with the author, Prague, Czech Republic, October 2006. This interview took place before the Virginia Tech massacre.

183 Roth is referring to the October 2006 Amish school shooting, when milk truck driver Charles Carl Roberts shot five girls dead and injured five others before committing suicide.

184 Interview with the author, Los Angeles, USA, January 2008.

for all movies submitted for a rating. As a result of this flagrant violation of the MPAA rules, the Board issued a 'month-long suspension of the ratings process,' which meant that *Captivity* would 'not be eligible for consideration by the ratings board until on or after 1 May 2007, and [would] be given no priority scheduling at that time.'[178]

Joffé's film finally opened in the US on 13 July, to disastrous reviews (no press screenings were organised before the release) and equally bad box office returns. Horror website Bloody-Disgusting later named it the Worst Horror Film of 2007, noting: 'This isn't just the worst horror movie of the year, or even the worst movie of the year … it's one of the worst films EVER MADE.'[179]

Sadly, the negative attention given to *Captivity* affected the reception of Eli Roth's *Hostel: Part II* when it opened on 8 June.

Not unlike the After Dark Films production, *Hostel: Part II* first caught the eye of moviegoers when, less than two weeks before Christmas 2006, a teaser poster showing a close-up of a piece of meat appeared in theatres and caused controversy. The ad, which had been approved by the MPAA, was particularly smart: as graphic an image as can possibly be, it was nothing you couldn't find at the butchery department of the nearest supermarket. It also illustrated Eli Roth's point that in the first and second film, human beings were objectified and treated like meat. Over the next three months, the image was followed by two others: one, bloodless and slick, of a woman's body holding its own severed head, was first seen at the New York Comic Con and on the Internet in February; the other, combining the previous two and showing the shadow of the body and the head superimposed over the meat photo, appeared in some theatres shortly after the After Dark advertising debacle. Unsurprisingly after the debate caused by the *Captivity* campaign, an additional two ads, released a few weeks before the opening of the movie, were much more restrained: the first showed a woman (actress Heather Matarazzo) hanging upside down on a grey background, her screaming face hidden by the title; the other was a simple shot of Roger Bart in his butcher's apron, a barely visible drill in his hand.

But no amount of restraint or cleverness could have saved *Hostel: Part II* from the tidal wave of criticism and controversy that would accompany its release. 'Nobody knew what the first movie was [when it came out]; it wasn't a threat to people, it came out of nowhere,' Roth explains[180]. 'But then it got into the culture, it was this new wave of films and people had their knives out for me. A lot of people were bashing the sequel before it even came out. With the second one, the reviews became confessionals; they weren't even talking about the film, they were afraid that people would say they liked that sort of thing. People were terrified that if they reviewed the film and gave it a good review, people would think that they endorsed that behaviour.' While the BBC, *Variety* and *The Hollywood Reporter* were amongst those few mainstream critics who appreciated the sequel, others returned to the torture porn debate. A low point was reached when Hot Button blogger David Poland publicly admitted watching an illegal copy of the film, an in-house pirate version circulating in the US a couple of weeks before the release, and described one of its scenes, Heather Matarazzo's death, as 'the most disgusting, degrading, misogynistic, soulless shit I have ever seen in a movie that is going to be released widely in this country.'[181] Says Roth: 'Poland bought a copy on the street and fast-forwarded through it; he watched one scene and then he'll justify what he did, like he's a moral crusader and he did the right thing by not paying to see the movie. He thought it made him look like a better person. But you don't make a movie like that without knowing you're going to offend some people. The smart people get it, and the ones that rebel against it are often the ones that end up looking stupid.'

What many reviewers didn't seem to notice was that *Hostel: Part II* was in many ways a direct answer to the criticism directed against the first one. Picking up where the previous film left off, *Hostel: Part II* opens with the end of Paxton's story before concentrating on a group of three female art students on a trip from Rome to Prague, who are lured to the notorious hostel by Axelle (played by Vera Jordanova), a model they meet in one of their classes. Putting girls in the lead roles was a risky move, but Roth makes his protagonists more likeable than *Hostel*'s

boys, eases off on the sex and gore, and turns the 'female victim' stereotype on its head in a finale reminiscent of Lorena Bobbitt's infamous act of revenge and emancipation.

In parallel, the writer/director also shows the inner workings of the criminal organisation by following the journey of the two men (played by Roger Bart and Richard Burgi) who paid to kill the girls. Not only does this move make the story more suspenseful – the lack of dread and anticipation being one of the main flaws of the first film – but it also gives viewers a different, powerful perspective on the events. 'I wanted to make a movie about the dark places that people go to and how every human being, no matter how normal and nice, is capable under the right circumstances of doing something horrific,' Roth says[182]. 'I think that's scarier to people than a guy with a mask chasing people with a chainsaw. The people doing the killing aren't necessarily bad people; they've just been driven to this place by boredom and insanity, and that makes them more real. I think when people watched *Hostel* they thought of the Iraq war and the hostages and Al-Qaeda decapitations, but I think right now the fear in America is your next-door neighbour. They're scared of the person next door who's never done anything wrong, because of that guy who went out and killed those girls at the Amish school[183], it's the most horrific thing you could ever conceive of, and this person never committed a crime in his life. Rapists and serial killers, you know where you stand with them. You know what they do. But these people out there who are now kidnapping people, you used to go to church with them, they'd baby-sit …'

Hostel: Part II is on the whole less bloody than the first instalment, but one can only wonder how an R-rated film got away with as graphic an image as the close-up seen in the end sequence, when one of the killers gets his comeuppance. 'The MPAA is great,' Roth comments[184]. 'Any time I approached them and we discussed as filmmakers what the point of the scene is, they really get it. I said if you don't show it, people are going to be thinking about it, but if you show it, it actually makes the scene a little less horrific and more like a cheer. I was careful about how I shot it; I obscured part of the dick so it wasn't technically full frontal, it wasn't erect and it wasn't

Hostel: Part II.

149

Saw IV.

a sexual situation. During the scene where he's trying to rape [Lauren German's character Beth], you never see anything. But during this scene it's important, because it's not going to upset anybody. We've been building that tension, and after that scene with Heather upside down, we need that relief where everyone can cheer. I'm not ending the movie on a depressing note.'

Not all rating boards were as understanding, however, but as Roth discovered, different things would upset different people. 'Comedy usually only plays in the culture where it was made, but horror is universal. But it's interesting to see what scenes they consider scarier in different countries. In Germany, they made us cut the scene with the kids playing soccer with the head! I guess kids really did that in Germany, I guess they were afraid they would copy it, I don't know! In Japan, the censors didn't let *Hostel* in theatres, but they let *Hostel: Part II* in theatres. They didn't like the American disfiguring the Japanese girl.'

Released in blockbuster season, and up against *Ocean's Thirteen*, *Hostel: Part II* stood little chance and opened at a disappointing $8.8 million: half of the first one's opening box office take. 'We had two studios [Lionsgate and Screen Gems], so neither felt 100% ownership of the movie, and they each gave it 50% of the release, thinking, it's *Hostel: Part II*, it can take care of itself. They assumed it would automatically be *Saw II*; they were already talking about the *Hostel* franchise. They forgot that the first one came out in January.'

Combined with the bad results of Robert Rodriguez and Quentin Tarantino's *Grindhouse* in April and Juan Carlos Fresnadillo's *28 Weeks Later* in May, *Hostel: Part II*'s mediocre opening incited film analysts to believe that the genre had reached the end of its cyclical popularity, and that horror was, once again, 'dead'. In the words of the *New York Times*: 'Moviegoers put a nail in the coffin of a dying horror boom this weekend.'[185] But the summer already saw some colour back on the cadaver's cheeks with *1408*'s $20 million opening, and in the fall, *Halloween*, *Saw IV* and *Resident Evil: Extinction* brought the genre back to life.

As violent as *Hostel: Part II*, Darren Bousman's *Saw IV* came out just before Halloween, unaffected by the whole torture porn hoopla, and opened at $31 million before grossing an additional $32 million by December in the US. Just as gory as its predecessors, this fourth instalment seemed to target exclusively the most rabid fans of the series, as the numerous convolutions of its plot made it impossible to follow for anyone lacking a deep knowledge of the saga's earlier events and protagonists. Still, the franchise shows no signs of slowing down, *Saw V* being, at the time of writing, directed by production designer David Hackl and scheduled for a 24 October 2008 release; and *Saw VI* being already in the works, with editor Kevin Greutert set to helm.

The MPAA may have been more inclined than ever to give a wide array of pictures an R-rating, but the wave of ultra-violent films observers now referred to as 'hard R' was a concern to MPAA chairman and Chief Executive Officer Dan Glickman, who realised that the rating included too large a range of scenes, from the supernatural shocks of *Dead Silence* to the severed penis of *Hostel: Part II*. Torn between the demands of parents no longer able to deduce from the rating whether a movie was suitable for their kids, and the insistence of the studios to get rid of the NC-17 rating, Glickman publicly called, in March 2007, for the creation of a new intermediate certificate. No agreement has so far been reached, but the debate clearly threw light on a certain unease in the existing system.

185 'Box Office for Horror Movies is Weak, Verging on Horrible', Michael Cieply, *NY Times*, 11 June 2007, http://www.nytimes.com/2007/06/11/movies/11hostel.html?_r=3&oref=slogin&oref=slogin&oref=slogin
186 Email interview with the author, March 2007.

'See! Two great movies for one low price!' (*Grindhouse*)

One of the most highly anticipated movies of the year, *Grindhouse*, a double feature inspired by the exploitation films of the seventies, was the brainchild of Robert Rodriguez and Quentin Tarantino, who each contributed one half of the bill.

Grindhouse opens with Rodriguez's *Planet Terror*, a zombie flick following go-go dancer Cherry (Rose McGowan) and her ex El Wray (Freddy Rodriguez) as they fight to survive a living dead epidemic. Fun, outrageously bloody and filled with action, great music and snappy dialogue, the segment would have been close enough to the feel of a 42nd Street B-movie, had it not been for its excellent cast and top-notch special effects. Clocking in at ninety minutes, *Planet Terror* suffers from minor pacing issues and could have been a bit shorter, but is on the whole a greatly entertaining gorefest.

The second part of the anthology is Tarantino's *Death Proof*, about a stunt driver called Stuntman Mike (an incredibly charismatic Kurt Russell) planning the killing of two separate groups of girls with his death-proof car. The film is structured in two acts: the first, a sort of extended opening scene introducing Russell's character, ends in a very impressive car crash but is otherwise too long and way too chatty; the latter, in which Stuntman Mike messes with the wrong girls (Rosario Dawson, Zoe Bell and Tracie Thoms, all amusing and likeable), is much more original and tense, and its finale was certainly the best 'girl power' scene of the year.

But for many, the biggest draw of the movie was the break between the films, when a selection of fake trailers was shown (another trailer, Rodriguez's *Machete*, also appeared before *Planet Terror*.) Directed by Edgar Wright (*Don't*), Rob Zombie (*Werewolf Women of the SS*) and Eli Roth (*Thanksgiving*), each one compiled the best, bloodiest and funniest scenes of homage to the slashers and exploitation films of the seventies and early eighties. Says Roth of his contribution[186]: 'Quentin showed me the *Machete* lobby cards that Robert did, and asked if I wanted to do a trailer. I immediately knew what I wanted to do: *Thanksgiving*. It's the dream

Grindhouse: Death Proof. Grindhouse: Planet Terror.

151

slasher film I've secretly wanted to make for years. My friend Jeff Rendell and I wrote an outline for it years ago, and have always been talking about when to do it. This was the perfect opportunity, and Jeff flew to Prague and played the Pilgrim, the killer in the film. I got to live out my eighties slasher dream project.'

The concept of *Grindhouse* was original and daring, the directors adulated, the reviews glowing, and the promise of the excesses the two mavericks had in store made horror fans salivate with anticipation. Yet the movie was a crushing box office disappointment; opening early April in the US on 2,624 screens, it only returned $11.5 million on its $60+ million budget, and grossed a total $25 million in the country during its eleven-week run. Once the initial shock had passed and analysts started to ponder, the reasons for this failure seemed clear. How could a 195-minute, $60 million homage to a sub-genre few were familiar with (what percentage of the movie-going population remembers 1974's *I Dismember Mama* or 1975's *Ilsa, She-Wolf of the SS*?) ever have been profitable? A vanity project financed only thanks to the two directors' clout, *Grindhouse* confused even those who did get the concept: how could a slick, star-studded blockbuster replicate the feel of exploitation films, even with the odd scratches and missing reels? Too obscure, violent and long for some, too neat for others, the movie simply didn't have massive box-office appeal, despite the combined power of the filmmakers' names.

Consequently, *Grindhouse* was cut in half for international release. Extended cuts of *Planet Terror* and *Death Proof* opened separately abroad, often months apart, and while many fans saw this as a simple attempt to charge the admission price twice, the move not only made sense commercially but also artistically, as Tarantino himself pointed out in a 2007 interview: 'Especially if they were dealing with non-English language countries, they don't really have this tradition. Not only do they not really know what a grindhouse is, they don't even have the double feature tradition.'[187] The filmmaker further explained that he and Rodriguez had made feature-length versions of their films before cutting them down to 90 minutes each for the double bill, so restoring them to their full length was more acceptable than it originally seemed. In the US, *Death Proof* and *Planet Terror* came out separately on DVD, and as in the international release, the trailers were missing from both releases.

The Gore the Merrier

Hostel: Part II, *Saw IV* and *Grindhouse* weren't the only brutal, R-rated pictures the studios released that year, far from it. Most of 2007's significant genre productions were adult horror films, and they were met with varying degrees of success, which on occasion seemed inversely proportional to their quality. With relatively few sequels and remakes and a good diversity of projects, it may have seemed for a brief moment that Hollywood was finally taking horror seriously. Besides the films falling under the 'torture' label, a series of violent movies came out that did not resort to supernatural scares.

One of the only follow-ups of the year, *The Hills Have Eyes II*, from Fox Atomic and German director Martin Weisz, came out in March 2007. Written by Wes Craven and his son Jonathan Craven, it focused on a group of National Guard trainees who unfortunately run into the killer mutant clan during a rescue mission. Mixing *The Hills Have Eyes* with *The Descent*

The Hills Have Eyes II. Vacancy.

187 'Tarantino Chops Feature-length *Death Proof* for *Grindhouse*', *Rotten Tomatoes*, 4 April 2007, http://uk.rottentomatoes.com/news/comments/?entryid=412023

and a hint of Iraqi combat situation, this sequel was undeniably inferior to Aja's remake and received generally poor reviews at the time of its release, but was, despite its pacing issues and underdeveloped characters, a fun and gory, if cheesy, guilty pleasure. 'When I originally read the script I immediately thought of one of my all time favourite movies ever: I just love *Aliens*,' Weisz explains[188]. 'I was like, wow, soldiers, caves, mines, mutants! I was immediately attracted; it was a chance to at least come close to the idea of having darkness, suspense, and people not knowing what's around the corner.' Much more ambitious in scope than the first one, but made on a similar budget, *The Hills Have Eyes II* may have suffered from the complexity of its script and the amount of characters, sets and stunts involved. 'We had to make some compromises to make it work in the time that we had, because we had such a quick turnaround. We have 42 days to shoot and have to deliver it on 16 February, so the turnaround is so quick that even if we'd had more days to shoot, it would have cut the time we have for post-production. We only have three weeks for editing.' In any case, *The Hills Have Eyes II* proved profitable, opening widely with nearly $10 million grossed in its first three days, and an additional $10 million during the rest of its run in the US.

The following month, Screen Gems released *Vacancy*, a thriller directed by Nimrod Antal and starring Luke Wilson and Kate Beckinsale. The story of a couple realising that the dodgy hotel room they're in is the scene of a snuff movie and they might well be the next victims, *Vacancy* is a rare example of a film which would have been interesting and successful with a smaller budget than its reported $19 million and unknowns in the lead roles. Surprisingly slick for such a gloomy exploitation script, its look would have been more fitting to its stripped-down narration, had it been grittier and closer to the snuff films and low-rent motels the plot describes. This tight little suspense drama is also hampered by its main characters, who are unlikeable and played by strangely out-of-place recognisable Hollywood actors; but despite these flaws and a few small incoherencies, Antal's movie is thrilling and unpretentious enough, and it paid back its initial investment during its time in US theatres.

The only high-profile genre remake to come out this year was also one of the most controversial. Rob Zombie's update of John Carpenter's *Halloween*, the 1978 classic which defined and popularised the slasher sub-genre, mixed in prequel elements and elaborated on the original's opening scene in which a five-year-old Michael Myers murders his sister. The film shows Myers's evolution from unloved and abused child to Dr Loomis's patient to homicidal maniac. Unfortunately, what seemed like a good idea, humanising a character formerly known as The Shape, in reference to his robot-like demeanour, works against Myers's strength as an unstoppable killer. No longer the mysterious, quasi-unbeatable menace he was in the previous eight instalments in the saga, Myers isn't exactly your next-door neighbour either, as the second half of the movie inexplicably changes the pace and depicts him as 'pure evil', a killing machine which has little to do with the kid we saw at the beginning. Neither freak of nature nor *Hostel*-like realistic murderer, Myers also isn't the implacable menace Carpenter created. In the classic *Halloween*, his on-screen time was so limited that an entire fan film has been made about his

Halloween.

188 Interview with the author, Ouarzazate, Morocco, October 2006.

actions between two appearances[189], the remake features him in practically every single scene. The same over-explanatory approach can be found in Zombie's treatment of the death sequences: if Carpenter used little blood and relied on camera moves and timing to create dread, the remake revels in gore and lingers on each killing, forgetting in the process to inject any kind of tension into the plot.

Like his previous films, Rob Zombie's *Halloween* is beautifully photographed and features great music and a cast of genre faves (from Malcolm McDowell and Brad Dourif to Udo Kier and Danny Trejo) but brings little new to the Michael Myers mythology, and doesn't allow the filmmaker's unique style and vision to shine through. Still, this $20 million (estimated) picture raked in $30 million on its 31 August opening weekend and a worldwide total of $78 million in theatrical sales. It also whetted the audience's appetite for slasher remakes, as the *Prom Night* redux would prove the following year.

Finally, opening in the States on 9 November, first-time director Franck Khalfoun's *P2*, co-written and produced by *High Tension*'s Alexandre Aja, pitted a young woman (Rachel Nichols) against a psychotic security guard (Wes Bentley) in a parking lot on Christmas Eve. Unfortunately, the charm of this linear and mildly entertaining little thriller wears off in its second half, due mostly to Bentley's over-the-top and sometimes downright laughable performance as the killer-with-a-bright-smile. A commercial failure in the US, *P2* was delayed to May 2008 in the UK, not the most appropriate time to release a Christmas-themed movie.

'You scream, you die.' (*Dead Silence*)

Not every R-rated film centred on realistic enemies in everyday situations, however. 2007 also had its share of supernatural villains on offer, including vampires, monsters, religious freaks, singing barbers and killer dolls.

Saw director James Wan made a much-awaited comeback with *Dead Silence*, an old-school ghost story revolving around Jamie (Ryan Kwanten), a young man whose wife was killed just after receiving a strange doll in the mail, and who slowly understands that her death is linked to the legend of a murdered ventriloquist called Mary Shaw. Written by *Saw* partner Leigh Whannell, *Dead Silence* is, as is often the case in this sub-genre, visually stunning; each doll is striking and the evil Mary Shaw is genuinely creepy. With some chilling scenes (like the one in the cupboard under the sink) and amazing sets, Wan and Whannell gave the movie a unique and eerie mood, but the plot and characters could have used more development. The concept is promising, the settings and props look good, but the storyline seems rushed, as if too many ideas had been crammed together without taking the time to find a coherent line between them, and the protagonists and dialogue are bland. Rumours of studio interventions plaguing the production might offer an explanation for this semi-failure, but whatever the causes, one can only admire Wan's determination to present fans with something different rather than cash in on the planetary success of his first feature. 'After *Saw*, there was a lot of pressure for us to come up with something groundbreaking and shocking and all that,' Wan told Horror.com in 2007[190], 'and I think in a lot of ways, psychologically, we went against that. We were like, you know what? We're not going to do that. We're going to do something that people are familiar with, and we're going to tell that story a bit different. We found a new twist for a story that people are used

P2. Dead Silence.

189 Bryan Kupko and John Slade's *Halloween Revisited*, 2006.
190 'James Wan and Leigh Whannell on *Dead Silence*', Staci Layne Wilson, *Horror.com*, 15 March 2007, http://www.horror.com/php/article-1548-1.html

to.' Unfortunately, these good intentions were not rewarded, and the $20 million *Dead Silence* scared up less than $8 million on its March opening.

Even more unusual was Tim Burton's *Sweeney Todd: the Demon Barber of Fleet Street*, based on a musical by Stephen Sondheim. Starring Johnny Depp in the titular role and Helena Bonham Carter as Mrs Lovett, the owner of the pie shop who uses the meat of the barber's unfortunate victims, this dazzlingly beautiful horror musical was too gory for general audiences and too full of songs for genre fans, which may explain its poor commercial reception: a $9.3 million opening for a $50 million budget. Despite gorgeous photography and production design, great performances and a strong screenplay, the constant singing of odd rhythms and melodies put off many viewers, who simply could not take one more song. Still, critics and foreign audiences loved it, and *Sweeney Todd: the Demon Barber of Fleet Street* went on to win two Golden Globes and be nominated for two BAFTAs and three Academy Awards.

Frank Darabont's *The Mist*, the adaptation of one of Stephen King's best novellas (published in the 1985 collection *Skeleton Crew*), also turned out to be a bitter box-office disappointment. The story of a small Maine town suddenly engulfed in a thick mist inhabited by quasi-Lovecraftian monsters, *The Mist* had been a long-time project for Darabont, who had acquired the rights thirteen years prior to the making of the movie. The writer/director chose to stay close to the original material, taking few liberties and only changing the ending, opting for a much more controversial and pessimistic finale which was heavily debated by fans and critics. Dark, intense, atmospheric but relatively low on gore, Darabont's film may emphasise its underlying message – your fellow man is just as dangerous as the monster outside – too heavily and lose some breath in the second half, but it is still a gutsy and haunting effort, and a worthy entry into the slimy creature sub-genre. Opening on 2,423 screens in late November, *The Mist* sadly raked in a mere $8.9 million during its first weekend, and ended its seventeen-week course at $25 million nationally. Not bad, but hardly the hit it deserved to be. 'This was always going to be

Sweeney Todd: The Demon Barber of Fleet Street. The Mist.

a very bleak film and that meant it would never get blockbuster money,' Darabont explained in a 2008 interview with *Total Film*[191]. *The Mist* would later be released in a special edition DVD coupled with a black and white version of the movie.

Proving that there might well be some kind of divine justice, religious blockbuster *The Reaping*, starring Hilary Swank as a college professor investigating the recurrence of the ten plagues of Egypt in a Louisiana town, didn't do too well either. Full of ugly computer-generated effects and stereotypical characters, this silly cross between *The X-Files* and *The Omen* starts off intriguingly enough, but soon piles up incoherencies and predictable happenings. With an estimated budget of $40 million, *The Reaping* opened at $10 million, but paid back its initial cost and then some with the combined results of national and international theatrical sales (a total $62 million).

The story of a small Alaskan town attacked by a gang of vampires during the month of winter night, *30 Days of Night*, directed by David Slade (*Hard Candy*) and adapted from Steve Niles's eponymous best-selling comic book of 2002, was thankfully more successful at the box office. Gruesome and dark in every sense of the word, *30 Days of Night* presents bloodsuckers that aren't beautiful and seductive, like the suave creatures filmmakers of the previous decades depicted, but cruel, savage, animal-like monsters: an interesting – if far from unique – twist on the mythology. 'We set out to make a very ballsy movie,' Slade told *Rue Morgue* magazine in 2007[192]. 'Not fantasy. Not romance. I don't want the audience to feel safe.' But while *30 Days of Night* offers some great effects and chilling scenes, and the basic concept, similar to *Frostbite* but more adult in its execution, is excellent, the film suffers from a lack of structure, its protagonists spending most of its two-hour length hiding and waiting in a snow-covered night time environment whose dullness seems to reinforce the sensation that little happens. Still, Slade dared to deliver a dead serious and original take on an old and oddly unpopular creature, and fans appreciated the move, as *30 Days of Night* opened at nearly $16 million in October 2007 and grossed over $39 million in the USA.

One of the very few PG-13 releases of the year (along with teenage werewolf stinker *Blood and Chocolate* and predictable countryside chiller *The Messengers*, the latter produced, like *30 Days of Night*, by Raimi's Ghost House Pictures), *1408*, by Swedish director Mikael Håfström, was one of 2007's biggest successes, opening above the $20 million mark at the end of June (and over £1 million in the UK in September), and grossing nearly $72 million in US theatrical sales alone. Based on another short

The Reaping. 30 Days of Night.

story by Stephen King, but much lighter in tone than *The Mist*, this essentially bloodless tale of a paranormal investigator (John Cusack) spending a night in a haunted hotel room offered exactly the kind of mild, accessible scares summer audiences craved. But while the first act, where Cusack's unlikeable but three-dimensional character is warned against staying in the room by the hotel manager (an excellent Samuel L Jackson), brilliantly creates anticipation and prepares the audience for the shocks to come, the rest of the plot merely puts the protagonist through a series of increasingly odd and disparate occurrences, from apparitions to dimension shifts to snow storms. And if some of these supernatural events are reasonably spooky or surprising (the ghost falling off the window, for example, is a great touch), their lack of coherence, coupled with the absence of a backstory for room 1408, makes it decidedly less threatening, and the horrendous happy ending is likely to leave horror buffs with a bad aftertaste. But even though genre connoisseurs may not find much they haven't already seen in *The Haunting*, *The Shining*, or any number of haunted house features, *1408* still offers enough fun little frights to be an enjoyable ride, at least in its first half. After all, didn't the tagline warn that 'no one lasts more than an hour'?

'Jason, Freddy, Michael. We all need someone to look up to.' (*Behind the Mask: The Rise of Leslie Vernon*)

If 2003 had witnessed the resurgence of seventies horror, 2007 (and in a smaller measure, 2008) would see the release of a few productions directly inspired by eighties slasher films. Centring around relentless and often supernatural killers and featuring pretty young boys and girls meeting their doom one by one in a variety of gory ways, these features were the direct descendents of *Friday the 13th* (1980), *A Nightmare on Elm Street* (1984) and *Halloween* (1978). Interestingly for a sub-genre which produced so many bad films, the 2007 batch of slashers would include some of the best productions of the year.

A prime example of this neo-splatter trend is writer/director Adam Green's *Hatchet*. Starring Joel David Moore, Mercedes McNab, Kane Hodder and cameos from Robert Englund and Tony Todd, this 'old-school American horror', as the tagline put it, pits a bunch of lost tourists against disfigured and allegedly dead maniac Victor Crowley (aka Hatchet-face) in the New Orleans bayous. Green's intention was clearly to create a new genre icon, on a par with the killers he grew up seeing in the eighties. 'We won't know for twenty years if he can actually stand next to the likes of Freddy and Jason, but they were certainly the inspiration behind this sort of character,' the filmmaker says[193]. 'Way back in the day we had monsters like Dracula and the Wolf Man; years later we had the new era of Freddy and Jason, but we haven't had anything like that in about twenty years. The key ingredient is a simple and easily repeatable backstory that creates the mythology of the villain. Freddy was a child killer who got burned alive by the parents and now he stalks the children's dreams. Jason drowned as a boy and is back to avenge his mother's death. Victor Crowley was accidentally killed by his own

1408. Hatchet.

father after a prank went wrong.' The tale was already told in the movie trailer, which focused on establishing the character, and the backstory is repeated in the first part of the film, before the protagonists face the murderer. 'In this kind of film, less is more. Does the killer look cool? Is he unstoppable? Will he kill you in inventive and outlandish ways? Does he keep coming back? Those are usually the key ingredients.'

Bloody, over-the-top and deliberately schlocky, *Hatchet* is filled with silly characters and humorous scenes, yet manages to take its horror very seriously. Green's film is a true love song to eighties slashers, but a certain amount of post-modern, tongue-in-cheek comedy is necessary

191 'The Fog of Gore', Buzz, *Total Film* 143, July 2008, p 20.

192 'The Bloodsuckers of Barrow, Alaska', Liisa Ladouceur, *Rue Morgue* 72, October 2007, p 50.

193 Email interview with the author, January 2008.

to defuse the cheese associated with a sub-genre whose conventions are well-known to post-*Scream* audiences. 'I don't think there will ever be a true '80s slasher revival,' Green admits. 'Despite what Hollywood may say now, the slashers of the eighties were actually made to be serious fright-filled films and I don't think they realised until part 5 or 6 of a franchise just how silly they were and how much the audience liked the fun of them. With *Hatchet*, I took the stuff I missed about horror (the monster, the mythology, the non-CGI effects, the in-your-face gore) and essentially slammed it into a comedy. It's not a spoof, it's just fun. Unlike most of the horror films made today, *Hatchet* was more along the old grindhouse tone. No one walks out of it disturbed or really scared. You're laughing and cheering more than screaming.' In this regard, Green's film – and the following titles – are similar to Ryan Schifrin's 2006 *Abominable*: all are made by self-proclaimed horror fans, and if they wear their love of old-fashioned films on their sleeves, they also bring a touch of self-awareness to update their respective sub-genres for new audiences. Says Green: '*Hatchet* was shot in 2005 but Victor Crowley was created way back when I was just eight years old, in 1983. At the time we were making it, I had no idea about movies like *Behind The Mask*, *Abominable*, or *Wrong Turn 2*, which were also recapturing and celebrating the spirit of the eighties monster/slasher film style. What's most interesting is that each of those directors are now amongst my closest of friends, and we all met doing the festival circuit with our films, which were merely the films we wanted to see. I think it's really indicative of our age and a reflection of the films that inspired us as children in the eighties.'

Shot on a shoestring budget (an estimated $1.5 million), *Hatchet* seemed destined to go straight-to-DVD, had it not been for its makers' determination. Capitalising on the buzz generated by the movie's festival screenings around the world, from Tribeca to the London FrightFest and Sitges, they gathered an impressive cohort of fans into the Hatchet Army, an ever-growing mailing list alerting its members of every new screening and asking them to spread the word. Green and his producers also had the inspired idea to use a rejection letter from a studio as a promotional tool ('It's not a remake, it's not a sequel, and it's not based on a Japanese one') tapping directly into horror buffs' hope to see original R-rated productions flourish at the box office, without necessarily pushing the boundaries of what is acceptable on screen, since the filmmaker described it as 'a film that reminded everyone that horror does not have to be depraved, sickening and realistic in order to elicit a reaction.'[194] Green's efforts paid off, and *Hatchet* was eventually awarded a small theatrical release in the US in September 2007 and in the UK in October.

With cameos from Robert Englund (again!) and Zelda Rubinstein, *Behind the Mask: the Rise of Leslie Vernon* took humour and post-modernism a step further. The story of an aspiring supernatural killer, Leslie Vernon (Nathan Baesel), whose training is followed by a film crew, the first half takes the shape of a mockumentary, as Vernon's preparation for his first killing spree is seen through the lens of the camera crew, in the style of *The Blair Witch Project*. The realism of the format contrasts amusingly with the absurdity of the plot – the characters live in a world where Freddy Krueger, Jason Vorhees and Michael Myers are as real as Charles Manson and John Wayne Gacy – and co-writer and director Scott Glosserman exposes all the clichés of the genre as Vernon creates his own back story, picks his final girl or plans his future victims' reactions. The second half of the film is a more classical slasher, in which Vernon applies the principles he explained in the first part and cleverly subverts them. Funny and personable in the beginning, Baesel turns into a disquieting figure the moment he slips on his mask, and if the third act of the movie is never scary, it is directed seriously, like a real slasher, and never falls into spoof territory.

'We shot [it] in the classic slasher style which today we're quite familiar with and desensitised to,' says Glosserman[195]. 'Therefore I was able to stay as true to the template as I could, because the audience would on the one hand identify it as genuine horror, but also view it in its dated context which is endearing, nostalgic and almost humorous.' The mockumentary was approached in a similar way. 'I wanted my actors to play their docu-world roles as truthfully as they'd play any drama,

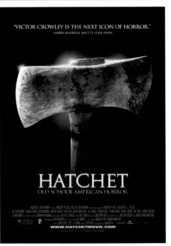

Hatchet.

194 'American Willies', Adam Green, *Film4 FrightFest Programme Collector's Edition*, August 2007.
195 Email interview with the author, September 2006.

158

because the comedy was going to be derived from the outlandishness of the situation. That's the difference between satire, what we did, and spoof. Parody/spoof hams everything up by overacting and overwriting... I decided that the *Blair* docu-style world had to be as real as possible. The dialogue had to be authentic because it was going to become stilted and campy when we got to horror. The aesthetic had to be video, like a newscast, because we'd be on grainy super 16mm to make it look like the classic slasher films when we got to horror. There couldn't be any music in the docu-world, but we'd have heavy scoring from beginning to end of the horror segments, and so on.'

Like *Hatchet*, *Behind the Mask: the Rise of Leslie Vernon* was made by a fan for the fans, and requires a certain knowledge and understanding of the slasher rules. This prerequisite may be one of the factors explaining the lack of enthusiasm with which the movie was met outside the genre community; the mix of comedy and horror, as for *Slither*, may also have contributed to the distributors' puzzlement. After a token theatrical release (72 screens over three weeks) in the US in March, it came out on DVD in June.

A low-budget, direct-to-DVD sequel to a four-year-old movie, *Wrong Turn 2: Dead End* had little chance to be any good, but first-time director Joe Lynch, a die-hard horror fan like Green and Glosserman, managed to beat the odds. 'The first *Wrong Turn* did well enough on DVD that [Twentieth Century Fox] thought, we could make more money off that title,' Lynch explains[196]. 'I was in Tokyo shooting a video for a videogame network, and I got a message asking me if I'd be interested in *Wrong Turn 2*. I replied right away and said, you had me at *Wrong*! They had a script written by Al Septien and Turi Meyer, who are doing *Smallville*. They're really good. They sent the script over and I read it on the train from Tokyo to Osaka and I have to admit, for all the flaws and clichés that I thought were in there at the time, there was a world of possibilities there, especially to make something that I would want to see.' Where other candidates saw little more than a quick cheque and a calling card, Lynch saw potential for a good feature. 'I started storyboarding the entire first scene and I wrote a twenty page bible of what I wanted

Behind the Mask: The Rise of Leslie Vernon.

196 Interview with the author, London, UK, August 2007.

to do, everything from the tone, the style, the way I wanted the characters, I had everything mapped out before I went in the room. I walked in with my storyboards and cardboard cut-outs when no one had come prepared, and I guess they liked what I did. If anything, I think it was mostly the passion that I showed that they liked.'

Lynch's enthusiasm paid off. *Wrong Turn 2: Dead End* is unpretentious and highly entertaining, thanks to the filmmaker's sense of timing, his understanding of the genre and his love of blood and guts, more than to the story itself, which sees a group of reality show contestants getting picked off by a family of deformed backwoods cannibals. The tone is set from the opening scene, in which a young actress gets cut in half after taking a wrong turn on the way to the show's base camp: outrageous, gory, fast-paced and acutely aware of the schlockiness of its subject matter. And if the first *Wrong Turn* was a clear homage to the survivals of the seventies, its sequel harks back to the excesses of eighties splatter films.

Wrong Turn 2: Dead End.

'At that time I was watching a lot of movies from the eighties, *Evil Dead II*, *Street Trash*, *Return of the Living Dead*, and I was thinking, where are the bygone days of having fun with a horror movie? At that moment *Hostel* had just opened at number one, so it was the advent of realistic horror, but I wanted to make something fun. For instance for that scene at the beginning of the film, in the script it ends with a cut to black right when the axe comes down but I thought, I want to go further, I want to have fun with this, I want the audience to scream and laugh and go, 'Did I just see that?' And that's what I remember watching *Evil Dead II*. That's what I got when I watched *Friday the Thirteenth: Part IV* when Jason slides down the machete. It's those kinds of gag moments that FX artists like Tom Savini had on the audience. It wasn't just trying to disturb you; it was a little bit of everything. It was horror and action and comedy – and not even comedy, more like a sense of humour. Not like too much winking at the camera but at least you knew that you were going to have fun.'

Wrong Turn 2: Dead End delivers fun in spades. The movie surprised audiences, critics and producers alike when it premiered at the London FrightFest, then when it was screened at Fantastic Fest and in Sitges. Still, it was released on DVD as planned. '[Fox] scheduled it, budgeted it and presold it as direct-to-DVD and my goal from the beginning was to make a movie that people would see on DVD and go, why wasn't that shown in theatres? I wanted to bring a grander scope to the film because the first movie was two groups or three groups and that's it, you don't get anything bigger within the woods. I wanted to broaden it a little bit, even down to shooting stuff from fifty yards up in the air, to open it a little bit. It's strategies like that that make people think it's bigger than they should have expected. Once Fox saw the film they thought it could go into theatres. There's been talks about it, but what they wanted most was to put it out on Halloween, because in the US it's the best market for horror films, especially one that has a brand name but not the critical laurels or a good buzz. Luckily for us we have both so far. But a $4 million splatter film could not open in June, in the summer, against all the blockbusters.'

Finally, starring an out-of-control Crispin Glover as two evil twins playing a deadly game with five college friends camping in their neighbourhood, *Simon Says*, from writer/director William Dear, is a competently made, mildly amusing but formulaic slasher. Glover's over-the-top one-man show will make viewers smile and cringe in equal measure, but this decent yet very traditional movie is unlikely to leave any lasting impression.

Something in the air clearly must have called for slashers, as from the *Halloween* remake to 2008's *All the Boys Love Mandy Lane* and the *Prom Night* and *April Fool's Day* reduxes, Hollywood would come back several times to the simple stalk'n'slash pattern, taking it dead seriously or with a grain of salt, and bringing in varying degrees of innovation.

Maintain the Quarantine!

Zombies were once again popular in 2007, starring in several productions including *28 Weeks Later*, an excellent sequel to Danny Boyle's *28 Days Later* (2002), a film that had jumpstarted the living dead craze throughout the world, despite the filmmaker's insistence that his infected humans were actually still alive[197]. Helmed by Spanish director Juan Carlos Fresnadillo (*Intacto*), who co-wrote the script with Rowan Joffe and Jesus Olmo, *28 Weeks Later* takes place six months after the outbreak, when the US army monitors the repopulation of London by placing the survivors in a protected area on the Isle of Dogs while the rest of the capital is systematically cleaned. But a new arrival carrying the Rage virus soon spreads the disease throughout the safe zone.

When a follow-up to Boyle's hit was announced without the original cast, writer and director, horror fans, always a protective bunch, were extremely apprehensive. But the second film told a different story, on a bigger scale, and involved new and equally well-constructed characters: it elaborated on the premise of the original and offered a fresh and unique take on the catastrophe. Possibly more realistic even than *28 Days Later*, *28 Weeks Later* shows survivors caught between the plague and the US military, who shoot everyone, sane or sick, in the colonised district once the situation has got out of control. Mixing fears of widespread infection (whether from bird flu, SARS or mad cow disease) with a criticism of the invasion of Iraq (the enemy having changed from isolated British soldiers to organised American troops), Fresnadillo focuses on a family with two children, and while the emphasis is clearly put on the emotional, human side of the events, the gore and scares have not been forgotten. 'I think this family drama is what makes it a bit different from lots of horror sequels about pretty people being chased for ages,' producer Andrew McDonald says[198]. 'We wanted a balance between a tense, threatening scary movie and a believable drama.' The film ends on a dark note, suggesting the possibility of a sequel which is, at the time this book goes to press, rumoured to be in the works.

Reviews were enthusiastic. CNN described it as combining 'traditional B-movie virtues – economy, invention, sinewy narrative spine – with the eerily resonant spectacle of a 21st-century metropolis stripped of its citizenry,'[199] while *Empire* praised it for its 'bigger action, more amazing deserted (and devastated) London sequences and biting contemporary relevance.'[200] But released on both sides of the Atlantic in May 2007, less than a week after mega-blockbuster *Spider-Man 3*, *28 Weeks Later* opened in the US at just under $10 million, slightly less than Boyle's *28 Days Later* had raked in on its first weekend, and ended up grossing less than the original in both countries.

Simon Says. 28 Weeks Later.

197 See the chapter on 2002.

198 Interview with the author, London, UK, October 2006.

199 'Review: *28 Weeks Later* thrillingly effective,' Tom Charity, *CNN*, 11 May 2007, http://www.cnn.com/2007/SHOWBIZ/Movies/05/10/review.28weeks/index.html

200 Kim Newman, *Empire Online*, May 2007, http://www.empireonline.com/reviews/ReviewComplete.asp?FID=133187

Released in September, *Resident Evil: Extinction*, a third take on the popular computer game, had more luck at the box-office. A post-apocalyptic western in the tradition of *Mad Max* (1979) and *Mad Max 2* (1981), set in the Nevada desert, *Resident Evil: Extinction* only had its zombies, the main character (Alice, played by Milla Jovovich and this time cloned in dozens of copies) and the evil corporation in common with the first instalment. The tone of the film and its scope could not have been more different. Directed by Russell Mulcahy (*Highlander* (1986), *Razorback* (1984)), this fast and dumb entry features some good zombie make-up and some horrible computer-generated effects, but doesn't have nearly enough plot twists to keep viewers awake over the course of its 95 minutes.

More entertaining was Scott Thomas's *Flight of the Living Dead: Outbreak on a Plane*, previously known as *Plane Dead* (until New

Resident Evil: Extinction. Fido. Flight of the Living Dead.

Line bought US distribution rights and imposed a title change). This was basically a living dead version of *Snakes on a Plane*. Consciously cheesy, this silly tongue-in-cheek effort was perfect for midnight screenings, and was a minor hit at every festival where it was screened, from Brussels to Sitges. It came out straight-to-DVD in the USA in October 2007.

Another DVD release, *Fido*, from Canadian director Andrew Currie, was praised by the specialist press for its witty social satire. This story of an undead human trained as a house pet even graced the cover of *Rue Morgue*, which dubbed it 'the zombie comedy with brains.'[201]

But although it wouldn't hit the rest of the world before the following year, the real zombie sensation of 2007 was *[Rec]*, from Spanish directors Jaume Balagueró and Paco Plaza. Following a TV crew, a handful of cops and firefighters and a few families trapped in a quarantined building, the movie takes place mainly in one location, over one night, with a small group of people, and the events are entirely seen through the crew's camera[202] (another undead film shot on a handheld camera would come out around the same time: the zero- budget British effort *The Zombie Diaries,* which premiered at FrightFest in August after a 'Zombie Walk' gathered hundreds of fans on Leicester Square). Realistic to the extreme, *[Rec]* takes its time to establish the premise, but quickly starts building up tension as soon as the first infected human appears and ends with all the shocks, thrills and heart-stopping jump-scares of a good funhouse ride.

'The idea came up during a conversation about the horror movies that we liked, why so many horror movies aren't scary, and how to reach a higher level of tension in film,' Balagueró explains[203]. 'We thought, why not use the language of live television? We thought we could place a camera with someone who is part of the story. We wrote a very simple script, without any dialogue because we wanted our actors to improvise.' To make the protagonists' reactions as natural and spontaneous as possible, the two directors only gave their cast and camera operator the vaguest indications and never let them know in advance where the danger was, or when they would be under attack. 'The cameraman is a very prestigious director of photography, Pablo Rosso[204], and we told him he would also be an actor and he would have to act with the others in the story. We gave him full freedom; he didn't always know what was going to happen and he had various options to react.' This audacious method explains some of the movie's apparent loose ends, such as the sick Asian father who is mentioned several times but never encountered. 'He was in a room, and if the actors had entered that apartment, they would have found him,' the filmmaker continues. 'He wasn't in the basic screenplay, but if the actors had taken a different way [than the one we had planned], we would have added him.' For the same reason, the origins of the disease which turns the building's inhabitants into zombies isn't spelled out but only suggested through various clues the survivors find towards the end. 'The film is realistic, so we didn't want to explain everything in a conventional way. We gave elements and the viewers can put them together and understand what happened, just like in real life. It's not obvious, but everything is there. And some people have already come to different conclusions than what we had imagined.'

The experiment was risky, but it quickly became obvious from the reactions of the festival-goers who saw it first, that this Filmax production would be welcomed by the fans. A video surfaced on YouTube soon after the Sitges screening in October, showing the audience jumping, applauding, screaming and literally hiding their faces during one of the film's most frightening moments. With hundreds of thousands of people viewing this clip, it only added to the buzz the movie had already generated. Balagueró and Plaza's collaboration won two Goya awards (Best Editing and Best New Actress), as well as several prizes in Sitges, Gérardmer, Fantasporto and Brussels. [Rec] opened in Spain in November 2007, and in Japan and most of Europe the following May/June. As of July 2008, no date has been set for the United States; Sony's Screen Gems bought the rights and produced its own remake, to be released late 2008. 'We discovered the remake through the Internet,' the co-director continues. 'They hadn't told us anything; they just made the film. They invited us to visit the shoot and it was exactly the same thing [as our film]. They shot the same movie scene by scene, but of course not with the system we had used.' Chances are that Balagueró and Plaza's terrifying original won't be shown on a big screen in the US until well after the release of the American version. In any case, the two writers-directors are already at work on a sequel.

[Rec]. The Orphanage.

'A tale of love. A story of horror.' (*The Orphanage*)

28 Weeks Later and *[Rec]* were not the only noteworthy European films of the year. Besides delivering one of the best zombie movies in years, Spain would also add a little masterpiece to the ghost sub-genre, while France would once again stun and delight horror buffs with yet another shocker.

First-time director Juan Antonio Bayona's *The Orphanage* (*El Orfanato*) follows Laura (Belén Rueda), a woman moving with her son Simon and her husband into a building which used to be the orphanage where she grew up. Simon soon starts mentioning mysterious friends he's made in their new home, and when he disappears during a party, Laura becomes convinced that he has been abducted by the ghosts of her former orphan companions.

Executive produced by Guillermo Del Toro, winner of three Academy Awards for his wonderful fantasy drama *Pan's Labyrinth* (2006), *The Orphanage* feels akin to the Mexican director's previous work, particularly *The Devil's Backbone*, which also features a ghost haunting a Spanish orphanage. Using the ghosts as symbols of the past and emphasising the human side of the story, Bayona's movie is, like *The Devil's Backbone*, atmospheric, at times terrifying, and utterly touching. Sure, this old-fashioned tale of love, loss and motherhood is reminiscent of several classics – *The Others* (2001), *The Changeling* (1980), *Poltergeist* (1982) or even *Dark Water* (2005) come to mind – but the characters are so well written, their emotions so believable, and the various elements so admirably tied together that the result is a unique experience, from the beginning to the heartbreaking end. Destined to please and surprise genre buffs and neophytes alike, Bayona's film, despite the familiarity of its themes and its settings, is neither an homage picture made for die-hard fans nor a rip-off for the ignorant, but an extraordinary piece using these influences and transcending them in a poignant ensemble. With Gothic chills,

201 *Rue Morgue* 68, June 2007.

202 The concept isn't new. An episode of the horror anthology series *Urban Gothic*, screened on Channel 5 in the UK on 26 December 2001, utilised the exact same premise. *The End*, written by Andrew Cull, postulated that the world has been devastated by a virulent virus which turns people into insane zombies, and follows the attempts of a small group, trapped and barricaded in a house, to survive. In the same way as *[Rec]*, all the footage seen comes from a camera used by one of the human survivors.

203 Interview with the author, Brussels, Belgium, April 2008.

204 Rosso had previously worked with Plaza on *Second Name* (*El Segundo Nombre*, 2002) and Balagueró's *To Let* (*Para Entrar A Vivir*, 2006).

The Orphanage. Inside.

suggestion and mounting dread, *The Orphanage* was the ultimate antidote to the excesses of the contemporary wave of ultra-violent horror, relying on sound, moody photography and the remarkable performance of its lead actress rather than graphic effects or jump-scares.

The film's broad appeal was reflected in the response it received from both mainstream audiences and the horror community. Coming out in Spain in October 2007, it became the top-grossing movie of the year in the country; it also raked in over £1.5 million in the UK and $7 million in the US, an impressive accomplishment for a foreign language and subtitled release. 'I don't believe in genre,' Bayona told IndieLondon in 2008[205]. 'The moment I started working on the film I felt free to do what I wanted and go where I wanted … The things that make movies alive are not the genre but what lies beneath. Here, that's a mother's unqualified love. That's why the movie has done so well in Spain and abroad. You can't pigeonhole it.' Bayona's first feature won seven Goya Awards (including Best Screenplay and Best New Director), the Grand Prize of Gérardmer 2008, as well as awards in various festivals around the world; it was also Spain's submission to Best Foreign Language Film at the 2008 Academy Awards.

'*The Orphanage* was nominated for fourteen Goya Awards, but we'll never see a horror movie at the Césars,' complains Julien Maury[206], co-director, with Alexandre Bustillo, of French shocker *Inside* (*A l'Intérieur*). 'In France, horror movies are exploitation, popular films, but not real movies. Horror is still seen as a sub-genre, a part of pop culture that people look down upon. And when your investors think that way, it's a real problem.'

Maury and Bustillo's *Inside*, released in France in June after premiering at the Cannes Film Festival, was the latest in a series of increasingly violent and/or disturbing horror films produced in France since the turn of the millennium. Focusing on a pregnant woman alone at home on Christmas Eve and harassed by a mysterious female stalker who seems to know her personally, this simple but incredibly nasty, gruesome and realistic effort immediately caught the attention of the international horror community, drawing comparisons with *High Tension* and Gaspar Noé's *Irreversible* (2002), yet it went all but unnoticed in its home country. 'People say there's a new wave of horror filmmakers in France, but the truth is, it's still as hard to get a horror movie financed and they're not that successful in the country,' Bustillo explains[207]. 'There have been a few since *High Tension*, but with a couple of possible exceptions, none of them has been commercially successful. We're still waiting for a hit to start a real wave of French horror productions.' Its box office results, similar to *High Tension* or *Maléfique* (2002), showed that no matter the quality of the movie, word of mouth or publicity campaign, genre pictures always attracted the same 100,000 audience members, a ridiculous number next to *Saw II*'s 620,000 viewers, or the 816,000 tickets sold for *Silent Hill*, an American film from a French director. 'People don't really believe in French horror,' Bustillo continues, 'They'd rather spend their money on American movies, which have bigger budgets. And so since French movies are not very profitable, you get smaller budgets, and the movies look even cheaper to the audience. Also if your movie gets a 16-rating, theatres are no longer interested. We got 90 screens, and we had to fight for each one of them. They say the kind of people who go see 16-rated movies are troublemakers.' Stuck in a never-ending cycle of low sales and lower budgets, French genre filmmakers seem doomed to produce films under €2 million ($2.5 million, give or take) if they want to recoup their investment.

And if the budget doesn't allow for name actors or groundbreaking special effects, what better way to make people talk than to up the gore and the shocks? Brutal and relentless, *Inside* is, from its opening shot (a car accident seen from inside the pregnant protagonist's stomach), technically flawless and magnificently orchestrated, but devoid of humour or sub-plots, calls forth no other reaction than disgust and nausea. Pitch black from the very start, the tone leaves little doubt as to the conclusion of the drama, and the violence soon reaches numbing, *Grand Guignol* degrees. Yet Béatrice Dalle, in quasi-Goth apparel, gives a haunting performance as the craziest boogey-woman in recent history, Alysson Paradis's brooding, aching widow is equally impeccable, and love it or hate it, no viewer will remain indifferent. 'Our goal was not to shock,' Maury says. 'The idea came from having a friend who was pregnant, and wondering what she could feel when she was alone at home. The violence and the story came from there. We never

205 '*The Orphanage*: Juan Antonio Bayona Interview', Jack Foley, IndieLondon, http://www.indielondon.co.uk/Film-Review/the-orphanage-juan-antonio-bayona-interview
206 Interview with the author, Paris, France, January 2008.
207 Interview with the author, Paris, France, January 2008.

wanted to shock for the sake of shocking. We just knew it wouldn't have a happy ending, it'd be a real horror film, not one of those films where the lead actress fights the whole movie through and ends up with a couple of scratches on her face.'

Ironically, *Inside*, the antithesis of traditional Hollywood horror, caught the eye of studio execs, and former TV cameraman and short film director Maury and ex-film reporter Bustillo are as of June 2008 negotiating their first steps in the US film industry. After being linked for months to a remake of Clive Barker's *Hellraiser*, which they quit when their script was discarded by the Weinsteins, they seem to have set their sights on the sequel to Rob Zombie's *Halloween*. They also keep open the possibility of financing and shooting another movie in their homeland, as Bustillo concludes: 'It's easier to get your movie made in the US, but we'd really like to stay in France as much as possible. France has all the actors and technicians necessary to make good movies. All we need is audacious producers. We don't know yet if our second movie will be French or American [and] we don't care, we just want to make the films we love.'

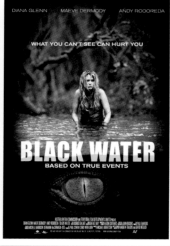

'Welcome to the terrortory' (*Rogue*)

If Spanish and French homes weren't safe that year, New Zealand and Australia, on the other hand, more than ever feared Mother Nature.

Crocodiles were particularly popular. Besides Michael Katleman's *Primeval*, an American film set in Burundi, no less than two crocodile movies were made and set in Australia. The best was certainly *Rogue*, from *Wolf Creek* director Greg McLean, the story of a group of tourists stranded in a swamp in the Outback, and preyed upon by a man-eating reptile. With solid characters and good performances from its entire cast – including Radha Mitchell, Michael Vartan and John Jarratt – McLean's second feature is as suspenseful and realistic as can be (although wildlife specialists may spot a few inaccuracies), keeps things simple and entertaining, and relies more on anticipation and dread than gore and graphic deaths. Avoiding the excesses of other killer crocodile movies, the Australian filmmaker crafts a straight-faced and entertaining horror adventure, and its scaled star, whether lurking underwater or running in plain sight, is scary and convincing. *Rogue* came out in Australia in November, but didn't get more than a limited release (ten theatres) in the United States.

A similar but largely inferior tale of survival in hostile crocodile territory, David Nerlich and Andrew Traucki's *Black Water* toured festivals in 2007 before opening in Australia in April 2008. '[*Primeval* and *Rogue*] were not released until well after *Black Water* completed filming,' says Nerlich[208]. 'However we did know these and some other crocodile films were coming. It's very strange just how many croc films appeared around the same time. It's been unlucky for us but didn't stop us.'

Last but not least, from New Zealand, a nation known for its sixteen to one sheep-to-humans ratio, Jonathan King's *Black Sheep* was built around the amusing idea that genetically modified sheep could turn against the population. Unfortunately, if played straight, the concept could have made for an extremely funny – and vaguely disturbing – little film, King, obviously taking a leaf from Peter Jackson's early work, made sure every scene was so outrageous, every character so caricatured and every performance so overacted that the result ends up closer to a spoof than to an actual scary movie. Some gags elicit smiles and the infected animals look pretty impressive, but *Black Sheep* is hardly the Kiwi answer to *Shaun of the Dead*, as some claimed at the time.

Rogue. Black Water. Black Sheep.

208 Email interview with Grégory Cavinato, June 2008.

2008:

Terror has evolved.

(Tagline for *The Ruins*, 2008)

AS OF JULY 2008, WHEN THIS BOOK GOES TO PRESS, LITTLE CONCLUSION CAN be drawn from the events and the box-office results of the year. America is absorbed in the run-up to the November presidential elections, with Democrat Barack Obama and Republican John McCain set to start debating soon. The Olympic Games are about to start in Beijing, China, but the nation's international policies and continued disregard of human rights have eventually and suddenly caused public opinion to shift towards a boycott of the Games. China also made headlines in May, when the Sichuan province was hit by a disastrous earthquake which killed nearly 70,000: one of the deadliest in world history.

In cinema, the hyper-violence wave has now affected mainstream filmmaking, the new version of *Rambo* being little more than a torture film with a little bit of action thrown in; and Paul Thomas Anderson's *There Will Be Blood* and the Coen brothers' *No Country for Old Men* – a B-movie starring Javier Bardem as an unstoppable killer in the vein of Michael Myers or the Terminator – winning BAFTAs and Academy Awards in all the major categories.

And while horror movies have seen steady good success commercially, no major hit stands out. Remakes are back with a vengeance, R-rated horror is still the dominating trend, and the United Kingdom has a plethora of genre films waiting to be released.

Reality Movies

Developed around the same time as Plaza and Balagueró's *[Rec]*, several other films shot on handheld cameras to heighten the realism of the story and place viewers in the middle of the action would be released in 2008. Inspired by *Cannibal Holocaust* (1980), *Man Bites Dog* (1992) and *The Blair Witch Project* (1999) as much as by reality TV and news reels, these features had no star names, often low budgets, and could be considered a natural evolution for the post 9/11, YouTube generation, for whom grainy footage of executions of Iraqi dictators and planes crashing into the World Trade Centre are as commonplace as home-made videos of dancing dogs and skateboarding cats.

Matt Reeves's *Cloverfield*, though more science fiction than horror, deserves a mention for being the leader of this wave of 'shaky camera' films. With an ad campaign focused mostly on the Internet, like that for *The Blair Witch Project*, this J J Abrams-produced creature feature kept its title and the nature of the threat hidden from the public until a few weeks before its January release and generated an unprecedented buzz around the first teaser trailer, released in July 2007. Presented as footage found on a digital camcorder, *Cloverfield* has no music or non-diegetic sound, lacks some scenes (when the battery runs out, for instance), and shows the entire monster invasion from the point of view of the characters, making the audience feel as though they are part of the action. If the movie itself has its flaws (slow beginning, hollow characters, no third act to speak of) and the shaky camera moves caused motion sickness for some, the scope of this $25 million story and the effects involved combined with the relative novelty of the filmic style made for an amazing movie-going experience. *Cloverfield* stomped its competition to the ground with a $40 million opening, and ended its theatrical run at $80 million, a number it more than doubled with its $90 million in foreign sales.

George Romero's *Diary of the Dead* used the same principle of showing the action through the lens of a protagonist. But unlike *[Rec]*, *The Zombie Diaries* or *Cloverfield*, this low-budget, back-to-the-roots story of a group of students caught in the middle of a living dead invasion has a music score, slick photography, editing and even a particularly annoying voice-over, which all naturally ruin the effect of the handheld camera style. The same filmmaker who gave the world the ground-breaking *Night of the Living Dead* in 1969, one of the most realistic horror films of its time, doesn't dare exploit the home-made video format to its full extent; instead of using it to increase tension, he utilises it to pontificate about the value of the new communication tools available to the people, as opposed to official media which, according to Romero, are deceitful and manipulating. Far from 'an underlying threat of social satire,' as one of the character says, the writer/director makes his message front and centre throughout the film, insisting on the authenticity of the testimony these new technologies allow to create, and wondering, as he did with much more subtlety in all previous entries of his zombie saga, if the living deserve to live despite the way they treat the dead and each other.

Of course, Romero has always been known as the thinking man's horror director, and the parallels between *Night of the Living Dead* and the Vietnam War, or *Dawn of the Dead* and the rise of consumerism, have filled entire books. But with these earlier efforts, the filmmaker still focused on creating characters and situations and telling a compelling story; whatever social comment filtered through was the result of a natural, unconscious thought process. *Diary of the Dead* on the other hand gives the plot a backseat and lets the message drive the movie; rather than giving the audience some food for thought, it pre-chews it and rams it down the viewers' throats. Pitting unlikeable characters against the sort of pathetically slow zombies *Shaun of the Dead* so brilliantly ridiculed, this pretentious entry marked a step back for a filmmaker until then known for his innovative flair. The success of *[Rec]*, a movie which built on Romero's heritage while adding its own stamp, made this failure all the more striking.

Cloverfield. Diary of the Dead.

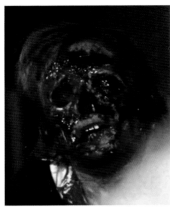

The Signal.

The Signal, a three-segment movie written and directed by David Bruckner, Dan Bush and Jacob Gentry, may not have resorted to the cameraman-amongst-the-characters ploy, but it did turn the limitations of its tiny budget into an advantage by filming with a handheld camera and opting for gritty, naturalistic photography. Each part of this triptych concentrates on a different character – or group of characters – facing a sudden surge of aggressiveness caused by a mysterious signal emitted on television, driving people to random acts of violence. All three stories take place around the same time in the same city, and the protagonists meet and interact at various moments, giving the movie a narrative unity; but each segment has its own tone, the first one being the scariest and the second introducing some humour, for instance. 'The Signal basically is a love story with a horror element and some comedy,' producer Alexander Motlagh says[209]. 'We were trying to give it a unity, but it all just came about naturally. It's three different styles, three different filmmakers with different tastes and different favourite horror films.' The variations work well for the first two parts, but the movie loses its breath in the last third, when the action moves from the characters' homes to a train station. Although *The Signal*'s victims are alive and breathing, the movie is in several ways – storyline, themes, structure – similar to a zombie flick; but its filmmakers fight this classification. Says Motlagh: 'The dead are not rational, but in our film, the people who commit those crimes are not mindless. In their minds what they're doing makes sense.' Co-director Jacob Gentry adds[210]: 'It's a reaction to zombie films, but it's not technically a zombie film. I think we were trying to recreate the same kind of aesthetics, but offer a different perspective. Here they're just people like you and me, and the signal just gives them a tipping point. Like the kind of things you only do when you're drunk. We feel it's more apocalyptic, more interested in how the apocalypse will happen.' Coincidentally, at least two novels were released in 2006 that described similar situations: Stephen King's January 2006 novel *Cell*, about a signal emitted through mobile phones and driving their users criminally insane; and David Moody's July 2006 *Hater*, in which random people suddenly resort to acts of extreme violence for trivial reasons. Eli Roth was attached to direct an adaptation of the former, while Guillermo Del Toro has bought the rights to the latter. 'There's always waves,' Gentry comments, 'and as a filmmaker you can't really analyse them. It's not deliberate. We move with our feelings and our inclinations, and our intellect just catches up. Every time you talk about a visceral reaction, like horror, something that gets inside our subconscious, it's hard to be intellectual about it.'

The Signal came out in February 2008 on 160 screens, and unfortunately made practically no money: $251,000 after four weeks with an average of $905 per theatre, despite decent reviews and a good advance word since its Sundance premiere. In a strange twist of fate, two people were stabbed during a screening of the movie in Fullerton, California in February 2008. The victims didn't know each other or their aggressor, who managed to leave the theatre by the back door, and the attacks didn't seem to have any apparent motive. To paraphrase the tagline: Did he have the crazy?

With *[Rec] 2* and *Quarantine* in the works, and Oren Peli's haunted house movie *Paranormal Activity* bought by DreamWorks who plans to both distribute it and remake it with a bigger budget, the handheld camera style may be more than a passing craze; but just as for every trend horror goes through, abandons, and comes back to eventually, only time will tell how long it will last.

Your Movie Could Be Next!

After a short break in 2007, where Rob Zombie's *Halloween* was the only notable redux, remakes were back in force in 2008, with many more in preparation for the following year.
J-horror adaptations proved to be a particularly enduring trend. Relatively cheap to make (generally around $20 million), often bloodless and PG-13, they almost systematically returned their investment despite generally bad reviews. Why stop if the audience asks for more?

Eric Valette's *One Missed Call* and David Moreau and Xavier Palud's *The Eye*, released in January and February respectively, both marked the first steps into Hollywood for the French directors, who'd made themselves noticed with their first low-budget genre feature. Both productions were also rumoured to be heavily controlled by the studios, and the resulting movies

209 Interview with the author, Sitges, Spain, October 2007.
210 Interview with the author, Sitges, Spain, October 2007.

did not conform to what their helmers originally had in mind. Re-cuts were ordered on both and some scenes of *The Eye* were even re-shot by a different director, Patrick Lussier (*Dracula 2000*). '[Co-producer] Paula Wagner had very specific ideas about what she wanted,' Palud says[211]. 'She doesn't know much about horror films but she wanted to change a lot of things. We had people in the studio on the other hand who understood the genre and backed up our decisions, so we were always caught in the middle of those two

sides. We even had to fight to keep the poster that we wanted.'

Their homeland offering limited possibilities for horror productions, French genre directors have long been tempted to flee to Hollywood. But what they went through there wasn't always exactly what they'd envisioned, and most seem to have found the experience unpleasant, from studio interference to lack of freedom in the choice of material (the majority end up with remakes – *The Hills Have Eyes* is another example – or videogame adaptations, like Xavier Gens's *Hitman* (2007) or Christophe Gans's *Silent Hill* (2006).) 'Some people only make a movie in France to get noticed abroad and get bigger budgets,' says *Inside* co-director Alexandre Bustillo[212]. 'But bigger budgets mean less control, and that's not something we're interested in. I'd rather wait and work on smaller budgets right now, and be able to say the movie's actually mine. But Xavier Gens for example, he knew he wouldn't have a lot of control on *Hitman* but he wanted to have that experience as early as possible in his career so it wouldn't be too hard to deal with it. Now he knows it'll be easier for him to get a bigger budget based on his name. It's a different approach …'

For studios, hiring a European or Asian filmmaker has obvious advantages. Says Valette[213]: 'I guess that in the mind of a producer, picking an inexpensive foreigner who's proved himself in his home country to direct the remake of a movie which has been successful in another country is the best way to limit the risks and maximise his profit. And at the same time, the foreign director has an artistic aura, or an exotic flavour.'

The lack of creative freedom may be a high price to pay to become bankable, recognisable names in the US film industry, but for Valette, Moreau and Palud, the bet seems to have paid off. *The Eye* opened at $12 million on nearly 2,500 screens and grossed a total $31 million in the States, and with a similar opening, *One Missed Call* ended its course in the US a little under $27 million. Valette is currently in post-production on *Hybrid*, a killer car movie filmed in Canada. As for Alexandre Aja, whose first Hollywood picture was also a remake, he is now prepping an update of Joe Dante's *Piranha*, to be filmed in 3-D for a 2009 release, and his latest feature *Mirrors*, a revamping of the South Korean hit *Into The Mirror*, comes out in August 2008.

Other Asian adaptations planned or released in 2008 include *Shutter*, an extremely banal ghost story by Masayuki Ochiai (who had in 2000 written and directed a wonderfully terrifying segment, *One Snowy Night*, in the four-part Japanese anthology *Tales of the Unusual*); and *The Uninvited*, a remake of *A Tale of Two Sisters* curiously titled after another South Korean success, whose date has been pushed back to 2009.

The Eye.

211 Interview with the author, Brussels, Belgium, April 2008.

212 Interview with the author, Paris, France, January 2008.

213 Email interview with the author, January 2008.

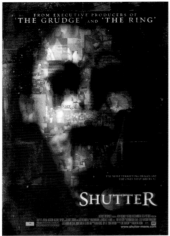
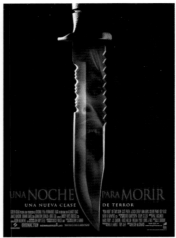
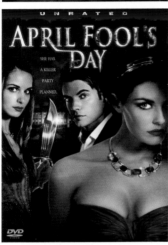

Classics are no safer than Asian movies, and the rights to everything from Universal horror and Euro-thrillers to slashers and exploitation gorefests seem to be up for grabs.

Prom Night, an abysmal PG-13 version of the already dreadful 1980 Jamie Lee Curtis vehicle, directed by Nelson McCormick (who also wrapped an update of *The Stepfather*), opened in the US in April to poor reviews but excellent box office, raking in over $20 million in its first weekend. Another slasher remake, Mitchell Altieri and Phil Flores's *April Fool's Day*, was less lucky: it went straight-to-DVD in late March and was practically unnoticed. Other stalk'n'slashes considered for the redux treatment include *My Bloody Valentine*, with Patrick Lussier attached to direct in 3-D.

Don't let its title fool you: *Funny Games US*, which sees German writer/director Michael Haneke reprise his own 1997 shocker with a bigger budget, takes itself much more seriously. This pointless exercise is eerily similar to the original, only slicker and less daring, but takes a new, vaguely unpleasant meaning in the post-*Saw* and *Hostel* context of 2008: when the home invaders turn to the camera to ask viewers if they enjoy the show, the question appears less as a game played with the audience than as a way for the cult filmmaker to distance himself from the sadistic excesses on display and to blame moviegoers for the success of hyper-violent films. The joke was on him: out in March on 274 screens, *Funny Games US* grossed a mere $1.3 million over the course of seven weeks.

Last but not least, Universal finally greenlit a remake of *The Wolf Man*, which had first been announced in March 2006. Scripted by Andrew Kevin Walker and David Self and starring Benicio Del Toro in the titular role, this update of the 1941 classic is directed by Joe Johnston, after the departure of Mark Romanek a couple of months before the scheduled start of the shoot. The movie, which was filmed in London and features special effects from veteran monster make-up artist Rick Baker, is slated for an April 2009 release.

The Only Thing We Have to Fear ...

Shutter. Prom Night. April Fool's Day. Funny Games. Wolf Man.

In the second half of the year, *Masters of Horror* creator Mick Garris announced that IDT and Showtime would not renew his contract for a third season, but that the show had found a new home at Lionsgate. The company soon signed a deal with NBC, and the resulting series, now titled *Fear Itself*, would be shot in Edmonton, Canada. The change caused a mini-stir in the horror world: how could a director-driven series which prided itself on giving complete freedom to the filmmakers, survive on network television?

Potential censorship, however, wasn't the only hardship *Fear Itself* would have to overcome. Garris only just had the time to collect the first drafts of the thirteen new scripts for the show when the writers' strike started on 5 November 2007. Being a member of the WGA (and having himself penned a couple of the show's screenplays), Garris was forced to suspend his activities on the series. 'There were a lot of producers who continued producing [during the walkout],' he told *Fangoria* in 2008[214]. 'Technically, this is a Canadian show and not an American show, so getting Writers Guild of Canada members was not a problem. Once the strike happened,

I could have technically stayed on as a producer, but my duties would have included hiring people to continue work on the scripts in place of Writers Guild of America members, and to be involved in notes and things like that, and I found that untenable. The Writers Guild strike was a very important one, and it was very crucial to me to fulfil the requirements of my guild and not be there in Canada supporting people who were taking the place of those writers.' Meanwhile, Lionsgate hired local writers to rework the episodes according to NBC's suggestions and demands, so that when the strike ended in February 2008, Garris chose not to continue in the role of executive producer. Following his departure, several filmmakers, including John Carpenter, who'd worked on both seasons of *Masters of Horror*, quit the production.

Still, *Fear Itself* managed to secure several cult directors for its first season, including returning directors Stuart Gordon, Brad Anderson and John Landis, and newcomers Darren Lynn Bousman and Ronny Yu. The series debuted on 5 June 2008 with Breck Eisner's *The Sacrifice*, based on a short story by Del Howison; NBC declared itself 'content' with its 5.2 million viewers.

As for Garris, he is now preparing a feature film adaptation of Stephen King's *Bag of Bones* scripted by Matthew Venne, and Tobe Hooper is attached to direct one of his scripts, a ghost story called *Dead*.

'What are you afraid of?' (*The Strangers*)

Besides PG-13 remakes and a watered-down version of *Masters of Horror*, 2008 had its share of original R-rated horror, both from independents and from the studios.

Mitchell Lichtenstein's *Teeth* was one of those films which, by their subject matter as much as by their content, are bound to puzzle rating boards and distributors. A very literal adaptation of the myth of the *vagina dentata*, it tells the story of Dawn (Jess Weixler), an innocent teenage girl who, at the same time that she finds herself attracted to a classmate, discovers that she has teeth 'down there'. In equal measure dark teenage comedy and gross-out horror, *Teeth* takes the time to introduce its characters and hint at the girl's anatomical abnormality before revealing it fully in a scene which would make any male viewer squirm. The tone is humorous and slightly cartoonish, but one still feels for Dawn and her unusual situation – at least until the third act, when the movie turns to pure *Grand Guignol*. With a none-too-subtle commentary on the power of female sexuality and the (very literal) horrors of adolescence, Lichtenstein's film was, strangely enough, the third release in less than a year to contain graphic scenes of castration, after *Hostel: Part II* and British film noir *WAZ*. Premiering at Sundance in January 2007, it toured festivals for a full year before receiving a token theatrical release (four screens) in the US; obviously afraid the movie might not get an R-rating or might be impossible to promote[215], distributors didn't bite right away, even though advance reviews were enthusiastic. A smart and daring film, *Teeth* received a real theatrical run in the UK in June 2008 and can now be found on Region 1 DVD, although Wal-Mart took it off its shelves shortly after its release.

Another female-centric teenage horror comedy was *All the Boys Love Mandy Lane*, about a young girl who, having become suddenly popular over the summer, accepts an invitation to a weekend party in a ranch with her classmates. Directed by newcomer Jonathan Levine, *All the Boys Love Mandy Lane* not only adopts a woman's point of view but is also one of those rare slashers to offer three-dimensional characters with complex relationships. Levine actually focuses so much on exploring the psyche of his teenage protagonists that the dramatic components of the story are much stronger than the scary moments or the deaths, which don't seem to blend in the mix. This is both the movie's greatest quality and most annoying flaw: as fresh and intelligently constructed as it may be, it just doesn't work as a horror movie, and its absurd resolution makes it all the more disappointing. *All the Boys Love Mandy Lane* came to UK cinemas in February 2008, and is set for an August 2008 release in the United States.

Also expected in August – though the date has been shifted around several times – is Ryuhei Kitamura's adaptation of Clive Barker's short story *The Midnight Meat Train*, in which a photographer

Teeth. All the Boys Love Mandy Lane.

214 'Losing the Fear', Abbie Bernstein, *Fangoria*, May 2008, http://www.*Fangoria*.com/fearful_feature.php?id=6734

215 Rejected posters for *Teeth* included, in the UK, an X-ray of a girl's body with teeth between her legs …

Midnight Meat Train. Jack Brooks: Monster Slayer. The Strangers.

216 'UK Audiences Surf Horror
Wave', Ali Jaafar, *Variety*, 20 June
2008, http://www.variety.com/article/
VR1117987843.html?categoryid=25
20&cs=1

hunts down a serial killer in the Subway. Starring Vinnie Jones, Bradley Cooper, Roger Bart and Brooke Shields, it is the first of a planned series of features based on Barker's short stories, collected in several volumes with the generic title *The Books of Blood*. The second film, *Book of Blood*, stars Doug Bradley and Simon Bamford, both of whom played Cenobites in Barker's *Hellraiser* movies, with Bradley playing lead Cenobite Pinhead, and was shot in Scotland in the first half of 2008 by John Harrison. The third, *Dread*, directed by Anthony DiBlasi, is set for a 2009 release.

Rogue Pictures' *The Strangers*, a home invasion movie from first-time director Bryan Bertino and with Liv Tyler, was first presented to fans at the 2007 Comic-Con in San Diego, but wasn't released until late May 2008, when it opened in the US with an impressive $21 million in its first weekend. Carter Smith's *The Ruins*, another holiday-from-hell tale, set in Mexico and adapted from a best-selling 2006 novel by Scott Smith, came out a month before and took $8 million in its first three days.

Other 2008 US releases included *Jack Brooks: Monster Slayer*, the funny comic-bookish story of a plumber who uses his fits of anger to fight supernatural creatures, directed by Jon Knautz and starring Trevor Matthews and Robert Englund; Englund also appeared in *Zombie Strippers!* alongside porn star Jenna Jameson. With *Teeth*, *Zombie Strippers!* and *Jack Brooks: Monster Slayer* all aiming to make viewers smile as much as wince, it seems the comedy-horror genre, usually a sign that scary movies are reaching the end of their popularity, is back in fashion again.

'UK Audiences Surf Horror Wave' (Variety headline, June 2008)[216]

In the United Kingdom, the popularity of horror shows no sign of waning, and 2008 offered fans a large selection of both supernatural and realistic villains, from vampires and zombies to serial killers, satanic priests and even children.

Naturally, a couple of horror comedies were released, results of both the *Shaun of the Dead/Severance* successes and the usual downward curve the genre follows after a peak of popularity. Paul Andrew Williams's *The Cottage* – about a couple of incompetent kidnappers (Reece Shearsmith, of *League of Gentlemen* fame, and Andy Serkis) struggling first with their feisty victim (Jennifer Ellison), then with a homicidal farmer – was the most successful, artistically and commercially.

Williams's second feature after his acclaimed 2006 drama *London to Brighton*, *The Cottage* is, much like Robert Rodriguez's *From Dusk Til Dawn* (1996), divided into two distinct parts: a gangster story and a horror comedy. But unlike its predecessor, it takes the movie two acts to get to the scary part, and while the kidnapping is amusing to watch, with its typically British humour and Serkis's excellent performance, gorehounds will wait impatiently to have their fill, the last third of the film being where all the frights and deaths occur. Still, the payoff is worth the wait, as Williams makes up for the relative unoriginality of his subject by adding touches of dark comedy to the shocks and a delicious dose of insanity to the ensemble. Unfortunately, *The Cottage* wasn't much of a hit in the UK, despite positive reviews and an opening on 260 screens in March.

Newcomer Kit Ryan's *Botched*, a horror comedy starring Stephen Dorff and Sean Pertwee, could have been seen as oddly similar – this time a heist goes wrong and the thieves find themselves trapped in a building with a bunch of mysterious and possibly supernatural killers – had its tone not been so different. If the movie features a few nasty deaths, its silly humour overpowers the scary side of the story, and unlike *The Cottage*, where the jokes arise out of the protagonists' insufficiency and the over-the-top nature of the situation they find themselves in, *Botched* pokes fun at everything, including its villains, who are so ridiculous they are hardly frightening.

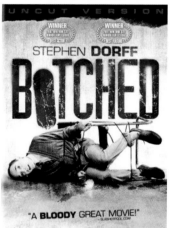

More unexpected was Hammer Films' return from the dead after nearly three decades of inactivity. Best known for its gothic horror pictures starring Christopher Lee and/or Peter Cushing from the late fifties to the late seventies, the legendary British company, which had left an indelible mark on the genre, had closed its gates in the eighties, after years of stagnation. But in 2007, the brand – and its back catalogue – was sold to Dutch consortium Cyrte Investments, whose plan is to release a steady flow of horror features from 2009 onwards. To test the waters and show fans that Hammer was definitely making a comeback, production started in the second half of 2007 on a low-budget online serial called *Beyond the Rave*, starring Nora-Jane Noone (*The Descent*), Leslie Simpson (*Dog Soldiers*) and Jamie Dornan (*Marie-Antoinette*), and with a cameo from Hammer favourite Ingrid Pitt. Premiering on the social networking site MySpace in April 2007, the twenty-part mini-series follows Ed, a soldier whose girlfriend has disappeared and is found hanging out with a group of vampires in the underground party scene. While many fans saw little more in the label's resurrection and first effort than a way to cash in on the Hammer name without actually keeping any link with the features that made the company successful, the film seemed to be embraced by the online community, and its page gathered over 30,000 'friends' in a matter of weeks.

Proving that zombies were still popular in the land of *28 Days Later* and *Shaun of the Dead*, Matthew Hope's *The Vanguard* and Steve Barker's *Outpost* (not to be confused with Neil Marshall's long-rumoured project of the same name) both involved the dead; and if the latter came out direct-to-DVD early in the year, the former is, as of June 2008, still touring festivals in search of distribution.

Amongst the other planned or past releases of the year in the UK are Julian Doyle's *Chemical Wedding*, co-written by Iron Maiden frontman Bruce Dickinson; Jake West's zombie/battle-of-the-sexes picture *Doghouse*; Simon Aitken's vampire tale *Blood & Roses*; Phil Claydon's horror comedy *Lesbian Vampire Killers*; and *Eden Lake*, from first-time director and *My Little Eye* scripter James Watkins. *Eden Lake* sees a young couple battle a band of children during a weekend at the countryside (children being a decidedly popular threat, with amongst others George Ratcliff's thriller *Joshua*, two aforementioned shockers with twist endings, and Tom Shankland's *The Children*, another UK production, also featuring evil kids). Realistic and brutal, *Eden Lake* is set for a September release in the UK. Watkins also penned the screenplay for Jon Harris's *The Descent 2*, which will see Sarah (Shauna McDonald) return to the cave in 2009.

The Cottage. Botched. Beyond the Rave.

Frontier(s). Martyrs.

'Warning from the Classification Commission (*Frontier(s)*)

France once again produced a handful of exceptionally graphic pictures: *Frontier(s)* (*Frontière(s)*), in which after a (fictional) presidential election, a group of young rioters flee Paris and find refuge in a countryside hostel whose owner isn't as well intentioned as he seems; *Martyrs*, about a girl found on the side of a road after being missing for over a year; and *Vinyan*, a France/Belgium/UK co-production which sees a couple fly to Thailand to look for their child, who disappeared in the 2004 tsunami. Directed by Fabrice du Welz and starring Emmanuelle Béart and Rufus Sewell, the latter is set for a late September release in France and Belgium.

Writer/director Xavier Gens waited over a year to see his first feature *Frontier(s)* released around the world; his second effort, videogame adaptation *Hitman*, came out in the US in November 2007, two full months before *Frontier(s)*'s French opening. Heavily inspired by *The Texas Chain Saw Massacre, Hostel* and *The Descent*, to which it pays direct homages, this hyper-violent film was given a 16-rating in its homeland (and an NC-17 certificate when After Dark released it in the States; the company even marketed it as 'the first NC-17 horror film in theatres') with the express condition that the filmmakers warned the audience about its content on the poster. Turning this demand into a selling point, the marketing team for the film wrote the warning from the rating board in giant letters behind the main image, *à la I Am Legend*: 'This movie piles up extremely realistic and harrowing scenes of butchery.'[217]

Indeed, the ordeal the young protagonists go through is shown in graphic detail, and the general tone certainly isn't fun. In the first half, Gens maintains a pretty high degree of realism in the situations and the unlikeable characters he depicts, and cleverly gives us some hints that things are about to go downhill for them. But in the last part of the film, when the main villain is revealed to be a Nazi patriarchal figure and Dr Strangelove look-alike, the story loses much of its credibility, and its political subtext – France is falling back into extremism – is seriously deflated once it becomes clear that the innkeepers aren't everyday people but demented, inbred, ridiculous freaks. Still, the pitch black tone and oddness of the storyline are enough to make the movie a must-see, and Gens a talent to watch for the future. Extremely bloody, *Frontier(s)* opened in France after a successful festival run which included Sitges and Toronto, and enjoyed a very positive buzz in the United States when it came out on DVD in May.

Pascal Laugier's torture film *Martyrs*, screened in Cannes in May 2008, may well push the frontiers of the genre even further. Hyped since its premiere as one of the most gruelling and extreme movies ever made, it was landed later that month with an 18-certificate, the equivalent in France of economic censorship as few theatres will dare show it, little advertisement will be possible, and no television network will be allowed to broadcast it before midnight. Laugier, backed by the Society of Film Distributors and supported by horror fans who organised a petition and even a demonstration, appealed the decision; the Commission changed the rating to 16 in late June 2008. 'Fifteen years ago, it would have been impossible to dream about making horror films in my country,' Laugier told Shocktilyoudrop in June 2008[218]. 'The whole system rejected the very idea of genre culture. Now … the French market has opened. It's a very good thing … The problem right now in France is the general climate. Again, some people think violent movies should be taken out from the multiplexes. There are a lot of debates, political discussions about the influence of nasty images on young people. It's always the same old story: any time a society is hard, unfair and brutal, horror movies are accused of everything.'

Italy also produced a horror feature in 2008: Dario Argento's *Mother of Tears* (*La Terza Madre*), the much-awaited third part of the director's *Mothers* trilogy, which began with *Suspiria* (1977) and *Inferno* (1980). Starring Argento's preferred cast of Asia Argento and Daria Nicolodi as well as a host of TV actors, *Mother of Tears*, scripted by Adam Gierasch and Jace Anderson in collaboration with the Italian filmmaker, is unfortunately as far from the masterpiece most expected as could possibly be. Rushed, incoherent and filled with bad performances and clunky dialogue, it is mostly worth seeing for its cheese value (audiences in some European festivals dubbed it *Mother of Tears of Laughter*); although judging from online reactions, it seems some

217 'Avertissement de la Commission de Classification: Ce film accumule des scènes de boucherie particulièrement réalistes et éprouvantes.'
218 'Exclusive Interview: *Martyrs* Director Pascal Laugier', Ryan Rotten, *Shocktilyoudrop*, 23 June 2008, http://www.shocktilyoudrop.com/news/topnews.php?id=6654

Mother of Tears. Dark Floors.

diehard fans appreciated its stylish atmosphere and are willing to give it another chance in a couple of years, stressing that some of Argento's best works were also decried upon release.

In Spain, Gonzalo López-Gallego's *King of the Hill* (*El Rey de la Montaña*), a brutal survival tale in which a man (Leonardo Sbaraglia) lost in a rural area is hunted by invisible killers, drew some attention at the Toronto Film Festival and the Sitges festival in 2007, and is expected to come out in September 2008 in its home country. Intriguing in its first fifteen minutes, the movie, like its main character, quickly has nowhere to go and the final revelation, similar to several other films released around the same time, brings little to the action or to the genre.

Finally, 2008 saw the release of the first ever Finnish horror movie: *Dark Floors*, directed by Pete Riski and starring Lordi, a five-member monster rock band hailed as national heroes since their 2006 win at the Eurovision song contest. The presence of the popular band ensured publicity for the film, but also had obvious disadvantages, which may well explain the film's lack of bite and the blink-and-you'll-miss-them appearances of the creatures. Says singer and lead villain Mr Lordi[219]: 'The thing is, people here in Finland, they think that even though we've been saying so many times that this is a horror film, in their minds this is going to be a family movie. They don't listen to what we're saying. Also they know what we look like, it won't be a surprise, so the movie is not so much about the monsters.' While the plot and characters are not very developed and the pacing is slightly off, the musicians' efforts to be taken seriously as genre icons are commendable, and their make-up, slightly refined for the movie, certainly looks impressive. Hardly a hit in the making, *Dark Floors* is nonetheless an amusing, cheesy and visually striking guilty pleasure.

219 Interview with the author, Oulu, Finland, August 2007.

Conclusion:

"The oldest and strongest emotion of mankind is fear.'

(H P Lovecraft)

AS WE APPROACH THE END OF THE FIRST DECADE OF THE NEW MILLENNIUM, it is clear, looking back, that we no longer live in the flourishing and apparently secure world of the 1990s. Terrorist attacks have exposed our vulnerability; misinformation and disorganisation have shattered faith in our governments; natural disasters have challenged the notion that our place on Earth is assured. From bombings and school shootings to hurricanes and viruses, death can occur anywhere, anytime, to anybody. Rich and poor, young and old, no one is safe, and we are all increasingly aware of it.

Society has changed and grown more complex, and horror has gone back to the basics. Scary movies no longer need action, adventure or thriller elements to appeal to the masses, and the fears they challenge us to confront are simple and primal: death, pain and destruction. Playing on universal anxieties, they are a way to express our discomfort with the state of the world; and the parallels between current events and the themes explored in these fictional works evidence the link between their newfound mainstream appeal and our real-life anxieties. Horror movies are, after all, as much about the time they are made as the world they are set in.

As a result, the genre has for the past few years enjoyed an unusual degree of acceptance – if not respectability – from producers, critics and audiences. Horror is no longer the dirty word it was ten years ago. Scary movies are no longer shameful guilty pleasures. This situation, and the emergence of new technologies which have made filmmaking more accessible than ever, allowed hundreds of writers and directors to develop and release an impressive variety of productions. The 2000s have witnessed the birth of many talents, and given the genre a few masterpieces.

As the biggest trends of the decade – torture films, zombie flicks, J-horror, Asian remakes – are starting to show their limits and no major success has yet come to replace them, it seems

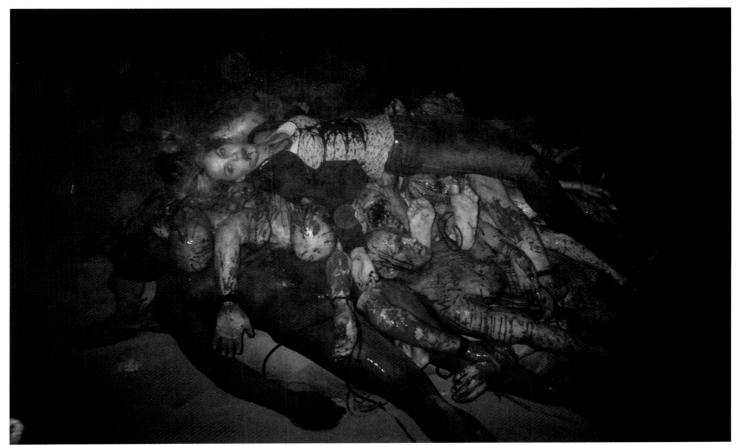

Midnight Meat Train. The Wolf Man. Vinyan.

the genre may be reaching the end of this cycle of popularity. But if scary movies become fewer and far between in the coming years, be sure that another hit, another crisis will spark a new wave of interest soon enough. Make no mistake about it: horror, the genre most embedded in our subconscious, most linked to our primal fears, most appropriate in times of tension, will return.

You see, horror never dies.

Bibliography:

Books

The Monster Show: A Cultural History of Horror, David J Skal, Plexus Publishing, 1994

The Rough Guide to Horror Movies, Alan Jones, Rough Guides, 2005

The Horror Film: An Introduction, Rick Worland, Blackwell Publishing, 2007

Danse Macabre, Stephen King, Hodder, 1981

Horror: The Definitive Guide to the Cinema of Fear, James Marriott and Kim Newman, Andre Deutch, 2006

Beyond Horror Holocaust: A Deeper Shade of Red, Chas. Balun, Fantasma Books, 2003

Shockmasters of the Cinema, Loris Curci, Fantasma Books, 1996

The FrightFest Fearbook Volume I, Alan Jones, Revolver Books, 2006

Psychos! Sickos! Sequels! Horror Films of the 1980s, John Stell, Midnight Marquee, 1998

Necronomicon: Book Five, edited by Andy Black, Noir Publishing, 2007

Zombiemania: 80 Movies To Die For. Dr Arnold T Blumberg and Andrew Hershberger. Telos Publishing, 2006

Book of the Dead: The Complete History of Zombie Cinema, Jamie Russell, FAB Press, 2005

Gospel of the Living Dead: George Romero's Visions of Hell on Earth, Kim Paffenroth, Baylor University Press, 2006–

J-Horror: The Definitive Guide to The Ring, The Grudge and Beyond, David Kalat, Vertical, 2007

The Ring Companion, Denis Meikle, Titan Books, 2005

Lurker in the Lobby: A Guide to the Cinema of H P Lovecraft, Andrew Migliore and John Strysik, Night Shade Books, 2006

Screams and Nightmares: The Films of Wes Craven, Brian J Robb, Titan Books, 1998

John Carpenter, The Prince of Darkness, Gilles Boulenger, Silman-James Press, 2001

The Unseen Force: The Films of Sam Raimi, John Kenneth Muir, Applause, 2004

30 Days of Night.

Crystal Lake Memories: The Complete History of Friday the 13th, Peter M Bracke, Titan Books, 2006

The Evil Dead Companion, Bill Warren, Titan Books, 2000

The Sleaze-Filled Saga of an Exploitation Double Feature: Grindhouse, Edited and designed by Kurt Volk, Titan Books, 2007

Websites

The Internet Movie Database, http://www.imdb.com

Rotten Tomatoes, http://www.rottentomatoes.com

Dread Central, http://www.dreadcentral.com

Shock Til You Drop, http://www.shocktilyoudrop.com

Bloody-Disgusting, http://www.bloody-disgusting.com

BBC Film, http://www.bbc.co.uk/film

Box Office Mojo, http://www.boxofficemojo.com

All Movie Photographs, http://allmoviephoto.com

Titles Index:

In this index, the films discussed in more length have those page numbers highlighted in bold text. Other titles are only listed when there is some significance to the mention of the film in the text. Brief, throwaway references to titles are therefore not included in this index.

Black Sheep.

Cursed.

Mother of Tears.

The Orphanage.

The Wicker Man.

About the author:

AXELLE CAROLYN HAS BEEN a horror fan for as long as she can remember. Brought up on a steady diet of scary movies and Stephen King novels, she soon began contributing to several genre websites, then to *Fangoria*, *SFX*, *L'Ecran Fantastique* and *The Dark Side*, for whom she conducted hundreds of interviews and covered dozens of festivals and film shoots. She has a monthly column on horror movies on the entertainment website IGN.com, and recently started writing fiction.

Axelle is also an actress, and her credits include Universal Pictures' *Doomsday* and Celador's *The Descent 2*.

She lives in London with her husband, writer/director Neil Marshall.

Other Film Books from Telos Publishing

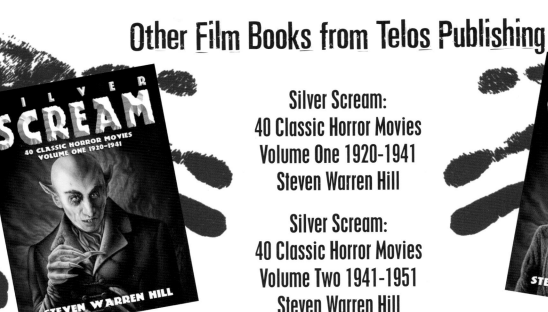

Silver Scream:
40 Classic Horror Movies
Volume One 1920-1941
Steven Warren Hill

Silver Scream:
40 Classic Horror Movies
Volume Two 1941-1951
Steven Warren Hill
(forthcoming)

Zombiemania: 80 Movies to Die For
Dr. Arnold T. Blumberg
& Andrew Hershberger

Taboo Breakers:
18 Independent Films
that Courted Controversy
and Created a Legend
Calum Waddell

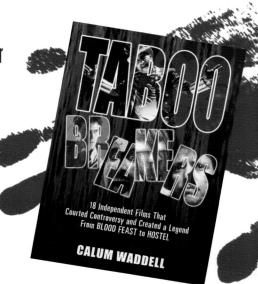

A Vault of Horror
Keith Topping

Beautiful Monsters: The Unofficial
and Unauthorised Guide to the
Alien and Predator Films
David McIntee

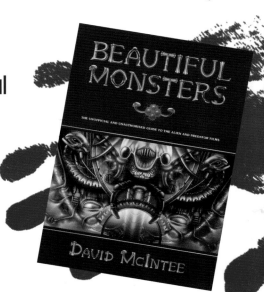

www.telos.co.uk